FLOWERS AND ASH

BRENDA BAKER

ISBN 978-1-7387835-2-6

To my husband, Nicholas.
Thank you for your support and enthusiasm.

CONTENTS

PROLOGUE

Wrunwicks: page 1
Stonebridge: page 5

AN AGE OF PEACE

Chapter 1 – Chapter 20

WINTER'S FLOWERS

Chapter 21 – Chapter 50

APPENDIX

Moon Cycles O/O: page 437
The King's Canons: page 438

Dear Reader,

I started writing *Flowers and Ash* as a short story in 2018, but it kept growing as stories sometimes do. Eventually, I had to accept that a short story, it wasn't. So I set my goal on a novella to the same effect. Fortunately, it did stop growing in 2020 with the first of many book drafts.

In going from that initial short story to the book you're about to read, I realized just how little I knew about my chosen world. This led to massive amounts of research and a collection of books on the Middle Ages that continue to keep me company as I write.

That is not to say *Flowers and Ash* is an accurate depiction of the medieval period. Not at all. It did, however, serve as a vibrant material for weaving the story.

And while the characters are fictional, I did make an exception for Ewart and Roy. These two characters were named after my late father and brother respectively. However, any dialogue, events, or circumstances involving Ewart and Roy in the book are completely fictional and not meant to be an accurate characterization of my father and brother in any way. In naming the characters after Dad and Roy, I wanted to honour their memory the best way I knew: through the written word.

Before you turn the page, I'd also like to take this opportunity to thank you for reading *Flowers and Ash*. I hope you enjoy it. Take care and until next time.

Brenda Baker
caffeinatedramblings.org

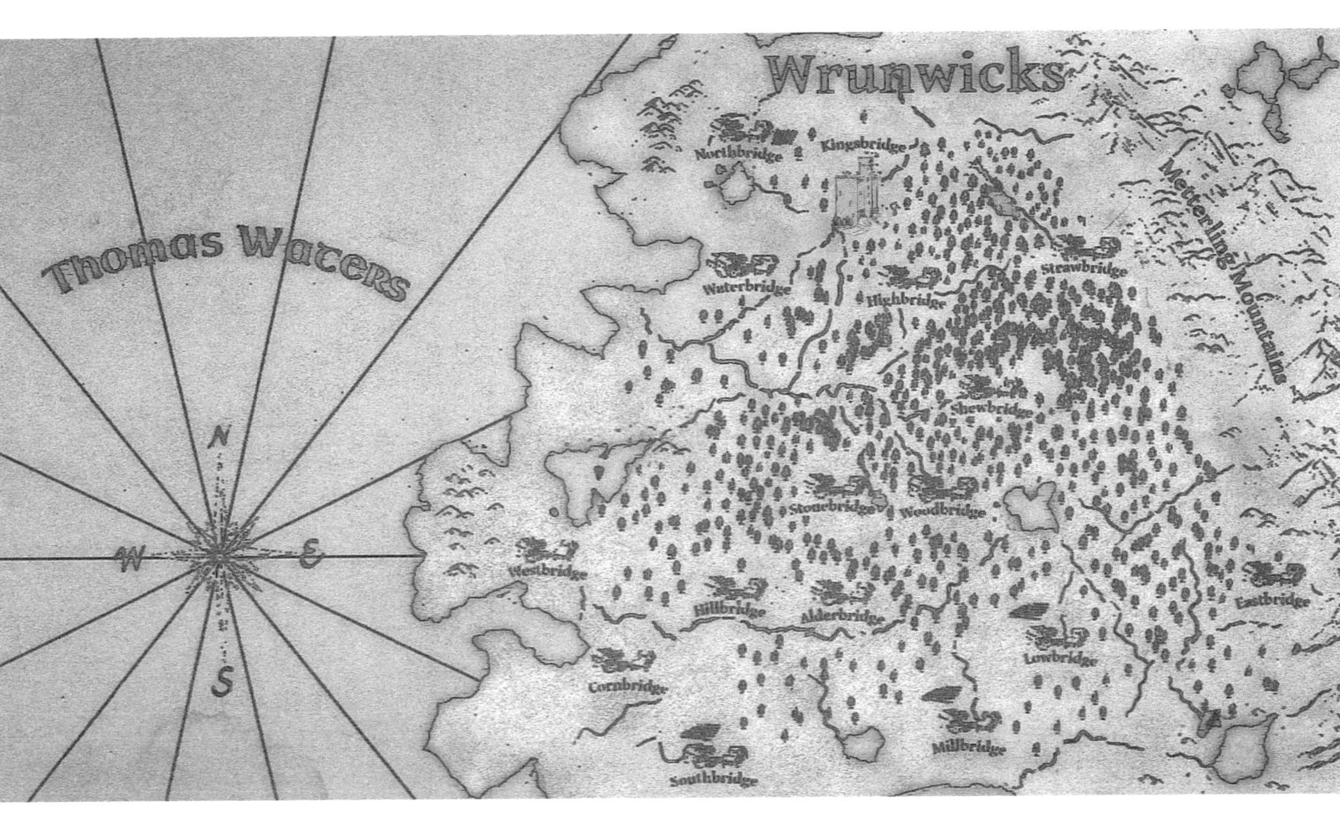

Wrunwicks
Metterling Mountains
Thomas Waters
Northbridge
Kingsbridge
Waterbridge
Highbridge
Strawbridge
Shewbridge
Stonebridge
Woodbridge
Westbridge
Hillbridge
Alderbridge
Eastbridge
Cornbridge
Lowbridge
Millbridge
Southbridge
N
E
S
W

Wrunwicks

In 1035 KR, Conrad Salt made a discovery. When the water from Thomas Waters evaporated, it left behind a curious white substance. And while Mr. Salt found the instance somewhat intriguing, he saw no use for the white grains, thus moving on to more important matters. But after dropping several of the grains onto his food one day, he noticed the rabbit's pleasing flavour. News of his latest discovery eventually spread throughout the land. Villages to the west and south of Wrunwicks began collecting their own salt, as it came to be known.

Then, in 1041, Alphonse Albridge discovered salt allowed meat to last far longer than the traditional smoking method. A wondrous discovery that caused the western and southern villages to increase the cost of salt beyond people's ability to pay. Each lord argued for the right to be the only salt provider to the central and mountainside villages. The ensuing war lasted for more than fifty years.

In 1094, King Lazoran passed away in his sleep. King Lazoran II accepted the crown among the cheers and celebrations of his loyal subjects. The new king multiplied his army threefold and led his knights to end the bloody war. The king's army gave the warring villagers a common enemy. When the villagers conceded to the king's mighty army in the historic battle of 1095, King Lazoran II travelled to Stonebridge, where he addressed the people.

The king divided salt distribution between three of the villages. He gave the other two villages the right to trade honey along with Stonebridge to reward its generosity during the war. A wise man, the king issued a new canon. Both salt and honey would be sold for an equally reduced price. Whether the villages agreed with the new law was of no consequence. The army had shown its strength.

In 1121, King Lazoran II died of an unknown disease like his father before him and, like his father before him, left the throne to his eldest son. A young and arrogant King Lazoran III dissolved his father's army, declaring the knights redundant in an age of peace. The people of Wrunwicks agreed with the king's sound reasoning as custom demanded.

Over a hundred years had passed without war or incident when in 1236, the vanishings began. After the fourth vanishing, people in the small town of Stonebridge began to fear the wrunwick had returned. A creature that once terrorized the land of Wrunwicks, only to disappear centuries ago.

Books described the wrunwick as cowardly creatures despite their size, who preyed on the young and helpless alike. The wrunwick never came near the villages, preferring to hide in the forest, or so the story went.

For you see, those with many stories to tell were considered blessed, regardless of their circumstances. Those with much coin were considered of good fortune. Of the two, the people of Stonebridge valued stories the most.

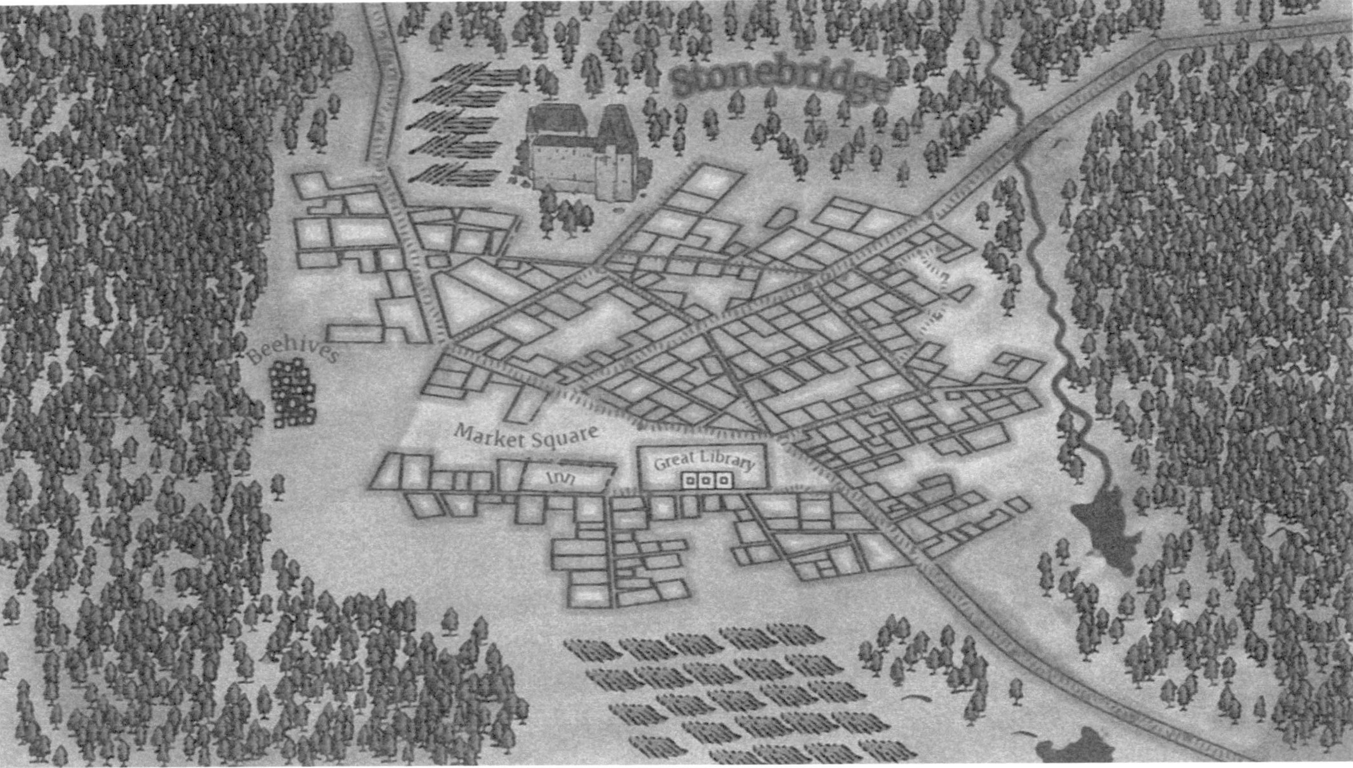

Stonebridge
Beehives
Market Square
Inn
Great Library

Stonebridge

1248 KR, Neomoks

The sun always rises on a new day. An age-old saying the good people of Wrunwicks knew well. Passed down from generation to generation like the beloved stories of old and new, it spoke of hope and purpose. Today was no different.

Surrounded by a forest spanning much of the kingdom, Stonebridge was located in the mid-belt of Wrunwicks. The people of Stonebridge travelled to the neighbouring town of Woodbridge and villages, but few ventured to the high or low belts. Throughout the snow season, passage was often unpredictable and dangerous. During the growing and harvesting seasons, duty precluded men and women from straying too far from home.

A township of 3,763 citizens according to the manor's records, Stonebridge marked the passing of time by its two moons and each season's toil. With the snow behind them once again, the people of Stonebridge were hoping for rain and sun. The growing season had just begun, and everyone looked forward to another fruitful year.

Today was the first day of Neomoks, dedicated to their Divine Mother to mark the new year and official start of growing season, humbly noted by appeals to Utaika for a plentiful harvest.

Nailed to a post in the market square, a notice informed every citizen past fourteen of their assigned field duties and work teams. The notice was carefully prepared by the lord's steward, who oversaw the manor's regional interests. The king's ordinance allowed shopkeepers to remain open when not in the fields, giving them a final chance to earn their yearly wron, payable to the lord's steward after the harvest. Any man without a shop or trade would not pause until the end of harvest, his dues paid with sweat alone.

Apart from children, the only names not included on the duty's rotation list were those of their lord, his servants, and the elders. Women deemed too old were also missing from the list. Instead, they were assigned permanent kitchen duty, effective on Mother's Day. It was a time-honoured system the people applauded for its efficiency and fairness.

The pig awarded to the two most productive teams was lauded as an example of their lord's generosity. In return, eager townsfolk tended the manor's crop without question or complaint. During the harvest festival, the lord's steward announced the winning teams. The festival and its prize were the two most anticipated events of the year and a welcome distraction from the vanishings.

So as the bells of dawn rang through the busy town, the first teams assembled in the crop fields to start their day of plowing and seeding. Shops opened their doors while women shooed children off to the Great Library, where elders shared the stories lived by them and their ancestors. Elders also taught the children reading, letters, numbers, and each of the king's thirty-four canons. Every child would stand before the elders at the age of fourteen to demonstrate their knowledge of the canons. If a child recited the canons to the elders' satisfaction, they could join their parents full-time to learn the skills of adulthood. The elders' citizen clearance offered a long-anticipated time of pride for all parents.

The Great Library was another source of pride for the good people of Stonebridge. Finished in 1196, it was deemed the most distinguished library in Wrunwicks. Built with the same colourful stone used throughout the renovation period initiated by the proud and ambitious King Lazoran III, the library walls rose above market square and symbolized hope for tomorrow. Over the years, the library had acquired a substantial collection of books from every belt across Wrunwicks, including Stonebridge. And just about all respectable folk in Stonebridge visited the Great Library at least once a year. Some visited often. One such visitor was Lisette, daughter of Sam and Nora Steels.

Part One

An Age of Peace

King Lazoran II
Stonebridge, 1095 KR

Good people of Wrunwicks, there can be no peace in times of greed. We must not seek riches of the purse but of the heart in its stead. May the hearts of our people be forever true and just in their pursuit. May we share this story and the many stories to come with humble breaths, uniting us all through each telling.

For Wrunwicks belongs to each of us. Through cooperation and wisdom, the people of our land know peace once more. My knights share many stories of your courage and hospitality. It be with a hopeful note that I observe our renewed fellowship. The people of Wrunwicks will surely prosper in their united purpose with such noble hearts.

Chapter 1

On a sleepy afternoon during the harvest of her eighth year, Lisette snuck past the Great Library's yawning doors. Inside the main hall, she beheld the endless rows of books. They seemed to have a life of their own. Covered in leather and bright fabric, the books called out to her young imagination. And so began her visits to the Great Library.

Though at eight years old, she was not yet permitted to touch the books or enter the reading chambers, where elders taught the children to read. She had to wait another two years before opening one of the brightly bound books, many of which were scribed in the large scriptorium behind the library.

During her tenth year, Lisette borrowed and read *Cinderella*, the beloved story of the girl with a tyrannical stepmother. Her love of reading forever sealed between the pages of that first library book, Lisette read whenever time and season permitted, borrowing and returning books once every fortnight.

Nine years later, Lisette kept her frequent visits to the library during the snow moons. But during the growing season, Lisette, like every other person with citizen clearance, belonged to a field team. Duty meant fewer visits to the library until after the harvest festival.

For her first rotation of the season, Lisette was on kitchen duty with her stepmom. This morning, however, she was going to the waterfalls with her friends: Aspen, Calder, and Ewart. It was the first time in two years that all four were assigned the same rotation schedule.

"Mind, ye'll need to be back to help with supper," Nora said as she placed some bread in a small pouch. "Your father be so fixed on winning that pig, he forgot that he'll need to eat."

"I'll be back by the third bell," Lisette promised, grabbing a piece of bread to take with her.

"'Tis a stroke of luck your friends are free today of all days," Nora said in her usual carefree manner. "Mother's Day, no less."

Lisette hugged her stepmom, spilling wayward crumbs down Nora's generous backside. After losing her mother, she was nervous when her father remarried. Having read *Cinderella* just one moon cycle before the wedding, an image of the evil stepmother remained all too vivid in her mind. But her fear proved unfounded. A warm-hearted woman, Nora treated Lisette like her own blood, never having any other children.

When Lisette had asked her stepmom about it some years ago, Nora laughed and said one daughter was enough. "I'll have more than my share of grandchildren when ye marry," she had gone on to add.

At nineteen, Lisette still had plenty of time before considering the outlandish prospect. As per the king's fourth canon, no man or woman could marry until their twenty-fifth birthday. She let go of her stepmom. "Calder told Mr. Brackins he'd finish building Lord Sumunder's chair before sunup tomorrow morning." Lisette gulped down the last drop of ale. "And build the second one by day's end for half the coin. He knows Calder's word be true. Aspen started supper for her mom last night."

Nora ushered Lisette out the door. "Don't forget to bring back that fish. I already promised some to Ewart's mom for supper."

The streaming sunlight chased the night's shadows from Lisette's thoughts. Sitting on a tree that fell victim to the tragic snowstorm of 1243, her mind was free to wander. She followed the light's checkered pattern through the woods.

The yearly escapes to Rocky Falls began the spring after her mother vanished. At first, they amounted to no more than a climb up to the cave behind the falls. Then at thirteen, she looked down at the swirling waters below, only to imagine a different girl than herself. She would imagine a girl filled with adventure, diving into its bone-chilling depths. After four years of escaping by herself, she invited her friends.

And from that year forward, soon as the lord's steward posted the duty notice, they would huddle around the curly-edged parchment to learn whose rotation schedules corresponded. Whoever's schedule agreed with Lisette's would accompany her to the falls. But as the years passed, they all began to make the trek to Rocky Falls whenever their field duty permitted, come rain or sun. It was their secret tradition, which her friends promised to share only with each other. From the beginning, Lisette had trusted them to keep their promise. A trust neither had broken.

Not one to sit for long, Ewart climbed a young ash tree to take in the view. Although Calder and Ewart were both past the age of boyhood, Calder liked to tease Ewart about being a child in poor disguise. Ewart often countered by telling Calder that he was being groomed for eldership before his time.

"I can see Stonebridge from up here," Ewart sang out.

"Has it changed since we left?" Calder asked lightly.

Ewart placed a hand over his eyes and squinted. "I can see Jistana in the kitchen with her mom. Is that Clarence outside their door?" He paused, continuing to squint into the distance. "Might he be looking for your girl with the ruby lips?"

Calder sprang from the fallen tree to grab a branch. "Your lips are far too bold, my friend. I challenge ye to a duel so I may strike those vile words from your balshan tongue."

"There be nothing quite like a duel to warm the blood." Ewart scrambled down from the ashwood. "Are ye to defend the lady of your courtship?" He picked up a branch of his own.

"I be courtin' no girl, so don't listen to what they say," Calder replied in the same playful tone. "Clarence best watch his step, should what I hear be true. Jistana be nobody's fool and won't be swayed by a few sweetened words."

Aspen turned to Lisette. They rolled their eyes in response to the men's antics. They had known each other for so long that little surprised them anymore. The oldest of the group, Calder would be twenty-five on his birthday. And while his birthday was only four moon cycles away, he had shown no interest in finding a wife. But it never stopped Ewart from teasing his friend.

Ewart assumed position with his right leg forward and knees bent. "On guard, my cheeky friend."

Calder grinned. "We'll see about that." He lunged his branch toward Ewart's shoulder.

Ewart blocked it, then stepped back and jumped on the rock

behind him with an exaggerated leap. "A tepid move at best. It'll take more than a sharp tongue to defend your lady's honour. Surely it be worth more sweat than that."

Thanks to many years of practice, both men were excellent swordsmen. The elders offered early morning lessons to children from the age of fourteen to seventeen after their citizenship clearance. Lessons were originally open to boys only, but when a young maiden repeatedly found herself in trouble, she was ordered to learn the art of sword fighting to keep her busy.

Depending on who told the story, it was a plan that worked so well, the young maiden forgot to marry. Others speculated the maiden was so busy learning to fight, she never learned the pleasing skills of a wife. In either case, the elders opened up lessons to include girls. The first time Lisette heard the story, she sent a silent note of gratitude to the fabled maiden. And like her friends, she continued to practice what she had learned all those early mornings at the Great Library.

"Are ye to cower on your mighty horse," Calder said with a sly grin, "or fight me like a man?"

"I prefer to fight on my own terms." Ewart jumped sideways from the rock. "A knight's heart be mightier than any beast's."

The men danced around, executing a series of strikes and blocks. They were as inwardly alike as they were different in appearance. Ewart's green eyes, sandy hair, and slight build contrasted sharply with Calder's stockier frame, dark brown eyes, and hair so black it was almost blue. But if a person were to look more closely, they would notice the same unflinching twinkle in both men's eyes.

Ewart's branch dodged around Calder's attempt to block it. "May love find ye ready and willing when it sings your name," he said, resting his branch on Calder's chest.

"How about we try focusing less on Calder's heart and more on getting to the falls," Aspen advised, mimicking the stern tone elders often used when a student failed to remember a canon.

Known by townsfolk for its violent beauty, Rocky Falls was part of a river system that emptied into the lake below, where it maintained course to another lake near the crop fields. Rising scarcely higher than a house, the falls redeemed themselves by the sheer strength of their waters. The stillness of the woods provided a stoic backdrop for the falls' pounding energy.

Letting memory guide their steps, Lisette and her friends dared the twelve-foot cliff to the cave's entrance. Standing inside the mouth of the cave, they looked down, exhilarated and wet from their passage through the thick curtain of water.

Lisette ignored the gloomy cavern behind them like every year. Located near the top of Rocky Falls, the cave saw few visitors. And the purpose of their trip was a showdown with fear, not the cave's lonely secrets.

Ewart jumped first, followed by Aspen. Next, it was Lisette's turn to test her courage. Frowning at the waters falling and crashing ever downward in a constant rush, she eyed the distance between herself and the lake below. It was the same distance as last time and every other time since her first attempt.

"Why do ye put yourself through this?" Calder asked gently.

Lisette looked down at her sodden friends. Aspen was rubbing her hands against the rising winds. "Why can't I jump?"

"Ye have more sense than they do," Calder replied, placing a hand on her shoulder.

"How long have we been friends?"

"Ye were already old when I met ye. Tis part of your charm."

Lisette punched Calder in the arm. "Are ye saying I'm boring?"

"Not in the least. Anyone can jump through a waterfall. That be easy. Just follow the person in front of ye. How many can make up their own mind?" Calder waved to their friends. "Let's get out of here. We'll need something to show for our trip."

Calder followed Lisette down the rocky cliff to where Aspen and Ewart were waiting. Aspen shook out the skirt of her dress and tucked the hem back over her belt.

Ewart grinned with a mixture of sympathy and mischief. "Best be leaving the stuff of fools to soft wits like me."

Lisette knew they would not question her failure to jump. They never did. Every year, she walked to Rocky Falls, determined that this year, she would conquer the falls. And every year, she walked away defeated.

Chapter 2

ocated in the west end of town facing the local villages, market square was the heart of Stonebridge. From the square, Stonebridge sprawled out in every direction. The square housed the largest and most respected shops in town, along with the Great Library and Wolf Moon Inn, the most prestigious inn within the lordship.

Many of the shops were shuttered for field duty, their wooden signs creaking in the wind. With wrons due after harvest, most shopkeepers preferred payment in coin during the growing season, but a few still accepted goods from their most loyal patrons. The tailor's shop where Lisette purchased her sewing materials was closed, as was her father's smithy.

With their morning lessons completed, the children drifted out from the Great Library to help in the fields. Dressed in waves of green and blue, the elders gathered for their daily meet by the well. Rebuilt after the fire of 1168, the well's casing reflected the stone found throughout the entire kingdom. The ancient well was also the only trusted source of fresh water for the township.

Lisette switched her attention to the butcher shop. It was open for business. "Maybe we should barter for some fresh deer meat to celebrate the beginning of another growing season." She held out the fish in her hand, knowing full well how ludicrous she sounded.

Meat from the butcher was a luxury afforded to few townsfolk outside Lord Sumunder, elders who were each paid a yearly coin by the manor for their contributions to the township, traders, and wealthy shopkeepers.

"It'll take more than fish with the new ordinance," Calder said. "I'd be happy with some custard pie."

The king's latest ordinance banned commoners from hunting deer to supplement their meat supply. It also reduced a butcher's allowance from six to three deer for the year. Townsfolk read the new ordinance and went about their day. They saw little value in complaining. Nor did they see the value four years ago when King Eldridge sent a notice throughout Wrunwicks inviting young men to participate in the newly established Knights Memorial.

The ceremony allowed the men of Wrunwicks to compete in a jousting or sword tourney for its unique prize, the right for a man to represent his fellow citizens in matters of their lordship. People's excitement soon turned to disappointment when they discovered the memorial's date. It would occur just one day before the first aromons of Laromoks, during the busiest moons of harvest and a time when no town or village could afford to lose their workers. The elders deemed the men's lack of participation another sign that subjects were more than happy with their king's reign.

"I was talking to a man from Woodbridge last night," Ewart said. "Word has it the deer are vanishing along with the people in the high belt. The king fears there'll be none left to hunt."

Lisette turned to look at Ewart. He possessed a quiet charm that appealed to parents. "King Eldridge should try hunting rabbit like the rest of us for a while." She looked over at the elders again. They were already engaged in a heated discussion. "What do ye suppose they're saying?"

"They've been holding meetings at the inn all winter," Aspen replied. "My father said the innkeeper ran out of wine."

"Meanwhile, the vanishings continue." Lisette was tired of hearing the elders needed more time to discuss the situation. Like just about all townsfolk, she respected the elders' sound judgment, but none of their meetings had yet to produce any suggestions or solutions. "How many people must we lose before acting?" she asked.

"The elders say we need more information," Calder replied.

Lisette threw Calder a sharp look. "That information won't be coming any time soon, if ever." As she spoke, Lisette heard the scorn in her voice. Anger would not bring their people back. "I'm sorry, Calder. Ye didn't deserve that."

Calder shrugged it off. "I hope ye're wrong about the elders."

Nora passed a trencher to Ewart's mom. "Mirken just the way ye like it."

"I'll be sure to fry some for your next field rotation," Ewart's mom promised.

"Biddle-babble," Nora replied. "There be plenty to go around. Ye know how much I love your boiled beans."

While Nora spoke to Ewart's mom, Lisette scooped the pottage into bowls and placed them on the table. Like many kitchens in Stonebridge, the table rested near the back wall, establishing a safe distance from the hearth and busy cooking area. Next to the table, an old wooden ladder led to the bedchambers upstairs. The chambers extended past the kitchen and over the back tewk or wash chamber, as their lord liked to call it. After supper, benches from the table would be placed in front of the hearth to take advantage of the fire's warmth and extra lighting for the nightly chores.

Nora bid the woman a good night, then turned to Ewart. "She don't look so good, your mom."

"Winter's been hard on her this year, I'm afraid. The warmer weather should brighten her cheeks."

"Aye. Our Divine Mother will see to her better health." Nora scooped a second ladle of pottage into Ewart's bowl. "Did ye do any bone carving this winter?"

"Not much, but I started a pipe a few nights ago." Ewart offered Lisette's father a grateful smile. "A way to thank ye for the morning away from the shop."

"Ye can thank Lisette for that," Sam replied between mouthfuls of his wife's treasured pottage, made extra thick to honour their guest. "She can be very persuasive."

Nora straightened her apron and sat down to eat. "Lisette takes after her father." She looked at Sam and grinned. "Just today, I told Fellis if I see her husband helping himself to the crop again this year, I'll be asking that ye escort him to the crop marshal. Imagine everyone doing the same. Winter would be very lean indeed."

"Always thinking of everyone else, my beautiful Nora," Sam said, glancing up from his bowl. "Let's hope Fellis shares your warning with her greedy husband."

Listening to her parents, Lisette's thoughts went back to the vanishings as they too often did. "When do ye think the elders will come up with a plan to find our people?" she asked her stepmom.

"Ye know the elders like to keep those things to themselves. Mrs. Grimly said her husband comes home from the inn full of wine and old tales about the wrunwick. They'll run out of their precious swig soon enough."

Lisette knew the stories well. They all did. Most dismissed them as legends meant to scare the children and stop them from going too far into the woods, although a few still believed them. Fact or fable, the vanishings breathed new life into the faded stories of their ancestors. Townsfolk shared their own opinion of the vanishings, blaming the mythical creature. But despite everyone's willingness to speculate, the truth remained unknown.

"If the people have their way, we'll have enough stories to share for years to come," Lisette said.

Nora nodded. "There be no shortage of imagination, it seems."

Chapter 3

hree fortnights passed. And with the growing season in full swing, the elders released students from their lessons and stories. The children spent their days scaring away birds and rodents while their parents tilled the fields, taking care to uproot the first Balsha grass from the ground. If allowed to grow, the deadly weed would spread throughout the fields, decimating all crops along the way.

As the townsfolk worked, they weighed in on the vanishings. A man had recently failed to return from a trip to the forest for kindling, prompting fresh speculation. Mothers forbade their children from venturing past the crop fields.

Working next to Nora, Lisette paused while a woman shared the story about how the wrunwick boiled their victims alive, making pottage from the bones. Workers listened in silence. Observing their hunger for every cursed detail, it occurred to Lisette that tales inspired by the vanishings were of greater interest to people than the truth behind them. But people deserved to know the real story. They all did. She looked to the sky, and in that instant, Lisette found the answer to her long-growing frustration. Like the weeds in her hand, she would get to the root of the danger threatening their people.

❧

While the fifth bell sounded across the fields, Lisette found Aspen hurrying home along with the other field workers. Tomorrow marked the start of a new rotation, so Lisette reasoned it was as proper a day as the next to make good on her plan.

"I have an idea how to solve what be happening to our people," Lisette whispered after catching up to Aspen. "But ye must swear not to tell anyone."

Aspen turned to her in bewilderment. "What do ye mean? What idea?"

"I'm afraid to say." Lisette looked around to ensure that no one was listening. "Just keep your ears open. Trust me, ye'll know if it works."

❧

The next day at noon, Lisette summoned the courage to approach the elders before she had time to change her mind. The elders were meeting at their usual place near the well. After they granted their permission for her to speak, Lisette steadied her hands. She had one chance to get it right.

"There was a young maiden who lived with her father and step-mom. The young maiden's stepmom treated her with love and devotion. A kinder woman ye will never find in all of Wrunwicks. She loved her stepdaughter as her own and had no other children.

"Then, when the young maiden was of rightful age, she dreamed of adventure and exploring the land. Oh, the stories she could tell upon her return! Hence, when the people of her town began to vanish, the young maiden knew what she had to do.

"And so she called upon those brave enough to travel with her. Together, they would find the truth. They would uncover if the wrunwick had returned and if they were killing the brave people of Stonebridge."

Pausing, Lisette allowed her words to sink in. The elders waited. The water carrier filled his barrels and pretended not to listen. She cast an eye over the well. Her mouth was dryer than wool, but she didn't dare stop long enough for a drink of water. She forced herself to continue.

"Although the young maiden was eager to begin her adventure, she knew to seek the counsel of her esteemed elders. The maiden hoped the wise elders might offer their advice before sharing her story with the brave townsfolk. And perhaps they would grant the maiden their blessing. For the time had come to put an end to the vanishings. It was time to act."

Lisette stopped there and waited for them to address her plea. The elders possessed keen minds despite their reluctance to act. And without their approval, she had little hope of anyone joining her or obtaining permission from Lord Sumunder and the privy council to leave.

At last, it was Mr. Walling who spoke. "I've known ye since birth, Lisette. Tis clear your story be just beginning. Though tis quite unheard of for a girl to lead a journey of this import, particularly during the growing season. But perhaps tis high time for a change. I presume your parents have given their permission."

Lisette nodded. If they knew the truth, they would never grant their blessing. She placed both hands in the plackets of her skirt and crossed her fingers so hard they hurt.

"Very well, then." Mr. Walling studied Lisette. "We will present your case to the lord and his council before day's end. They need answers too. The vanishings that plague our fair town cannot be allowed to go on." He looked to see if any of the elders disagreed with him. "We would not normally grant our blessing so easily, but these are far from normal times," he said when no one raised an argument.

Lisette tried to hide her sense of victory, although she could not stop the smile that made its way across her face. She knew asking for permission to leave on such a journey had been a bold request. Some were bound to call it shameless at the very least.

"Be here tomorrow by the third bell," Mr. Walling continued. "We will spread word of your story. May the adventure ye seek be only the start of many stories to come. Ye have our blessing in this matter."

Lisette bowed in gratitude. "Thank ye, Mr. Walling," she said, not yet old enough to address an elder by their given name. "I swear to return with the truth and the stories of our journey. Now I must return home to share the news with my mother." She bid the elders a quick farewell before one of them found occasion to dispute Mr. Walling's decision.

❧

During her return home, Lisette prayed to Utaika for guidance. Sam listened to his wife and often asked her opinion on matters of business. If she could convince Nora, her father would be more likely persuaded. She needed Nora on her side. Still dazed by her meeting with the elders, Lisette ran through the kitchen door. Nora was at the butcher's table skinning a rabbit.

"There ye are. Come now. Ye can help with this rabbit." Nora gently peeled back the skin on the rabbit's legs. She had already started a new winter tunic for Sam.

Unsure where to begin or what to say, Lisette blurted out the news of her plan to find out what was happening to their people, her subsequent meeting with the elders and her petition to leave Stonebridge. The words spewed out in a tangled mess.

Nora listened without so much as a sound, her eyes growing wider with each word. "Surely, such a burden be best suited to men with experience," she said after Lisette had finished speaking. "Ye've never been past Woodbridge, and that was years ago. How in the name of our Divine Mother did ye persuade the elders to bless such an idea?"

Lisette shared the story she had told the elders. "They'll be meeting with the lord and his council by day's end. Their minds are made."

"All that wine be dulling their wits," Nora said. "There be no other reason to let a young maiden go on such a dangerous journey without her parents' permission. Tis against the canons, for king's sake. I'll be sharing a piece of my own mind with Mrs. Grimly. Maybe she can sharpen her husband's senses."

"The vanishings have to stop. We can't allow them to continue any longer." Lisette recognized the stubborn look on Nora's face. She had to convince her, or the journey was over before it began. "I told the elders I have your permission."

Her stepmother's eyes grew wider still as the creases in her forehead deepened in an unfamiliar frown. "And now they'll share that with the council. If they should learn the truth, ye'd be thrown in a cage. What possessed ye, Lisette?"

"They won't. Unless we tell them. This be something I have to do. I grow more frustrated with each vanishing and can no longer wait till someone else finally decides to do something about it. By then, who knows how many will have disappeared? Will ye grant me your permission? Please, Mom."

Nora sighed, pulling the skin off the rabbit. "My dearest and willful Lisette," she said after a long pause. "As ye know, I'm hoping ye'll have many children someday. But only our Divine Mother knows that. And it be your life, not mine. Ye still have years before taking a husband. Now be the time for ye to walk a different path, it seems. I can only hope that path brings ye home safe."

Lisette squeezed her stepmom. "I knew I could depend on ye. Tonight, I'll need to convince Dad."

"No need to worry about that." Nora's face softened. "Ye know how he listens to me."

"My father be a very wise man." Lisette had never known her stepmom to be serious for long.

"Aye, that he be," Nora agreed, regaining the sparkle in her eyes.

As Lisette helped Nora prepare supper, she gave thanks to Utaika for the woman who had raised her. There was no other talk of Lisette's going away until her father arrived home.

Complaining of a bad back after another day of damage done, Sam took refuge by the hearth. Nora informed him of Lisette's news. Sam sat staring into the fire, silent and still as a rock. When Nora finished, Lisette backed her stepmom's words with a reminder of all those missing, then waited for the most important approval of them all. After what seemed like the passing of three bells, he turned toward Lisette. She searched her father's face for a clue to his thoughts. He looked calm. And for the briefest moment, Lisette glimpsed a sadness lurking below the surface.

"I always knew ye were strong of mind and heart," Sam said at last. "With your nose more often stuck in a book or sewing project, ye never gave us any trouble. No maiden has ever taken a journey such as this, but who am I to discourage my only child."

As her father spoke, Lisette realized how lucky she was to have parents who paid no heed to the opinions of others. In supporting her quest, they risked attracting the criticism of those who valued tradition more than their children. "I won't be gone any longer than necessary," she said. "Once I discover what or who be causing our people to disappear, I promise to return."

Lisette looked around their kitchen. It was as unassuming as her stepmom. She paused. Her eyes settled on a shelf over the salt meat barrel. Nora's most prized possessions were still the flowers she had picked for her as a child, kept in a wooden box for safekeeping. Smiling at the memory of Nora placing one of the flowers inside its new home, Lisette took in the faces of her parents. And like the flowers in their box, the image of her parents sitting by the fire would last forever inside her heart.

"How many are ye hoping will answer your quest?" Nora asked.

"I haven't given it much thought, nor have I told any of my friends. I can't expect them to leave everything behind for me."

"I'm sure ye'll find enough brave souls once ye share your story," Nora said with her usual optimism.

"I know I'm asking a lot of the townsfolk." Lisette hoped it wouldn't turn into something ugly. "But I can't be the only one in need of answers."

"Biddle-babble. If I was younger, I'd join ye myself. I was known to stir up a little trouble from time to time," Nora replied.

"Dad would be lost without ye," Lisette said, grateful to Nora for not repeating her initial doubts on the matter.

"Aye. Your father be best suited for the iron he hammers." Nora reached for her husband's hand.

Following Nora's cue, Sam rose from his bench and accepted his wife's hand. "Lisette be right. I'd be ruined without ye, my wise and beautiful Nora. May we dance tonight and all the nights of our twilight years."

"I might not be as young as I once was, but I'm still not old enough to consider my twilight years," Nora teased her husband.

"Ye'll never be old to me." Sam led Nora to the middle of their kitchen.

"I've gotten too old for flummery, dear husband," Nora said with a twirl to the left.

While her parents danced to the murmuring of the fire, Lisette questioned if she would ever find such happiness. She still missed her mother every day, not that anyone could have expected Sam to raise his daughter alone. She was happy he found his second chance at love, though she still wondered what happened to her mother all those years ago. One of the first to vanish, Lisette held little faith that her mother lived. But try as she might to ignore it, the last flicker of hope refused to die.

Those first vanishings were declared accidents beyond anyone's control. It was impossible to accept that reasoning now. Thinking back, Lisette asked herself if it was ever truly possible. How does a person disappear without leaving a single trace? Save for a basket in Lisette's chamber, her mother may as well never existed. She saw no point in mentioning it to her parents. They didn't have the answers any more than she did.

Lisette stoked the fire. "I think I'll do some reading."

"Don't stay up too late," Nora said, letting go of Sam.

"I won't." When Lisette was younger, Nora would brush her hair before bed, sharing stories of her childhood.

"I see now it was courage that coloured your hair," Nora said and planted a kiss next to the star-shaped birthmark on Lisette's forehead.

Chapter 4

True to his word, Mr. Walling had spread the news about Lisette's speech. So as the chantry bells rang noon, townsfolk drifted from fields, shops, and homes to hear what Lisette had to say. On seeing the number of people flocking to the square, Nora tutted in surprise, telling Lisette she could not recall a single time work had been interrupted during the growing season, making today's call to meet an unprecedented event.

Lisette nodded in agreement, the full weight of her venture turning both feet to stone. She looked around for her father, but he was reshoeing Lord Sumunder's mare and said he might not be able to leave the smithy. It was just as well. If today's address turned ugly, she didn't want him to witness her failure.

She forced her legs to move, twisting her way through the sweat and noise. When she emerged from the crowd with Nora, Lisette turned to her stepmom. Nora looked ready to take on the wrunwick if necessary.

"Tell them what ye told me," Nora said earnestly. "Make them understand. I'll be right here if ye need me."

The podium loomed in front of the well. Lisette could feel the people's excitement breathing down her neck like an unseasonably warm wind. The crowd stood back and waited. She left her stepmom to join Mr. Walling on the podium. Townsfolk gawked in anticipation, whispering to each other as she passed.

How are they going to react? Will they accept what I have to say or laugh me off the podium? Who am I to think I can learn what be happening to our people? I must be out of my mind. Lisette climbed the four steps onto the podium. It was around nine feet long and five feet wide. Older folk said it was once used for hangings. *Maybe they'll hang me for dog madness. Can they hang ye for that?*

Lisette forced her fears aside and hoped no one could see how scared she was. Speaking with a confidence she wished were true, Lisette adapted her story for the townsfolk. She skipped over any reference to her stepmom, speaking instead of murdering monsters drenched in the blood of their people. She spoke of the need for answers, no matter how grievous those answers might be. The townsfolk stared with their mouths open in shock and disbelief. She finished by inviting others to join her quest.

The townsfolk continued to stare. No one stirred in the noon-day sun. Lisette stared back, hoping she hadn't gone too far in her address. But people needed to listen. Nora smiled encouragingly. Lisette returned her stepmom's smile. What would she do without stepmom? Nora looked fearless in a wall of faces, strengthening her own determination to see the day through. She held her ground. Time stretched to the sky, trailing behind a lone cloud.

Mr. Walling approached Lisette and turned to face the crowd.

"Those who answer Lisette's call will be relieved of their field duties and this year's citizen wron. Once again, Lord Sumunder and his privy council have shown themselves to be generous and wise. Who will be brave enough to answer the call? Who will be brave enough to join Lisette's quest?"

Lisette looked down at the crowd, hiding her surprise. No one had ever been exempted from wron before.

"I'll join ye!" Roy shouted. "If my parents approve, of course."

Waking from their stupor, the townsfolk turned to Roy. Voices broke out in a sputter of confusion. Lisette ignored the voices. She located Roy's eager expression.

"Ye can count on us!" Ewart and Henry sang out.

"Me too!" Aspen said. "I could do with a quest."

"It'll be the adventure of a lifetime," Calder added.

Lisette followed the voices of her friends and smiled in relief when she spotted the rest of their group. "Thank ye, dear friends. Together, we'll uncover the truth behind these vanishings. Our people deserve to know what happened to their loved ones."

Silence fell over the crowd once again, apart from a thin cord of indistinct chatter to her right. Their lord's sanction outweighed any criticism they might harbour.

"I also need to thank our wise lord and elders who have blessed this journey." She smiled at Mr. Walling before casting an eye over the crowd. A few of the older folks looked away. Several more looked skeptical, but others were smiling. She returned their smiles, mentally thanking Mr. Walling.

"Why don't we meet at Black Boar Tavern tonight to discuss the matter?" Calder suggested.

"Will everyone be able to make it after supper?" Lisette asked.

The group of friends nodded. It was settled then. Those who disagreed with her words would save their judgment until her back was turned.

Night crawled over shuttered homes and shops as it crept through the streets of Stonebridge. On Brewering Street, Black Boar Tavern welcomed loyal patrons inside its walls, long stained with a thick layer of soot. One of many such establishments on the bustling street, Black Boar served the usual cheap wine, overpriced mead, and ale. Most patrons preferred a mug of sweet ale. It quenched the summer thirst and filled empty stomachs during the leaner moons of winter. A tavern without ale was a quiet place indeed, unlike the noise drifting from Black Boar's open door.

A pungent bouquet of stale wine and freshly brewed ale greeted patrons before entry. The rowdy tavern amounted to a large square chamber filled with empty wine and salt meat barrels that served as tables. Barrels offered the advantage of being easily grouped by those looking to unwind with a game of dice. Lisette scanned the tables for her friends.

The young patrons sat near the fireplace. At seventeen, Roy was scarcely old enough to frequent the tavern. Town lords determined at what age his citizens could drink with adults. To coincide with the entry to apprenticeships, Lord Sumunder declared seventeen the rightful age to be weaned from childhood. Until then, children drank the weaker ale, almond milk, and water. For special occasions, they sometimes drank sheep or cow's milk sweetened with honey.

"My ale be growing warmer by the score while ye stand there," Aspen shouted above the din.

Lisette paid for her wine, thanked the owner, and went to join her friends.

"When ye said ye had an idea, ye weren't kidding," Aspen said, watching Lisette pull up a stool next to her. "Imagine us travelling across Wrunwicks. Who would've thought such a thing possible?"

"I didn't want ye to feel pressured into joining me. I don't know how long our journey will last or what be in store for us," Lisette explained. "Then there was getting the elders to agree without anyone knowing my plan. I didn't know if it would even work. Ye know how Stonebridgers like to exaggerate."

"How did ye manage to get the elders' blessing?" Ewart asked.

"I told them the same story I told the townsfolk, more or less."

"Release from field duty be almost impossible to gain," Ewart observed. "After Mr. Walling announced the wron exemption, I'm surprised more didn't offer to join ye."

"Everyone has their eye on that pig." Lisette grinned. "They'll have to beat my father first."

"As your friend, I wouldn't dream of letting ye go without me," Aspen said. "I spoke to my parents earlier, and Father gave me his approval. Now, if Mom has her way, she'll talk him out of it. But I'm old enough to go without their permission. Who knew turning twenty would bring such good fortune?"

"My mother was reluctant at first," Roy said. "But then Father said I'd return a man, whatever that means."

They chuckled at the baffled expression on Roy's face. The youngest among them, he also had the greatest sense of humour.

"With any luck, ye'll discover his meaning by journey's end," Calder said.

Roy flashed the grin that had many a young maiden more than a little charmed. "Ye'll have to ask me when we return."

"Your fanciers will miss ye," Lisette teased.

A loud cheer rang out from the other side of the tavern. Lisette spotted Vincent approaching their table. It was a poorly kept secret that he despised her. No one knew why, save for Lisette. She had caught him stealing from the baker's shop when they were children. And while she had never told anyone, Vincent nursed his hostility like a mother nursing her baby.

"Well, well. If it isn't Lisette and her squawking buffoons come to grace us with their presence," Vincent drawled. "I should wish ye luck on your quest I suppose, but we all know I wouldn't mean it."

"If it isn't Vincent and his bumbling wit," Lisette said in a tone drier than her wine.

"When can I expect the overdue pleasure of bidding ye farewell?" Vincent asked.

Henry smirked. "How be your lovely sister? Still frequenting the Balsha district?"

"Malicious rumours spread by people like ye." Blood rushed to Vincent's ears. "My sister be no topa. Married close to a year now."

"We haven't had time to decide," Lisette said, pretending to be distracted by the game of dice at a nearby table.

Catching her eye, Ewart spoke up. "We'll be leaving in four days. So if ye would excuse us, we were about to leave."

"Lest we keel over from the stench of your rotting breath," Henry quipped.

"Don't let me be the reason ye're delayed." Vincent bowed with one hand over his knee.

Lisette acknowledged Vincent's hand with a dismissive nod. It was the only sign of disrespect a patron dared without risk of being thrown onto the street. She expected no more and certainly no less from her childhood enemy. "Fare ye well, Vincent. And good health to your family."

"Four days *would* give us time to prepare," Calder said when Vincent had left.

"We could meet in the square after the first bell." Lisette looked at her friends and smiled. She should've known they would never abandon her.

The noise in the tavern rose along with people's spirits. Townsfolk liked their drink even more than they liked playing dice. Although most made it home without incident, the occasional misfortune was inevitable when tongues became too loose. In rare cases, a man lost his life. The soon-to-be travel companions left the tavern to those still celebrating another day behind them.

They walked the maze of empty streets following the familiar route that ended with Ewart's house. After Roy turned the corner onto Miller Street, Lisette and Ewart were the only two remaining. Lisette glanced at Ewart. It was high time to ask about their trips to Rocky Falls.

She had avoided the question for long enough. It was just easier to forget about it until she faced the falls again. But if she were to find the courage to leave Stonebridge, she needed to find the courage to speak with Ewart first. It was far less intimidating than broaching the matter with everyone at once, and she had known Ewart since she could walk.

"I've been meaning to ask why ye never say anything about me dragging us to the falls every year but not once jumping myself." Lisette let out a sigh of relief. She should've asked years ago.

Ewart threw her a quick look. He appeared taken off guard by the question. Across the street, a woman blew out the night lantern hanging by her front door.

"Ye don't drag us to the falls," Ewart said slowly. "We go because we want to. As for ye not jumping, I can only assume ye have your reasons. We respect that. Ye'll tell us when ye're ready."

"But what if I don't really have a reason at all?" Lisette paused before voicing her greatest fear. "What if I'm nothing more than a scared rabbit and just too afraid to jump? What if I'm only kidding myself into thinking I'll ever have the courage?"

Ewart looked at her and smiled gently. "Last I heard, rabbits don't give speeches or go in search of their rabbit friends. If they did, Stonebridge would be overrun. Ye're braver than ye think."

"Have ye ever spoken to a rabbit?"

"Not recently. But I'll be sure to ask the next time I see one."

"Did ye speak to my father yet?" Lisette asked, steering their conversation back to the more pressing matter at hand. An entire year stood between her and Rocky Falls, unlike their journey. And maybe rabbits did go on quests. She would find out soon enough.

"This afternoon. Your father knows a young man in need of an apprenticeship. He said I'm welcome back when we return home and warned me to keep an eye on his only daughter."

They had arrived in front of Lisette's house. Ewart bid her goodnight with a promise to meet in the morning. His house being next door, he walked the six paces and saluted before going inside.

Lisette entered the kitchen where Nora had taught her how to cook and sew. On her way to bed, she checked the fire cover and picked up Nora's book from the floor, placing it on her stepmom's bench. Mouser was asleep in the middle of the bed when she closed the door to her chamber. He woke to greet her and joined his owner on the pillow. That night, she dreamed of giant rabbits attacking Stonebridge.

Chapter 5

For Lisette and her loyal band of friends, the next three days were filled with preparations. Townsfolk nicknamed them the Truth Seekers, counting on them to solve the mystery of more than a decade or perhaps even centuries. Folks who disagreed with their quest kept a careful silence, at least in the company of busy tongues. They dared not contradict their elders, which would break the eighth canon. And so praise of the Truth Seekers circulated without contest.

When Lisette heard the nickname, she prayed they could live up to people's expectations, despite her claim of similar persuasion during her speech. A promise, she knew, was one thing, but making good on that promise was cut from a different cloth altogether. She vowed to earn the people's trust in them. The truth was out there somewhere. They just had to find it.

On the evening of the third day, Stonebridge prepared to honour the Truth Seekers. The much-lauded event was to be held in the main hall of Wolf Moon Inn. Everyone was invited, including Lord

Sumunder and Lady Constance. What began as a tiny spark, had grown into a bright flame of hope, lighting the heart of Stonebridge with it.

To feed that flame, work in the fields had ended with the chimes of a single bell. The bell announced it was time to gather in celebration. So when the fifth bell rang through the streets a short while thereafter, townsfolk were already spilling onto the square, their arms filled with pots and trenchers.

As people entered the hall of Wolf Moon Inn, they placed their contributions to the evening's feast on the banquet table. It overflowed with food, generously prepared for the occasion. Pottages, meat pies, fried fish, and puddings were all offered. There was even ale, courtesy of the innkeeper.

All but three of the tables were pushed up against the walls to provide additional space for guests. The stairs were cordoned off to discourage anyone from straying into the wrong bed. Beneath the oversized stairway, the right side corner had been cleared away for music, a must-have for any Stonebridge celebration.

The lutists were already playing when Lisette arrived with Sam and Nora. Her parents went to find a spot for Nora's egg pudding at the banquet table nearby. Egg pudding had always been one of Lisette's favourite dishes. A fact that Nora could not resist pointing out on their way into the inn.

Given the number of townsfolk present, Lisette suspected her parents would be gone for a while. Nora loved to gossip as much as the next person. And Lisette knew her father would oblige his wife. He always did. Seeing Aspen, Lisette made her way over. Aspen was talking to her mother and older brother.

"Ye're going to look like soft wits travelling in those clothes," Erwin said to his sister just as Lisette joined their company.

That afternoon, Lisette had drawn a promise from Aspen, who agreed she would let her mother know about their riding outfits. Aspen's mother was not one to hold back her opinion, and Lisette figured it was best to avoid any surprises before their departure. The sour look on Mrs. Greene's face said that Aspen had kept her promise.

"Ye picked up the wrong impression," Lisette said before Aspen had a chance to respond. Erwin's mouth had the distinct habit of annoying her. "It just so happens that I managed to find used ones in good repair. The outfits just needed a few minor adjustments." She smiled at Aspen. "I even had enough coin left to buy us hooded mantles," she said, referring to the shoulder-length garments which had recently become popular among nobles and commoners alike.

"Riding outfits are for men," Erwin said with his mean blend of defiance and insolence.

"Then we'll have to make do," Lisette replied. "Riding outfits are far more practical."

"Do ye already have yours?" Mrs. Greene asked her daughter with a cold expression.

"Yes, Mom." Aspen stared at the floor.

"Women travelling in men's clothing of all things. I never heard the likes in all my years. Preposterous," Mrs. Greene said, stiffening her back in readiness for battle. "I wish ye had spoken to me first."

Aspen lifted her head. "I didn't think it was worth the topic of conversation."

Listening to Aspen and Mrs. Greene, Lisette felt sorry for her best friend. Mrs. Greene could freeze the sun with a mere glance if she fixed her mind on it. "Trousers will protect us better than our dresses," she said politely, not wanting to further incense the woman. "And we may be travelling for some time."

"I can no longer tell Aspen what to do," Mrs. Greene said. "But know that it be against my better wishes. Are your parents aware of this?"

"They are," Lisette replied. She refused to say more. It was none of this woman's business what her parents thought. "Perhaps we should see what splendours the good people have provided for us this evening," she continued, ignoring the full plate in Mrs. Greene's hands.

"I can go with ye," Aspen said a little too quickly. "I haven't had a bite since this morning."

Lisette recognized the desperation in her friend's eyes. Aspen gave her the same look whenever she needed to escape her mother.

※

Hungry guests rallied around the banquet table in their quest for food. Going straight for Nora's egg pudding, Lisette filled her plate bearing the inn's mark, a wolf standing inside a crescent moon to guide travellers on their journey. The wolf symbolized loyalty to their king, lord, and land.

"Henry's here," Aspen said, helping herself to a piece of fish.

Henry stood next to a barrel, drinking his ale and scanning the hall. Upon seeing them, he waved.

"Let's see what he be up to," Aspen suggested. "It'll give Mother some time to dampen her tongue."

Lisette waved to let Henry know they had spotted him. "That might take longer than the banquet." She hurried to join Aspen, who was already five steps ahead of her.

"Quite the turnout," Henry remarked when Lisette and Aspen joined him.

"Ye know Stonebridgers, always up for an excuse to celebrate." Lisette dug her fork into Nora's egg pudding.

"Ye think Lord Sumunder and Lady Constance will join us?" he asked.

"They always come to our weddings." Aspen studied the floor. "The innkeeper expects they'll show. He didn't strew the lavender for us."

As if on cue, Lord Sumunder and Lady Constance entered the hall. Before she married Lord Sumunder, Lady Constance had been a commoner like the rest of them. But after his first wife died in childbirth, the youth and beauty of Mr. and Mrs. Fern's only daughter had so charmed their lord that he soon asked for her hand in marriage. They married on the day of their lady's twenty-fifth birthday. Now pregnant with her first child, Lady Constance was finally beginning to fill out her dress. Most women would have been showing two moon cycles ago.

Lisette was pleased to see Lady Constance wearing the gown she had sewn for her. While common women wore kirtles outside their linen smocks, Queen Harriet and the ladies of Wrunwicks liked to add the more sumptuous layer with kirtles made of fine wool or silk, often dyed to complement their gowns.

Made of pale-yellow velvet, their lady's gown had the same long sweeping sleeves worn by Queen Harriet in the Great Library's high portrait. The gown's sleeves and V-neck displayed their lady's dark blue kirtle. Lisette had also included side lacings in the gown's bodice. Lady Constance could ease the lacings as she grew with her baby.

"I swear Lady Constance be shinier than a new sword," Aspen said, admiring the handsome couple.

Lisette smiled proudly. "Tis my best work to date."

The hall had grown quiet. It was the first time Stonebridgers dared invite their lord and lady to an event other than weddings.

But Kurt, their innkeeper and host, had insisted, declaring the evening to be no ordinary affair.

Arriving at the table setting prepared for them, Lord Sumunder and Lady Constance stood facing the townsfolk. The innkeeper's oldest son rushed to fill the silver goblets of their most honoured guests. Kurt's younger son scurried to their guests' side with a washbowl and drying cloth. The innkeeper liked to remind folks that even he knew the importance of good manners.

"Fine people of Stonebridge, I thank ye for this most gracious invitation. Like everyone here this evening, it be my keen wish to celebrate the courage of our young band of Truth Seekers. And like ye, I look forward to their return and the stories they will share with us. Let us toast to their good health and safe passage home." Lord Sumunder raised his goblet along with Lady Constance. "Let us also toast the wisdom of our elders."

"Hear, hear!" the townsfolk sang out, raising their mugs. They waited for their lord and lady to take the first drink.

"When I'm heavy with child, I'll drink honey water too," Aspen said, watching Lady Constance.

"Have ye read the book?" Calder asked.

"No, but what be good for our queen and lady, be good enough for me."

"Ye, my dear Aspen, will never be a lady," Henry said.

Aspen elbowed Henry's arm. "Your opinion counts less than that of my shoes."

Lisette shook her head in amusement. She had picked up the book once, aptly titled, *The Growing Baby*. The book's author advised expecting moms to drink honey water as the preferred means to sweeten a baby's disposition. Expecting moms dismissed the book until Queen Harriet began following the author's advice over two decades ago. Soon after, all the ladies in waiting were imitating their queen, followed by commoners with honey to spare.

"I don't think we'll need to worry about motherhood or good graces any time soon," Lisette said, her amusement turning to laughter.

"Now, let us enjoy this lavish feast." Lord Sumunder's voice boomed across the hall.

After Lord Sumunder and Lady Constance sat down to eat, the privy council and senior elders resumed their seats at the two side tables. The town's people went back to their celebrations.

While Lord Sumunder and Lady Constance enjoyed their meal, Lisette went with Aspen and Henry to hunt down the rest of their friends. Aspen spied Calder near the door. He was talking to Ewart and Roy.

"I guess Vincent couldn't resist the free food," Calder said, looking over Henry's shoulder.

Lisette had also spotted Vincent on the way over. "As long as he keeps a safe distance, I'll keep mine. But he shouldn't be a problem. He'd never risk the attention of so many elders or Lord Sumunder. Vincent be nothing if not a coward."

"Speaking of food," Roy said. "I was talking to Kurt earlier, and he invited us to stop by tomorrow to pick up some leftovers."

"A generous offer," Ewart said. "We could pick them up before saying our farewells."

The lutists increased their tempo with the town's favourite. A lover of music, Roy tapped his foot in response. A woman walked up to Lisette and hugged her. As a dear friend of Nora's, Lisette considered Edith part of the family.

Edith wrapped her arms around Lisette. "I wanted to personally wish ye a safe and fruitful journey. Tis about time someone offered to find out what be happening. Never ye mind the folks who say otherwise."

"I only wanted to do right by our people, Aunt Edith."

"Well, ye succeeded." Edith released her. "Your mother be so proud of ye."

"I only hope we can live up to everyone's faith in us."

"Ye will. I can feel it in my bones. I be needing to get back to my husband now, but I'll see ye tomorrow at the square." Edith wished the others safe passage and left with feet quicker than their lord's prized horse.

"I didn't realize how much support this journey would receive." Lisette watched Edith skirt around the horde of merrymakers.

"The townsfolk want answers as much as we do," Calder said. "We've lost too many good people. And for the first time since the vanishings began, they might get those answers."

After their honoured guests finished eating, Kurt helped his sons push back the tables to make room for dancing. The lutists played a melody composed for the noble couple. Soft and upbeat, the tune attracted smiles from the townsfolk. Lord Sumunder and Lady Constance danced inside their circle of admirers. Throughout Wrunwicks, the people danced to honour Utaika and to celebrate peace between the land belts. Through story, the elders of every town and village guaranteed the Salt Wars and its lessons survived in people's memories.

Lord Sumunder and Lady Constance finished their opening dance and approached the Seekers.

"Please allow me to offer my blessings." Lord Sumunder pulled a small leather purse from his belt. "To assist with your quest."

"That be most charitable," Lisette said, taken aback by the gift.

"But I'm not sure we can accept such generosity, my lord."

"Then I shall have to insist," Lord Sumunder said. "It will be my honour." He gestured to include all six comrades. "In exchange, I ask that ye visit the manor upon your return so that we may hear the details of your venture."

"The honour will be ours, my lord." Lisette bowed gratefully.

"And now we must be off." Lady Constance placed a hand on her stomach. "I fear I've had enough excitement for one evening."

"Of course, my lady." Ewart held their lady's hand and bowed.

Lord Sumunder handed the purse to Lisette. "May this coin provide some of what ye need."

Lisette accepted the gift. "May your baby be born strong and healthy."

They watched as Lord Sumunder and Lady Constance took their leave. Lisette was still trying to make sense of what had just happened. A commoner never disobeyed their lord. She looked down at the purse. It weighed heavy in her hand. She had no idea where their journey would take them. The extra coin could prove helpful, and she couldn't give the purse back. She fastened the drawstring around her belt loop.

The Seekers danced next to the other guests, ate until their stomachs hurt, and drank until it was time to say farewell to the evening. Townsfolk filled the square with cheerful hollers before disappearing down shadowed roads. Tomorrow would bring more sweat, but tonight the town's men and women had no care for the hardship that awaited them. Among the boisterous cheers and lighthearted banter of neighbours, the Seekers promised to meet at dawn.

Chapter 6

efore work the next morning, townsfolk gathered in the square. Lisette and her friends hugged their families for the last time. Roy's mom wiped her tears. Mrs. Greene frowned while Aspen teased Erwin about missing her. Sam gave Nora his new pipe for safekeeping. Lisette summoned a smile for her parents, hoping it held more confidence than her heart.

Reaching into his blacksmith apron, Sam gave Lisette a copper sprig inside the traveller's moon. "I finished it last night after the banquet."

The brooch was given to loved ones on the rare instance they were expected to be gone for either length of time. The sprig served to remind its owner that no matter how far they travelled, they had a home waiting for them. Moved by her father's gesture, Lisette hugged him for the second time. "Thank ye, Dad," she said. "I'll wear it proudly." She fixed the brooch to her green leather jacket, placing it just above her heart.

"Know that our love travels with ye." Sam glanced at Nora. "We'll miss ye every day that ye're gone from us."

After speaking with Roy and his parents, Mr. Walling stopped in front of Lisette. "Allow me to wish ye a safe return."

Lisette bowed. "Thank ye once again for blessing this journey."

Mr. Walling shook Sam's hand. "Ye have a fine daughter there."

"Tis sure as the moons," Sam agreed. "I always knew Lisette was destined for great things."

Lisette turned to her father. She suspected he was exaggerating for Mr. Walling's benefit.

"Our young Seekers will make us all proud," Mr. Walling said.

Sam nodded. "They'll have many stories to share."

"If the rumours be true, people are vanishing across the entire land," Mr. Walling said gravely. "I ask myself what our good king thinks of the matter."

"If he has an opinion, tis unknown to me," Sam replied.

"Or to any of us." Mr. Walling bowed and took his leave, informing them he still needed to speak with Henry and Ewart.

Lisette turned to her stepmom, who had stopped crying. The two of them had spent nearly every day together since her parents' wedding. She would miss her stepmom as much as her father.

When Lisette had mentioned the idea of replacing her dress with riding clothes, Nora pointed out that it would protect her legs from Daisy's saddle. She went on to call the tradition of riding in a dress silly and impractical. "If anyone has a problem with it, let them come to me," she had said in conclusion, raising a fist covered in rabbit's blood to show her resolve.

Lisette hugged her stepmom. "I'll miss ye." She paused, remembering the look on Nora's face that day in the kitchen. "I'm blessed to have ye as my mother."

"Who am I to argue with such a smart daughter," Nora replied, recovering her sense of humour.

Lisette let go of her stepmom to see how the others were faring. Roy caught her gaze and winked. They had met earlier in front of the inn to pick up their provisions. Then after they arrived at the square, townsfolk offered more food to take with them. Roy joked they would not go hungry, regardless of whatever else befell them. The elders had given them swords for protection.

"I hope ye never have cause to use them," Mr. Walling had said, studying their group. "But ye're a sharp lot, and it will do my old heart good to know ye can all defend yourselves if necessary."

Lisette hoped they would never have cause to use them as she looked around at her friends.

Their parents and well-wishers were gone. Soon, everyone would be busy tackling the day ahead. Lisette was relieved. Saying farewell to her parents proved harder than addressing the townsfolk. She brushed a hand over her brown woollen trousers and checked Lord Sumunder's purse beneath her jacket. The purse pulled on her belt. Her riding boots felt equally awkward with their heavy wooden soles. She had promptly removed the spurs and given them to the surprised cobbler. She would not be using spurs while riding Daisy.

Noticing Ewart's boots, she tried folding the stiff leather uppers to a more comfortable position. It worked. *At least now I can bend my knees.* She looked over to where their horses waited. It was time to go, or the day's sun would be wasted.

They rounded up their horses and took the west road out of Stonebridge. Lisette had a copy of her book tucked away with her few belongings. Granted permission by the bookkeeper to pack the book, its presence provided a sense of comfort. And as they began their journey, Lisette vowed once more to bring home the truth. She also vowed to return each of her friends to their families.

A mid-morning sun peeked through the trees as they entered the forest, taking the trade route along Stonebridge River. Riding north to the first bridge, then following the eastern river, they should cross the bridge over Woodbridge River in seven days. From there, they planned to ride north until they met the river running eastward into Shewbridge.

Based on her map, Lisette guessed it would take another fortnight to reach the township. But having never travelled beyond Woodbridge, neither of them knew for certain. Rumour had it that several people had vanished from Shewbridge, so it seemed like a good place to begin their search. The amount of time their journey took mattered little to them.

With the dry weather of summer settling in, traders would soon begin their delivery of honey, beeswax, salt, spices, and lady's fabrics to the townships. Traders also shared gossip and carried letters to people on their route, depositing them at the shops in townships. Respected for the goods and information they carried, traders earned coin from both their lords and shopkeepers. A trader's house was often distinguished by its wealth and size.

Many travelled vast distances, requiring them to be gone for long periods of time. The greater the distance, the more coin a trader earned for his trouble and the more servants he owned to sweeten his wife's temper.

But with few traders on the road this early in the season, the first day of their journey was uneventful. And as the sun began its reluctant descent behind them, they set up camp in a small clearing a few paces from the road. Their horses cooled and fed, the Seekers shared a meal of cheese, bread, and salted meat. Unaccustomed to riding for such a long time, they nursed their aching bodies. After the sky spilled its treasure chest of stars across the land, they settled down with their thoughts. Lisette gazed up at the sky. To the west, she could see the Hiros star belt from the knightly symbol for hope. It watched over her as she fell asleep. The fire kept watch along with the stars until it too succumbed to the night.

The Seekers repeated the same routine for three days and three nights until they crossed the first bridge. To their left, the eastern river twisted through the forest like a bustling caterpillar. Tired of salted meat, they decided on some fresh fish for supper.

They gathered kindling for a fire, searched for sticks to serve as fishing spears, sharpened the ends, and dried the tips over the hot flames. They would try their luck from the riverbank, choosing a grassy stretch where the two rivers merged and mirkens would be plentiful.

Lisette kept her eyes peeled on the river and waited. Spotting the telltale green and silver just below the surface, she aimed for the mirken. It darted around a nearby rock.

"I caught one!" Roy cried out.

"Another one like that and we'll be feasting like the lords of Wrunwicks," Henry said, admiring the mirken Roy held in the air.

"I see ye haven't lost your touch." Ewart jabbed his stick into the river, missing his target. "If I had to depend on my fishing skills, I'd starve," he mused aloud.

"Caught one!" Aspen said just as Ewart finished speaking.

In the distance, two riders appeared from the north. They had no wagons, meaning they weren't traders but simple travellers like themselves. Only these riders were travelling at a much faster pace.

"It looks like we're about to have some company," Lisette said.

Calder looked up from the river. "They're not wasting any time by the looks of it. Where do ye suppose they're headed in such a hurry?"

"Your guess be good as mine. I wager we'll learn soon enough."

Lisette soon proved correct. The riders crossed the eastern river bridge and rode up a few moments later. They came to a stop, maintaining a polite distance between themselves and the Seekers.

"Greetings, fellow travellers," one of the men said, taking stock of the group. "And who might ye be?"

"Humble citizens from the good town of Stonebridge," Calder said. "And ye are, kind sirs?"

"We travel from Highbridge on our way to Woodbridge," the man said. "I received word that my father be missing for almost two moon cycles now, so I'm on my way to investigate."

The man's words reminded Lisette of the days after her mother had disappeared, knowing the man's father would have left no clue of his whereabouts. The vanished never did. "Sixteen people have disappeared from Stonebridge," she said. "It be the reason ye see us today."

"Are ye looking for your people?" the other man asked.

"That, kind sir, be a story best shared over a meal," Ewart said.

"We'd be honoured if ye joined us." Roy pointed to the mirken on the ground.

"We made good time today, and our horses are tired," the first man said. "They could use a break."

Roy managed to spear three more fish before the evening meal. The mirken were a good size, so along with the fish caught by Aspen and Henry, there was more than enough for everyone. They sat to eat their meal on a small green patch near the eastern river. The first man introduced himself as Chester and the second man as Hubert.

They were both old enough to be addressed by their family names, although Chester insisted such formalities were unnecessary.

After a mouthful of fish, Calder paused and turned to Chester. "Highbridge be a long way from here."

"We've been on the road for many days with many more to go."

"Did ye see anything unusual?" Henry asked, enjoying his ale courtesy of the innkeeper.

Chester shook his head. "We heard stories of people vanishing across the land, but we saw nothing to explain why. Tis a strange thing."

"A strange thing indeed," Calder said. "The people of Stonebridge fear the wrunwick have returned from below."

Hubert washed down his bread with a swig of ale. "Tis the same in Highbridge. I've always considered stories about the wrunwick to be nonsense, schemed up to scare children into behaving. A cruel joke in the name of our land."

"The lack of answers has given new life to the stories of old," Lisette said. "Without answers, the stories will keep growing, and fear will spread. We're hoping to find the truth behind what be happening to our people."

"An impressive task for a group so young," Chester replied. "Ye can't be any more than eighteen at most."

Chester's words struck an unwanted chord. Try as she might to squash her doubt, Lisette sometimes found herself wondering if their journey was a quest of fools, best left to the more experienced as Nora had suggested. "Nineteen, kind sir," she replied. "Our age won't stop us from at least trying. Doing nothing certainly hasn't worked."

"Don't let her smile trick ye. A more determined woman, ye'll never meet." Henry raised his mug to Lisette.

"Wise words for someone so young," Chester said. "Doing nothing rarely achieves the desired outcome. "Tis why we travel to Woodbridge. I find it near impossible to believe that someone could disappear so completely. And no one has seen fit to look for him. Tis unconscionable. Surely a man's life be worth more."

"After my mother vanished, I spent months waiting for her to come home."

"I remember the townsfolk talking about it," Ewart said. "I was just a lad myself then, and ye looked so lost."

"Where are ye headed in this search of yours?" Hubert asked.

"A lot of people have vanished from Shewbridge," Lisette said. "Or so we've heard. We'll be travelling there to start."

Hubert appeared deep in thought for a moment. "We were in Shewbridge during the moons of aromons. The folk there be scared and wary of strangers. They say the wrunwick took their people. I thought it the nonsensical ramblings of over-ripe imaginations."

"If my father be out there, I'll find him," Chester said. "Wrunwick or no wrunwick. But now, fair hosts, we must be off to make use of the sun's final light."

The Seekers wished them well and set up camp for the night. They were in no rush, keeping an eye along the way for the feared wrunwick or the slightest clue to the mysterious vanishings. That neither of them could say what such a clue might look like was of no consequence, they listened and watched with one eye open while they slept, the river babbling on about monsters and people disappearing inside their hungry bellies.

Before dawn, they made a quick meal of bread and cheese, splashed the sleep from their faces, and prepared to leave. The sun rose to greet them as they set east. And while the bridge faded into the distance, Lisette asked their Divine Mother to watch over them.

Chapter 7

The journey from Stonebridge to Shewbridge took eighteen days. Travelling the eastern river into Shewbridge had taken just nine days, a full five days less than Lisette's initial prediction. Not that anyone was complaining. After the last eighteen days of camping under the stars and swatting forest flies, they were looking forward to sleeping in a bed. Their backsides ached from too many days in a saddle, and provisions had dwindled to mere crumbs. They fastened their eyes on Shewbridge.

A mile outside of town, the trail began to widen. Eight paces or more outside Shewbridge, dirt gave way to stone. They rode into town. During the renovation period, King Lazoran III ordered a single design for every township in Wrunwicks. It guaranteed that Shewbridge resembled every other town with its stone houses braced against winter's snow-padded winds. And like every other town, the main roads would converge at the town square.

Continuing along the eastern road, they listened to the sounds coming from the square. They had arrived on market day. Music and voices drifted through the empty streets, blending with a faint whiff of pottage simmering over their fires. Lisette took a wistful breath. The smell reminded her of home.

When they reached the inn, the Seekers rode around back and left their horses in the stables, paid for their chambers, deposited their few belongings, and met outside. The square overflowed with townsfolk, villagers, stalls, and carts. Market day occurred twice a moon cycle during the growing season and shut down every shop on the square, giving everyone the chance to earn some extra coin before wron was due.

Women sold their sewing and baked treats, with hopeful suitors paying too much for the pies and puddings of maidens. Men sold chests, pipes, bowls and any other wooden items that were easily carried or carted. The local butcher kept the cheapest meats for his stall to offer those without enough coin to enter his shop. And no market was complete without music and storytellers. It lent an air of celebration to the day.

Dividing into pairs, the Seekers went to find the latest gossip, agreeing to meet back at the inn later to share their findings. If the people of Shewbridge were scared, it was nowhere to be seen this afternoon. Lisette and Aspen began their search with a stall over-seen by a woman selling armlets.

Picking up one of the bands, Lisette showed it to Aspen. "The green stitching be perfect for ye."

"The stitching be of admirable quality, but I'm not sure if I can afford it."

"How much?" Lisette asked the woman.

"Four wrunsos for the set."

"Ye've mistaken us for rich, kind woman." Lisette admired the armlets. She waited for the woman's next offer.

The woman picked up a set of armlets with white bands and dark blue stitching. She handed it to Lisette.

"I can add these to sweeten the deal," the woman said with an eager smile. "See how they match your eyes."

Pretending to briefly consider the woman's offer, Lisette turned to Aspen. "What do ye think?"

"It be a fair price for such exquisite work."

"We'll take them." Lisette handed the woman a wren. "Lisette, daughter of Sam and Nora Steels. And this be Aspen, daughter of Walter and Eleanor Greene."

"Where might ye be from, Lisette and Aspen?" the woman asked, returning six wrunsos to Lisette's hand.

"Stonebridge," Lisette replied. "And what may we call ye?"

"Mrs. Fardon be the name. What brings ye all the way to Shewbridge during the growing season?"

"We're hoping to find out what be happening to our people."

Mrs. Fardon looked like she had just heard a strange noise in the dark. "'Tis said the wrunwick have returned from below."

"The people of Stonebridge fear the same," Aspen said. "But we've seen no evidence of their presence."

"The forest keeps many secrets and only reveals what it wants when it wants. Ye best be careful, fair maidens of Stonebridge. Our people report hearing many a curious step during their travels."

Lisette and Aspen reassured Mrs. Fardon they would indeed be careful, then bid their farewells, informing the woman they had much to see at the fine market of Shewbridge.

"That went better than expected," Aspen said once they were out of earshot.

"Lord Sumunder's purse be proving useful, it seems. What do ye think she meant by strange sounds?"

"We'll need to keep our eyes and ears open on our way to Straw-bridge." Despite the sun's warmth, Aspen pulled her jacket tighter.

They walked several paces to where a dozen or more spectators encircled a band of performers. Inside the festive circle, minstrels played a rousing tune on their gitterns and lutes. The music created a festive background for the colourful troupe. They were telling the popular ballad of King Lazoran II. And while the bard spoke, his troupe enacted the words. People watched in fascination, shouting their support and applauding throughout the performance.

The bard concluded his ballad by urging everyone to celebrate the dawn of peace with them. The performers began a lively dance as the minstrels increased their tempo. Onlookers cheered, joining the dance. Lisette hooked her arm in Aspen's and twirled, once to the left and once to the right.

She had forgotten what it was like from the other side of the table. At home, she often shared a stall with Nora to sell her sewing projects. Nora had insisted after seeing her work, saying she could earn a few wrunsos. Nora was right as usual. She smiled to herself, remembering the ever-present sparkle in her stepmom's eyes. A few paces to her left, she saw a group of children playing bone circles, a favourite game of her own as a child.

"Ye think they'd mind if we joined them?" Lisette pointed to the children.

"They might think us a little old. Remember when we were that young?"

"Maybe we'll just watch," Lisette said. "But I'm not promising anything."

They joined the children who were watching the game. A large pebble sat in the middle of a rock circle. The closest bone to the pebble received three points. Any other bones still inside the circle received a point each. The most trusted player kept score in the dirt. Lisette looked over. The score was 15–12.

A girl of about ten examined Lisette with the often shameless curiosity bestowed upon children. When the score tied, the girl clapped in excitement, her attention diverted for the time being. But when the game resumed, she looked up at Lisette again.

"Your hair looks like fire."

Lisette kneeled to face the child. "A gift from my mother."

"Where did she get it?"

"I'm not sure, but her hair was the same colour."

The girl stared at Lisette's forehead for a moment. "Did she give ye the star too?"

Lisette smiled. "She did. When I was very young, she said it was a gift from my great-grandmother, who had one just like it."

"Why are ye dressed like a man?" the girl asked next.

"My friend and I lost all our dresses."

"How?" she asked.

What do I tell her? "We forgot to put them away."

"All of them?" The young girl looked shocked.

"All of them. Isn't that right, Aspen?"

"Tis. And now they're in the land of lost dresses," Aspen said, looking appropriately serious.

Lisette nodded in agreement and prepared herself for the young girl's questions about the mysterious land of lost dresses. Luckily, the young girl appeared happy with Aspen's explanation.

"Can I tell ye a secret?" the girl asked her instead.

"Sure. I love secrets."

She gestured for Lisette to come closer.

"My brother saw a monster," she whispered in Lisette's ear, then looked to see her reaction.

"What may I call ye, little one?" Lisette whispered back. "My friends call me Lisette."

"Katherine."

"Well, Katherine, that be a really big secret. Have ye told your parents?"

Katherine shook her head. "We're not supposed to go into the woods."

"The monster be in the woods?"

Nodding slowly, Katherine's young eyes held the full weight of her secret.

"I tell ye what. Tis our secret now, so let me worry about the monster. And I promise that when I find him, I'll destroy him for ye. That sound good?"

Katherine nodded once again. She smudged dirt in the palm of her hand. Lisette grabbed a little dirt from the score square, and the two shook hands. Their secret was sealed with Lisette's impulsive promise. They watched the remainder of the game. Katherine made no further reference to monsters, clapping whenever a boy of about twelve scored a point.

When the game ended, Lisette turned to her new friend. "It was nice to make your acquaintance, Katherine. I won't forget our promise."

Red Squirrel Inn teemed with patrons and high spirits inside the main hall. An iron candle wheel hung from the centre of the hall, throwing a warm light over the stone walls and guests. A maiden carried trenchers laden with food to a table where three travellers waited. The innkeeper's wife disappeared into the buttery to refill an empty pitcher. Lisette and Aspen sat with their friends, enjoying their own fresh pitcher of ale after supper.

Henry took a quick swig. "She be scared, tis all," he said, laying down his mug. "Who can blame her with all the talk about strange noises."

"But ye didn't see her eyes," Aspen said. "She believed it."

"I'm sure she did." Calder leaned forward on his bench. "Kids believe all kinds of things."

Ewart turned to face Lisette. "It was probably a bear or some other animal."

"Maybe," Lisette agreed. She cupped her face in both hands, an old habit from childhood. Her father had tried breaking her from the habit to no avail, calling it improper for a young girl at the table.

"Ye have to admit how wild it sounds." Henry's eyes glowed in the soft light from their table's candle.

"Wilder than strange noises in the woods?" Lisette asked.

"Another product of people's imaginations." Ewart refilled his mug from the large pitcher.

The men had encountered several people who spoke of the woods with fear, talking about strange sounds in the distant hills. When placed alongside Katherine's claim of a monster in the forest, it made the stories difficult for Lisette to dismiss, despite her mind's best effort. Somewhere inside those stories hid the truth.

Roy looked around the table. "Something be causing people to vanish."

"We can't jump to conclusions," Ewart said. "Nor can we throw our good sense to the winds. I don't own much to begin with."

Lisette recalled Katherine's scared voice. *My brother saw a monster.* Katherine had clearly believed it, regardless of whether it was true or not.

A guest who looked to be in his thirties approached their table. He lifted his mug toward the man sitting at a far table. "We heard rumours of two women dressed in men's clothes. I thought I'd see for myself. We're honest shopkeepers from a nearby village and could use a much-needed distraction from our troubles."

Ewart studied the shopkeeper. His expression suggested he had already cast the man as unworthy of their time. "There be nothing for ye here."

Lisette sat up straight. "Ye must be referring to us, kind sir," she said in her most sober voice. "I'm guessing ye'd like to know what happened to our dresses."

"If ye would oblige a poor shopkeeper's curiosity, milady."

"We lost them." Lisette confronted the man's rude stare with her own steady gaze.

"Surely, ye take me for a fool. What ye say be impossible."

"Have ye ever lost a dress?" Lisette knew she was being stubborn and silly, but the man's insolence defied her understanding. While she could appreciate and respect a child's innocence, this man should know better than question a stranger so brazenly.

"No, but—"

"Then how would ye know?"

"Prithee, milady. Know what?"

"That it be impossible to lose a dress, kind sir."

The man continued to stare at Lisette, his face now flushed with anger. "Ye'll have to forgive me. I mistook ye for a maiden of good breeding."

"And I mistook ye for a man of good manners. It seems that I was wrong. But ye, sir, weren't mistaken. If ye were so fortunate as to meet my parents, they would assure ye of the same."

"Then I wish your family the finest of health," the man said. He looked around the table. "And good health to ye, as well."

"To good health." Ewart raised his mug.

The others followed Ewart's lead, raising their mugs to the man. "To good health," they toasted, then waited for the shopkeeper to raise his mug in turn.

The red-faced man failed to return their demonstration of goodwill as expected. After a final look at the Seekers, he scurried back to his table.

Lisette's friends were grinning from ear to ear. She grinned back, not sure what had possessed her.

"I always knew ye had it in there," Calder said, tapping his chest. "Ye hide it well, but I can see it sometimes, especially when Vincent crawls up from underneath."

"We don't have time to entertain dastards," Lisette replied, still surprised by the boldness of her words.

"Hear, hear," Aspen said. "Maybe he'll think twice the next time he needs a distraction."

Chapter 8

Before dawn, the Seekers packed their provisions bought at market and set out, travelling north along the river. They journeyed for one fortnight plus a day, stopping each night to rest beneath a thick blanket of stars. They planned to stop in Strawbridge next, with Lisette estimating four more days of travel at their current pace.

On their sixteenth day of travel, Henry signalled for them to stop. "Did anyone hear that?"

They scanned the forest. There were no other souls within view save for a rabbit munching on some wildflowers.

"Who travels these woods to disrupt my sleep?" A voice asked, rising above the Seekers.

"Who travels these woods?" The voice asked again, louder now.

Lisette looked to Ewart, who shook his head in bewilderment. The question seemed to have come from their right.

"Who speaks?" Lisette called out to the forest.

"Tis I, Grand Oak of Evergreen Forest." The voice sounded through the trees. "Who wakes me from slumber?"

Lisette heard stories about talking trees as a little girl, but those were fairy tales told to children as they fell asleep. This voice didn't live inside a fairy tale, and the tree that stood less than twelve feet away was not the result of someone's imagination.

The Grand Oak's thick eyelashes were made of leafy twigs, which hung from a face old as the mountains and gentler than a warm summer breeze. Her giant branches extended no less than a hundred feet in every direction and clear across their path some six feet above the ground. Awe-struck, Lisette admired the Grand Oak's extraordinary size.

Regaining some small measure of composure, she dismounted to bow before the Grand Oak. "We are the Truth Seekers of Stonebridge, Grand Oak. We travel in search of the people who have vanished from this forest." Lisette's voice shook with wonder, for even her wildest dreams paled in comparison to this moment.

The others dismounted to bow before the Grand Oak. Lisette knew she looked just as dumbfounded as her friends. *How is this possible? We can't all be imagining together.* Lisette resisted the urge to pinch herself.

As the Seekers bowed before her, the Grand Oak opened her eyes. They were a dark, mossy green. "There be no need to bow, Truth Seekers of Stonebridge. Rise so that I may see your faces." The Grand Oak's voice drew life from deep inside the earth.

Quick to obey, the Seekers straightened to face the Grand Oak, who chuckled in a low, rumbling echo that shook her branches and released a sudden cloud of emerald greens into the air. The massive cloud separated into hundreds of extraordinary creatures. Less than two hands tall, the tiny creatures flew down to inspect the Seekers. They looked human but with pointed ears and hair in different shades of green like their wings.

"Meet the fair folk of Evergreen Forest," the Grand Oak said. "There be no need to fear their presence. They mean ye no harm."

The fair folk darted around the Seekers, whispering to each other as they went. The Grand Oak observed with affection while the fair folk satisfied their curiosity.

A fay grabbed Lisette's finger and giggled. "Pleased to meet ye," she said.

Lisette smiled as the fay shook her hand. "Pleased to meet ye as well." She noticed the fay's bright green eyes, which lit up her face.

"Ye say people are vanishing from my forest? I have been asleep too long, for I am unaware of this. But I will ask the other trees." The Grand Oak closed her eyes.

The Seekers waited before the Grand Oak. Their host appeared to be sleeping. The fair folk disbanded and flew off into the woods. Lisette admired the elegance of their flight. Next, she turned to admire the Grand Oak, a name that fell far from fact. The Grand Oak was so much more than a tree. And when she spoke, it was as though Utaika's spirit filled each breath. While Lisette marvelled at the thought, the Grand Oak opened her eyes.

"The trees tell me there exists an encampment of what might be wrunwick north of Metterling Mountains," the Grand Oak said. "The trees near the campsite are young, so they have never observed a wrunwick before."

"The wrunwick disappeared hundreds of years ago." Aspen looked dazed.

The Grand Oak moved her eyes to the left. "When the wrunwick disappeared, no one ventured to say how or why. The reasons were left to invention. And over the course of time, the wrunwick became legend, never to be seen again. I was younger then, but I heard whispers of their savage nature. We all did. The trees that witnessed the gruesome killings mourned along with the people of Wrunwicks. It was a dark time for everyone."

Lisette looked to her friends. "We're already on our way to Strawbridge. Maybe we could ride north from there."

"The wrunwick were known to be quick and even quicker to slaughter the people of Wrunwicks. If they have indeed returned, then ye will need to be cautious and use your heads," the Grand Oak said.

"We have a map to show us the way, Grand Oak. Each of us promised the good people of Stonebridge to bring home the truth. It will be our honour to fulfill that promise." Lisette glanced over at Ewart.

"We could set course in the morning." Ewart smiled in the late-day sun. "The greater part of today has passed."

"Hear, hear," Roy said quietly. "We can set up camp early."

The Grand Oak invited them to spend the night beneath her branches. While they ate next to the stream wrapped around their host's immense trunk, the Grand Oak asked them more about Stonebridge and the vanishings. After they had obliged the Grand Oak, Calder asked if there were any other trees like her.

"There are two more. But only one of us be awake at any given time. I sent a signal to the other oak upon my awakening, so that she may sleep when it befits her. It be our purpose to watch over the forest and its creatures."

"Excuse my manners, Grand Oak, but why haven't we heard of ye before?"

"But ye have, Calder. Remember the stories ye heard as a child."

Lisette wondered how the Grand Oak knew of their fairy tales and how she was able to communicate with the other trees. A feat that was nothing less than astounding. She looked up at the centuries-old tree. To live for hundreds of years would bring more knowledge than any of them could ever imagine. The Grand Oak commanded respect with each word she spoke.

"Do ye wish to ask me a question, Lisette?" the Grand Oak asked.

Lisette hesitated. She watched a group of fays enjoying a meal of strawberries to her right. "We thought the stories were just fairy tales," she said, looking up at the Grand Oak.

"As do most people. They forget what they once knew."

"What is that, Grand Oak?" Aspen asked.

"Magic exists all around us."

"Magic?" Roy asked, the last of his bread gone.

"Each fay possesses a form of magic. Florette can harness the power of Arias, the giver of winds and Utaika's firstborn child. Arias cannot be seen but remains our constant companion. And like the winds of Arias, Florette can move unseen throughout the land."

The fay who had shaken Lisette's hand earlier sat on a large rock next to them. Unlike the other fair folk, Florette had forsaken the forest in favour of their company.

When the Grand Oak grew quiet, Florette turned to Lisette. "I can also share my power with others."

"That sounds like a useful ability," Lisette replied.

Florette nodded. "It keeps us hidden from humans."

"*We're* human," Lisette said. She liked Florette very much and couldn't resist teasing their new friend.

"But your hearts are pure."

Roy clutched his chest. "There goes my reputation."

"Your secret be safe with us," Ewart said earnestly, contradicting the laughter tugging at his lips.

Florette's wings fluttered ever so slightly. "With me too."

"Thank ye, Florette," Roy said. "At least I can believe ye. I'm not so sure about this fellow right here. What do ye think?"

Ewart placed a hand on his chest. "Now tis my heart that be crushed."

"A heart can be fixed," Henry said. "Mine having been crushed on many occasions."

"Your mouth being the cause of that," Calder remarked for the umpteenth time.

Aspen stood, brushing her trousers to remove any crumbs that might have fallen. "At least your hearts are safe during our journey."

"Speak for yourself," Henry said. "There be maidens in every town."

"And just as smart as the maidens back home," Calder replied with a low chuckle.

As the evening wore on, the fair folk kept to the forest, feeding the rabbits, squirrels, and deer that visited the Grand Oak. Florette stuck with Lisette. After their handshake that afternoon, they had become instant friends. Florette sat with her by the fire, listening to their reflections on back home and their journey thus far.

When the sun gave way to the moons as it always did, the fair folk settled down for the night, draping the Grand Oak in brilliant greens once more. The Seekers gathered their blankets and lay down in pursuit of sleep. The forest grew silent.

As she gazed up at the stars, Lisette wondered if the forest had been named after the fair folk. She liked the idea. It would mean her ancestors not only knew about magic but they had also celebrated its existence.

Chapter 9

A deer wandered through the campsite, waking Lisette before the sun. The fair folk were already busy feeding their hungry wards. Florette flew over to Lisette and offered her a strawberry. Lisette gratefully accepted. Fresh berries were a welcome change from their regular diet. She would have thought it impossible to tire of fish. But after the twentieth meal since leaving Stonebridge, fish was losing its appeal. The others stirred and sat up, rubbing the sleep from their eyes.

"I trust ye slept well, Seekers," the Grand Oak said. "The clouds bring much rain. And not a day too soon. The forest needs water."

"It hasn't rained in nearly a fortnight," Roy said. "The land grows dryer by the day."

"Best we be leaving early then," Calder replied, accepting a strawberry from one of the fays. "We'll want to get ahead of it."

"Utaika always sees to her children." The furrows deepened around the Grand Oak's grateful smile. After one of her long pauses, she suggested that Florette travel with them to Metterling Mountains. Florette's magic, the Grand Oak explained, would help protect them on their journey but warned that it should never be misused or used without good reason.

"We'd be proud to have Florette accompany us," Lisette replied.

Florette flew over to stand inside Lisette's hood. "I'm happy it pleases ye," she said, addressing the Seekers. "Ye bestow me a great honour."

❧

Shortly after leaving the Grand Oak, the Seekers fell into a reflective silence. Florette rose from Lisette's hood to claim her seat on Daisy's upper back and sat facing Lisette. She held onto the mare's dark brown mane to steady herself.

"Do ye think the wrunwick have returned, Lisette?"

"It be too soon to say. We can't rule out the very real possibility of something far less strange just yet. Maybe the mountains will give us some answers."

"What kind of answers are ye expecting to find?"

"That, Florette, remains a mystery. Who knows? But we set out to find the truth. And no matter what that truth might be, we'll face it. I can promise ye that much."

"But there are so few of us, how can we ever hope to defeat such fierce creatures? When the wrunwick first ruled this land, no one could stop them."

"As a little girl, I read about the wrunwick and the terror that reigned over our people. No one dared to confront the wrunwick because of their size and strength. I'm afraid too. We all are, but we can't allow fear to keep us from fighting back. And if the wrunwick have truly returned, we can't allow the age of terror to reign as it once did."

Lisette told her about Katherine and the young girl's brother. She explained how Katherine's words had originally seemed like the imaginings of a frightened child who might have heard too many stories created by the vanishings.

"What do ye suppose now?" Florette asked.

"I wish I knew. I didn't believe in fair folk or talking trees until yesterday."

"The clouds are moving in. We should keep watch for shelter. It seems the Grand Oak was right," Ewart said. "The mud'll be difficult for the horses."

Lisette and the others looked to the sky. The clouds were dark and heavy, giving them anywhere from a few moments to a few miles. She hoped they had enough time. The horses would soon need their shoes reset. Lisette had witnessed the damage caused by improper shoe care and muddy conditions all too often. She petted Daisy's shoulder, wishing they had taken the time in Shewbridge to visit a blacksmith.

"Florette, I need ye to see if there are any caves nearby," Lisette said. "Don't stray too far and be careful. We're not accustomed to this part of the forest. Can ye do that?"

"Ye needn't worry about my safety. I promise that no one will know of my presence."

They wished her luck and a swift return. Florette gave Daisy an affectionate scratch behind her ear and flew off in search of shelter. Although brand-new to the group, they had grown quite fond of their new friend. It was clear to Lisette the fay's lighthearted spirit lifted their own.

To the Seekers' collective sigh of relief, Florette returned sooner than expected. Her wings quivered with excitement.

"I had faith in ye, Florette." Roy grinned at Lisette. "What did I tell ye?"

"Tis natural to worry." Lisette returned Roy's grin, knowing he was just as happy to see their new friend as she was.

"I found what appears to be a cave nestled inside a hill," Florette said. "It be a short ride from here. I can take ye there, but I must warn ye. Outside the cave, there stands a creature with the upper body of a man and the lower body of a horse. He has wings like a bird and carries a bow and arrow. He also looks upset and confused. More confused than upset, I think."

Lisette remembered reading about such a creature. The books called them taupaks. But those stories were widely accepted as myths. Yet after meeting the Grand Oak and befriending Florette, she was open to the possibility of anything. She suddenly felt as though she had turned upside down in a world turned inside out.

"Did he see ye, Florette?" Lisette asked.

"I was veiled by the winds of Arias. As soon as I found the cave, I hurried back."

"What do we do now?" Aspen surveyed their group.

"We still need shelter from the rain when it gets here. And we've already committed to facing the wrunwick if they've returned. Surely, we can face this one creature." Roy reached for his sword.

"I read about such creatures," Lisette replied. "In books, there exists both good and evil taupaks." She stopped. *Are we really talking about taupaks?* "Maybe it would be wise for us to approach with caution until we know more." She stopped again. The ground was spinning. "With the help of Florette's magic, we could approach unseen to observe the creature before acting."

"Let's hope this taupak be one of the good ones," Ewart said with a wry grin. "But we won't know until we see for ourselves."

"To adventure!" Roy raised his sword to the sky.

"To courage!" Aspen raised her sword in turn.

"To truth!" Lisette and the others joined in.

"To us!" Florette sang out from Lisette's hood, grazing Lisette's cheek with her fist.

Florette motioned for them to stop. "We're almost there. The cave be through the trees in that direction." She pointed to a couple of trees to her right. "I think it might be wise for us to veil our presence before entering this part of the forest."

"Will the taupak be able to hear us?" Ewart asked. "The thought of getting to the cave without making at least some noise be near absurd. And if the creature can hear us, all the magic in Wrunwicks won't do us much good."

"The winds of Arias bond us to the air around us. It'll be impossible to see or hear ye. To each other, we'll appear in our natural state." Florette left the warmth of Daisy's back to begin.

"Have ye used your magic on humans before?" Henry sounded skeptical.

"It was a long time ago now, but I once knew a young girl from a small village. We'd veil ourselves to hide from her cruel parents. She outlived her husband and two sons. Ye won't even notice the difference. All ye need, be a kiss from me to cast the spell. When ye want to end the spell, ye can rub the kiss with spittle to remove it."

"What are we waiting for, Seekers?" Roy pointed to his cheek with a look bordering on mischief. "Florette, ye can kiss my cheek first."

"Ye seem to be enjoying our situation." Henry sounded much less eager than his younger friend.

Appearing charmed by Roy's enthusiasm, Florette flew over to plant a gentle kiss on his cheek. She then flew to Shadow, planting a kiss under the mare's dark brown forelock. Shadow neighed before disappearing with her master. They stared in amazement at the spot where Roy had been.

"Roy, are ye still with us?" Henry inquired of the air.

"He be safe on the other side. Now, who would like to go next?" Florette studied the Seekers from where she had kissed Shadow.

"I'll go!" everyone said at once.

Florette started with Henry and hurried to complete her round. She finished with Lisette, kissing the star to the right side of her forehead.

In less than a song, they were headed to the cave. The path was clear except for the occasional rabbit or deer. Lisette concentrated on the woods before her, steering clear of the low-hanging and fallen branches. Calder rode with her while Aspen and Henry led the way through the dense forest. Ewart and Roy completed their line of faith. They would need to trust themselves and each other if they were to face whatever waited at the cave and Metterling Mountains.

"Where do ye think the taupak might have come from, Lisette?" Calder asked. "Surely, if taupaks lived in these woods, we'd know. Shewbridge be only four days ride from here, five tops. The towns-folk would know of their presence, and word would've spread."

"I can no more know that than what lies on the other side of Thomas Waters. We left home in search of answers. But all we have so far are more questions." Lisette paused to think for a moment. There was so much they didn't understand. Maybe it was for the best. Maybe they weren't ready to understand yet. "I've learned there are many things about our land that we don't know. Perhaps it be the first step in our quest for the truth."

"Do ye think tis possible for land to exist across the waters?"

"Two days ago, I might've rejected the notion without a second thought." Lisette turned to smile at Florette, who had returned to her seat on Daisy's back. "It seems anything be possible."

"Inside our limited knowledge, it be impossible I think to know with absolute certainty, but I can't accept that we're alone in all of Wrunwicks." Calder ducked to avoid a tree branch. "There must be land with people who look and wonder as we do."

"The story of Thomas Waters always made me laugh as a child," Lisette confessed. "A man rides to the ocean, only to turn back when he couldn't find a place to cross without being swallowed by waves higher than his horse."

Before Calder had a chance to respond, Florette rose from her seat and pointed to the steep hill a few paces ahead. "The cave be just beyond that hill."

"Time to see what waits for us," Roy said.

Lisette looked behind her and smiled at Roy. "We should've put ye up front."

Ewart chuckled. "And have me travel back here by myself?"

"We can't all be in the front," Lisette teased. "These woods are scarcely passable now. I can only pray our efforts aren't defeated."

Chapter 10

eaching the top of the hill, Lisette spotted the entrance to the cave. Located at the foot of a second impassable hill, a traveller could easily miss the cave's whereabouts. There was no sign of the creature.

"We should proceed with caution," Lisette advised as the first raindrops began to fall. "Our taupak may not be far."

They made their way down the grassy hill. With little more than five paces left between them and the cave, they heard the taupak approaching from the woods.

"Quick!" Lisette instructed. "To our right!"

The creature cleared the woods, his arms laden with branches and twigs. His coat was a warm chestnut brown with wings the span of an akivor, one of the largest birds in Wrunwicks. The taupak's wings were two shades darker than the fur coat covering his entire body, apart from his face, shoulders, and arms. A set of pointed ears protruded through his long black hair, which also feathered out from his forearms and fetlocks.

Unaware of their presence, the taupak disappeared inside the cave, returning moments later to retrieve four rabbits next to the cave's entrance. He scanned the area and went back inside the cave.

"A magnificent creature," Aspen said, looking toward the cave.

While Aspen spoke, they could hear the taupak moving inside the cave. The rabbits suggested he would be making a fire. They listened as he went about his task.

Ewart calmed his horse. "He doesn't appear dangerous or wild. His face shows intelligence, and his actions are those of a civilized creature. Though we'll still need to be careful, I think we should approach the taupak with our swords down."

"I'm inclined to agree with Ewart," Lisette said. "What say ye, Seekers?"

"We didn't ride this far only to back down. I say we remove our veils and make ourselves known." Roy rubbed the kiss from his cheek.

"Then we're in agreement. I'll speak to him." Lisette gave her forehead a quick rub before gently wiping below Daisy's forelock. She rode over to the cave and stopped some three paces from the entrance.

"Kind sir, the Truth Seekers of Stonebridge seek your counsel. May we call upon your presence before us?" In books, taupaks could always speak. She hoped the books proved accurate. It would certainly make communication with this taupak much easier. *What if he speaks, but I can't understand him?* Straightening her back, Lisette heard the approaching sound of hooves. He appeared to be in no rush.

"Humans, why do you request my presence? What do you want of me?" the taupak demanded, his hind legs hidden inside the cave.

Lisette smiled in relief. His speech belonged to an unknown patink, but she understood him. "My name be Lisette, daughter of

Samuel and Nora Steels. We seek the truth behind the vanishings of our people."

"Daughter of Samuel and Nora, you may call me Mhutig, son of Hyrek and Wiolas from the land of Krousus. I was on my way home from a hunting trip with my brothers and went to gather wood for the fire. But after climbing that hill"—Mhutig pointed behind Lisette—"I found myself here. When I tried returning to my brothers, they were nowhere to be seen. And the forest I knew had been replaced by this one."

"Ye say that ye're from the land of Krousus. I've never heard of it. Is it located somewhere in the far reaches of Wrunwicks?" Lisette felt dizzy again.

"I see that you are all soaked. Please, why not join me inside the cave where it is dry? We can continue our conversation away from this rain."

The Seekers dismounted, tied their horses to the trees next to the cave's clearing, and followed Mhutig inside.

The cave's chamber was bigger than Lisette expected. With an entrance of about four feet wide and seven feet high, Mhutig had to bend his upper body to compensate. However, once inside, the cave revealed its true size. After a quick inspection, she guessed the cave's chamber to be at least thirty feet wide and twenty feet high. There was plenty of room for everyone.

Mhutig went to check on the fire, allowing Lisette the chance to sneak a closer look at their host. He would make a formidable ally. His broad, muscular build would provide strength against any enemy, not to mention that he towered over them by a good two feet. And yet the lightness of his bearing implied speed and agility.

"Never judge a cave from the outside," Ewart said, interrupting Lisette's thoughts.

"Or a taupak, for that matter." Lisette continued to observe Mhutig, who was still tending to the fire. It was a modest fire with the larger branches on the bottom. And placed at the back end of the cave, the fire remained far enough from the cave walls to avoid heating the rock. A rabbit lay next to the fire, skinned and ready to cook. A pile of smaller branches and twigs lay stacked out of harm's way. She noticed Mhutig's belongings. Next to the kindling rested a saddlebag with a wide leather belt, a long sword, and a bow.

The fire stoked, Mhutig joined the Seekers. "Now we can talk, Seekers of Stonebridge. You mentioned your people disappearing."

Henry explained to Mhutig about the vanishings occurring throughout Wrunwicks. He also shared people's fear the wrunwick had returned from legend to terrorize their people once again.

"In the land of Krousus, there lives a band of monsters we call karupas. A dangerous breed of cave dwellers who hunt the humans of my land. Some of us have taken to hunting down karupas. Many believe our ancestors conjured the monsters with dark magic."

"Where be this place ye describe to us?" Henry asked. "Is it on the other side of the ocean surrounding our land?"

Henry's question struck Lisette as odd. He had always mocked the idea, but she was happy he asked. Mhutig never answered when she asked earlier. *Could he be from a strange, unknown land somewhere in Wrunwicks?* She studied Mhutig, waiting for his answer.

"On the other side of the ocean?" Mhutig stopped to ponder the question. "Of that, I cannot speak. But Krousus is surrounded by a vast ocean with many lands. We don't know exactly how many, for no one has made a journey that far or wide."

Lisette looked over at the fire. In the blink of an eye, the remote possibility of another land had become a reality. Calder's theory no longer seemed so implausible. Maybe another land did exist across the ocean, too far to travel in a batek. Well suited to the lakes of Wrunwicks, a batek could never withstand the force of Thomas Waters.

When she glanced back at Mhutig, it dawned on her that other than herself, they had not introduced themselves to their host. "Ye'll need to forgive us, Mhutig, we aren't normally this rude. This be Henry, son of Gus and Eugena Traveen of Stonebridge."

The others introduced themselves next. Florette waited for them to finish before venturing from the safety of Lisette's hood.

"And who might you be?" Mhutig asked with a gentle smile.

"Florette, daughter of Leander and Hyacina. Pleased to meet ye." She flew over to shake Mhutig's hand.

"Pleased to meet you, Florette. We have fair folk in Krousus as well. Noble creatures, indeed."

"I'm afraid the fair folk of Evergreen would pale by contrast."

"Humility is a rare quality in my experience. Come, let us enjoy a meal together. What do you say?"

Relinquishing Mhutig's hand, Florette nodded her agreement.

Lisette could see that Florette was impressed by Mhutig. She suspected they all were. It was one thing to read about taupaks. But to meet one was incomparable to any story.

"Although I have little to offer, I hope you will help me celebrate our new friendship." Mhutig met Lisette's eyes.

"We'd be honoured to share a meal with ye," Lisette said. "We also have provisions. So between us, it'll be a feast sufficient enough to convince kings."

Lisette and Roy went to check on the horses. Rain quenched the earth beneath an untamed sky. Ignoring the pounding rain and wind whipping at their faces, they led the horses to where the trees were thicker and would provide better shelter from an unforgiving storm. Once their horses were fed and given a drink, they inspected the area one last time and ensured each horse was secure, then ran back to the cave.

Aspen and Mhutig were cooking the last rabbit while the others busied themselves with preparations. When everything was ready, they settled down to enjoy their meal, complete with bread, wine, and sweet biscuits. Calder had laid out his camp blanket for Lisette, Aspen, and Florette to sit on.

"If the rain cooperates, we'll be able to resume our journey in the morning. The mud will dry, and we could still reach Strawbridge before day's end," Lisette said between mouthfuls of sweet biscuit.

"Strawbridgers have lost even more people than Shewbridge if the rumours prove themselves. There has to be a connection there somewhere to what the Grand Oak said," Ewart replied.

Roy turned to Mhutig with an inquiring look. "Do ye plan to stay in this cave for long?"

"I have waited two days for my brothers to find me. Or I, them, but it seems neither will happen."

Lisette saw the opening she needed to share her idea. "I propose that ye accompany us, Mhutig. We could use someone like ye on our side. Just as we hope to discover the truth behind the vanishings of our people, maybe ye'll discover what brought ye to our land and find your way home."

"I see no point in remaining here any longer. It would be my honour to join your group." He raised the mug borrowed from Roy. "To friendship."

"Strong and sure." The Seekers raised their mugs to their new friend.

That evening, the Seekers shared the stories passed down by their elders. Mhutig delighted them with stories of his son's antics.

"How old is he?" Aspen asked.

"Ten. In two years, he can begin training for war," Mhutig said with obvious pride.

"Twelve seems so young to consider war," Calder said.

"Taupaks have been at war for many years. The opowaks fight to take over our kingdom. Their victory would mean the end of humans and taupakian rule. While many taupaks welcome the end of humans, they are not willing to lose the war."

"Do taupaks hate humans that much?" Aspen asked.

"It shames me to admit it, but many of them do, unfortunately. They see humans as weak two-legged animals, unworthy of living among us."

Lisette found the description repulsive. and realized how much she took for granted. To her, taupaks were also very different. *Who decides what form be better?* Her thoughts were interrupted by Henry, who was telling Mhutig about the Salt Wars.

"I foresee no peaceful end to the wretched war between taupaks and opowaks," Mhutig admitted once Henry had finished. "The opowaks will accept nothing less than victory."

"Do they look like ye?" Calder asked.

"Opowaks are a little shorter and broader with horns and thick foreheads. They possess no wings. Although a taupak's wings are of little use, limbs inherited from our first ancestors. Our wings give us no advantage against their endless quest for power."

"Then I'm happy we met ye and not an opowak," Roy said, helping himself to some more rabbit.

Roy's comment broke the tension, and the conversation shifted to lighter topics. Aspen shared their encounter with the Grand Oak and fair folk of Evergreen Forest. Mhutig informed them that in Krousus, fair folk were respected for their sizable courage and the same humility he had witnessed in Florette.

"The fair folk of Evergreen once shared this land with its people. But people grew scared when the wrunwick forced them to retreat into their homes. Some accused fair folk of hiding wrunwick in the forest." Florette's eyes went from bright green to dark.

"Did they?" Henry asked.

Roy booted him in the shin. "Of course not." He rolled his eyes.

"It was a joke." Henry rubbed the spot where Roy had found his mark. "Ye didn't have to kick so hard."

"It wasn't funny," Roy said. "And I scarcely touched your leg."

Henry turned to Florette. "Please forgive me, my fair lady." He placed a hand on his chest. "Or my heart won't recover this time."

"'Tis not for me to break a young man's heart," Florette replied.

"And ye, Roy," Henry continued. "Will ye deign to forgive my crude manners?"

Roy scrambled to his feet and bowed. "I'll not be known for breaking the heart of a loyal friend."

Lisette was well used to her friends' shenanigans, but Mhutig wasn't. And she didn't want him to get the wrong impression. "Please excuse my friends. They're completely harmless."

"I have two younger brothers at home, so no excuses needed."

Henry grinned. "We're going to get along famously."

Roy went to stand by Mhutig and began to sing:

> *There once was a beautiful maiden*
> *with ice in her eyes and fire in her soul.*
> *All the boys fell at her feet.*
> *But she neither saw nor heard their sorrow.*

Maisy had eyes for one man, they said,
who was blind to her beauty.
George was his name. Brave and bold,
he feared neither man nor beast.

For George was too slippery for them.
For George was too slippery for them!

The Seekers happily joined in:

With ice in her eyes and fire in her soul,
Maisy knew what she must do.
A cake of honey and oats, Maisy did make.
A cake of honey and oats, Maisy did make!

Alas! Poor George didn't stand a chance.
His eyes sweetened with honey,
he asked Maisy to marry him.
No words ever sounded so sweet to the beautiful maiden.

And the ice in her eyes began to melt,
soaking the ground beneath her feet
where the teardrops grow.

Afraid Maisy would slip through his fingers,
George wed his sweet honey that very same day.
On that very same day, they did wed!

And a happier man ye never did see.
And a happier man ye never did see!

They spent what remained of their night revisiting tales of their childhood alongside Mhutig's company. A charming and gracious host, Mhutig insisted on keeping watch over them and the fire as the night grew late, explaining that he needed little sleep compared to humans.

When Mhutig finished speaking, Florette shared how fair folk slept in cycles, sometimes lasting for entire seasons. Outside of their regular sleep cycles, fair folk preferred short naps during the day and night. Although, as Florette quickly pointed out, she would not be napping during the day on their journey.

Upon hearing Florette's revelation, Mhutig invited her to keep him company between naps. Florette promptly agreed. The Seekers sealed the deal with a round of sleepy smiles and a loud yawn from Aspen.

Chapter 11

At daybreak, they set out for Strawbridge with Mhutig, the once distant bridge between friends and strangers crossed overnight. After yesterday's dark skies, the sun's cheerful ascent renewed Lisette's faith in their quest. She had made a promise to the people of Stonebridge, and she would keep that promise. Fear, she reasoned, was a poor excuse to stay home.

If they had stayed in Stonebridge, they would never have met the Grand Oak, Florette, or Mhutig. Who knew what else awaited them on their journey? *Not opowaks, hopefully.* Like Roy, she was happy they had met Mhutig and not one of his enemies. Lisette cringed at the thought. Their encounter would have been a far worse experience.

They had travelled for about five miles when the trade route peaked through the trees. Everyone agreed it was best to stay on their current path, avoiding traders and other travellers. Mhutig's presence would undoubtedly startle the most seasoned trader or unsuspecting traveller.

The terrain was rough going, but Lisette was grateful for the shade provided by the forest. She looked up to hail the enormous redwoods scattered among the lower pine trees. Redwoods were said to be the tallest trees in Wrunwicks. The thick roots of the red giants covered the forest floor. Admiring a redwood to her left, she guessed they could all fit inside its massive trunk, Mhutig included if they squeezed together. She looked toward Mhutig and smiled at the thought. He didn't strike her as someone who liked tight spaces. Turning her attention to Roy and Ewart, she heard the homesickness in Roy's voice.

"I hope my father be doing well at the bakery," Roy said quietly. "With my brother gone, he has no one to help out besides me. I suggested he take on a new apprentice during my absence, but he insisted on waiting for my return. I wish to Utaika he weren't so hardheaded."

"I may know someone like that," Ewart replied. "Remember the time Harold challenged ye to a sword match? He was three years older than ye and a lot more experienced. Ye had little more than a year of training, but that didn't keep ye from accepting. Harold may have won the match, but ye held your own."

"I was only fifteen and didn't know any better," Roy said after a quick laugh. "If he were to challenge me now, I'm not convinced I'd accept so easily."

"Nonsense. I've never known ye to back down from anything in the seven years we've been friends."

The thunderous sound of feet crashing through the woods brought everyone to a sudden halt. Mhutig withdrew his sword, with the Seekers following suit. The crashing grew louder until a monstrous beast appeared before them. The beast wasted no time on introductions. Instead, it jumped in front of Henry. And with the sweep of one arm, sent him stumbling through the air. Henry landed in a heap no less than ten feet from his horse. Lisette watched in horror as his body landed on the ground.

The beast was about to sweep Aspen off her horse when Mhutig charged toward it. He pierced the beast's heart with a single thrust of his sword. Crying out in protest, the one-horned monster clutched its chest. Blood gushed from its hand. Toppling to the ground in a last fit of rage, it landed with a deafening thud, shaking the ground beneath their horses.

Lisette bolted from her saddle, ran to where Henry lay with his face in a patch of moss and placed a trembling hand on his back. She wanted to scream, but what good would it do? The others quickly joined her. Calder helped her turn over Henry's limp body, careful not to cause further injury.

Unable to tell anything from Henry's lifeless condition, Lisette placed an ear on his chest and listened for a heartbeat. The others stood in shock. Lisette felt an invisible hand squeezing the air from her lungs. "I can hear his heart beating," she managed to say.

"We need to know if anything was broken," Ewart said. "That creature threw him pretty hard."

"Here. Try these smelling herbs." Mhutig withdrew a small pouch from his saddlebag.

Calder took a pinch of herbs and waved them over Henry. The putrid smell filled the air, biting Lisette's nose. Henry remained unconscious.

"It isn't working," Calder said to Mhutig.

"Keep trying," Mhutig advised. "It can take a few moments."

Calder continued to wave the herbs in front of Henry, whose nose began to twitch.

"What be that awful stench?" Henry asked, opening his eyes. "What have I done to deserve such punishment?"

Lisette breathed a loud sigh of relief. Florette flew over to kiss Henry's forehead.

"Ye gave us quite the scare," she scolded.

"I'm not going to disappear, am I?" Henry asked with a weak smile. "I wouldn't want to end up lost somewhere."

Pretending to be insulted by his question, Florette placed both hands on her hips. "The magic doesn't work by accident."

"Am I happy to hear that," Henry said.

"Anything feel broken?" Roy asked.

"My entire body hurts, but I don't think so." Henry struggled to sit up. "I've never felt more alive." He glanced over at the lifeless creature. "That thing, whatever it be, can't say the same."

"It is a karupa like the ones I mentioned yesterday," Mhutig said. "Other taupaks along with myself have formed an alliance to protect humans from these monsters."

"I don't think I'd enjoy your land," Henry replied. "Too much war and violence."

"It must have arrived here in the same manner ye did, Mhutig," Aspen said.

"For the sake of your land and people, I hope he is the only one. We should proceed with caution, nonetheless." Mhutig turned to Florette and smiled. "Perhaps it would be wise to veil ourselves for the remainder of our journey to Strawbridge."

Glancing at Mhutig, Lisette noticed the forced broadness of his smile. After her mother disappeared, her father would look at her with a smile that grew wider with each passing day. But no matter how wide her father's smile grew, it never reached his eyes. Mhutig's eyes were just as worried.

"Will ye be okay to ride?" Calder observed Henry for either sign to the contrary.

"I think I can make it. Just give me a hand to stand up."

"Ye're one lucky dastard," Calder said, after helping Henry limp back to his horse.

"Let's hope there be plenty more luck to go around," Henry grunted, then flung his leg over Mystery's back.

"What should we do with him?" Aspen asked, looking over at the karupa. "It be hard to miss."

Even in death, the karupa looked ready to strike at a moment's notice. Covered in a thin layer of large grey scales, it had towered over Mhutig's head by at least three arm lengths. The monster could easily crush a person with its bare hands. Lisette forced her eyes away from its cold, unblinking stare.

"We could cover him with branches and let Utaika take care of the rest," Ewart said.

"Or we could just leave him be." Henry winced as the colour drained from his face.

"The monster deserves nothing more than to be left under the rain like a diseased rat," Lisette said. "But if someone were to come across his body, it could cause panic. We should at least try to cover it up."

"I can no more argue with your reasoning, Lisette, than argue with the rain. And while I'd love to help, it might be best for me to sit this one out," Henry replied.

"I think we can manage on our own." Ewart grinned at Henry. "But don't get too used to it."

"Let's get it over with, then." Roy dismounted from his horse.

They went to work using rocks, fallen tree branches, moss, and whatever else they could find to hide the karupa's body. Florette stayed with Henry to keep an eye on him. When the Seekers were done covering the body, they stared at the mess of debris.

"I'm not convinced it'll fool anyone," Calder said. "It'll take a lot more than branches to hide something that big."

Florette flew over to a nearby redwood and placed her palm on its trunk. The roots around the karupa stirred, scarcely noticeable at first. Moments later, the roots separated and rose from the earth, beginning a slow march over the karupa's inert form. As the roots inched their way over the karupa's head, arms, and legs, they picked up speed, seemingly encouraged by their progress. The roots intersected and twisted over the karupa's midline, then maintained course until their tips reached the other side, tunnelling their way into the earth. When the roots settled back down, all that remained was a jumbled mass of roots.

"A person would need to be very curious to dig through that," Lisette said, staring in amazement.

"They'd be in for a nasty jolt. I've never laid eyes on anything so ugly," Calder replied.

Florette flew back and sat to face Lisette. "The trees were happy to help."

Ewart let out an admiring whistle. "Ye'll need to remind me to never challenge a redwood."

Chapter 12

The Seekers kept a watchful eye on the forest. It looked peaceful. As part of their lessons, elders taught children to respect the land and its creatures. An animal could not be killed for pleasure alone. And neither part of an animal was ever wasted, the same for trees. In return, Utaika blessed the land and its people with long growing seasons, fertile soil, and abundant forests.

Now the forest hid an evil presence: karupas from a mysterious land. Lisette could not imagine their Divine Mother ever creating such a destructive creature. It would have killed them all without reason or provocation. Were the vanishings related? She looked to the sky in search of an answer. The sun retreated behind a passing cloud. *Even the sun be afraid. What chance does a rabbit have?* She pictured a rabbit peeking out from its burrow, only to retreat at the first sign of danger. She looked to Mhutig next and knew that he would never retreat from danger. Sensing her gaze, Mhutig turned and smiled. Lisette returned his generous smile, grateful to count him as a friend.

"Are there many karupas in your land, Mhutig?" she asked.

"Too many by my count. I was relieved to see that one travelling alone. They often travel in small packs since the Order of Taupaks was formed. A way to defend themselves, I suppose. Not that it does them much good in the end. But here in a strange land like myself, they may think differently."

"Could there be more we have yet to encounter?" Lisette asked.

"If there *are* more, at least now we have the advantage of being invisible to anyone but us," Mhutig replied. "I only hope there are no other travellers in this forest today."

"Those poor unfortunate souls won't have a taupak to protect them," Henry pointed out.

"My presence here may not be so accidental after all." Mhutig smiled at Henry.

"Ye said that ye hunt karupas. Does that mean ye're a member of the Order of Taupaks?" Roy asked.

Mhutig nodded. "There are many who disagree with us and the hunting. They argue that it is not our place to interfere or destroy another creature without provocation. But humans are no match against their size and strength. We hunt between battles with the opowaks."

"The people of Wrunwicks are no more equipped to fight them than yours," Roy said. "I fear the age of peace has made us weak."

"And yet, here you are," Mhutig replied.

"We'll have to warn the people of Strawbridge. They deserve to know of this new threat," Ewart said.

"We'll also need to explain Mhutig's presence to them," Calder said. "They've never laid eyes on a taupak before. It'll be somewhat of a shock."

"Just as we have come to appreciate Mhutig's alliance, so too will the townsfolk." Lisette grinned at their new friend.

Calder was about to respond when Florette lifted her arm from Lisette's hood to signal her travel companions.

"Does anyone hear that?" she asked.

They stopped to listen and scanned the forest. A fox scurried off while an eagle squealed from above. To their right, they heard the steady thump, thump of footsteps approaching from the south.

Lisette's heart pounded in response. She took a deep breath and turned to face her friends. "As long as we stay out of its direct path, we should be safe. It shouldn't be able to detect us with our veils. This time, we have the advantage."

The others nodded, listening as the footsteps maintained their steady approach. Mhutig appeared deep in thought.

"From what I can hear, there are two sets of feet." Mhutig's ears twitched in concentration. He pointed to his left. "Whatever is headed our way will be here before the sun crosses that tree."

"Perhaps tis best to keep moving," Henry said. "I feel like an ant next to a shoe, even with the veil."

"I have to agree with Henry," Aspen said. "And we still need to get to Strawbridge."

"What do ye think, Mhutig?" Lisette asked. "Should we wait to confirm the presence of more karupas, or should we keep going?"

"If more karupas have indeed arrived in Wrunwicks, they will eventually find their purpose," Mhutig replied. "They make up for their lack of wit with their sense of smell. In Krousus, they stay away from the villages to avoid any taupaks who might be waiting. But if they discover that the people here are alone and defenceless, they could attack an unsuspecting village."

Thinking over Mhutig's words, Lisette paused before speaking. She wanted to agree with Henry and put as much distance between themselves and the karupas as possible, but they had a promise to keep. "Henry and Aspen are wise to be concerned. We've already witnessed the destructive power of these monsters. And our veil hasn't been tested against them, so the decision to stay can't be mine alone. What do ye say, Seekers? Do we stay, or do we head for Strawbridge?"

"We stand our ground," Roy spoke out. "It be time to answer the question of who we are. Are we cowards? Or are we the Truth Seekers, defenders of Wrunwicks?"

"To truth and courage." Ewart raised his sword.

"To Wrunwicks," the others chimed in.

"That settles it, then," Lisette said. "Now we wait and hope those footsteps don't belong to karupas."

"But in case they do, we'll need a plan of attack," Roy said, holding Shadow's reins tighter than a set of clamps.

It was now impossible to ignore the footsteps' rhythmic thud, growing louder with each breath. It was also obvious the footsteps belonged to something much larger than any animal known to Wrunwicks.

"Karupas." Florette's wings fluttered nervously.

"It might be wise for everyone to take shelter in the woods," Mhutig said. "Florette's veil should hide your presence, or at least long enough for me to destroy the karupas. You will be safer there."

"And ye?" Ewart asked. "What of your safety?"

"One taupak against two karupas is seldom a fair fight," Mhutig admitted. "But Florette's veil will help even the odds."

"Could ye not use your bow and arrow in place of your sword?" Calder asked.

"A karupa's scales are soft, but the thick, rubbery skin underneath is exceptionally strong. We've tried flaming arrows, but their skin doesn't burn so easily, allowing them to survive longer than any other creature known to us. And a wounded karupa is even more dangerous," Mhutig explained. "My sword was forged and sharpened to destroy any karupa it meets."

"By the sound of it, ye won't have long to wait," Lisette said, listening to the footsteps.

As the footsteps closed in, the horses raised their heads and flicked their ears in alarm. The Seekers led their horses into the woods, leaving Mhutig in the middle of the clearing. When they reached the bottom of a wooded hill next to a redwood tree, the Seekers stopped and waited.

Lisette watched while Mhutig kept his ears glued to the woods. Before leaving him to fight, he had explained his need to be as near both karupas as possible when he struck the first blow. The closer he was, the greater his chance of victory. Once the karupas learned of his presence, they would attack as one.

A short time passed when two karupas emerged from the woods and onto the clearing. Mhutig jumped in front of the karupas and raised his sword, reminding Lisette of a knight in battle. He aimed for the chest of the nearest karupa.

Striking just below the karupa's heart, Mhutig's sword sliced upwards. It yelped in rage. The second karupa lashed out, missing Mhutig's back by inches. And while the first karupa careened to his death, the second one found Mhutig's hip and cried out with the same blood-hungry rage. Its voice was higher than that of the first karupa. A female, Lisette realized in disbelief.

Mhutig's legs buckled from the impact. The karupa flared her nostrils. Although she might not be able to see her attacker, she could definitely smell him. Punching the air, she found Mhutig's front leg and struck him again. Mhutig looked small compared to the towering karupa. Watching the staggering scene in front of them, Lisette gasped in horror as the karupa hit Mhutig again.

"We can't just stand here while he loses," Roy said.

"We have to help him before it be too late." Calder sounded even more frustrated than Roy.

Roy seized Shadow's reins. "What are we waiting for?"

The Seekers raced to help their friend. Florette gripped Lisette's hood as they broke through the woods and charged the clearing, their swords raised for battle.

The karupa thrashed the air in search of her attacker. Mhutig leaned back. The karupa's left arm struck him in the stomach, sending Mhutig to his knees. His hind legs wobbled. He straightened his wings to steady himself.

"I told you to remain in the woods!" Mhutig shouted, blood spurting from his mouth.

The first to arrive, Calder thrust his sword into the karupa's lower thigh. He managed another strike before the karupa flung him from his horse.

"Humans!" the karupa shrieked, grasping at the air.

Roy shoved his sword into the other thigh and ducked to avoid the karupa's arm as it swooped through the air. Roy struck the karupa's thigh again. Pressing his wings against the ground, Mhutig stood up and leaped forward, plunging his sword into the karupa's heart. The karupa let out a final shriek, searched the clearing for her killer, then joined her mate on the ground.

Aspen ran over and fell to her knees next to Calder's lifeless body. Calder had not moved since the karupa flung him from his horse. Lisette and the others joined them. Observing Calder's face, Lisette knew there was no need to check for life signs. Calder's blank expression told Lisette that he was gone. The rock beneath Calder's head was stained a dark red. Aspen's weeping was the only sound in the clearing. Oblivious to the blood and tears, Calder lay quiet beneath the late afternoon sun. Lisette kneeled and cradled Aspen, who wept from the river of shattered dreams.

Calder's death struck Lisette harder than a karupa's fists ever could. Seeing him lying there sucked the air from her lungs and filled her with a grief so profound, it crushed her mind and body. Just moments ago, Calder had charged through the woods, riding next to them, full of life and energy. Nothing could have prepared her for this.

Florette flew over to Calder and closed his eyes. She placed a gentle kiss on his forehead. Glancing around at the Seekers, she flew back to Lisette's hood and rested her head on Lisette's shoulder.

Mhutig cleared his throat. "Calder was a man of towering courage. Never have I witnessed anyone charge a karupa so fearlessly," he said. "I will be forever in his debt. And yours, Roy."

Lisette looked up, her eyes widening at the sight of two birds flying around the karupas. She had never seen birds with such bright colouring or bald heads. She closed her eyes, then looked again. The birds were still circling the karupas. "Are those birds from Krousus, Mhutig?" The ground was spinning all around her.

Mhutig examined the birds for several moments. "We do, but I have only seen a few with the bold red feathers of those two. Their brown feathered cousins are far more common."

"I've never heard of anything like them in Wrunwicks."

"In Krousus, we call them purifiers. They feed on the dead like those karupas and any other creature that would otherwise rot," Mhutig replied. "These could be from some other part of Krousus where I have yet to travel."

Ewart's eyes went from Aspen to Lisette. "We'll need to bring Calder with us to Strawbridge, so he can receive a proper burial."

While Ewart spoke, the purifiers began to clean the bones of the karupas, unmoved by their new surroundings.

Lisette was still cradling Aspen. She searched for the strength to brave their new reality. The karupas meant the people of Wrunwicks faced a vicious enemy. And she had promised herself to bring everyone home safely. A promise she was no longer able to keep. "He'll ride with us one last time," she said, wiping Aspen's tears from her cheeks. "Calder will be given the burial of a hero. We'll share his story with the people of Strawbridge, and word of his courage will spread throughout the land. His story will be passed on to our children and theirs, where he'll live for eternity."

"And with us," Aspen whispered.

Roy went to retrieve Calder's horse and led the old steed to his master. Ewart and Henry hoisted their friend onto Moonlight's back. They pulled Calder's blanket over his body so that he could travel undisturbed. Roy reached for Moonlight's reins. He would lead the horse and his master to Strawbridge.

"It be time for us to go," Lisette said.

Aspen nodded, and they stood for the first time since kneeling beside Calder. Lisette wrapped her arm around Aspen's waist and guided them toward their horses. Florette's calming presence gave her the strength she needed to help Aspen. Their horses waited in silence, munching on the tall grass at the edge of the clearing. She helped Aspen onto Silver's back.

The purifiers were still tearing into the karupas. It would be long past the time sensible folk went to bed when they arrived in Strawbridge. Lisette was past caring. There was nothing sensible about this day.

"May the rest of our journey to Strawbridge be uneventful," Roy said, casting a final look backwards.

Chapter 13

fter a day forged in horror, the Seekers arrived outside Strawbridge. Given the night's sizable headway, they had expected the town to be dark. But to Lisette's surprise, the town still burned bright through the trees. They stopped at the edge of the woods some twenty paces from Strawbridge and considered the lights ahead.

"The townsfolk must keep late nights," Henry remarked.

"We should proceed with care," Lisette cautioned. "The people will be frightened at first. They'll need time to adjust."

"I don't think we'll have long to wait for their reaction once we enter the township," Ewart replied.

"Perhaps it would be best for me to wait here for now," Mhutig said. "I do not wish to alarm anyone."

"Nonsense," Ewart said. "Ye're one of us now. And we never leave our friends behind."

Lisette turned to Mhutig. "He be right. We might not have known ye for long, but friendship be based on trust, not the amount of time we've known each other."

"I am honoured by your words," Mhutig replied. "I, too, count all of you among my own."

"We're all grateful to have ye here with us," Aspen said. "Together, we'll honour Calder's sacrifice."

"To Calder," Roy said.

"To our dear friend," the others said quietly.

"Well, I think it be time for us to meet the townsfolk," Roy said.

"Something tells me tis going to be a welcome to remember," Henry replied, his voice laced with exhaustion.

"I fear that to be an understatement." Lisette signalled Daisy to continue. She would take them into Strawbridge.

They followed the northeast road to market square. When they passed the first homes, townsfolk peered out their windows to see what was causing the late disruption. The slow clipping of iron on stone ricocheted off the town's gloomy walls. Lisette stared straight ahead, determined not to falter. She recalled Calder standing next to her at the falls.

"Why do ye put yourself through this?" Calder had asked with unfailing compassion.

Ye weren't supposed to die. The final bells rang out, announcing curfew. Lisette straightened her back against the ominous sound. To be out past curfew without a warrant could land a person in the cage. But the people of Strawbridge ignored the bells, pouring onto the street for a closer look.

Before long, the Seekers were surrounded by men and women with their mouths hanging in disbelief. It was impossible to move beyond the crowd packed in around them. *At least they didn't bring weapons.* Lisette confronted the mob of wary faces.

"We are the Seekers of Stonebridge," she said. "And this be

Mhutig of Krousus, our friend and ally. Please, don't be afraid. Mhutig's size and strength are matched only by his sympathy for the people of Wrunwicks."

"What be this aberration?" a man inquired from the growing swarm of people.

"A taupak and protector of the people," Lisette replied in the calmest voice granted to her. She wanted to acknowledge their fear. By anyone's standard, Mhutig was an extraordinary sight.

"A taupak?" the man asked.

Lisette took a deep breath, spotting another man to her right who was watching Mhutig with unnatural loathing. She shuddered at the cruelty in his eyes but knew it was critical to display reason and respect. "Kind sir, a taupak be a man with the strength of the mightiest horse and the heart of the strongest among us. As ye can see, he has the lower body of the animal whose strength he owns."

"There exists no such creature!" a man shouted from inside the crowd.

Refraining from pointing out that Mhutig's presence proved otherwise, Lisette searched for the face that went with the man's rough voice. She found him staring at her no more than five feet away. "'Tis true that taupaks don't exist in Wrunwicks, but Mhutig be from a different land."

"A different land? Sounds like the biddle-babblings of a mind softer than wool!" a woman shouted. "Do ye bring proof of this?"

"We don't, but our journey has scarcely begun," Lisette admitted. "As the Seekers of Stonebridge, we hope to prove its existence and uncover why the people of Wrunwicks are disappearing."

"Two days ago, a band of three men went to find the source of thunder coming from the forest," the woman replied. "They have yet to return. Are ye able to find out what happened to them?"

"We've seen no sign of the men ye speak of, kind woman. I wish we had. Too many of our loved ones have vanished." Observing the faces caught in the glow of sleepless lanterns, Lisette decided it was time for Mhutig to quiet their fears. Until then, they would not hear beyond their own voices. The townsfolk needed to see him as they did. "Please, let us give Mhutig the chance to speak." The crowd stared up at Mhutig, and an image of Stonebridgers gawking up at her sprang before Lisette.

"I know my appearance must seem strange and frightening to you, noble people of Strawbridge." Mhutig studied the flickering faces before him. "But allow me to assure you that I am not your enemy, and I mean you no harm. In Krousus, I swore an oath to protect the people of our land from creatures who would see them annihilated."

"Have those creatures also made their way to Wrunwicks, taupak?" a young man inquired from the outskirts of the crowd.

"I fear the thunder you heard coming from the forest may have been such a creature. In Krousus, we call them karupas," Mhutig replied. "They are people's greatest enemy. And although we were successful in destroying the three we encountered here in your land, one of them took down our friend before its death."

The townsfolk turned their attention from Mhutig to Calder. Lisette watched their expressions. Some of the men removed their hats. *Tis a start.* Sensing Daisy's growing agitation, she patted the mare's neck, their signal for Daisy to lower her head. Within a few short moments, Lisette felt the stress drain from Daisy's body.

The young man moved through the crowd to stand in front of Mhutig. "Who be the fallen one?"

Lisette could see the man was not afraid of Mhutig. Taking a closer look, she suspected he feared little of anything.

"This be Calder," Aspen replied before Mhutig had a chance. "The son of Clarence and Anna Reed."

"And who might ye be?" the young man asked.

"Aspen, daughter of Walter and Eleanor Greene."

"'Tis a pleasure to meet ye, Aspen. My friends call me Deidrik, son of Lloyd and Hazel Black. May I ask what happened to your friend?"

Lisette wondered who the man was. When Deidrik spoke, she noticed the townsfolk listened fully. It suggested the people of Strawbridge held him in high regard, an unusual honour for someone so young.

"Like the good people here, we too heard the roar of footsteps in the forest," Aspen said. "We had already fought and destroyed our first karupa. A more savage beast ye've never laid eyes on with the skin of a yeiat, but near tall as a house and stronger than any creature known to Wrunwicks. We waited to see if the footsteps we heard next belonged to more of those vile creatures.

"Mhutig instructed us to wait in the woods while he readied himself for more battle. When two karupas appeared with teeth thicker than my wrists, we watched as Mhutig killed the first beast with a single strike. But the second karupa wasn't so easily killed. Unable to stand by, we charged the clearing to save our friend and defend our land.

"Calder reached the beast first and struck with all his might. The karupa knocked Calder from his horse, causing him to bang his head against a sharp rock. In the end, Calder's bravery allowed Mhutig to destroy the karupa and save the rest of us."

Townsfolk listened to Aspen's story in shock. Grief ran through her words like a river in spring. When Aspen finished speaking, Deidrik turned to Mhutig.

"We're honoured by your presence in Strawbridge," Deidrik said. "And by yours as well, Seekers."

"The honour be mutual," Lisette said. "We hope to provide Calder with his final words during our stay. In the meantime, we'll need lodging."

"My inn be always open to visitors!" a portly man shouted from the crowd, creating a brief ripple of laughter.

"Then we'll gladly stay, kind sir," Lisette said.

Florette relinquished Lisette's hood to take her seat.

"Who do we have here?" Deidrik asked.

"This be Florette. A fay of Evergreen Forest. Without her help, we might not be here as well," Lisette said. She wanted to do right by Florette, whose skill far outweighed her size.

Deidrik bowed. "It sounds like another story worth hearing." His eyes were bright with interest. "I have a feeling we'll be old friends before long."

Lisette felt eyes on her and noticed the same man who had been watching Mhutig earlier. The cold in his eyes reminded her of the karupa's dead stare. She held onto Daisy's mane to ward off a chill. Whoever the man was, he despised strangers.

When Deidrik finished speaking, the crowd appeared calmer. Lisette turned to Ewart in relief. The town's reception was better than she had dared to hope. Ewart nodded and jumped to the ground. The worst was over. Lisette and the others dismounted to face the townsfolk from a more even footing.

Men and women walked up to shake their hands and welcome them to Strawbridge. A few paused to shake Mhutig's hand, but most were still too afraid. The people were clearly spooked by all that was happening, not that Lisette could blame them. Along with the vanishings, their world had just been turned upside down.

Elbowing his way through the crowd, the portly man broke through the wall of people. "Greetings, kind travellers. I've room for everyone at the inn, though I'm not sure ye'll fit comfortably, Mhutig. The inn's chambers are a little small for someone of your size. I'm afraid ye might not fit."

"Perhaps you would know of somewhere else I could rest for the night," Mhutig said. "I require simple lodging."

"There be a large stable behind the inn. I fear tis not befitting a gentleman, though," the innkeeper replied, sounding apologetic.

"It will be more than sufficient."

"My friends call me Bernard." The innkeeper extended his hand to Mhutig.

"Bernard, it is." Mhutig shook the innkeeper's hand.

"Before we leave for the inn, I can introduce ye to Albert, our most esteemed caretaker in all of Strawbridge," Bernard said. "He'll take excellent care of your friend and prepare him for the burial."

"No need, Bernard," said a wizened man, who had just emerged from the crowd.

"Albert, old fool. I should have known that ye wouldn't be far behind," Bernard said.

"I be simply doing my best to welcome our visitors," Albert said to his younger friend. "And tis my duty to ensure the fallen one be taken care of."

"The townsfolk won't sleep much tonight," Bernard said.

"'Tis not every day we receive a taupak and a fay in Strawbridge," Albert replied. "Reason enough to break curfew, I think."

A man rode up to the crowd and dismounted. The people quickly separated to let him through. Dressed in a dark green jacket and overcoat of fine wools, the town lord made his way toward the Seekers, stopping on occasion to speak with his citizens.

When he reached the end of the town's people, the Seekers bowed before their lord, then waited in silence for him to address them. Lisette hoped their lord's cordial expression was a good sign.

"It seems your presence has caused quite the commotion," the lord of Strawbridge said at last.

"My lord." They bowed again.

"At ease, young travellers. Allow me to introduce myself. Lord Stanley at your service."

"We are the Seekers of Stonebridge," Lisette replied, regretting the tremor in her voice. *Stand your ground.*

"And ye, kind sir?" Lord Stanley asked, removing his gloves.

"Mhutig of Krousus, my lord."

"A pleasure to meet ye, Mhutig." Lord Stanley offered his hand in friendship. "To what do we owe the pleasure of your visit?"

Mhutig shook Lord Stanley's hand. "We come in search of a place to rest and bury our brave friend."

As the two spoke, Lisette listened with growing respect. Lord Stanley appeared clueless to the fact that Mhutig was a taupak. *Maybe he's seen one before.* She chased the idea from her mind. *Not unless he's been to Krousus.*

"Ye've come to the right town. The people of Strawbridge are some of the truest in all the kingdom. I see that ye've already met Bernard." Lord Stanley turned to look at the innkeeper. "Knowing Bernard, he has already offered ye shelter."

"Aye. That I have, Lord Stanley," Bernard replied. "But I fear my inn isn't big enough to accommodate Mhutig."

"Ye're more than welcome to stay at the manor, Mhutig," Lord Stanley said. "I know someone who would love to meet ye. Your friends are also welcome to stay."

"A most esteemed offer, my lord. But if it pleases ye, we will accept Bernard's charitable offer." Lisette suspected Lord Stanley's invitation was a simple demonstration of manners, which betided them to politely decline. And they had already accepted Bernard's offer. To accept now would insult the innkeeper's kindness.

"Then I insist ye join me tomorrow for the evening meal. We can exchange stories and discuss your friend's burial."

Lisette saw Aspen watching them. She looked lost, and her eyes had aged twice since yesterday. They met at the Great Library when Lisette was ten. Aspen had already been taking lessons for a year by then. Forming an immediate friendship, they shared the secrets that all girls share. When Aspen had confessed her love for Calder, she vowed to wait for him, no matter how long it took. And she made good on her promise, waiting the four years after, dreaming of the family they would have someday. Now he was gone, taken from them in a single act of savagery.

How do ye recover from that? Lisette mustered a smile for her dear friend. Aspen would need her to be strong. Willing herself to focus, Lisette switched her attention back to Lord Stanley. He was addressing the townsfolk.

"Kind people of Strawbridge, the Seekers are weary of mind and body, as we all are. Let us get some rest before the sun rises once again."

Lord Stanley was right. Lisette was exhausted and knew that her friends must be as well. She was grateful to see the townsfolk leave for their homes. The day had cost them more than any coin could ever replace.

Chapter 14

The Seekers rode to Albert's house with Calder. Next door, the chantry's bell tower sliced through the darkness, silent and unswayed. Ewart and Roy lifted Calder from his horse and carried him into the care chamber, located at the rear of the house. The Seekers accepted Albert's offer to stay for ale. When the candle dipped past the next karpal score, they bid the caretaker a tired goodnight. And with Calder in Albert's capable hands, they followed Bernard back to Mountain Inn.

Lisette soaked up the quiet of the square. King Lazoran II kept an ever-vigilant eye in front of the library, about half the size of the Great Library in Stonebridge. Down on his luck, a dog scrounged for food. Roy threw some bread onto the street.

"Ye best be careful, or every stray this side of Strawbridge'll find ye." Bernard slowed in front of the inn.

"I'll take my chances." Roy threw another piece of bread out for the dog.

With the horses sheltered for the night, their owners went to pay for their chambers. The men requested a private chamber each. Lisette offered to share a chamber with Aspen and Florette. She reasoned it wouldn't be good for Aspen to be alone. Nor did Lisette wish to be alone with her thoughts.

Florette flew next to them up the stairs. Lisette unlocked the door to their chamber. A table mellowed with age greeted them by the doorway. To their right, a washstand rested beneath the only window. Two beds welcomed them from the middle of the small chamber. The beds looked clean and inviting.

Lisette plopped her saddlebag on the table and collapsed onto one of the beds. Florette sat on the pillow next to her.

"Bernard keeps a proud inn," Aspen remarked, slumping onto the other bed.

They could hear Roy and Ewart talking in the next chamber. Henry had remained downstairs, taking Bernard up on his offer to finish the night with a mug of ale. To neither friend's surprise, Henry had required no convincing, saying it would ease the pain from his bruised ribs.

"I guess none of us are ready for sleep yet," Lisette said, referring to the voices next door.

"I'm afraid that if I close my eyes, I'll see Calder lying there with his head on that rock," Aspen replied.

Florette flew over to the window. "It be calm out there now," she said, looking down at the square.

Lisette noted the kalpar candle above the table. It would be light in around three scores.

"Did ye find it strange so many people were still up by the last bell?" Aspen asked, lying down on her side to gaze at Lisette.

"I could feel their panic. The vanishings and strange noises breed dread among them." Florette flew back to the bed.

"Ye felt their panic?" Aspen asked.

"I can feel people's emotions," Florette replied.

"How does that work?" Aspen hoisted herself up on one arm.

Florette crossed her legs on the pillow. "I can't sense every emotion, mind ye. Only the stronger ones. Lord Stanley be pleased by our presence. He was especially happy to see ye, Lisette. It was as though he recognized your face."

"I never met Lord Stanley until tonight. Maybe he recognized something else. Fear, maybe? The people here are certainly scared." Lisette recalled their lord's brief conversation with Mhutig. "He did seem charmed by Mhutig, though."

"Lord Stanley's heart be pure in the same way your hearts are pure," Florette said.

"Can ye also read our thoughts?" Aspen asked.

"Sometimes."

"I guess the Grand Oak forgot to mention that part," Lisette said, removing her boots.

Aspen traced the blanket's delicate pattern with her fingers. "Calder's parents deserve to know of his passing."

"How do ye tell someone their son has died?" Lisette asked. When her mother vanished, no one ever spoke of it with her, including her father.

"News of Calder's passing will hurt the entire town," Aspen said. "We all knew there were risks involved when we left Stonebridge, but I don't think anyone knew how great those risks were."

"I promised myself that ye would all arrive back home safely," Lisette said.

"We accepted this journey of our own accord," Aspen replied. "Ye're not responsible for our safety."

Next door, Lisette heard Ewart speaking to Roy before taking his leave. Roy's chamber fell silent. She hoped the men would get some sleep but suspected they were all in for a long night. Sleep was best left to dreamers.

Aspen walked over to the window and stared at the night sky. "I think we all wanted to be part of something bigger. I know I did."

Lisette turned toward Aspen to see how she was faring. She looked restless. They wouldn't be going to bed any time soon. It was just as well. "Remember when Calder and Ewart read *Balsha's Reckoning*?"

Aspen laughed for the first time since seeing Calder lying on the ground. She walked back to her bed. "How can I forget? They spent their time arguing over whether Balsha should have punished the knight and what the author's message was."

"Calder argued the knight only wanted revenge. Ewart argued the knight's actions were true, but Balsha stole the opportunity to justify his claim on another soul." Lisette pictured the two of them at the tavern in one of their friendly debates.

Florette flew over to sit next to Aspen. "Calder was a man of honour, and he loved ye both very much. He held a special place in his heart just for ye, Aspen."

Lisette sat up straight on the bed. What did that mean? She saw the surprised look on her friend's face. "Would ye be up to saying the last words at Calder's burial?" The question escaped before she realized it was there. Last words were always delivered by the father or other male kin. But with no kin available, Lisette could think of no one more deserving than Aspen.

"Maybe it would be best for one of the men to do it." Aspen's eyes were round as full moons.

"But would ye like to?"

"The people here don't know us, and we don't know them, not yet anyway. Introducing me as the consecrator might not be the best way to start. They just met Mhutig. That might be enough shock for now."

"But would ye like to?"

"I'd be honoured, but ye know tis against the rules."

"Haven't ye ever asked yourself why a woman can never be the consecrator?" Lisette said, surprising herself with the question. It had never occurred to her until now.

"We've always found the practice strange," Florette said. "But the Grand Oak said it wasn't our place to interfere, telling us that a river must follow its own course."

"I wish she was here to explain." Lisette watched while Aspen stared at the blanket. Life be so unfair. "Are ye up for it?"

"When a fay passes on," Florette continued, "the Grand Oak always begins the ceremony. Next, family members share their loved one's memories with the rest of their kin and friends. In this manner, a fay's memories are preserved and become part of all those inside the circle. The ceremony takes at least two kalpar scores to complete. Fair folk have many kin and even more friends. After the passing of memories, a fay be given new life through the same dirt that gave life to Wrunwicks. When the Grand Oak sleeps, a friend or family member begins the ceremony."

"I wish we could pass our memories of Calder on to the people of Stonebridge," Aspen said, appearing miles away.

"Tomorrow, we could introduce ye as the head of ceremony to Lord Stanley. Ye can still honour his memory," Lisette said.

"We can mention it and decide from there."

Lisette knew not to push the matter further. A woman sharing the last words was unheard of in Wrunwicks. Although there was no canon against it, she knew her request would be unprecedented and would require Lord Stanley's blessing.

Chapter 15

akened from a string of troubled dreams, Lisette snuck down to the square while her chamber mates slept. The market shops were already open for business. She heard a familiar banging as the blacksmith forged iron into submission. The cobbler was setting up an outside table with his best shoes and boots. A few women had gathered in front of the butcher shop.

Crossing the square to the tailor shop, she was relieved to see that it was also open. Pleased that no one had interrupted her along the way, Lisette opened the door. She wanted to get back to the inn and surprise Florette with her idea. Florette was one of them now, a Truth Seeker. And to let Florette know how much she valued her, Lisette wanted to create a new outfit to offer as a gift. The fair folk all wore clothes made of leaves and other materials from the forest, well suited to the woods in which they lived but not for riding. She hoped to make Florette an outfit similar to hers and Aspen's.

Inside the shop, Lisette started over to where a man inspected the linen samples on a table. She heard the voices of two apprentices drifting from the back sewing chamber. In the right corner of the shop, a spinning wheel rested next to a basket of combed wool. The wheel's placement would allow the tailor easy oversight as the spinner worked. The spinner's absence could only mean she was on field duty. The tailor paused to observe Lisette as she approached. She was about to introduce herself when the tailor raised his hand in protest.

"There be no need for introductions, young Seeker," the tailor said. He finished inspecting the linen and placed it on top of the carefully stacked samples. "My friends call me Herman. What can I do for ye this morning?"

Lady Constance always requested the finest materials for her gowns, but they were less practical and expensive. Lisette preferred to work with wool. After informing Herman what she needed, the tailor went to retrieve some samples from another table and hurried back. Lisette chose the softest two. Once cut, they would make a fine jacket and trousers. She asked for a needle, scissors, and thread.

"Ye won't be making much with those." Herman retrieved an old patch of linen from the shelf behind him. "Will ye be needing the items wrapped for half a wrunso?"

Lisette smiled and nodded, wishing she had thought to bring her saddlebag to spare the unexpected expense. The tiny scrap of linen would have been offered at no cost in Stonebridge. She also wanted to get back before Aspen and Florette noticed her missing and didn't want to entertain the tailor any longer than necessary.

Most tailors snubbed their noses at the work of a seamstress, who learned to sew from her mother and through years of practice. Tailors still excluded women from their guilds, while the growing preference for a seamstress among the ladies of Wrunwicks incited further scorn from guild members. So Lisette accepted her package, bid the tailor a quick farewell, and set out for the inn.

Back inside their chamber, Lisette found Aspen and Florette still asleep. Determined not to nap during the day, Florette slept for longer periods at night. Smiling at the sight of their sleeping faces, Lisette crept to the side table, stored the packet in her bag, and went down to the main hall.

Roy and Ewart were seated at a table with Deidrik Black. The men appeared to be in good spirits and enjoying each other's company. Bernard placed a large trencher of cheese and smoked meat on the table, reminding Lisette that she had not eaten since the morning before.

"Good day to ye," Deidrik said when she arrived within hearing distance. "I happened to be staying at the inn, so I figured I'd join ye this morning."

Lisette had assumed Deidrik lived in Strawbridge. When he beamed the same easy smile from the night before, she wondered what had brought him to Strawbridge. Nestled at the foot of the mountains, Strawbridge was not the kind of town that a person passed through on their way to somewhere else.

"Aspen and Florette still sleeping?" Roy asked.

Lisette nodded. "We were up to see the sunrise." She took a seat next to Ewart.

"We haven't seen Henry yet either," Roy said. "According to Bernard, they were also up until the early morning light."

"Aye. He was feeling no pain when he went to bed." Bernard poured a mug of ale for Lisette.

"In last night's excitement, I neglected to mention I'm from Kingsbridge," Deidrik said. "I like to visit my sister and her family here in Strawbridge when I get a chance, which isn't often enough. Although my sister would disagree, then tell ye I'm too protective."

Lisette wondered why he wasn't staying with his sister instead of at the inn. "The people of Strawbridge appear to trust ye."

"I've been visiting Strawbridge for the past six years. The townsfolk are used to seeing me around."

"Were ye here when the three men vanished?"

"I arrived two days before they left. Bernard's son was among them. Like his father, Adler be a good man with a generous heart."

"Adler be hardheaded like his mother," Bernard replied. "Once his mind be made, there be no changing it."

"There've been far too many vanishings in our land. Tis long past the time to put a stop to it," Lisette said after trying the meat. It tasted even better than it looked. She took a second piece and placed it on her bread.

"A few have vanished from Kingsbridge as well," Deidrik said. "People are nervous."

"The people back home are scared too. And when we visited Shewbridge, it was the same there." Ewart took a swig of ale. "From what we've seen, they have good reason to be afraid."

"Ye said last night that ye're hoping to discover why people are disappearing. Have ye found anything so far?" Deidrik asked.

"Other than karupas?" Ewart placed his mug back on the table. "We've been advised there might be a band of wrunwick in the northern part of the mountains."

Deidrik stared at Ewart in surprise. "Impossible. The wrunwick are legends created by our ancestors around campfires to keep themselves busy. Those stories have never described them in any detail, except for their size and tempers. If such a creature did exist, wouldn't we have more details of what they looked like?"

"I might have agreed with ye at the beginning of our journey." Lisette helped herself to another piece of meat. "But with all that's happened since we left Stonebridge, I can't help thinking there be much about our land we don't understand, including the existence of monsters and other kingdoms."

"I'll admit Mhutig's presence would suggest there be something very unusual going on in Wrunwicks." Deidrik glanced at Ewart. "And the presence of karupas, of course. The idea of another land be an old one, but people have largely accepted it as biddle-babble. Ye mentioned proving it. A tall promise."

"Calder once spoke of the possibility to me." Roy tore a large piece of bread from the trencher. "And like most, I dismissed the idea. But now, I'm convinced it has to exist. Mhutig has no reason to lie." He popped the bread into his mouth.

"It be a lot to absorb for anyone," Lisette said.

"When do ye plan to leave for the mountains?" Deidrik asked her.

"We haven't decided yet. We've accepted Lord Stanley's supper invitation for this evening. But after tomorrow, we'll have no other reason to stay longer."

"I'd be honoured to accompany ye on your quest," Deidrik said. "I was planning to stay in Strawbridge for a while longer, but my sister will be happy to get rid of me, even if she'd never admit it."

Taken off guard by his offer, Lisette turned to look at Roy and Ewart.

Ewart shrugged his shoulders. "Another man can't hurt."

Lisette left the men to inquire about a bath. Seeing that one of the doors was open, she went to speak with the bath maid, who introduced herself as Radira. The chamber had a fireplace with three large pots boiling, an oversized copper tub in the middle of the floor, and a thick wool towel next to it on a small table. The tub was partially filled with fresh water. Lisette asked if it was available.

"Ye be in luck." Radira reached for a bucket and began scooping water into the tub from one of the pots, checking after every few buckets until the water was sufficiently warm to the touch. She added a few drops of rose oil when the tub was half-filled.

Her bath ready, Lisette thanked the young maiden. Radira lit the karpal candle and told Lisette she would return in one score. Alone in the steamy chamber, Lisette undressed to wash the travel from her aching bones. Still not used to travelling over such long distances, her skin was cracked and raw. Lisette winced as she sank into the tub. The water stung her thighs and rider's seat. She waited for the pain to subside.

Soon as her skin adjusted to the water, she leaned back against the tub. The copper was warm and smooth. She had never bathed in anything other than a wooden tub covered in scratchy linen. Allowing herself the uncommon luxury of soaking in the fragrant water, Lisette thought about the wool samples. And for the first time, she worried if Florette would want something more practical than her dress. *If not, the wool can be made into something else.*

Her thoughts drifted to Calder. Although they were both from Stonebridge, she didn't speak to him until she was fourteen. She was attending the harvest festival with Aspen that year and had just finished her first field rotations.

She was joking about her hands never recovering when Aspen spotted him standing near the statue of King Lazoran II with a small group of friends. Aspen was immediately smitten by his good looks. But approaching a strange man was considered brazen at best. So they kept a safe distance for then, and Aspen admired him from afar.

After they had joined Ewart later that afternoon, Lisette asked him if he knew the man hanging around the Great Library. She knew Ewart would think nothing of her question. When Ewart identified Calder as a friend, Lisette asked if he could introduce them, thus helping her to win Aspen's challenge to approach and introduce herself. It was an impulsive lie, but Aspen played along without missing a step.

Calder quickly shook their hands after Ewart had introduced them. Like Ewart, he was unaware of anything out of the ordinary. He remained unaware of Aspen's feelings for him throughout their friendship. Calder's blindness to her love did little to sway Aspen. A romantic, she held onto hope, insisting the day would come.

Florette's observation suggested that Calder might have loved Aspen after all. She almost wished Florette had not said anything, fearing it had broken Aspen's heart even more. *Happy endings are for the lucky few.* Another part of her wished they had not left Stonebridge. *Calder would still be alive if I had just minded my tongue.* "What was I thinking?" she asked the cooling bath water. *Who am I to think I can find the answers? Who are we, for that matter? Who are we to take on this journey, the wrunwick, or karupas?*

Lisette glanced over at the candle. Her time was almost up. She dunked her head in the water, stepped out and patted herself dry, dressed in her usual brisk manner, and headed for the door, making sure to leave it open. The bath chambers were at the end of a long corridor off from the main hall. On her way to the stairs located at the other end, she peeked inside the main hall to see if Ewart and Roy were still there. They were gone.

Next to the stairs, a short, narrow corridor stopped before a set of doors. Last night, Bernard had said the chamber was reserved for the private meetings of miners and tradesmen, explaining that Strawbridge owed its size to the neighbouring mining camps.

The miners who married and settled in town divided their year between living in the camps and living with their families in Strawbridge. Young, unmarried miners also liked to visit the town, causing new inns to be built. Bernard had boasted that Mountain Inn was the original inn of Strawbridge, renovated to attract new patrons. The number of men in the main hall suggested that Bernard had succeeded. No one noticed her, being preoccupied with their own affairs. Lisette welcomed their lack of curiosity, further scanning the hall for Aspen and Florette, but she saw only strangers. She went in search of a quill, ink, and parchment. If Florette agreed to a new outfit, she would need to trace the pattern.

"There ye be," Aspen said when Lisette entered their bedchamber. "We were growing worried something happened to ye. I checked the main hall, but ye weren't there. Ye took a bath?"

Lisette nodded. "Did ye eat anything?"

Aspen shook her head. "I'm not hungry."

"Ye need to eat."

"I had some cheese," Florette said, drying her hands next to the basin.

Lisette laid down the quill and inkpot, then retrieved her package. "I have something for ye, Florette." She placed the package on her bed and opened it.

"What is it?" Florette flew over to inspect the green and brown samples.

"It might not look like much now, but if ye'd like, I could sew an outfit for ye like ours."

"Using this?" Florette looked confused.

"The wool be thin and soft, making it easy to cut and sew. But only if ye would like."

Florette ran her hand over the material. "An outfit like yours?"

"A jacket and trousers fit for a fay. It be the finest wool the dress shop had to offer."

"At home with the Grand Oak, I can make a new dress whenever I want. But I haven't taken the time since we left."

"Is that a yes?"

Florette smiled brightly. "Your intentions are pure."

"I can vouch for Lisette's skill as a seamstress." Aspen sat on the bed next to Florette. "She's been sewing for many years and even made a dress for my mother once."

"When will it be ready?" Florette asked.

Lisette retrieved the string from her book that served as a page marker and divided it into sections of one finger width apart. "We have time before we need to be at the manor, so I can start now. It may be dark by the time we get back, but I can sew before bed. And I'll get up with the sun tomorrow to finish. Sewing be best done with natural light." She measured Florette's inseam.

"I should see about a bath," Aspen said on her way to the door. "I'll be too sore to ride soon."

"Florette and I can stay here while I work on her outfit," Lisette replied as she wrote down their friend's inside trouser length: half the string plus one finger width.

Soon as Florette's measurements were noted on the best piece of parchment that Bernard could find, Lisette began to outline the pattern. Florette's legs were scarcely thicker than twigs. All the fair folk had the same build, giving them an ethereal quality. As she drew the tiny pattern, Lisette remembered the many dolls' outfits she had sewn over the years. The most popular dolls remained kings, queens, knights, and the fair folk of children's lore. *No one seemed surprised to see Florette. Mhutig's arrival took care of that.*

"People simply forgot the stories were real," Florette said.

Lisette glanced up. It seemed Florette could read minds more than just sometimes. "There be no written description of the wrunwick anywhere. Do fays know what they look like?"

"It was considered a bad omen to speak of them. People believed it would summon the wrunwick to their village. Fair folk spoke of the wrunwick with great caution. A few whispered of giant one-horned monsters."

"Like the karupas?" Lisette stopped with her hand in midair.

"The whispers only spoke of their size and horns."

"Why didn't ye mention something sooner?"

"I didn't want to alarm anyone. I still don't."

Lisette thought about Florette's words as she finished outlining the sewing pattern. *Could the wrunwick and karupas be the same creature from their legends? How? What did it mean?* And yet, it somehow made sense. She felt herself turning upside down again. "It might just be an ugly coincidence."

"Should we tell the others?" Florette inspected what would be her first jacket.

"Let's wait until after Calder's burial." Lisette wanted to give everyone a chance to grieve without the intrusion of this latest news. "Besides, it might be a false alarm. And it won't change our minds, regardless if both monsters are the same or not."

Chapter 16

The fifth bell chimed as the Seekers set out for the manor. An early afternoon visit with the caretaker had reassured them Calder would receive a hero's parting. During their visit, Albert suggested they ask Lord Stanley to send the news of Calder's death home to Stonebridge. Ewart had promised Albert they would broach the matter.

Lisette still needed to mention the delicate matter of Aspen sharing the last words. It would be too late once they reached the manor. She mentally crossed her fingers. They were her closest friends, but it scarcely guaranteed they would accept her proposal, going against a longstanding and respected tradition.

"I know tis customary for another man to recite the last words in place of the father or other male kin." Lisette looked around to ensure everyone had heard her. "But it occurred to me that Aspen would be equally suited."

The group came to a standstill. In lighter times, Lisette might have laughed at their expressions. They looked like their horses had just been stolen from underneath them.

"What makes ye the judge of that?" Henry asked. His eyes had turned stone cold.

Good question. "Calder and Aspen were very close." Lisette groaned inward. *Is that the best I can come up with?*

"We were all close," Ewart said.

"And Ewart knew him longer than any of us," Henry argued. "Do ye agree with this, Aspen?"

"I said we could discuss the matter with Lord Stanley," Aspen replied.

"'Tis unthinkable," Henry spat out.

"But why is it so unthinkable?" Lisette asked patiently.

"A woman has never said the last words," Henry replied.

"Why would ye suggest that Aspen do it?" Roy asked.

"Why not? There be no canon against it." Lisette directed her answer toward Henry.

"Ye would have us throw away one of our most time-honoured traditions that easily?" Henry asked.

"We wouldn't be throwing it away, just making an adjustment," Lisette said.

"'Tis no minor adjustment," Henry rebutted.

"But why?" Ewart's eyes searched Lisette's.

What could she say? Aspen loved him? He loved her? Lisette loosened Daisy's reins and sighed. "I wish I knew for certain, but my heart tells me it be the right choice."

"We have to trust ourselves first," Florette said from her seat. "It be the only true map."

"And what does your map say, Florette?" Ewart asked.

"Our hearts will point us in the right direction."

I hope ye're right, my friend. Lisette straightened her back. "Why don't we wait to hear what Lord Stanley has to say?"

"He'll think the sun melted our brains," Henry said, his face red by now.

"Lord Stanley appears to be a man of sound reason, so let his words speak for all of us on the matter." Lisette suspected that one man's reason was another man's folly, but she wanted to end their argument. No good could come of it.

The others reluctantly agreed, and they resumed their trip in woeful silence. *This be taking a toll on everyone.* Although Aspen rode beside her, she seemed oblivious to Lisette's presence. *Some things can never be mended.* Again, Lisette brooded over the wisdom of their journey. *If we hadn't left Stonebridge, Calder would still be alive.*

"And the people of our land would continue to vanish," Calder whispered through the trees bordering their path.

I'm losing my mind. "Maybe the sun did melt my brain," Lisette said out loud.

Ewart rode up to join Lisette. "Calder believed in what we're doing. He admired ye for taking a stand."

And look where that got him. "If Lord Stanley agrees for us to use one of his pigeons, we'll need to write a message for his parents." Lisette brushed a fly from Daisy's shoulder to stem the tears.

"I'll write the message." Ewart placed his hand on hers. "We all miss him."

"We're almost there!" Roy's voice sounded ahead of them.

"So we are." Lisette was grateful for the distraction. It would not help the others to see her cry, especially Aspen.

Lisette wiped the tears that managed to escape. She could see the manor's roof peeking over the tree line.

"How do ye suppose Mhutig made out last night?" Ewart asked. "In all my years, I've never heard of a lord inviting a single commoner to stay at the manor before, much less a taupak.”

“It was a first for me too. Lord Stanley did seem taken with Mhutig.” Lisette signalled Daisy to slow down.

In full view now, the manor was a massive stone structure with a wall extending a couple hundred feet on either side of the gate. Inside its wooden gate, the manor rose some ninety feet into the air. It was a daunting sight.

“Ye could stack a good six houses inside there,” Lisette said. “Tis even bigger than Lord Summunder’s.”

As they approached, Lisette could see a man standing at the gate in the late afternoon sun. He waved when they came within a few paces. The man’s demeanour reminded her of the townsfolk who waited to greet the lord of Woodbridge during one of his visits to Stonebridge. The comparison was absurd. *My mind be muddier than a clod of dirt.* Lisette looked over at Aspen, relieved no one could hear the biddle-babble inside her head. Shaking the nonsense from her thoughts, she stopped in front of the manor gate.

Ewart removed his hat. “Good afternoon, kind sir.”

The man bowed. “Lord Stanley be expecting ye.”

“There be no need to bow before us. We’re nothing more than common folk from Stonebridge. My friends call me Ewart. What may we call ye?”

“Halden Shoemaker be the full name given to me at birth, but ye can call me Halden. It serves me well enough, so I’ll keep it for now.” He glanced toward the manor. “Lord Stanley instructed me that we’d be receiving guests of foremost importance today. And that I should escort ye immediately to the great hall.”

Ewart dismounted. “But first, allow me to introduce everyone.”

The Seekers dismounted. Lisette recognized the look on Ewart’s face as he introduced their group. Quiet by nature, Ewart seldom had a lot to say. Most times, he required only a few words. His face often said the rest for him. And right now, his face told Lisette he found their alleged importance to be amusing indeed.

They followed Halden through the gate. To their right, Lisette heard the calming sound of horses coming from the stables. She gave Daisy an affectionate pat on the shoulder. Utaika had seen fit to make them perfect. They were loyal, hardworking animals who asked for little in return, but after travelling from Stonebridge to Strawbridge, their horses were now in dire need of reshoeing.

"Let's get your horses settled away, shall we?" Halden pointed to the stable door. "This way."

They trailed behind Halden. Three stable grooms met them inside and took the horses.

"They'll be well provided for," Halden said, watching the men lead the horses to their stalls. "Don't mind them. They're much better with horses than people. Time to get ye to the great hall."

Lisette inquired about a reputable blacksmith or farrier. Halden informed her the manor had a farrier and would reshoe their horses. Lisette reached for her coin purse.

"There'll be no need of that here, my lady," Halden said. "Our farrier receives a fine wren for his services. Come now. Lord Stanley waits for ye."

The courtyard smelled of cooked meat and fresh bread. Men and women went about their business and paid no heed to them. A woman, whose face told the story of many years lived and gone, scurried to the kitchen with a basket. Chickens, sheep, and at least three dogs all proclaimed their stake in the land beneath their feet. The sun winked through the apple trees populating the entire courtyard. In full bloom, the trees' bright pink flowers danced with the warm winds of Arias while the birds sang to their neighbours.

Lisette noticed a young girl standing behind one of the taller trees. The girl was watching them with the wide-eyed questioning of children. Lisette waved to her. The young girl waved back and, apparently deciding they were harmless, ran to greet them with her doll in tow.

"Well, hello there, little one," Lisette said when the young girl reached her destination. "My name be Lisette. What may we call ye?"

"Harmony. Cause my mom said on the day I was born, the sun finally came out after too many days of rain and thunder. The land was quiet and at peace again."

"That be a beautiful story, Harmony. Your mother sounds like a wise woman. Is she here at the manor?" Aspen's voice was softer than a fresh layer of snow.

Harmony shook her head. "This be Posey." She held up the doll for everyone to see.

"A pretty name," Aspen said.

Harmony stared up at Lisette. "Your hair be the same colour as mine. Mom says it means I have fire in my soul just like Maisy."

"Lord Stanley wouldn't want ye to hold up our guests. Why don't ye see if Miss Elsa needs help in the kitchen?" Halden gazed down at the young girl.

Harmony curtsied and said her farewells. She looked back and waved once more before disappearing into the kitchen.

"A sweet child," Lisette said as they made their way to the great hall. She counted four stained windows overlooking the courtyard.

"A bundle of energy, that one." Halden smiled with affection. "And here we are."

Lord Stanley rose from his chair and extended his arms in welcome.

The Seekers bowed and waited for their host to direct them inside the massive hall. The walls gave way to a vaulted light blue ceiling, ribbed from end to end in dark wood. From the wooden rafters, three oversized candle wheels hung from their iron chains.

A wide fireplace dominated the back wall. Its frame matched the grey stone encompassing two-thirds of the walls. Above their lower counterparts, white plastered walls showcased the vibrant tapestries hanging throughout the hall. To their far right, Lisette noticed a large panel painting of what looked to be a young girl with bright red hair. The child reminded Lisette of Harmony.

"Please." Lord Stanley smiled generously. "There be no need to stand on ceremony here. My cooks have prepared a proper feast for us, but first, let us sit by the fire. I would introduce ye to my steward, but he be visiting the villages where he prefers to spend his time. At least ye've met Halden, who works with Master Squires and will be the next steward." He directed them across the hall.

Mhutig was standing by the fireplace, where a man sat next to him dressed in the same expensive wool as Lord Stanley. The man's tunic and trousers were cut in a simple pattern and free of adornment, save for a wide leather belt.

The man stood to greet them with a warm smile. "Welcome to Strawbridge Manor."

"Seekers, this be Lord Aurik." Lord Stanley paused, glancing around at his guests. "My husband."

Florette rose from Lisette's hood to sit on her shoulder.

"Have ye been inside that hood this whole time?" Lord Stanley looked dismayed. "Ye have nothing to fear inside these walls."

"I haven't been around people since I was a child. The Grand Oak urged me to be careful," Florette replied but gave no further explanation.

Lord Stanley's face relaxed. "I hope ye'll learn to trust me in time." He pointed toward the chairs. "Let us take a seat."

The Seekers made themselves comfortable. Lord Stanley's words echoed inside Lisette's brain. *How is it possible?* It was forbidden for a man or woman to court another of their kind, a canon established by King Regwood in 1072.

"Ye must have questions." Lord Stanley sat back in his chair. "We knew it would come as a shock, but we're hoping to make a public announcement before too long. The township could use a reason to celebrate with all that's going on with the vanishings."

Lisette tried to gather her thoughts, but they were spinning too fast. King Regwood issued the canon after a mysterious disease killed hundreds of people in the high belt, including the king's firstborn son, who had married a young man from Northbridge two moon cycles before his death. Prince Regwoood's death left the king's younger and less favoured son, Prince Lazoran, heir to the throne. The king blamed his son's death on Utaika and declared the disease a punishment for the Salt Wars.

Henry shifted nervously in his seat. "Ye aren't afraid of punishment? The privy council rarely forgives those who break a canon. The first canon be clear. In Stonebridge, my uncle perished in a cage because of that canon."

Lisette glanced over at Henry. According to the retelling of events, King Regwood's order put an end to the disease. And the high belt prospered once more despite the ongoing war. The elders declared it proof of King Regwood's wisdom in the matter.

"Utaika was wrongfully accused of murder," Florette said from Lisette's shoulder. "Our Mother gives life. She doesn't take life."

Henry turned to Florette with unyielding defiance. "How do ye explain the deaths of those who are struck down by lightning?"

Florette held Henry's gaze. "Utaika can't control lightning in the same way that a human mother can't control every action of her children." She sounded like a mother speaking to her young child.

Lisette squeezed Florette's hand. In her heart, she knew Florette was right. And although she once questioned how King Regwood could ever be so cruel, she dared not question the first canon. No one did. Commoners obeyed the royal canon, or they risked the same fate as Henry's uncle. She buried her feelings on the subject three years ago and never looked back. Florette held onto her hand. Did she know? *Impossible.*

"How long have ye been married?" Roy asked their hosts.

"Six short moon cycles." Lord Stanley smiled at Lord Aurik. "But we've known each other since we were children."

"Are ye from here, Lord Aurik?" Ewart asked politely.

"I grew up in Highbridge, but I often came here to visit with my father."

"Would anyone like some wine? Some honey fire perhaps?" Lord Stanley observed the faces of his guests and chuckled. "Tis herbs boiled in water and sweetened with honey. That be all my cook will tell me, but I assure ye tis quite delicious and warms the body from the inside out." He motioned the servants forward with their pitchers and two silver trays with mugs.

"I'll give it a try," Roy said with a familiar curve of his lips.

"Me too. Why not?" Ewart leaned back. "Many thanks to our gracious hosts."

"I'll have some ale if ye have it." Henry looked skeptical. "I like to stick with what I know."

Lisette agreed to a mug of the honey fire. She tried catching Henry's attention. But it was useless. If he noticed her attempts, he also managed to ignore them. *Tis not the time to be stubborn.* Lisette had long accepted Henry's tendency to get his back up. Now she hoped he wouldn't say anything to offend Lord Stanley or Lord Aurik. She wrapped her fingers around the warm mug, taking a tentative sip. It was sweet with a slight hint of bitterness.

"My compliments to the cook." Lisette felt the tension leaving her body.

"Ye're not afraid of word making its way back to the king?" Henry directed his question at Lord Aurik.

"King Eldridge be aware of our marriage and offered his private blessing." Lord Stanley looked amused. "Queen Harriet and I share the same bloodline on my mother's side."

"The king be set to discuss the royal canon with his elders," Lord Aurik added. "He agrees with our queen that the canon be the rash mistake of a father who needed someone to blame for the loss of his son."

Lisette's face froze behind her mug. She had always struggled to believe or accept their Divine Mother would punish her children for the offence of others. Before King Regwood charged Utaika with the mysterious deaths, there were no bans placed on marriage. She used to dream how it must have been to love without fear.

"King Eldridge be a fair and generous king," Roy said.

"As I was telling Lord Stanley and Lord Aurik last night, we do not impose such restrictions in Krousus, although the opowaks despise humans for it," Mhutig informed them.

Lisette pretended to be preoccupied with her drink. She snuck a look at her friends. Notwithstanding Henry's poor temper, the others appeared in good spirits and unconcerned. If Lord Stanley's announcement had surprised them, it didn't show. *Henry needs a lesson in manners.* Lisette vanquished the thought. *Now isn't the time or place to start an argument.*

"Ye're very quiet," Aspen said in a low voice.

"The travel's caught up with me." Lisette reached over to gently embrace her friend's hand. "I'll be fine."

The servants readied the hall for their evening meal. A group of young men retrieved two tables from the far wall and set them in front of their lords' table. When the tables were straightened to their satisfaction, the men retrieved four long benches with seats covered in a dark red tapestry and placed them in front of the tables. Another group of servants adorned all three tables with pressed linen, smoothing the crisp white material as they went. A servant waited next to the right-side table with a small bench and chair. Lord Stanley thought of everything, Lisette mused.

More servants brought silver goblets, plates, and tableware from a side door. Lisette guessed it led to the kitchen. To the left of their lords' chairs, she noticed a goblet but no chair or bench. A servant pulled out their lords' seats and bowed.

"That be our cue, Seekers of Stonebridge. Quinlan does not like to be kept waiting." Lord Stanley rose to his feet. "Mhutig, ye will dine at our table. I have also taken the liberty of borrowing one of Harmony's miniature chairs for ye, Florette. I hope it be to your liking."

Florette flew over and sat down. The chair was perfect for her. Lisette and Aspen took their seats next to her. A servant appeared from the kitchen with an embroidered linen cloth over his arm. Washbowl in hand, he started with Lord Stanley. When her turn came, Lisette inhaled the sweet-scented perfume. At home, hand washing was thought a simple necessity before meals. The water was always cold, and adding flowers would be seen as frivolous pomp. This water was warm and with fresh teardrops. Frivolous or not, the water smelled like a wedding and delighted her senses.

"There ye be. We were going to start without ye." Lord Aurik's stern voice did little to hide his love for the child walking toward them.

"I didn't mean to be late. I was helping Erik carry eggs for Quinlan." Harmony hurried to the empty chair next to Lord Aurik.

"Those eggs must be very important," Lord Stanley remarked. "I trust that none were broken."

Harmony's eyes grew wide. "None, Uncle Stanley."

"Make sure she washes her hands thoroughly, Braxton," Lord Stanley said as the servant approached Harmony.

"I will, my lord." Braxton exchanged a wink of camaraderie with Harmony. He waited for her to finish, then disappeared back into the kitchen.

Next, several men and women appeared, reminding Lisette of street performers. The servants worked together in a skilled unison that only practice would afford, each tasked with their role to play. Within a few short moments, the tables overflowed with pitchers of spiced wine and ale next to trenchers of almond cream, mirken, and chicken.

Lisette had never tasted chicken outside of a pottage before. The people of Stonebridge valued chickens more for their eggs than their meat. After a chicken died, the meat was divided up and shared with the neighbouring family. She wondered what Nora would think of the chickens before them now. *The waste of perfectly good chickens*, Lisette could hear Nora say in her no-nonsense voice. Cutting a piece to try, she bit into the white meat with caution. It was surprisingly tender with a hint of ginger and cinnamon. She washed the chicken down with a sip of wine before trying the apple stuffing. It was the perfect blend of sweet and sour. "Your cook be very talented," she said to Lord Stanley.

"Quinlan learned the careful art of cooking from his father, who learned it from his father." Lord Stanley dipped a piece of mirken into the almond cream on his plate. "Quinlan's family has been with us for many generations."

"We were informed that ye have an impressive flock of pigeons," Aspen said, laying down her fork in favour of the wine.

"My father was a proud man who liked to show off his wealth." Lord Stanley pointed to the tapestry of a man riding his horse. "Woven shortly before his death."

"Ye have a lovely home," Ewart said with a quick look around the hall.

"It often feels more like a shrine than a home. But who am I to make light of my family's history? They stare down in judgment, made colder by the hall's near-constant draft." Lord Stanley turned to look at the panel painting behind him. "My sweet sister before the fever took her."

"We will remodel someday." Lord Aurik helped himself to some chicken. "Change can no more be stopped than the night sky."

"Will we be having tartes, Uncle Aurik?" Harmony stared at the mirken on her plate. "Maybe I'll save a little for Posey."

"The mirken or the tarts?" Lord Stanley's face brightened.

"The mirken. It has almonds in it. They're her favourite."

"Then perhaps Posey would prefer the almond cream," Lord Stanley continued.

Lisette's thoughts went to Harmony's missing parents. Where were they? She turned to Aspen, who, like Harmony, appeared un-impressed with the food on her plate. *What do ye expect? Tis your fault. Calder would still be alive if it weren't for ye.*

"We were hoping to send a message of Calder's passing to his parents," Lisette said a little louder than she intended.

"Of course," Lord Stanley replied. "They need to be informed. I have one of our fastest pigeons available for the task."

"That be most generous of ye, my lord," Aspen said in a rush of gratitude.

Once again, servants appeared with enough food to serve ten families. To honour their hosts, Lisette dutifully placed a mutton ball and some wine bread on her plate. She dreaded her next topic of discussion. Coin was seldom an appropriate matter for the table, but she wanted to get it out of the way.

"If it pleases ye, our lords, we have ample means by which to pay." *Let it not be heard the Seekers of Stonebridge are beggars.*

"We would be most pleased if ye accepted our help without payment," Lord Aurik replied. "In exchange, perhaps ye would oblige us with the telling of your journey after our meal."

"I'd be happy to," Roy said as he helped himself to a piece of custard pie.

Lisette threw Roy a grateful smile. She was lucky to count him among her friends. They all were. She knew how much Roy cared about Calder. And yet, he still managed his famous grin.

"Now isn't the time to give up," Calder whispered in Lisette's ear.

Lisette glanced around at the others. *I've officially lost my mind.* "If it also pleases ye, my lords, we can discuss Calder's burial."

"Albert assures me all will be in place for the ceremony," Lord Stanley said.

"I would also like to discuss the last words."

Lord Stanley's eyes filled with compassion. "Never an easy task. It fell upon me to recite my father's last words. Tis a day I will never be able to forget."

Supper out of the way, the Seekers settled in front of the fire with their hosts. After a second blueberry tart, Harmony hurried off to her bedchamber, promising to be back in time to say goodnight.

"A charming girl," Aspen said, watching Harmony skip down the hall.

"Her mother died last harvest." Lord Stanley paused. "So when her father disappeared some three cycles ago, we decided to care for her ourselves. Both her parents grew up on the manor, and we have always loved Harmony as our own. It felt like the right thing to do."

"She seems happy," Aspen remarked.

"Children are often stronger than they look," Lord Stanley said. "We do our best, but nothing can replace the loss of her parents."

Lisette pictured Nora and her father sitting in front of the fire. Next, she drifted to the day Nora had asked about her trips to the forest. Nora and her father had been married for nearly a year by then. Inside that year, she had come to trust Nora with her whole heart, so she told her stepmom the truth. Instead of the expected scolding, Nora hugged her and said that she missed her mother too. Nora went on to share stories of when she was a child, no older than Lisette. Nora never told her father, and it became their secret. Over time, Lisette grew to love Nora as much as any daughter loved their mother.

"Ye'll have to excuse me, my lords," Henry said, standing up. "I need to visit the ruchton."

"Rahak will show ye the way." Lord Stanley signalled one of the servants, who was helping clear the table.

Roy stood by the fire, ready to begin. While Rahak escorted Henry out of the hall, Roy began his rendition of their journey. A natural-born storyteller, he honoured their lord's request with gusto, recounting the details of their journey from the very beginning. Roy finished by sharing Calder's act of bravery and the subsequent killing of the karupa.

"Your friend sounds like a man of great courage," Lord Aurik said. "The words ye shared today will not be forgotten."

"Ye're most gracious, my lord." Roy bowed, then reclaimed his chair next to Henry, who had returned midway through the story.

Roy's story left the door open for Lisette to raise the matter of Calder's last words. "My lords, I know tis customary for our fathers or male kin to deliver us after death—"

"A tradition going back to the oldest tree," Lord Stanley said.

"Certainly, my lord. However, Calder has no family here. And while the honour would then be given to another man," Lisette said, glancing at Henry, "tis my wish that Aspen share the last words."

Lord Stanley studied Lisette for a moment. "I must admit tis an unusual request, but so are the circumstances of your friend's death." He spoke as though weighing each word. "What would your friend's parents say of this matter?"

What *would* they say? But they weren't there to ask. "We can't speak for his parents, my lord, so we're asking for your counsel in their stead."

"A heavy responsibility," Lord Stanley replied.

"I can see no reason to deny your request," Lord Aurik said. "The privy council would normally be consulted, but unusual times require unusual methods."

Lord Aurik's words reminded Lisette of what Mr. Walling had said just over one moon cycle ago. The full moons of uomons had passed and were due again in three days. And yet, Stonebridge felt closer to yesterday when she recalled the days leading up to their departure.

"My husband be very wise," Lord Stanley remarked. "And like him, I can think of no valid reason to deny your request. It will help prepare our people for the changes that await."

"The changes, my lord?" Ewart asked.

"The town's people know nothing of our marriage. It will no doubt be a shock to them when we make the announcement."

"But the servants . . ." Aspen said, sounding unsure.

"They know not to speak of it outside the walls of this manor. Most have been with my family for many generations before me," Lord Stanley replied.

"Ye aren't afraid they'll speak anyway?" Lisette asked. She had overheard Nora gossiping with one of Lord Sumunder's servants on many occasions. From those conversations, it was clear nothing was off-limits, including their lord's penchant for books deemed too lowborn for the lords and ladies of Wrunwicks.

"My servants are well provided for and want for nothing. Every servant be given a day once every fortnight to spend as they please. They would not risk their position here for the sake of spreading rumours."

Lisette doubted the veracity of Lord Stanley's reasoning but nodded in agreement. She hoped he was right.

"Ye're not concerned that we'll say something?" Roy asked.

"Ye have far greater concerns than us," Lord Aurik said. "I doubt ye have the time or the inclination to share tales of so little importance."

Lord Aurik's observation reminded Lisette they still needed to send word back to Calder's parents. "If it pleases ye, my lords, Ewart will write a message for Stonebridge at your earliest convenience."

Lord Stanley called to a nearby servant. "Your message will leave tonight," he reassured Ewart.

"Thank ye, my lord." Ewart bowed and followed the servant.

"When do ye expect to make the announcement?" Henry asked Lord Stanley.

"We're hoping to hear from the king by the end of the next moon cycle. King Eldridge was never a man to be rushed."

"Change is never easy," Mhutig said. "It will undoubtedly cause some growing pains."

"Growth be vital to the success of any society." Lord Aurik added a piece of wood to the fire. "To understand this, we need look no further than Utaika."

True to her promise, Harmony returned with an elderly woman to wish them goodnight. Lord Stanley introduced the woman as Halden's wife, Agnes.

"Married for thirty years," Agnes said proudly before escorting Harmony back to her chamber.

Ewart returned moments later. The sky had turned dark, and Lisette hurt from head to toe. She suggested they return to the inn. The others agreed, looking equally spent. Mhutig bid them safe passage along with their hosts. It occurred to Lisette that Mhutig was remarkably comfortable in the manor's ornate surroundings.

Pleased with her progress on Florette's outfit, Lisette lay in bed waiting for sleep to arrive. She drifted back to her conversation with Florette as they rode back to the inn.

"Lord Stanley holds a secret," Florette had said.

"A secret?"

"He keeps it hidden behind a door."

"How do ye know?"

"Secrets are quiet and prefer the dark. I can see the key, but a fay must never go through a locked door," Florette had explained.

Staring at the ceiling, Lisette wondered whether she owned a similar door and key. If so, could Florette see hers too? She had wanted to ask but feared what Florette might say. *Some things are better left in the dark.* Her mind wandered to Calder's parents next. What would they think of Aspen saying the last words? *Who am I to question tradition? What possessed me?* And try as she might, she could not find the answers. The questions still hung in the air, taunting her when sleep finally took hold.

Chapter 17

haken from a dream about faceless shadows spinning her faster and faster, Lisette sat by the window to watch the sunrise. She removed Florette's outfit from her bag. Careful not to disturb her friends, she sewed to the waking sounds of Strawbridge. Her fingers moved of their own accord. With the trousers completed and the jacket started last night, she should be finished before Florette woke.

A while after, the first bells joined the chorus of roosters to wake her chamber mates. Aspen rubbed the sleep from her eyes and pushed her pillow against the wall. She leaned back and adjusted her blanket.

"Someday I'll wake before ye." Aspen studied the doll-sized jacket in Lisette's hands for a moment. "How long have ye been up? It looks finished."

Florette flew over for a closer look. Lisette had just finished sewing the trim, using one of her sleeve bands to add a splash of colour to the green jacket. She removed the needle and held up her creation for Florette to see.

"Tis beautiful." Florette traced the stitching with her finger. "May I try it on?"

"I don't think it'll fit me," Lisette said with a bright smile, relief banishing her last remaining doubts on the matter.

Florette pulled up the trousers and removed her skirt. She guided her wings through the two slits in the back of the jacket, then tied the belt made with the material from the other sleeve band.

"If only the Grand Oak could see ye now," Aspen said.

"Thank ye, Lisette." Florette did one complete spin. The rider's outfit left just enough room to be comfortable. "I'll wear it with great pride."

"Ye honour me," Lisette said. "Tis not every day I get to sew for an Evergreen fay. Will ye be able to fly okay?"

Florette zipped around the chamber, returning to stand on the windowsill. "The material be light and comfortable. Tis perfect."

The Seekers rode to the caretakers. The men would carry Calder to the resting grounds in a burial box reserved for noblemen and women. Burial boxes were once used for fallen knights too, but peace meant no knights or heroes were left until now. Although Calder did not fall in a king's war, he gave his life defending Wrunwicks and Mhutig against their newest enemy. To them and Strawbridge, that made him a hero.

Calder was wrapped in a red burial cloth with a yellow tree outlined in dark brown stitching. The red symbolized courage, while the yellow tree symbolized Utaika and her infinite wisdom. The brown stitching symbolized Wrunwicks. The cloth was expensive, but Albert agreed to accept Calder's old steed as payment for any expenses, including the burial box.

Albert informed them Lord Stanley would lead the procession. That final blessing of their lord guaranteed the townsfolk would not dispute Calder's place among Wrunwicks' heroes. Lord Stanley and Lord Aurik arrived with Mhutig just as they were preparing to leave. Henry thanked Lord Stanley for his esteemed presence. Lord Stanley quickly dismissed his part in the ceremony as minimal.

As they marched to Forest Hills, people stopped in the streets and fields to watch them. Many saluted their respect. Lisette could not have hoped for a better response. She vowed to share the story of their kindness with Stonebridge upon their return.

A dense tree hedge belted the vast clearing that served as the town's burial grounds. On the far side, high shrubs cordoned the area reserved for nobility. Knights and soldiers lay in adjacent burial plots. Throughout the clearing, trees bloomed in magnificent whites, purples, and yellows. Overlooking the sacred trees were the hills that gave the grounds its name. To the east of Forest Hills, ran the river needed for consecration. In the remote distance, Metterling Mountains scraped the sky. Lisette spotted three elders waiting inside the soldiers' division.

Among them stood the master of ceremonies, dressed in his light purple robe with a tree stitched in white on the front. The elders watched as the men lowered the burial box into Calder's final resting place. A small sapling waited to be planted in its new home. Lisette looked down at the burial box. Calder was gone and would never know the love of a wife and children. He would never grow old. She cursed the karupa that took him from them. She cursed karupas' hate for humans and their evil presence in Wrunwicks. The master of ceremonies went to stand by the sapling. Lisette stared straight ahead. She pictured Calder as he rode toward the clearing and plunged his sword into the karupa.

The master of ceremonies began by introducing Calder and sharing the story of his arrival in Strawbridge. He then invited the Seekers to share their own stories about their friend. Lisette shared Calder's final act of bravery. Aspen shared the first time she met Calder in front of the library. When Ewart finished the last story, the master of ceremonies invited them to join him in the song of their ancestors. Their voices filled the air:

> *Oh Mother, sweet Mother,*
> *in ye, we trust. To ye, our hearts we too entrust.*
> *And on this day, we ask of ye, oh Mother, sweet Mother,*
> *the strength to let your child go, to let your child go.*
>
> *Oh Mother, sweet Mother, to ye, we entrust he who waits.*
> *And we shall not mourn our kin of yore, nor of today.*
> *And we shall not mourn but give thanks on this day,*
> *and the days of morrow.*
>
> *Oh Mother, sweet Mother, may ye guide our hearts.*
> *May ye guide us to wisdom and courage.*
> *Oh Mother, sweet Mother, may ye guide our hearts.*
> *May ye guide us on this day and the days of morrow.*
>
> *Oh Mother, sweet Mother, in ye, we trust.*
> *And to ye, our hearts we too entrust.*
> *May ye guide your child home.*
> *May ye guide your child home, oh Mother, sweet Mother,*
> *may ye guide your child home.*

When they finished singing, the master of ceremonies invited the consecrator to stand with him. Aspen wiped her tears, joining the elder. She stood straighter than a redwood tree.

Aspen's voice rang out loud and clear. "From bone to dust, may ye find eternal peace. And through our Mother, may your spirit travel across this land to learn the stories of our kin before us."

The master of ceremonies picked up the spade and gave it to Aspen. She removed the first soil to make room for the sapling. The elders lined up behind her. Each removed a spadeful. Lord Stanley, the Seekers, and Mhutig followed. Next, Aspen gently placed the sapling at Calder's feet, careful not to hurt the roots. She poured water from the river over the soil and scooped the wet earth into her hands.

"May this tree be made strong by ye. To this tree, may your spirit return when it has grown tall and proud, its flowers made brighter by your eternal light. May its roots be planted firmly in the ground to stand with your kin, old and new."

Aspen scattered the earth over Calder. Taking her time, she scraped the remaining soil over the sapling's roots, using her hands to tamp the soil as she worked. The consecration complete, Albert's sons returned the soil from Calder's grave. There was nothing left to say. Lisette looked to the mountains, wishing she would wake to discover Calder was alive and well. But there was no escape from this nightmare.

Chapter 18

After leaving Strawbridge that morning, they travelled east through the forest until reaching a grassy field where blue flowers grew wild and free among the soaring pine trees dispersed throughout the field. No more than a day's ride continuing eastward, Metterling Mountains presided over the land below.

Lisette waited for Henry to begin. When he asked to ride with her at breakfast, she knew he wanted to share a piece of his mind. Henry was a man of purpose, seldom acting without intent. She admired his steadfast resolve most times. And despite his tendency to be painfully blunt, she was happy for their friendship. On those occasions when his mouth ran away from him, he caught up to it more often than not.

Henry turned and studied her for a moment. "I know why ye requested to let Aspen share the last words." He turned to survey the large field. "I do. But I'm afraid it'll do more harm than good in the long run. Calder's parents are bound to be outraged."

"They'll understand with time." As Lisette spoke the words, even she had trouble believing them. Calder's parents honoured tradition as much as any good Wrunwicker.

"I know ye want to think tis true, but some traditions have been with us since our earliest stories. They can't be dismissed so easily."

"Even if that tradition lacks reason?"

"Tis not for us to question the wisdom of our ancestors."

"Our ancestors were human. They made mistakes too."

"Ye have a stubborn streak, Lisette, that serves ye well. But it'll catch up to ye someday."

Lisette suspected he was right. When they eventually returned to Stonebridge, Calder's parents would require an explanation for her choice. And she had no reason to expect their understanding. She didn't fully understand it herself.

"Until then, we have far greater problems to keep us busy. I'll worry about that when I need to," Lisette replied. She was tired of being on the defence. Right or wrong, it was done. She breathed a heavy sigh of frustration and looked to the mountains.

Reaching clear across the horizon to the north and south of Wrunwicks, the famous mountains scattered all cloud that dared to challenge their rightful place next to the sun. Relentless in their pursuit of greatness, Metterling Mountains rivalled the ambitions of any king and owned infinitely more riches with their vast supply of metal and stone. The southern mountains alone held several large deposits of the white plaster rock so coveted by King Eldridge and the lords of Wrunwicks.

Nicknamed Father Time, the ancients claimed the mountains were old as Wrunwicks itself, witness to the birth of Utaika and to that of her children. Unable to declare their love for her, the mountains spread across the land to protect Utaika and her many children from danger.

Admiring the mountains' immense size, Lisette asked herself where such danger might originate. From the other side? No one had ever crossed the mountains, so no one knew what lay beyond their unsurmountable height. Some believed a land much like Wrunwicks waited for them to explore. Maps supporting the idea of a neighbouring land included a lake on the other side of the mountains, much like the one she owned, Lisette imagined. Most simply rejected the argument. Idle musings of the rich, they called it. Regardless of who was on the right side of the popular debate, Metterling Mountains were an exceptional sight.

They would follow the mountains north and bypass the mining settlements. Neither of them knew how far they would need to travel or what they might find when they got there. And true to his word, Deidrik had joined them on their journey.

Lisette could hear him joking with Aspen in another attempt to lighten her mood. Sometimes he succeeded. When she had heard Aspen laugh for the first time since that night at Mountain Inn, Lisette's heart had felt a little lighter. Aspen had been gifted at birth with unfailing optimism. Utaika's assurance her spirit would not be broken by a mother's inability to show love of any kind. It had always struck Lisette as an ironic twist of fate that a woman like Mrs. Greene should have three children. While a woman like Nora, who had love to spare, should have no children of her own.

"If we continue east through the forest, we could follow the green belt to the north," Deidrik called out from the field's edge.

"The green belt?" Ewart asked.

"The grassy stretch at the foot of the mountains. Tis used by miners who've built shacks along the way."

"It might be best to keep inside the forest," Henry suggested.

Deidrik examined the trees to his left. "The miners say these woods are home to the restless souls buried inside the mountain after the mining accident of 1205."

"I doubt those poor souls mean us either harm," Henry replied. He leaned toward Lisette. "What do ye think?"

"We'll stick to the forest for today. If we're not wanted, I'm sure the ghosts will let us know."

It was late evening when they heard the faint roar of running water. Tracking the sound, they came across a waterfall that emptied into a small lake. Mhutig suggested they set up camp for the night.

"I can think of no better place to rest," he said, admiring the water tumbling over its rocky bed.

"Not even the manor?" Lisette asked.

Mhutig chuckled. "Lord Stanley and Lord Aurik are gracious hosts."

"Who wants to go for a swim?" Deidrik was already removing his boots.

"I could use a cool-off," Roy said without hesitation.

Down to their braies, the men jumped into the lake. Such a state of undress was forbidden in public. Deidrik pointed out they weren't in public after Lisette said as much. Henry, Ewart, and Mhutig joined them. Lisette sat watching them along with Aspen and Florette.

"Will ye not join us, my ladies?" Deidrik splashed the water, spraying himself and Mhutig.

"What would ye have us wear?" Aspen asked with an equal mix of shock and indignity.

"That, my ladies, be up to ye. But surely, ye're wearing smocks under your clothes."

Lisette felt her face grow red. A woman never dressed down to her smock, even women of disrepute. To be so shameless would earn a woman time in the cage district. Plus they were wearing men's shirts, nearly half the length of a smock. And while there were no elders to pass judgment, the cages loomed larger than the mountains in her mind.

"My clothes could use a wash," Aspen said, running a hand over her trousers.

"Mine too." Lisette removed her boots and jacket. She looked down at her shirt and trousers, ignoring the cage blocking her view as best she could. "Would ye like to join us, Florette?"

"Fair folk prefer flying to swimming."

"Maybe ye could keep watch for us." Lisette scanned the trees. "We can never be too careful."

They fell asleep beneath the stars while the water gurgled a cheerful lullaby. When the moons were high to the south, Lisette woke to the sound of Florette whispering in her ear.

"Do ye hear that?"

Lisette rubbed her eyes and stared into the dark. The embers from the fire flickered in the moonlight. She strained to listen. The usual sounds of the forest greeted her. Then she heard a branch crack. *Ghosts don't break branches.* Careful not to alert whatever was out there, Lisette crawled over to where Mhutig slept. She stood up and placed her hand on his back.

"Mhutig," she whispered. "Wake up."

Mhutig opened his eyes. "What is it?"

"Listen." Lisette tried to hide the panic threatening to overcome her good sense.

Another branch protested against its assailant, closer this time. Lisette's panic grew with the sound of each branch.

Mhutig's ears twitched. "Alert the others," he instructed.

Lisette hurried to wake her friends. They wiped the sleep from their eyes, staring up at Lisette in bewilderment until a muffled voice drifted through the woods. The voice belonged to a human, not a karupa. Who would be travelling through the woods so late? Ewart grabbed his sword and jumped to attention. The others scrambled behind him, forming a defensive circle with their swords ready. Lisette retrieved her sword and went to stand with her friends. Florette sat guard on Mhutig's back.

Five men emerged from the woods with their faces snared by the twin moons. Lisette recognized one of the men. It was the same man she saw staring at them on their first night in Strawbridge. His eyes were still just as cold.

Spotting Ewart and the others, the men froze. It seemed they had failed to anticipate anyone being awake, much less prepared to fight. The man with the dead eyes stood with one hand on the hilt of his sword. The other four men looked to him and waited. He was clearly the leader and puffed his chest accordingly.

"Seekers, our quarrel be with the beast, not ye," the man with the dead eyes said.

To Lisette, he sounded like a king commanding his people. Only a king would never sound quite so arrogant. A king ensured obedience through loyalty and trust. She reckoned these men dealt in vices, not virtues.

"A quarrel with Mhutig be a quarrel with us." Roy raised his sword a little higher.

"Are ye prepared to die by those words?" the man with the dead eyes asked.

"I am," Roy said.

"I'd advise ye to lead your men home before someone gets hurt, Melvin," Deidrik said calmly.

The man with dead eyes stared at Deidrik. A cruel smile snaked its way across his face. "Is that a threat?"

"Ye can't possibly expect to win this fight. There are more of us than ye," Ewart added.

Melvin snickered in the moonlight. "Women masquerading in men's clothes hardly makes them equals."

Inflamed by his words, Lisette aimed her sword at Melvin. "This one be mine."

Melvin positioned himself for battle. "On my signal, men. But leave the topa to me." He fixed his eyes on Lisette. "Now!"

Lisette could not have said where the rage came from, but she poured every ounce into her blade. Lunging, she aimed for his chest. Melvin's blade struck hers. The sound of steel colliding against steel filled her ears. The impact travelled from her wrist up to her shoulder. She leaned back to dodge his sword's lethal path, then swung back into ready position. He was bigger and stronger than her. *A sword fight be won with speed, skill, and wit, not strength.* The elders' words bounced off her skull.

She slowed her breathing and waited for Melvin to make the next move, looking for what that might be. *Patience.* He stepped to the right, glanced at her shoulder, and lunged his sword. She raised her sword to block the attack, then slid her blade over his until the tip grazed his neck. *A single move and ye'd be dead.* Calder's lifeless expression appeared before her. Melvin freed his sword and readied himself for the next strike.

"Ye're too slow, wench." Melvin's hands tightened their grip.

"And ye have the cunning of a rabbit." Lisette avoided looking at his leg, not wanting to give away her target. She swung her sword over and around her head, lunging forward once again to strike his thigh. Melvin's sword came down to block her attack, but he was too late. Her blade ripped through his flesh. Melvin staggered from the sudden impact. Blood gushed from his leg. He lost his step and toppled forward.

Lisette gave him just enough time to sit up before resting her blade on his shoulder. "I could finish ye, but I'm no killer." And for the first time since their fight began, she looked to see how the others were faring.

One of the men was about to plunge his sword into Henry's throat when a giant black cat with emerald eyes leaped onto his back. *Are those wings?* The cat forced the attacker to the ground, grabbed his sword between its teeth and flung it into the woods. The cat ran off in the direction of the sword. Henry's attacker heaved himself back up.

Henry stood with his sword ready. "Shall we continue?"

"I didn't agree to die." The man scampered into the woods.

The man's words reminded Lisette of the gash on Melvin's leg. She yanked her knife from its sheath and ripped the bottom of his trousers.

"Ye flatter me, but ye're not my type," he said.

"Dastards aren't my type." Lisette finished ripping his trousers. She wrapped the cloth around his wound. "Ye'll need to keep it in place, or ye could bleed to death."

"A true lady of mercy," he sneered.

"My conscience be worth more than the pleasure of watching ye die."

A sudden cry rose above the swords. Lisette looked to see one of Melvin's men fall to his death. Deidrik and Aspen stood over him. Blood dripped from Aspen's blade.

"Ye've led your men on a fool's quest." Lisette tightened the cloth around Melvin's leg. "That should hold until ye arrive back in Strawbridge."

Melvin leveraged the rock behind him to hoist his body into a standing position. "Friends, it be time for us to go and leave these balshaks to their fate."

Lisette felt almost sorry for the men. They were now grossly outnumbered and defeated. Enough blood had been spilled in hate's praise. The men withdrew their swords and wiped the sweat from their faces. All except one. The man glanced at Melvin and thrust his sword toward Roy's chest.

"Roy," Lisette sang out. "'Tis over."

Roy and the man were locked in position. A single move from either side would prove fatal for the other. Roy's sword was a breath away from the man's lips, who held his sword against Roy's chest.

"Lower your sword, Jacob," Melvin ordered.

Jacob pressed his sword a little harder against Roy's chest. "Tell this balshak to get his sword out of my face."

"If I wanted to kill ye, it'd be done by now." Roy edged his sword in closer.

"Big words for a balshan boy," Jacob retorted.

"Why don't ye both lower your swords at the same time, so no one gets hurt." Lisette glanced at Melvin. She needed him to pull back his mule. "Your man won't listen to me."

"The wench speaks to reason," Melvin called out.

Roy eased his sword away from Jacob's face and stepped back. Smirking, Jacob stepped back but kept his sword pointed at Roy's chest. They maintained their slow retreat until both men were out of harm's way.

One of Melvin's men ran into the woods and returned a short while later with their horses. He lifted their fallen comrade onto his horse. Jacob helped Melvin over to his horse.

Melvin stared down at Lisette. "Ye haven't seen the last of us." He chose not to wait for an answer. Instead, he turned his back and disappeared into the darkness behind his friends.

"He certainly has an instinct for drama," Lisette said, relieved to see him go.

Mhutig and Florette were still at their post by the trees. Lisette waved to Florette, whose eyes burned a hole in the dark. It occurred to Lisette there might be a connection between the pardela and Florette. Their eyes shared that same brilliant shade of green. While it was scarcely enough to connect the two, her instinct said it did. Rather than waste time speculating, she went to find out.

"We almost lost Henry tonight," Lisette said after resuming her position next to Mhutig.

"Everyone fought with courage," Mhutig replied. "You will have to forgive me, Lisette. I am unable to harm the humans I swore to protect."

"They were foolish to follow us," Lisette replied. "It seems we have another ally."

"Inside each fay lives the spirit of an animal," Florette said.

Lisette took in Florette's words. The pardela she saw had been of flesh and blood, not a ghostly manifestation of its spirit. "The pardela that saved Henry?"

"In times of need, I can transform into its likeness."

"Ye become a pardela?" Lisette checked to make sure her feet were still on the ground. Of all the possible connections she might have imagined between Florette and the pardela, this was not one of them.

"Every pardela be a fay in animal form."

"Pardelas are fair folk?"

"It depends on the fay. Lakiyas choose us."

"Lakiyas?" As she stared at her friend, Lisette felt thicker than overgrown wool. But it was all she could muster. Exhaustion had caught up with her.

"Our spirit animals. There are many different lakiyas."

"The Grand Oak never told us," Lisette managed to say.

"The Grand Oak frowns heavily on transformation," Florette replied. "The more we transform, the greater our chance of never being able to return to our original form. And should the transformation ever become permanent, we lose all memory of our former selves. Stories speak of fair folk going mad in the process."

"It can't be all bad. Ye saved Henry."

"I haven't transformed in many seasons. The Grand Oak sent me to protect ye, not watch ye die."

Chapter 19

he attack placed everyone on edge as they tried to make sense of what happened. Opting to follow the green belt, they travelled for three days without incident or karupas. A fact that did nothing to ease anyone's mind. A man had died. It mattered not that his death was in self-defence. He was gone. Deidrik said the man's name was Elmer, the new father of a baby girl and that townsfolk knew him as a good man.

Deidrik's words swept over Lisette like thunderclouds colouring her thoughts in shades of dismal grey. Too many families had already suffered the loss of a loved one because of the vanishings. At least Elmer's family could bury him, she kept reminding herself. A poor argument, but there was nothing else to hold onto. No amount of regret would bring him back. She could only hope it was the last time either of them would have to choose between their own life and that of someone else—or the rocks knocking against their skull. If the dastard had lived, she would have gladly shaken those rocks out through his ears. As it were, Elmer's daughter would grow up without ever knowing her father.

The fourth day was equally uneventful until Mhutig halted. He pressed his ears to the wind. Lisette stopped to listen along with the others. She trusted Mhutig's keen sense of hearing. It was faint, but Lisette could hear the footsteps. She concentrated on the incoming sound. The footsteps were different from those of a karupa. These were lighter, or at least for now.

"A karupa?" she asked Mhutig, placing more faith in his ample experience than her opinion.

"Too light," he said, still listening. "I hear two different sets of footsteps, one set lighter than the other."

"Maybe we should veil ourselves." Henry's nervous expression mirrored that of his companions.

"It served us no good the last time," Ewart replied. "Either way, we'll have to confront whatever it be. And this time, I'm not hiding in the trees."

Lisette stared at the only trees close enough to provide shelter along the green belt. To their right, the trees sloped upward with the mountains. But there was no way up the steep, rocky incline. The mountains might protect them from some imaginary danger on the other side, yet they offered no protection from the very real danger headed their way.

"We stand together." Roy grabbed his sword in anticipation of the worse.

"If it isn't a karupa," Deidrik said, "how bad can it be?"

The Seekers sat on alert. Their faces reminded Lisette of the day Calder was killed. They wore the same looks of horror, panic, and disbelief. And again, mule-faced stubbornness outweighed their rising sense of terror. She wondered if veiling their presence might be a good idea despite what Ewart thought. Even if it couldn't help them, she failed to see how it could hurt. Veiling had not caused

Calder's death. Nor did she believe that remaining visible would have saved him.

"Instead of sitting here waiting to see what we're up against, why don't we keep going to find out?"

Lisette turned to Aspen, struck by the newfound firmness of her voice. Aspen had always been a little too timid for her own good. Meeting Aspen's gaze, Lisette noticed the uncertainty in her friend's eyes had disappeared. In its place was something else. A strength that filled her entire being, adding a new depth and fire to her delicate features.

"Aspen be right," Deidrik said.

"That she be." Lisette smiled at her friend. "Time to see what we're up against."

They kept their eyes and ears peeled for the next twenty paces or so, then came to an abrupt stop. A woman draped in a sleeveless, light blue dress had just appeared on the horizon. Lisette gawked at the scene before her. The woman was running from a man with the lower body of a bull. The man's horns were bigger than those of karupas. Protruding from his wide forehead, two horns curved up and outward. Lisette frowned in alarm. Those horns could easily kill whatever, or whomever, they encountered. The woman must have seen their group, adjusted course, and was now running in their direction. She looked terrified.

"A human from Krousus," Mhutig said, racing toward the woman before anyone had a chance to react.

Mhutig ran ahead of the woman to shield her from the creature. The woman paused for an instant, glanced up at Mhutig and kept running.

"You have no business here." The creature spat on the ground. He flared his nostrils like a wild animal.

Mhutig raised his sword. "Humans are my business."

"So be it." The creature raised his sword in turn. "Filthy two-legs who mate with their own kind. Is this one worth your life?"

Mhutig thrust his sword toward the creature. "Is she worth yours?"

"My life isn't yours to take, taupak," the creature said, blocking Mhutig's sword. "It belongs to Kalaoun."

"Kalaoun has no stake in your arrogance." Mhutig aimed for the creature's heart, missing by no more than a few inches.

"Do ye think we should help?" Roy asked his friends.

"Mhutig doesn't look like he needs our interference," Aspen said with a hint of awe.

Lisette looked down at the woman, who had just caught up with them. She had never seen anyone with such pale complexion before. Lisette noticed the woman's ears next. They resembled Florette's and Mhutig's with their pointed tips, making this woman different than any other woman in Wrunwicks. Meeting the woman's eyes, Lisette felt herself drowning in eyes bluer than the summer sky. "My name be Lisette," she said, dismounting to regain her composure.

"Amelia," the woman said as she tried to catch her breath. "Thank Krousus you crossed my path when you did."

"If only we had crossed your path before that monster." Lisette glanced back at Mhutig and the creature. Near matched in height, the two seemed equally matched in battle, with neither of them looking ready to back down. Mhutig thrust his sword once again. "But if ye ask me, Mhutig's courage has the advantage."

"The prince is well known for his skill with a sword," Amelia replied.

"Prince?" Lisette asked, unsure whether she had heard correctly.

"Prince Mhutig is respected throughout the land for his sword-ship and kind heart."

The creature let out a yelp. Lisette looked over in time to see Mhutig remove his sword from the creature's chest. Blood gushed from the fatal wound.

"I'm only one opowak. You can't kill all of us." The creature swung his sword in a useless attempt to strike back.

"Let me worry about that." Mhutig wiped his sword on the grass.

"Fool—" The creature fell to the ground, his final words clenched between his teeth.

Mhutig looked to the Seekers with a reassuring grin and waved. He appeared confident and at ease. Lisette mused that he belonged in this moment, the triumphant protector of humans.

With his sword in hand, Mhutig left the two-horned creature to its miserable fate. A purifier circled from above. It swooped down to rid them of the dead intruder. Wasting no time, Wrunwicks' hungry visitor ripped the flesh from the opowak's face. Several more purifiers swooped down to take their place around the opowak's body. Lisette looked away in disgust, leaving the bright feathered birds to their monstrous feast.

Mhutig rejoined them moments later. He smiled at Amelia. "Welcome to Wrunwicks."

The woman bowed. "Thank you, my prince."

"You've come a long way from home." Mhutig held out his hand. "My friends call me Mhutig."

After a long pause, Amelia accepted Mhutig's offer of friend-ship. "It's an honour to meet you, my prince."

"How did you end up in Wrunwicks?" Mhutig asked.

"I was out gathering apples. And the next thing I knew, I was here, surrounded by karupas and opowaks."

"There are more here?" Deidrik asked, dismounting from his horse. "More of those balshan monsters?"

Amelia nodded. "A lot more."

"It is highly unusual to find opowaks and karupas in one place," Mhutig interjected.

"In Krousus, there are rumours the opowaks have joined forces with karupas among some of the villagers."

"I have yet to hear of such a depraved union." Mhutig kept a protective eye on the young woman before him.

"The rumours are only that for now," Amelia replied. "Who would believe such an alliance possible?"

"I might have been inclined to agree a short time ago." Mhutig looked around, meeting Lisette's eyes. "However, it does nothing to explain their presence here."

"After we met, ye told us the opowaks wanted to rule Krousus," Lisette said.

"An ambition the karupas have never shared," Mhutig replied. "The only ambition they know is the annihilation of humans."

"According to that ugly balshak," Ewart said, pointing to the opowak, "they share the same hatred."

"There has to be a connection," Henry said.

Mhutig sighed. "I fear we will find out soon enough."

"I can show you the way to their camp," Amelia said.

"Ye can ride with me," Aspen reached to help Amelia onto the mare's back.

Mhutig smiled at Aspen, then turned to Amelia. "The Seekers are a noble group, but it would make greater sense for you to ride with me. Aspen's horse will tire twice as fast carrying the both of you."

Amelia looked hesitant. "Ride with you, my prince?"

Mhutig chuckled softly. "There is no need to look so shocked. I promise you not to bite."

"In that case, I'd be honoured to ride with you." Amelia's eyes opened in dismay. "Not that I thought you'd bite, my prince."

"All I ask is that you call me by my given name."

"I will, my pr—Mhutig."

Listening to Mhutig and Amelia, Lisette decided liked their new companion with the most enchanting eyes she had ever seen and hair the colour of dark silver.

"We should prepare to leave for their camp," Mhutig said. "We could use a blanket to make you more comfortable."

Ewart folded his camp blanket and placed it on Mhutig's back. He linked the men's belts from their jackets together and used them to secure the blanket in place. Aspen and Deidrik helped Amelia climb up. Mhutig wrapped his wings around Amelia and instructed her to hold on. Once Amelia had found her bearings, they set out for the camp.

As they travelled toward the unknown, Lisette found plenty of time to question her good sense. She wanted to think of them as brave, but where did bravery end and reckless begin? How could a group of humans, a fay, and a taupak ever hope to defeat a group of karupas and now the opowaks? Two karupas cost Calder his life. How many would they find at the camp? And at what cost? But what choice did they have? Turn back in defeat? Then what? The list of questions went round and round in Lisette's head with no clear resolution.

The sun gave way to cloud, casting an ominous shadow over the land. Lisette surrendered her questions to the wind. She had nothing to gain from her gloomy thoughts except more shadows to haunt her dreams. Only Utaika knew the answers, but she rarely interfered in the lives of her children. Resigning to the uncertainty, Lisette rode up to Mhutig and Amelia.

"How long have ye been in Wrunwicks?" she asked their new companion.

Amelia's eyes darkened. "For twenty-three sunrises."

"A long time to be running for your life," Lisette said.

"They were sleeping on the morning I arrived not far from their camp. I walked with the mountains until I found a shack three days later. I stayed the night and filled my satchel with salted meat and jam before setting out again. I came across two more shacks along the way. I didn't see that opowak until it was too late. It feels like I've been running forever," Amelia replied.

"Fear will do that," Mhutig added. "You're safe now."

"I'd rather run across Krousus than face one of those monsters," Amelia said.

"Opowaks know no mercy. You were right to be afraid. The quickness of your legs served you well," Mhutig said, adjusting his wings to give Amelia a little more space.

"Itanuk has favoured me today."

"May she favour our journey as well. But in case she does not"— Mhutig turned to Florette—"we may be wise to veil ourselves before reaching their camp."

Florette's face lit up like a new candle. "At your service, my prince."

"In Wrunwicks, I own no such title, my loyal friend. To everyone here, I'm Mhutig, a strange creature in a land not my own."

"Why didn't ye tell us?" Lisette asked. She was still amazed by the discovery.

"I did not think it important or relevant to our circumstances and that of Wrunwicks."

Mhutig was right, of course. His title would not eliminate the threat to their people or bring them back, nor did it change their friendship. His title didn't change who he was. Lisette promised herself not to mention it again. She respected Mhutig, who seemed to want the matter closed. As his friend, she needed to respect his privacy.

Coming across a miners' shelter, they decided to spend the night. The shelter was made of wood from the tree thicket growing along the foot of Metterling Mountains. Amelia remarked that it looked like the shacks she had stayed in. Once inside, Lisette was surprised to note the shelter was outfitted for a more than a sufficient night's stay, complete with provisions, a fireplace and kindling, two trestles with a table board and bench, basic cookware, and the unexpected luxury of sheep skins to keep warm.

The shelter's low ceiling prevented Mhutig from entering, so he proposed to sleep outside and keep watch. Upon hearing Mhutig, the men also insisted on spending the night outdoors and dismissed Mhutig's protests to the contrary with the quick brush of a hand.

After their meal of rations, the women settled in front of the fire. There was plenty of wood for the night. In the morning, they could replace what they burned for the next visitors. Neither of them spoke of opowaks or karupas. Amelia sat next to Florette, staring into the fire.

Amelia looked toward Florette with heavy eyes. "The fair folk of Krousus hold much magic," she said at last. "We call them guardians of the land, sent by our Divine Mother to care for our forests and crops."

"The fair folk of Evergreen Forest live in harmony with all other creatures to honour Utaika," Florette replied.

"We know her as Itanuk, provider to all who believe."

"Mhutig and the opowak mentioned Kaloun?" The crackling fire warmed Lisette's cheeks.

Amelia smiled. "Ka-la-oun, the god of honour and justice. Many wars have been fought in his name." Her eyes turned a deeper shade of blue.

Lisette blinked. For better or worse, she was drawn to this woman. "Krousus sounds like a violent land."

Amelia's pale skin gave way to a sickly grey colour. "As much as we'd like to deny it, the capacity for violence exists within all of us."

"Are ye okay?" Lisette watched helplessly as Amelia laid a hand on the floor and slumped to the side.

Florette hurried to Amelia's side and listened to her chest. "Her heart feels weak, and tis beating too fast."

Amelia grabbed hold of Lisette's hand. "I don't feel so good," she whispered before falling unconscious.

Florette placed one hand above Amelia's heart and the other hand over her own. Florette's wings began to glow, followed by her entire body. Next, brilliant strands of emerald green light flowed from Florette's fingers and into Amelia's chest. Lisette watched in amazement.

Colour rushed back to Amelia's face. Her eyelids flittered, opening in time to see the last string of light disappear into her chest. She fixed her eyes on Florette. "I think you saved my life."

"The light of the pardela now resides within ye," Florette said softly. "Your heart beats slow and steady."

"Pardela?" Amelia looked confused.

"I shared the light of my spirit animal with ye. A most wise and courageous animal."

"How? . . . Why? You barely know me."

"Your heart carries no malice. The bodies of most humans aren't able to hold more than a grain of its light, but I sensed your body be different. When ye've fully recovered and no longer need its strength, it will return to me."

"Guardians of the emerald." Amelia sat up and smiled.

Chapter 20

In the days that followed, the Seekers extended their friendship to Amelia and shared stories about their land. Returning their trust with an unfettered heart, Amelia shared stories of her own, including the one about her ancestors. She told them of a people who fled their homeland in search of freedom. Shunned and feared because of their appearance, they sailed to Mesolak, a small group of islands in Krousus. The karupas' subsequent arrival challenged that freedom, but with the Order of Taupaks, they continued to live in relative peace.

"Because of your ears?" Aspen asked innocently.

"Our ears, skin colour . . . slow aging." Amelia fell silent, then patted her skirt. "In Mesolak, our legs make us deviants. So we live in villages apart from taupaks and opowaks, still shunned but no longer feared. They leave us alone, and we do the same."

"Your homeland, what do ye call it?" Lisette was intrigued. The more she learned about Amelia, the more curious she became.

Amelia steadied herself after Mhutig leaped over a wide creek that cut across their path. "Joro. According to our ancestors, it's a distant land somewhere in Krousus. But no one has ever travelled there."

"Do the stories tell how your people found Mesolak?" Ewart asked.

Amelia shook her head. "Only that Queen Cethina led them through an enchanted passage across the ocean. It was winter, and without her guidance, they might not have survived. We owe her our lives."

"A wise and powerful queen." Roy stopped to give Shadow a chance to drink from the next creek.

"Itanuk's youngest of four daughters. It's said that after Queen Cethina's birth, Itanuk's husband became jealous. He didn't like sharing his wife with a fourth child, so he left but still visits every winter to see his wife and daughters."

They were about half a day's ride from the camp. Mhutig suggested they veil before continuing. Not knowing what to expect when they arrived at the camp, everyone agreed to approach with caution and assess the situation before acting. To their relief, they had not yet encountered any other opowaks or karupas. The occasional miner who had crossed their path maintained a safe distance and left them to travel in peace. But they had not seen a miner or other soul in ten days.

"What do ye suppose those monsters are doing here?" Deidrik asked while Florette made her rounds to protect them from blood-hungry eyes.

"Whatever the reason, it can't be good for the people of Wrunwicks," Ewart replied.

"Karupas are not known for their intelligence or diplomacy," Mhutig said. "In Krousus, my brothers and I are able to protect humans from their savagery. Here, they have no such enemy. If left unchecked, they could eventually annihilate your people."

"We can't let them turn our land into a butchery." Roy's eyes burned with anger. "Karupas or otherwise."

Lisette shared Roy's anger. They all did. After she had mentioned the karupas might also be the wrunwick of old one night, they had all agreed it mattered little to their quest. A threat was a threat. Karupas or wrunwick, they could not be allowed to hunt their people like wild animals.

Mhutig examined the faces of their group before returning to Roy. "Our goal is to prevent that from happening. A heavy burden for anyone, but we will succeed."

⁂

Day ceded to night as they neared their destination. When light from the camp grew bright, Mhutig signalled for them to stop, pointing to a ledge about thirty paces from the camp and five paces up the mountainside. Between the ledge and the ground below, there rose the meagre semblance of a path between the rocks and stunted trees. Lisette nodded her understanding.

They approached the mountain with caution. They were veiled, but no one wanted to test the limits of Arias or her powers right now. Some twelve paces later, they arrived at the foot of the mountain. The ledge appeared large enough to accommodate them with room to spare. It should provide them with a safe vantage point to observe the camp.

Mhutig led the way up the mountain with Amelia, steering clear of the rocks and trees. The others followed in a single twisting line. It had not rained in several days according to the dry terrain, making it easier for the horses to climb the steep path. Lisette smiled up at Mhutig and Amelia, who waited on the ledge. Amelia sat atop the sheep skin borrowed from the miners' shack. Then one by one, they took their place overlooking the camp.

It was impossible to see how many opowaks and karupas there were, nor could Amelia tell them. In fear and shock, she had fled from the camp with little more than a glimpse at her surroundings. Mhutig speculated that her quick reaction had saved her. That, and the arrogance innate to opowaks.

Lisette glanced at their newest companion. Thanks to Florette, she had nearly recovered from her night at the shack. And thanks to the pardela's light, her eyes had acquired a green outer circle that, like the blue, changed from light to dark according to her mood. They were dark now.

"Seekers, remember to be patient," Mhutig cautioned. "We cannot defeat our enemy on faith alone or by attacking without a plan."

"I'm not ready to die just yet," Henry said.

"None of us are," Deidrik replied. "Let's hope it doesn't come to that."

Lisette could see at least a dozen karupas and opowaks. They were gathered round a fire over which a bear roasted, sending whiffs of scorched meat up into the night sky. Next to his opowak neighbour, a karupa turned the bear on its spit. The opowak must have said something funny, causing the karupa to laugh. It was an ugly sound. Lisette had never heard a live animal being sliced open, but she imagined it would sound much like that karupa.

"At least tis not a person," Roy said, shifting in his saddle.

"Karupas kill humans out of hate, not for food," Mhutig said. "But their hunger for human flesh is never satisfied."

The only structures were two broken-down buildings. Neither building was large enough to serve as viable shelter for the group of giants waiting to eat. Standing on an old mining site, Lisette guessed the buildings once housed the men who scratched a living from the mountain. She could also hear voices coming from inside the cave at the mountain's base. Similar caves were scattered across the mountains, offering easy access to the wealth inside. It seemed this cave now served as a foothold for whatever the karupas and opowaks were planning.

An opowak threw a chunk of meat inside one of the buildings. The building sprang to life as the sound of voices and feet collided.

"Those voices sound human," Aspen said, breaking Lisette's concentration.

"We need to see who be inside." Roy peered down at the camp.

Henry flinched. "Our veils won't save us from those balshan spawn."

Lisette agreed with Henry. The karupas' sense of smell was sharp as their souls were black. Good intentions would not save them if they were detected. And yet, they hadn't come all this way to turn around in fear.

"I'll go," Amelia offered.

Lisette frowned. "They'll detect ye too. Our veils can't hide us from a karupa's nose."

"I can do it." Florette rose from her seat. "They're not hunting pardelas."

Lisette glanced at the half-eaten bear. "They're not picky."

"Pardelas have no odour. I'll be fast."

"I say we give her a chance," Deidrik said. "Someone has to go."

Florette made no attempt to hide her transformation this time. She flew to the ground, shook out her wings, and stretched her arms to the north and south. The same lustrous green which had radiated from Florette's fingers to save Amelia now surrounded her in a wispy cloud of light. She began to morph into the animal revered in stories for its exceptional appearance.

As she began to morph, Florette's face, arms, and body merged with her animal form until there was no trace of her former self, save for those unmistakable green eyes. Her wings reached up and out, growing ever wider, covered in the same black fur as her glossy coat. Her transformation into the animal so lauded for its beauty was complete.

"Ready." Florette gave her wings a gentle shake. "I can't use these. My veil won't hide the turbulence created by their movement from keen eyes."

"I don't see either light inside those buildings." Henry gazed at Florette, sounding doubtful.

"Once my eyes adjust, I'll be able to see as though it were high noon," Florette replied.

"Travel lightly and be careful." Lisette had an inkling Florette's stubbornness rivalled her own. There would be no stopping her friend from going.

Lisette's heart flip-flopped once, then twice more, as Florette descended the mountain on her way to the camp. Florette sprinted past the rocks and trees, her feet scarcely touching the ground. She slowed to half speed a few paces out. Arriving inside the camp, Florette maintained a safe distance from the greedy circle of giants. They showed no knowledge of Florette's presence as she made her way to the nearest building. Lisette let out her breath.

One of the karupas threw a bone, nearly hitting Florette on her hind leg. Lisette gasped and slammed her mouth shut to stifle any further noise. Florette leaped forward, landing in front of the first building without disturbing a single rock. She walked over to the building's only window, raised her front legs to balance herself against the wall, and stretched her neck to peer inside the window. She proceeded to the next building, looked inside, then turned back toward the mountain. The brutes carried on with their meal. What was it that Henry had called them? *Balshan spawn.* Lisette liked it. An accurate term for murdering monsters, she mused.

The excitement shining from Florette's eyes as she leaped over rocks and shrubs ignited a light inside Lisette. She allowed herself to hope again. *What did Florettee see inside those buildings?* Lisette watched as Florette crisscrossed the mountain faster than a bird could fly.

Florette's eyes lit up the entire ledge. "The buildings are filled with people," she said eagerly. "Some look like Amelia."

"Then we need to free them." Roy reached for his sword.

Lisette felt a sudden urge to hug her young friend. Roy's heart was sometimes bigger than his reason. "We'll need to be careful."

"Is it wise to free them all at once?" Deidrik asked. He jutted his chin toward the camp. "Won't that alert them to our presence?"

Ewart turned to Roy with a pained face. "I hate to admit it, but Deidrik has a point. Tis bound to get their attention, even if Florette managed to veil every person down there."

Lisette's heart sank like a rock in a shallow pond. Ewart and Deidrik were right. To try and save the prisoners meant risking the lives of everyone involved. A risk she was not prepared to take. *So what now? We can't just leave them here. We didn't come all this way to cower like balshan rabbits. We're not rabbits. I'm not a rabbit.*

"Bravery comes in many forms," Florette said, still in her animal form.

"So do mice." Roy inspected the ground. "But I see none here."

The idea of doing nothing tied a knot in Lisette's stomach next to the sunken rock. She understood Roy's reaction. Wrunwickers were prisoners inside those buildings. They were loved ones with family and friends who missed and mourned them. Florette said there were people like Amelia in the buildings too. *What do the balshan spawn want with them?*

"Karupas have never been known to capture humans. It appears that opowaks have not only allied with karupas but have also found a way to control them."

Mhutig's words quelled the thoughts banging inside Lisette's head. Again, she wished they could charge the camp and free the prisoners.

"Better captured than slaughtered like pigs," Henry said.

Deidrik turned to Lisette. "We could seek the king's aid."

"I highly doubt King Eldridge would hear the likes of us speak." Aspen held Silver's reins in a grip so tight, angry white ridges ran free across her knuckles.

"He'll hear me speak," Deidrik replied. "As the court painter, the king has never turned me away."

"Are ye suggesting we leave the prisoners here?" Roy looked ill.

"If we are detected," Mhutig said, "the karupas and opowaks will not stop until everyone is dead. We cannot win against an army of that size—"

"We don't know that for certain," Roy interrupted.

Mhutig looked at Roy, pausing briefly. "I may not know why they are keeping prisoners, but I do know a karupa's hunger for blood. If we could free them without risking every life in those buildings and our own, I would be happy to fight."

"How do we know they won't slaughter everyone tomorrow?" Roy asked.

"If such was their intent, they would have done so by now," Mhutig said quietly.

Lisette asked Utaika for a way to save the prisoners. Were they really going to turn their backs on them? *Do we risk spilling their blood and ours?* In the most popular stories, a hero always saved the day. But this wasn't a story, and they weren't heroes. "Do ye think King Eldridge will help us?" she asked Deidrik, hating the defeat in her voice. *If only Father could hear me now, he wouldn't be so proud of me.*

"Don't let your pride lead ye astray," Nora had once said after hearing her boast about being a dressmaker for Lady Constance. Was she being proud now? Or was she looking for an excuse to cower inside her burrow, after all?

"The king can be a little blunt at times, but he be a kind man," Deidrik replied. "He will not see his people suffer."

"In the meantime, we leave them to suffer." Roy's voice shook with anger.

"We get it. We get it," Henry said.

We'll be fighting among ourselves before long. And to what end? An image of Calder reminded Lisette of a karupa's savage strength. She cleared her throat. "Neither of us wants to leave them here, Roy. But we can't possibly hope to win against that many balshan spawn. We owe it to our people to do this the right—"

"Doesn't mean I have to like it," Roy said.

"I don't like it either." Lisette glanced around at their group. "None of us do."

"We'll need more than our good intentions to defeat those ugly balshaks," Ewart said in a tight voice.

"Good intentions haven't done us much good so far." Henry watched with disgust as one of the karupas tore into the bear's leg.

Roy met Henry's eyes. "A visit to the castle it be, then."

Deidrik took Mossy's reins. "We have a long ride ahead of us."

They travelled throughout that night and the next day, wanting to cover as much ground as possible. Kingsbridge lay southwest of the prisoners' camp. The forest was thinner with fewer rivers so far north. Deidrik estimated their journey would take around twenty days if they made good time, less if they rode harder. It meant fewer stops and longer days if they were to succeed. Their quest for the truth had been replaced by a new mission: free the prisoners and defeat the balshan spawn, a term each of them borrowed. And while the exact means remained unclear, they were determined to accomplish both goals.

After nine days of travel and three days of rationing their water supply, they heard the welcome gurgle of running water. According to Lisette's map, they had finally made it to the river that flowed south through Kingsbridge and continued downstream past Waterbridge. At their current speed, they should see Kingsbridge in just over six days. Everyone was bone tired, including the horses. But neither horse nor rider was willing to slow down.

The tension created by their decision to leave the prisoners clung to the air like a late-harvest mist. Monsters were not only real, they were armed with a plan. And whatever that plan was, it could only spell disaster for Wrunwicks. Now it was them who needed a plan. The enemy could not be defeated by want or wishes alone, no matter how many times they wished it true. Facing their limitations was a sobering experience that no ale or wine could dampen. It was just as well since both were in scarce supply, Henry had pointed out one night around the campfire.

Lisette busied herself with getting to know Amelia, careful to ignore the question forming in her heart. It was not the time for self-absorption, Lisette reminded herself. They had more pressing concerns for now, like the future of Wrunwicks. An invasion by karupas and opowaks meant an end to the long-celebrated age of peace. The people of Wrunwicks were unaware of the danger that threatened their land, but Lisette feared a new age had begun. Time would decide the final outcome. She prayed it favoured them.

"There you go, lost inside your thoughts again." Amelia stood next to Lisette while the horses drank from the river.

Startled, Lisette felt the colour rush to her face. Amelia had a knack for making her blush. "Nothing more than the idle musings of a foolish heart."

"Musings of the heart are seldom foolish."

"Ye sound like Florette." Lisette emptied her waterskin over Daisy's neck.

"A wise fay," Amelia said with her cheekiest grin.

Amelia's humour provided a welcome relief from the prevailing dark mood. Lisette needed to believe they had made the right choice. At least the prisoners still had a chance at life beyond the camp. She refused to give up on them or their ability to save them. They just needed help.

"I'd settle for a small slice of that wisdom," Lisette said in the same lighthearted tone.

Amelia considered the group for a moment, then turned back to Lisette. "Roy looks much happier there now."

Roy stood adjusting his saddle next to Ewart, who was sharing the story about a fishing trip with his father. Roy chuckled as he listened to Ewart tell him about the fish that nearly got the best of him and his father. The two had been riding together since leaving for Kingsbridge. The day before, Lisette had thanked Ewart for keeping an eye on their youngest friend.

"Roy knows our choice to be true," Ewart had said to reassure her. "He just needs time to accept it."

Ewart's words had struck her as more than a little ironic and still did. They didn't set out from Stonebridge to turn around in defeat. But they didn't set out to wage a war either. Lisette watched Daisy drink from the river, recalling the last of their conversation.

"Tis certainly not the truth any of us wanted to find," she had remarked, "although I'm not sure what I was expecting."

"Our journey be far from over. There'll be other truths along the way."

"May those truths be a little easier on the stomach," she had said in conclusion.

Lisette refilled her waterskin, knowing there was no way she could wash the sour taste from her mouth. She offered a drink to Amelia. "Ye must be thirsty."

Amelia gulped down the water and passed it back to Lisette. "Thank Krousus you have but one sun."

Lisette glanced up at the late afternoon sun and poured another bag of water over Daisy. "Roy prefers action to words."

"Your king. What does he prefer?"

Lisette mulled over the question. Those who dared to defy a royal canon found themselves rotting inside a cage more often than not. But the canons long predated King Eldridge. "There's been no need for a king to act since before our elders can remember."

"All we know is conflict, and our weapons are no match against the karupas."

"Let's hope we can find a way to defeat them." Lisette patted Daisy's shoulder. "We'll also need to find a way to convince the king. Tis our only option."

Part Two

Winter's Flowers

Chapter 21

The Seekers arrived at the rolling hills of Kingsbridge six days later and headed straight for the castle. As they rode the well-beaten path, two green and white flags twisted in the wind. Lisette eyed the flags with mounting dread. They held neither plan nor invite on which to hang their hopes. All they had was Deidrik's assurance that King Eldridge would welcome their presence. Lisette hoped he was right. Commoners never announced themselves at court without just cause. What if the king refused to hear them?

Despite her concern, Lisette could not help smiling as she took stock of their group. They were a strange lot by any standard. Crusty travellers in need of a bath, a taupak, a fay, and a woman with pointed ears and skin so pale it was almost the colour of milk. Ewart had given their new companion his jacket after seeing her burnt arms one day. And although her arms were now protected, Amelia's cheeks looked like bright red apples. Glancing down at her trousers, Lisette's smile widened. *Add two women and a fay dressed in men's clothes.*

As they neared the castle, Lisette could see the royal crest on each flag: two swords over a stone bridge. The swords symbolized justice and the king's army, while the stone bridge denoted the king's strength and unity under his rule. They would need all four to defeat the monsters at Metterling Mountains.

Beyond the sun-drenched highlands, men and women stopped to look. Their fear and curiosity reminded Lisette of the night they had arrived in Strawbridge. Boys and girls stared from the safety of their mothers' skirts. The younger children strained to see over the wheat.

"Let's hope the moons bring a cold wind tonight," Deidrik said.

"I doubt there be a wind cold enough to stop their tongues," Ewart replied.

Roy tugged his ear. "Mine are burning already."

"Ye'd think they've never seen travellers before," Aspen said.

Lisette watched as the flags drew closer with each breath. What did fate hold in store for them? And what would the balshan spawn throw at the people of Wrunwicks? She noticed Florette studying her. "Do your magical powers include knowing the future?" she asked her faithful friend.

"Not even the Grand Oak can tell us that."

A short while later, Lisette slowed her breathing as they rode to the castle gate. Deidrik suggested it would be best if he spoke on behalf of the group, given his familiarity with the king. Lisette was more than happy to relinquish him the reins. It was one thing to visit Lord Stanley who had so willingly and warmly invited them to his manor, but they knew little of King Eldridge or his disposition. He was the sort of king who kept to himself, leaving regional matters in the hands of his lords. To the disappointment of townsfolk back home, King Eldridge had never visited Stonebridge.

Sensing her owner's tension, Daisy let out a loud snort. Lisette relaxed her body and spoke softly into Daisy's ear. "I'm being silly, girl. Neither of us has anything to worry about. Ye'll see."

"We've been spotted." Deidrik waved to a watchman in the tower.

The watchman waved back, then disappeared. The loud clanging of metal greeted them as the gate lifted. Unlike the wooden gate at Lord Sumunder's or Lord Stanley's, this one was forged of heavy iron with the royal crest engraved in the middle. Lisette guessed it was the original gate. Iron had largely fallen out of favour as a building material for the lords of Wrunwicks. Most preferred to use wood or stone. Wooden gates resembled doors that quietly opened onto the courtyard, unlike the castle's gate with its pull chains.

Two men waited beyond the gate with their swords and dour faces. Lisette snuck a glance at Deidrik. He looked unconcerned. *At least someone be smiling.*

"Surely there be no need for such posturing," Deidrik said to the men.

"The King advised us to ready our swords," the man in a red tunic said, eyeing Mhutig with an extra share of suspicion.

"But as ye can see, there be no need for your weapons." Deidrik gestured toward Mhutig. "My esteemed companion means ye no harm."

"King Eldridge received word of the taupak," the man replied.

"Then ye know I speak the truth." Deidrik dismounted. "I need to speak with the king at once."

The man in a plain brown tunic broke his stare down with Amelia. "What of the rest?"

"They're with me." Deidrik looked around the empty courtyard. "Where might we find our noble king?"

"The king be back from his hunting trip," the man in the brown tunic replied, his eyes darting from Deidrik to Mhutig.

Deidrik indicated for everyone to follow him. "Let's get our horses settled first, shall we?"

The Seekers dismounted and waited for Deidrik. The man in the red tunic gawked at Aspen.

Lisette offered her hand in friendship to the man in the brown tunic. "Lisette, daughter of Sam and Nora of Stonebridge."

The man hesitated, looking unconvinced while he scoured her face. She waited for him to make the next move.

Appearing to find a suitable answer to his inquiry, the man shook Lisette's hand. "William, loyal servant of King Eldridge."

Lisette looked around at their group. "We must seem very strange to ye."

"Mhutig, son of Hyrek and Wiolas of Krousus." Mhutig turned to Amelia. "And this is Amelia of Krousus."

William ignored the introduction. "We've heard rumours of the half-man, half-horse."

"I hope those rumours have fared me well," Mhutig said with an easygoing smile.

"The people of Strawbridge speak of ye with awe, but our king isn't so easily impressed." William kept one eye on Mhutig and the other on Lisette.

"A wise king must decide for himself what is true or not and act accordingly," Mhutig replied. "He rarely possesses the luxury of choosing what is popular."

Lisette wondered whether Mhutig was speaking from personal experience as a future king. Amelia once told her that, according to the castle servants, Mhutig and his father hadn't spoken to each other in almost a year. After an argument about his involvement with the Order of Taupaks, Mhutig was seen storming out of the castle to never return.

The man in the red tunic pointed his sword at Aspen. "And ye, what of your truth?"

"Come now, Geoffrey," William said quickly. "We don't aim our swords at ladies."

"Tis no lady like I've ever seen," Geoffrey said, withdrawing his sword nonetheless.

"What would ye know of ladies?" Aspen's voice was colder than winter's first breath.

Geoffrey stared at Aspen's clothes. "They don't steal men's trousers."

"Tis funny because I almost took ye for a peacock." Aspen's eyes lingered on the man's ornate tunic.

Lisette fought to suppress her laughter, remembering the tale in which Utaika transformed a man into a brightly coloured bird to punish him for his arrogance and vanity. Utaika named the now infamous bird after his favourite sword.

"Ladies and sirs, please. There'll be plenty of opportunities to banter at a later time," Deidrik said. "Right now, we have more pressing matters to occupy us."

Sun spilled through the stable's doorways and windows, bathing the walls in its warm light. A few of the stable's horses snorted their disapproval when they saw the newcomers. To the Seekers' left, a groom mucked the hay from an empty stall. In the next stall over, Lisette spotted a magnificent black horse. An older groom was brushing down the impressive animal and tossed them a quick look. He went back to the horse, whispering into its ear.

Two more grooms entered from a door at the far end. They

looked even more skittish than the horses. Lisette was grateful Mhutig had decided to wait outside with William. She looked to Amelia, who held the sheepskin, strap, and stirrups that Ewart had made for her with some wood and nails found at the miners' shack. Florette's light had done her well, and she appeared to have made a full recovery. The two grooms inspected their horses, seeming not to notice them.

"I think they may have forgotten their manners," Deidrik said with a bemused expression.

The dark-haired man turned toward them. "Please forgive our poor manners, Seekers. We're not used to receiving guests here at the castle. Our king often prefers the company of his horses to that of people. I'm Milton, son of Wilbur and Enid of Kingsbridge."

The man's reference to their nickname surprised Lisette. She couldn't remember either of them mentioning it.

"People are sharing tales of your adventures throughout Kingsbridge. Traders bring the stories with their salt," Milton continued. He turned to Florette with a smile. "Ye must be the famous fay of Evergreen Forest we've been hearing about."

Florette flew from Lisette's hood to shake the man's hand. "My friends call me Florette."

"And this be Victor, son of Basil and Mavis of Kingsbridge," Milton replied, indicating the other groom.

Victor's face relaxed. "Your horses look tired and thirsty. We'll take good care of them."

Remembering their own manners, the Seekers introduced themselves. Ewart was thanking Victor for his kindness when William ran in and announced that King Eldridge was expecting them in the round hall.

William and Geoffrey led the way to the tower. They followed the stone path twisting its way round the courtyard like a giant snake. Flowers bordered the path to prevent anyone from straying, their perfume clinging to the unusually warm breeze. Every flower in the courtyard had been forced into submission. The final effect was a dreamlike perfection that left Lisette cold. She preferred wild-flowers, growing free and untamed, not this show of wealth and control.

When they reached the tower, their escorts stopped. Smoke rose from the tower's chimney, rising ever higher until it claimed passage on the next cloud. A small child stuck his head out the door, then disappeared. Voices drifted from inside.

William turned to Geoffrey. "Wait here."

Geoffrey eyeballed Mhutig. "Ye'll need to stay this one out, I'm afraid." A brazen grin spread across his face. "Ye'll never make it to the rounder."

"The round hall be on the second floor," William explained, "and ye won't fit through the stairway."

"I'll stay too," Roy replied.

Lisette could smell a strange meat cooking. She wrinkled her nose in rebellion. Although neither of them had eaten since their meagre supper the night before, Lisette's stomach heaved at the very idea of food. Her eyes adjusted to the tower's dim light, she focused on the stairway with its high, narrow steps.

Several stairs later, Lisette spotted a doorway. She heard a loud, gregarious voice coming from the other side. Moments later, she heard a second voice. The lower, deferential tone of the second voice suggested it belonged to a servant. Lisette snuck a peek at Deidrik, admiring the calm but determined look on his face. No one had pried about his relationship with the king. Nor did anyone ask what he planned to say. They placed their faith in his word that King Eldridge would help them. They had no choice if they wanted to save the prisoners. Uncertain of what else to do, Lisette prepared what she hoped to be her most engaging and respectful smile for their king.

"The king be always in his best mood after hunting," William said, waiting by the door.

The walls inside the rounder were white like the rest of the tower and bare of any embellishment, apart from three intricately patterned wool and silk tapestries with busy hunting scenes. Two of the massive tapestries faced the length of a redwood table in the middle of the chamber. The third tapestry hung from the wall to Lisette's right. Two high windows flanked the fireplace opposite the door.

King Eldridge was standing in front of one of the windows. Known for his uncommon height, King Eldridge overshadowed the servant next to him. Although people spoke readily of the king's imposing stature, they failed to mention his equally impressive girth. The painting of King Eldridge hanging in the Great Library depicted a younger king half his size.

They waited by the door for the king to acknowledge them. He studied them in silence, eventually waving them into the chamber. Remembering Deidrik's instructions, the Seekers walked three paces, kneeled with their heads bowed, counted to ten, repeated the process, then stood up, waiting for the king to address them. Again, the king waved them forward. They joined him by the window.

"Word of your new friends precedes ye." King Eldridge fixed his eyes on Deidrik.

"So I've heard, my king." Deidrik bowed, then gestured to include their group. "These are the Seekers of Stonebridge."

"I've heard much in your regard, including the beast ye travel with. It seems ye've been busy." King Eldridge threw the remainder of his apple out the window. "Something for the birds."

The Seekers bowed. Florette's wings vibrated with quick bursts of energy next to Lisette.

"Tis an honour to meet ye, my king." Lisette's mouth was drier than wool. Meeting their king was proving more daunting than any crowd.

"Ye travelled from Strawbridge?" King Eldridge asked.

Deidrik bowed once more. "We seek the help of our wise king."

"Forever the charmer of fools, but I have enough people to kiss my ring."

Deidrik's body shook with laughter. "Forgive me, my king. I plum forgot in my absence." He winked at Aspen and shared what they had discovered.

King Eldridge listened with an unrivalled calm, nodding his head every few sentences or so. The servant's eyes were astonished. When Deidrik finished speaking, the Seekers waited for their king to respond. Lisette listened to the birds outside the window. Even to her, their story sounded fantastical.

"How did these monsters get here?" King Eldridge finally asked, breaking the silence.

"We don't know, my king," Deidrik admitted. "Nor do we know what their presence means exactly, but it won't be good for our people."

"Were ye able to confirm if these monsters are the wrunwick our people fear have returned?" the king asked.

"We did not, but they could well be monsters from our stories. There be no way of knowing with absolute certainty."

"Have ye shared this information with anyone else?"

"We wasted no time." Deidrik looked around at his watchful companions. "And came straight here. The journey took fifteen days despite our hastening."

"Good, good. No need to incite panic among the people."

"That isn't our goal, my king."

"And what of the beast that accompanies ye?"

"Mhutig, my king. He wishes only to help us."

"I prefer to arrive at my own conclusions," the king said quietly, directing his words at the whole group.

A servant entered to inform the king his evening meal was ready.

"I trust ye'll be staying," King Eldridge said. "My elders will want to meet ye."

※

Supper was to be served in the great hall, which the king said would also allow Mhutig to join them. The Seekers followed their king and his servant down the stairway and past the tower's kitchen. They walked past the armoury to a set of doors opening onto the great hall. At the opposite end of the hall, six men hovered near a fireplace that stood taller than either of them. Light filtered in from a series of high, narrow windows placed throughout the hall on both sides.

King Eldridge introduced his company of elders, who formed the castle's privy council. He finished with Master Furlow. "My oldest friend and castle steward," he added. "Without his wisdom and sage advice, this castle would fall to ruin."

The great hall's lavish decor contravened the king's exuberant praise of his steward. Next to silver and iron, copper was the third most expensive metal in Wrunwicks. A first glance told Lisette every portrait in the great hall was framed in the costly metal. Three-foot copper squares with branches punched into the metal wainscotted the walls. Made of wood, copper, and a large iron top rail, the king's throne presided over the hall from its polished five-step platform near the tower entrance. Lisette imagined the elders sitting in their chairs on either side of the throne, pronouncing judgment in the royal court.

While the king entertained everyone with his hunting exploits, Lisette admired the lavender and rose strewed across the grey and brown floor. The petals softened an otherwise stern hall. The door leading out to the courtyard opened. Lisette looked over to where Mhutig had just walked in. The sound of Mhutig's hooves on the stone tiles echoed through the hall as he approached.

King Eldridge and his elders turned to gawk at their latest guest. Recovering his senses, the king welcomed Mhutig to the castle and introduced him to the elders. Mhutig extended his hand in friendship to each of the elders. The men cautiously accepted.

Queen Harriet and Princess Rosalyn appeared from the tower entrance just as the king was directing everyone to the table. King Eldridge introduced his wife and only child. The queen and princess appeared unfazed by their guests, nodding politely throughout the introductions. Nonetheless, Lisette was heartened to notice the warmth in Queen Harriet's eyes, a welcome relief from the smug disdain expressed by the elders.

Seated at the table, Lisette went back to their evening at Lord Stanley's. In Stonebridge, townsfolk who met in the square took advantage to chat and catch up on the latest news. Their lords and king seemed to prefer meeting around food, and a lot of it. Before their meal at Lord Stanley's, Lisette had only witnessed so much food on one table for special events, during which the townsfolk gathered inside to celebrate. She recalled the carefully prepared food from their celebration at Wolf Moon Inn. Each dish would have used more stores than most families could afford. Lisette doubted King Eldridge suffered from such an affliction.

Master Furlow looked up from his chicken and bacon to study Amelia. "Might ye, by either chance, be Mhutig's kin?"

Lisette's spoon froze next to her custard. Along with their king and lord, people respected their elders above all others.

"Ye'll have to forgive my curiosity," Master Furlow continued, "but I couldn't help noticing your ears."

The king let out a roar. "Your cheek will always impress me, old friend."

Lisette bit down hard on her spoon. A surge of anger threatened to choke her. Amelia wasn't there to amuse anyone.

"Still your tongue," Calder whispered in her ear. "A fool with coin in the hand be a dangerous breed, indeed."

Lisette turned to observe her friend's face. Amelia betrayed nothing. She confronted the master elder's crude remarks with un-flinching restraint.

"We aren't related," Amelia said, stirring her soup. "But there is a story that speaks of a white taupak who fell so in love with a woman, he called upon a healer with magical powers to grant him human form. His wish granted, the taupak married the woman."

"That would explain the unnatural lightness of your skin," Master Furlow said glibly.

"What a lovely tale," Queen Harriet said. "We should all know such love."

"Our queen be a true romantic." King Eldridge squeezed his wife's hand. "It be one of her many virtues."

"And ye, Mhutig," Princess Rosalyn said, "do ye have someone to love?"

"My wife waits for me at home, my princess."

"This home ye speak of, please do tell us more." Princess Rosalyn examined Mhutig with open curiosity.

"It is much like Wrunwicks with its vast and plentiful forests," Mhutig replied.

"But with the hideous monsters ye've told us about."

"Yes, my princess. Although monsters rarely see themselves as such. They darken our islands in search of their next victim, so we hunt them to even the balance."

"What would ye call these monsters?"

"The enemy."

"Ye would have us slay this enemy in your place?" Princess Rosalyn asked bluntly.

"Please excuse my daughter's curiosity. She still needs to learn when to hold her tongue," King Eldridge interrupted.

Mhutig smiled patiently at the princess before directing his full attention to the king. He nodded in understanding. "I have a son who keeps me busy as well."

A group of servants placed trenchers on the table with a large assortment of meats. King Eldridge dug his knife in and filled his plate. He took a piece and chewed slowly to test the meat.

"The dastard almost got the better of me," King Eldridge said, observing Mhutig. "A deer made sweeter by the hunt."

"My brothers and I have spent many days in the woods." Mhutig held the king's gaze.

"Then ye'll try some. Not kin of yours, I hope."

Mhutig laughed good-naturedly. "Not that I'm aware."

Despite his easy response, Lisette noticed that Mhutig ignored the trenchers of deer meat in front of them. Fortunately, the king appeared too preoccupied with his own plate to notice.

An elder lay down the drink he was nursing. "How do ye and

your brave companions imagine us defeating this so-called enemy, Mhutig?"

"With men, lots of men. An entire army if possible," Deidrik asserted.

Lisette looked to where Deidrik sat next to Henry. They had entertained the idea of gathering enough men to fight the monsters stationed at Metterling Mountains. But neither of them expected their king to agree to such a plan. Nor did they know how to carry out a plan of that magnitude if the king did agree. The men of Wrunwicks had never been trained in battle. And like most, they were busy with their field and other duties.

"Where would ye expect to find this army of yours?" The elder's tone was skeptical, with the slightest hint of derision.

"'Tis why we're here." Deidrik met the elder's eyes.

"There has been no army since long before my first drop of ale." The elder poured himself another goblet of spiced wine.

"I wish the situation were different," Deidrik said. "But idle wishing won't rid us of these monsters."

Careful not to attract unwanted attention, Lisette observed the elders from behind the safety of her wine cup. They showed little concern for their group, focusing entirely on Deidrik and Mhutig. However, she drew no comfort from their cold expressions.

"I will not be remembered for being a coward." King Eldridge signalled a servant to approach. "Another pitcher of wine for our guests. And bring out the onion tartes."

"What do ye propose for us to do?" the elder asked.

"Create a new army," Deidrik replied.

Lisette sent a quick prayer to Utaika. Judging by the elders' hard noses, they would need all the help Utaika could spare them. She wondered if begging would make a difference to her prayer.

"There are no knights left to fill the role." The elder now looked at Deidrik with an expression often reserved for the soft-witted.

"No, but there are plenty of men with courage," Deidrik said. "We need not look far."

"Your faith be commendable as always, Deidrik," King Eldridge said. "Although a little misguided, perhaps. The threat of death tends to dampen a man's spirit."

"Make no mistake, my king. If they aren't stopped, there will be neither spirit left to dampen," Mhutig said. "Karupas will slaughter every human in Wrunwicks. As for opowaks, their role in all this has yet to be determined. They want to rule Krousus, perhaps they seek to add your land to their list of ambitions."

"If we were successful in defeating these monsters, what would stop more from coming?" King Eldridge asked.

"We don't know, my king," Deidrik said. "But we must act."

The king sighed. "For now, let us finish our meal. There's been enough talk about monsters for one evening. The elders and I have much to discuss."

King Eldridge's words precluded any further discussion of the matter. Lisette took a sip of her wine. She could scarcely taste the food on her plate. There remained nothing else for them to do now, except wait. And hope their journey had not been in vain.

Chapter 22

After they left the king and his elders to deliberate a course of action, Deidrik invited them to stay at his house. They gratefully accepted. Lisette was happy to see the distance increase between themselves and the castle. The meeting had taken its toll on all of them. King Eldridge and his elders were a daunting assembly by anyone's esteem. The highlight of the long, drawn-out evening had been when Queen Harriet wished them a comfortable stay in Kingsbridge before their departure. Their queen was a kind and gracious woman, unlike her husband.

Deidrik pointed to Lock Street and a house five doors up. They had arrived. Deidrik had yet to take a wife, so Lisette was surprised to see a candle burning in the main window. The matronly woman who opened the door and threw her arms around Deidrik appeared to be more than twice his age.

"I received word of your return from Rayley." The woman stepped back to take a closer look at Deidrik. She pursed her lips. "Ye've gotten thinner."

Deidrik laughed at the woman's expression. "Tis good to see ye too, Bertha. The townsfolk had a good look when we arrived outside the fields. Ye should've seen their faces. Twas a sight to behold."

"Ye bring guests too."

"That I do." Deidrik lifted the woman by the waist and carried her into the house. "Ye grow lighter with every trip. I see ye've been busy," he said, glancing around the kitchen.

Although the kitchen was three times the size of their kitchen in Stonebridge, it reminded Lisette of home with its modest but comfortable furnishings and familiar design. Enjoying the mouthwatering aroma wafting from the hearth, Lisette noticed the table had already been set with mugs and a trencher of cheese. A summer painting of a woman washing clothes in a river presided over the table.

"My mother," Deidrik said. "She became sick when I was a painter's apprentice. Her death left my poor father heartbroken. He joined her six moon cycles later."

"She was remarkable," Lisette said, admiring the painting.

"Will ye be eating?" Bertha smoothed out her dress. "I have more than enough to go around."

"It smells delightful," Ewart replied, eyeing the pot.

Deidrik took the opportunity to introduce everyone. Bertha's smile grew brighter with each introduction. She reminded Lisette of Nora. The woman accepted them without question or a single trace of fear as her eyes settled on Mhutig.

"My, ye be a sight for these old eyes if they be true."

Mhutig bowed before the woman. "Your charity honours me."

"I could really go for some of that pottage." Roy rubbed his stomach. "The day's been longer than we hoped."

Aspen insisted on helping serve their late-night meal. Florette carried the spoons, which were almost as tall as she was.

Basking in the warmth of their hosts' hospitality, the Seekers sat around the table chatting. Difficult as it was for Lisette to believe, the pottage tasted even better than it smelled. And for the first time that day, Lisette found her appetite. Bertha sat with them, sharing stories of her grandchildren and late husband.

"After Gerald died and I couldn't pay house wron, my daughter invited me to live with her in Ruderting, a village not too far from here. But I'd grown used to living in Kingsbridge, then Deidrik asked me to help out around here. Now, if ye ask me, he needs a wife to keep him company." Bertha elbowed Deidrik with comic force.

Deidrik pretended to nurse his arm. "None will have me. What am I to do?"

"Stay put for starters. That'd be what ye could do," Bertha said with emphasis. "Ye're not a young lad no more."

"On that, we can agree," Deidrik joked. "Maybe the princess will take a liking to me in my dreams. She waits for love, not more useless coin to fill her purse."

"The hungry might say otherwise. If ye ask me, ye'd be better off without a wife at all. Colder than a winter's day, that one."

"Maybe I should try my luck," Henry cut in.

Bertha looked at Henry in amusement. "Best of luck to ye, then. More than one young lord be still looking for his heart."

The next morning, one of the king's messengers arrived to summon the Seekers back to the castle at once. Thinking King Eldridge had come to a decision about the prisoners, they hurried back at full speed. Once inside the castle gate, William, Geoffrey, and four other men greeted them with dour expressions. William informed them King Eldridge urgently awaited their presence. Two of the men took their horses while the others led them to the great hall.

King Eldridge and his elders were sitting at the table. The king held a sheet of parchment in his hand. Melvin studied them from opposite the privy council. He looked more distraught than a caged rabbit, but Lisette saw the smirk behind his shifty little eyes. She felt a sudden urge to shove that smirk down his miserable gullet. The dastard's presence in Kingsbridge could only mean trouble.

The elders watched in silence. King Eldridge signalled for them to sit down. Mhutig stood at the end of the table where he faced King Eldridge. Lisette's heart pounded in her ears.

"Melvin and the signatory of this letter accuse ye of the most vicious crime within the canons." King Eldridge put down the parchment. "They say ye murdered a man from Strawbridge."

"*Ye haven't seen the last of us.*" Melvin's words churned inside Lisette's brain. The morning's bread churned even faster.

"Is this true, Seekers?" The king slammed the table with his fist. "The punishment for murder, as ye bloody well know, be death."

"Tis not, my king." Roy's voice shook. "The men attacked us in the woods. We acted in self-defence."

"Self-defence?" King Eldridge stared at Roy in disbelief. "All of ye against three men?"

"There were five men, my king." Roy's voice was scarcely audible now.

The council observed the Seekers. Lisette stared at the wall. She should have let the balshak bleed to death. Even at Melvin's five, they had outnumbered the men. The thirtieth canon also allowed citizens to defend themselves under the threat of death. Melvin's men would have gladly killed them all, but they couldn't prove it.

"Against nine of ye," King Eldridge bellowed.

"Amelia wasn't there." Roy studied a spot on the table.

"If I may, King Eldridge," Ewart said, "the man's death was a tragic accident. We all regret what happened that night."

King Eldridge picked up the letter again. "Regret will not bring the man back. Nor will it provide solace to his widow and child."

Watching King Eldridge wave the letter in anger, Lisette's heart pounded louder still. She forced the bread back down. The king had already made up his mind about their guilt. If the elders sided with their king, they could be executed by day's end.

Master Furlow examined Melvin. "Did ye speak with your lord and his council on this matter?"

"Given his affection for the Seekers and the gravity of the canon that was broken," Melvin said, "I thought it best for everyone concerned to bring the offence straight to our king."

"As for all matters that break canon, it falls to the council to pass final judgment." Master Furlow paused to look at King Eldridge. "This becomes especially important when there are no witnesses, and a life has been taken." He turned to Melvin. "I can assume there were no witnesses outside your group?"

"None, esteemed elder," Melvin replied.

"In that case, we will need to send word to the elders of both townships and await their arrival. We cannot judge the honesty of yourself or the Seekers without their consultation." Master Furlow directed his attention to Deidrik next. "We will wait for the elders to join our council before deciding your innocence in this matter or lack thereof."

Deidrik tilted his head in deference. "May truth continue to keep me company."

Relief poured over Lisette with a begrudging sense of gratitude for the master elder. He had spoken so crudely to Amelia the night before. But now they had a chance to prove their innocence.

"The council agrees with Master Furlow?" King Eldridge asked, looking around the table.

The elders nodded. "We are, my king," one of the elders said. "I would suggest keeping the Seekers confined until we know more."

"We have enough cages available," another elder said. "But I doubt them big enough to hold a taupak."

The image of a cage floated before Lisette. People often referred to them as widow cages. To be thrown into a cage during the cold winter moons meant near-certain death.

King Eldridge lingered over the suggestion, examining Mhutig. "Deidrik can return home. I trust him to remain in Kingsbridge. We could keep the Seekers in the cellar below the tower. It would be impossible to escape unseen."

"A gracious offer, my king," Deidrik said. "But if the Seekers will be staying in the cellar, I feel it best for me to join them. They're here because of me."

King Eldridge pondered Deidrik's words for a moment. "Your loyalty be commendable."

Lisette wanted to scream. The king may as well be discussing sheep shearing. *We should've taken our chances at Metterling Mountains.* She had never known the elders of Stonebridge to act quickly.

"Anger won't save the prisoners," Calder whispered beside her.

Nor will we. Lisette feared their journey to Kingsbridge had been in vain after all and would only bring their own demise.

The cellar was located on the opposite side of the tower from the great hall. William and his men led their prisoners past the tower stairs and straight to the entrance. A long chamber bereft of windows or heat, the cellar was cold and dark. Six wall torches provided the only source of light along the two rows of vaulted pillars. Lisette scowled at the rows of wine barrels lining the walls on both sides. She imagined the barrels looking back at them with indifference. Their situation was of no interest to the barrels. They were trapped inside a stone prison while Melvin roamed free.

"Ye suppose they'll let us have some of this wine?" Henry thrummed his fingers on the nearest wine barrel.

"King Eldridge was never one to deny himself the pleasures of life," Deidrik remarked.

"We could drink ourselves senseless." Roy stared down the length of the chamber.

"I'd like to roll a few barrels over Melvin," Lisette said. "Then stuff him in one."

"I wish ye hadn't stopped me from finishing Jacob," Roy said, continuing his inspection of the cellar. "Where do ye suppose those stairs lead?"

Lisette noticed the stairs at the far end of the cellar and the latch in the ceiling above. "My guess would be more storage. If the king keeps this much wine, he probably owns enough food to feed an entire village."

"This be all my fault," Aspen said with tears in her eyes.

"That dastard had it coming." Henry turned to face Aspen. "It could've been either one of us."

Florette flew over to one of the barrels and sat with her legs crossed. She looked completely oblivious to the morning's events. Lisette envied her composure while she, herself, fought for control. She now knew what it meant to hate, to truly hate another person. It gnawed on her heart like a hungry bear.

Chapter 23

ime in the cellar crept forward. The Seekers spent their nights sitting on the stone floor, brooding over their families back home and guessing how long it would take for the elders to arrive. They reassured each other the elders would eventually confirm their innocence. No one dared mention what would happen if the elders failed to believe them.

Servants brought food twice a day, bread in the morning and pottage in the evening. Both were served with copious amounts of ale, placing Henry in a constant stupor. And twice a day after their meal, William and Geoffrey took them outside the gate to stretch their legs. The two men stood in silence, pretending to watch the field workers. Lisette remembered hearing about breakers sitting in their filth, the accepted cost of breaking a royal canon. At least they were given a chance to use the stable's ruchton on their way back to the cellar. Unable to fit, Mhutig was given a stall to use.

Townsfolk and villagers trusted their elders' judgment in all matters of the court. The privy council had upheld the canons for generations. But under the threat of death, Lisette questioned how many breakers had truly earned their fate. And for the first time, Lisette began to question their trust in the seats of judgment. She had also grown so used to the upside-down feeling that it now felt normal. It was the world in which she lived that no longer felt right.

The long nights gave way to longer mornings with no word on the elders of Stonebridge and whether a message had been sent. They were outside the castle gate for one of their breaks when a servant ran out to speak with their guards. William and Geoffrey kept a suspicious eye on their prisoners as they listened. His errand complete, the servant hurried back to the castle. William called out to Lisette.

"King Eldridge requests your presence in the rounder at once," he said with a well-practised scowl.

Lisette's mind raced. There was no way the elders had arrived. It was impossible to make the journey in five days. But what else could it be? She waved to let William know she had heard him.

"What do ye suppose he wants?" Roy asked nervously.

"Maybe he's received word from the elders." Lisette looked around at their tired expressions. "I'll let ye know soon as I return."

King Eldridge paced the floor in the round hall, stopping in front of the fireplace. "Lord Stanley has sent an urgent message. He was injured during an attack on Strawbridge yesterday morning and has asked to speak with ye."

Lisette's jaw dropped. "Injured?"

"Attacked by the monsters ye spoke of."

"Strawbridge, my king?"

"His message contained very few details. It failed to include the extent of the attack."

Lisette tried to digest the news. Strawbridge had been attacked by karupas. What did it mean? Would the balshan monsters go after another town or village? She needed to tell Mhutig and the others. "Lord Aurik and Harmony?"

"He failed to say." King Eldridge poured himself a generous serving of wine. "For reasons I cannot fathom, the queen be quite fond of her nephew. A strange man with even stranger notions, our Lord Stanley. But when word of his injury finds her, the queen will undoubtedly want to know how he be faring."

Lisette knew she should say something about their queen and Lord Stanley. But what? King Eldridge didn't strike her as a man who heard anyone but himself. And she was nothing more than a commoner—a commoner accused of murder at that. Their king would hold no regard for her opinion.

"If I don't send ye, Queen Harriet would insist on going herself. I will not risk our queen's safety. William and Geoffrey have agreed to accompany ye."

"Even a mule can be persuaded to listen," Calder whispered in her ear.

Lisette took a deep breath. "Two of your men travelling with one woman may cause unwanted speculation. People will speak of the woman being escorted by the king's men." She paused, wanting to choose her next words carefully. "The vanishings have already created more than enough fear among our people. We cannot risk further exciting those fears."

King Eldridge waved his hand in dismissal. "Rumours are easily squashed."

"I'm inclined to agree with your wisdom, my king. But these rumours would be driven by an alarming truth. The attack on our people has begun and should word spread too far before an army can offer the promise of victory, panic may ensue."

"What would ye have me do?" King Eldridge asked, still pacing the floor in front of Lisette. "Lord Stanley was clear in his request and asked for ye by name, otherwise I would send one of the men. They seem more than sufficient enough. I'm not in the habit of sending maidens across Wrunwicks, especially those accused of murder. But the queen will be safe while we wait for your return. It seems ye left quite the impression.

Lisette ignored the inner voice mocking her every word. "Then perhaps it would be prudent to send at least two women and two men." She wanted to suggest more but was afraid to push her luck.

"Very well, the half-breed can go with ye. Any other travellers will be too busy with tales about her to wonder further." The king poured himself more wine. "Another mouth less to feed."

"A most wise decision, my king." Lisette bowed, careful not to betray her amazement. *Thank ye, Calder.*

William and Geoffrey escorted Lisette to retrieve Amelia and told her to be ready before the next bell. Lisette acknowledged them with a quick nod. Their situation felt like a bad dream. They were all facing an uncertain future, her friends inside their stone prison, herself and Amelia at the mercy of two strangers and whatever else waited in Strawbridge. Lisette pictured a karupa charging toward her and banished the image. Right now, she needed to tell her friends about the attack on Strawbridge.

The Seekers sat in nullified silence while Lisette recounted her meeting with King Eldridge. She saw her own disbelief staring back at her. After sharing how she had convinced the king to let someone accompany her, Lisette waited for them to react.

"It's only a matter of time before they attack again," Mhutig said. "They will not stop with Strawbridge."

Lisette met Mhutig's eyes, knowing in her heart that he was right. "We've never faced an enemy like this before. Even the wrunwick of old stayed away from our villages. I'm scared of what we'll find in Strawbridge."

"Why did the king choose me to go with you?" Amelia asked. "Of what possible use can I be in Strawbridge?"

Lisette hesitated for a moment. She refused to repeat their king's words. Amelia wasn't some idle curiosity. "Ye weren't with us that night in the forest when they attacked without provocation or reason. Ye had nothing to do with what happened and shouldn't even be in here."

"What about the rest of us?" Henry asked. "Why not ask for everyone to go?"

"I wanted to. Ye have to believe me on that." Lisette choked back the tears as she looked around at her friends. "I wish Lord Stanley had asked for one of ye instead."

Henry grunted. "I would've insisted. I—"

"Lisette did the best she could under the circumstances. None of us would've done any better." Ewart threw Henry a dirty look.

"My sister," Deidrik said. "She lives on Banner Street. It be on the outskirts of Strawbridge. Would ye be able to ask about her?"

Lisette nodded, sending a prayer to Utaika. She had forgotten about Ludara.

Florette left her station on one of the barrels to plant a gentle kiss on Lisette's forehead. "I'll ask the trees to watch out for ye."

Chapter 24

"Those two really know how to lighten the mood," Amelia said sarcastically.

It was day two of their journey, and their guards had scarcely spoken a word to them, keeping them well within their sight but out of hearing distance. Lisette was happy to oblige. She had no desire to talk with either of the men, who were only there to prevent them from escaping. Yet Lisette had no idea where they would run or why. It seemed their king was unable to understand the concept of friendship and loyalty. She would never abandon her friends.

"They have a very important job to do," Lisette said, mimicking the king's grave tone. "Ye, on the other hand, are little more than deer waiting to be slaughtered."

"You don't think the elders will find you innocent?"

Lisette considered Amelia's question. "There was a time I would've said yes without a moment's hesitation. Now I'm not so sure. I can only hope the elders are in a good mood on the day of our judgment."

"The elders here have a lot of power."

"The people of Wrunwicks trust their wisdom. And the king's."

"King Eldridge is much like King Hyrek. A brute."

Lisette's mind wandered back to the king's elders and Master Furlow in particular. "Power can turn men to swine."

Amelia threw back her head in laughter. "They make better pets than food." She glanced over her shoulder. "I'm amazed those two haven't started snorting yet."

The trade route to Strawbridge was hard-packed and dry, allowing them to reach the Strawbridge River seven days later. Following the river south, Geoffrey estimated they would reach the township in two days, three at most. Riding long past dark and before sunrise each day, he proposed they stop early to give themselves and the horses a much-needed rest. In agreement for once, Lisette and Amelia dismounted and led their horses to the river for a drink.

William suggested they hunt for rabbits to give everyone a break from salted meat. Amelia offered to go with him. Lending Amelia his bow and arrow, Geoffrey wished her good luck. The two went to gather wood for the rabbit they planned to bring back, leaving Geoffrey and Lisette to care for the horses.

"Aren't ye afraid we'll try to escape?" Lisette asked Geoffrey, who was watering down his horse.

Geoffrey inspected the sparse forest. "We'd find ye soon enough. There be nowhere to hide in these woods we can't go."

Lisette watched as William stopped again to check on Amelia. "Ye might want to tell that to William." Lisette patted Amelia's horse. "Good girl," she soothed. On loan from Deidrik, Lisette had fallen in love with the mare immediately.

"The last man who failed the king spent three days in a cage."

"Ye have to start trusting us, Geoffrey."

"So ye can plunge your sword the instant our backs are turned?"

Lisette sighed in exasperation. "Ye'd get along well with Henry."

※

Eating the last of her supper, Lisette heard the first warning. As she strained to listen, a cold sweat turned her skin to ice. She motioned for everyone to stop talking. The hair on her forearms bristled to attention. There was no mistaking that sound. Karupas. At least one, maybe more. "We need to find cover," she said, putting down her plate.

Geoffrey eyed her suspiciously. "Cover from what? We didn't see anything in the woods."

"Listen, balsh it." Lisette tilted her head to the left. "We have a karupa headed this way."

William jumped up and grabbed his sword. "I refuse to cower in fear."

"Your sword can't protect ye from karupas," Lisette replied. "Mhutig barely survived a battle with them."

Amelia threw water over the fire. "Fear isn't our enemy. Folly is. I'd rather not watch them slaughter you. As much as I'm tempted myself at times." She went to get more water.

Lisette searched the woods for possible shelter, knowing that hiding didn't guarantee their safety. "We can all be heroes another day. Right now, we're wasting time."

"Where do ye propose we go?" Geoffrey asked. "The trees won't save us."

Geoffrey was right. The scruffy trees were tall with narrow trunks in this part of the forest, offering no protection from a karupa bent on destruction. To stay would risk all their lives. Lisette shielded her eyes from the setting sun. She eyed a young mountain in the neighbouring distance and pointed southwest. "I say we head in that direction. We might be lucky enough to find a cave. In any case, it be better than waiting around here."

A steady thump, thump rose above the trees like a heart beating too fast. The blood-freezing sound grew along with the sound of water pushing and falling over itself. Lisette asked Utaika to guide their steps. She had called on their Mother so often since leaving home that she lost track at some point along the way and hoped Utaika's patience had not been exhausted.

As they rode toward the waterfall, she recalled the cave behind Rocky Falls. Parents forbade their children to enter, sharing tales of the yellow-eyed monster with teeth made sharp on the bones of children. Ignoring the old stories, Lisette had discovered the cave's chamber was at least ten paces deep and found solace in the only place that offered privacy after her mother vanished.

Alone in the chamber with her grief, she would let the tears fall with the same fury as the water outside. At thirteen, she dried her tears and turned her eyes to the falls, never going back inside the cave and never sharing her secret with anyone except Nora. If this waterfall hid a similar cave, it couldn't save them from the monsters lurking in their nightmares, but it might save them from the monster hurtling through the dark.

Pine trees enclosed the small pond glistening in the moonlight. At the right end of the pond, a large basin of water tumbled over the rock, spreading out in every direction when it reached the bottom. Lisette searched the rock for the entrance to a cave. She spotted it halfway up the waterfall. "The cave isn't too far up for us to climb. I think we can make it, but we'll need to be careful. Some of those rocks look pretty sharp." She glanced around at their group. They looked lost. "We'll need to leave the horses down here."

"Won't that alert the karupa to our whereabouts?" William asked.

"Can ye think of a way to get them up there?" Lisette examined the cave's entrance. "I don't think we have much of a choice in the matter."

"Karupas aren't usually drawn to the smell of a person's horse," Amelia said. "They aren't the brightest of creatures."

With their horses tied to the nearest trees, they tackled the steep climb up to safety, feeling their way over the jagged rock surface. The climb was slow and slippery. Rocks nearest the falls were smoother than the blade of a sword. Lisette instructed them to watch their feet and avoid the pounding water.

"Let's not take any unnecessary risks unless we have to," Lisette shouted as loud as she dared.

The others kept whatever objections they had to themselves, concentrating on their next step. William led their group, making his way up the mountain one rock at a time.

"Don't look down," Lisette advised when they were level with the cave. "Once inside, stay close. We made it this far."

Lisette was last with Geoffrey in front of her. She waited while he hoisted himself up. When Geoffrey's feet disappeared inside the cave, she grabbed hold of the ledge, used a rock to balance herself, then pushed herself up and onto safety.

The roar of the water filled the chamber. Lisette peered into the dark recesses of the cave and listened to the ever-nearing threat. The karupa's path seemed doomed to cross their own. They could only wait and hope they weren't detected inside their refuge. If they were detected, they could only hope the karupa would not deem them worth its trouble. But she suspected karupas never passed on the opportunity to kill a human.

She wrinkled her nose against the stench of spoiled eggs. The cave's chamber was small, but it opened up to three tunnels leading inside the mountain. She wondered where those tunnels led and how far they went. If the karupa did attack, the tunnels might mean an escape route. Lisette removed her jacket to shake off the worst of the water. She was shivering from tooth to toe, made all the worse by her wet clothes. The men sat near the entrance with their heads supported by the cave walls. Amelia wrung out the skirt of her dress.

"I'm going to check out one of these tunnels. We can always use a backup plan," Lisette said to Amelia.

William and Geoffrey opened their eyes to look at Lisette with a distrust most often reserved for breakers, reminding Lisette of Melvin's accusation.

"Don't worry. I won't run away," Lisette said. *Where do ye think we'd go?*

"Maybe we should come with ye," William replied, "just in case."

"The real danger be out there. Amelia can join me while ye keep watch here. Tis probably just a dead end."

Geoffrey grunted. "Don't expect us to weep over your graves."

Lisette tore three branches from the largest tree in the cave. Next, she located some moss. They would need a torch to navigate the tunnels. Reaching into the pouch on her belt, Lisette removed the fire striker and stone, then wrapped the moss around the stone and struck it until she saw a spark. When the moss finally caught fire, she lit one of the branches.

๛

The light bounced off the tunnel walls, creating shadows stumbling in the dark. Away from the falls, it was quiet, too balshing quiet. Stories of the yellow-eyed monster came back to haunt the silence. Lisette ignored the knot twisting in her stomach, refusing to let fear get the better of her.

The tunnel appeared to be part of a larger system, intersecting and branching off in no discernible pattern. Lisette marked the rock with her knife. A trick passed on by her mother during one of their visits to the forest for berries. "In case we get lost or should find ourselves wandering in circles," she told Amelia.

Amelia picked up a small rock and threw it into the emptiness stretching into more emptiness. "Where do you suppose it leads?" she asked.

"It could take days to find out." Lisette rubbed her eyes, certain she had seen a faint light in the far recesses of the tunnel. Was anyone else in the mountain?

"Maybe we should head back," Amelia said. "There's nothing here but rock."

"What do ye think that be?" Lisette asked. The light was bigger now and a shimmering blue. It was mesmerizing and not the light cast by a torch.

"Be what?" Amelia sounded confused by the question.

"That light up ahead." Lisette pointed with her torch.

"A light. Are you sure?" Amelia squinted in the dark.

Amelia's inability to see it puzzled Lisette. Was the dark playing with her mind? The light expanded until the tunnel was awash in a pale blue. The rock began to vibrate, scarcely noticeable at first, speeding up as the light grew brighter. The tunnel dissolved around her. Lisette reached for Amelia. She was gone.

The knot in her stomach unravelled, punching the air from her chest in a sudden, explosive burst. She kneeled on the tunnel floor, all that remained of the mountain. *A nightmare. It has to be a nightmare.* Keeping her hands on the ground, Lisette waited. A second wave of nausea forced the rabbit and bread from her stomach. Her head was spinning out of control. The mountain had given way to a black sky with stars above, around, and below her. There was no up or down. The sky reached forever in either direction.

She shook uncontrollably. It was dark and cold. The air burned her skin. She tried to shout, but her lips were too stiff. *I'll freeze to death before long.* She willed herself to get up, keeping her eyes on the tunnel floor. *Don't look down. . . . Don't look down. . . . Don't look down.* It felt like she was pulling the mountain up with her. *What happened to it? Where am I?*

Standing amidst the vastness of the scene around her, Lisette felt smaller than an insect. *How different their world must be.* Her entire body was numb. Turning around, she saw the same blue light from the rock tunnel. *Am I inside the light? Think, Lisette. Think.* The cold stuffed her head with wet wool. A star shot across the edge of forever, then blinked out of existence.

Lisette stared at where the shooting star had disappeared. *If I'm inside the light, there has to be a way out.* Her eyes dropped to the tunnel floor. Inside the mountain, the tunnel was wide enough for at least three people. Now it was half that width. Lisette's heart skipped a beat and knocked against her ribs. She kneeled back down on her hands and knees. Taking a deep breath, she started to crawl. The air froze inside her chest. *If ye can hear me, Mother, don't let me die out here.*

After what seemed like days, Lisette arrived in front of the light. It was spinning faster than her head. Unable to see around or through it, she placed her hand close enough to check for hot or cold. It was cold as the air but no colder. Lisette poked her fingers through the blue spiral, fully prepared to lose them. The air on the other side was warmer. She pushed her arm forward, reaching for the warm air. Better to lose an arm than her head, she reasoned. A hand grabbed hers on the other side. *Amelia.* Lisette held on. *Thank ye, Mother.* She felt a sharp tug on her shoulder. Amelia pulled again. Summoning the last of her strength, Lisette crawled through the light.

"You look frozen half to death," Amelia said, kneeling beside her. "What happened? One moment you were there, and the next thing I knew, you were gone."

Needles travelled up and down Lisette's body, stabbing every inch of her skin. "I was inside the mountain, only it wasn't the mountain. I could see stars and a sky blacker than ink. But it didn't look like our sky." She struggled to find the right words. "The stars were bigger, brighter. And some were clustered together in huge clumps of light. I know it sounds completely stewed, but it felt like the air was pushing and pulling me all at once, as though I was somehow being crumpled and ripped apart at the same time."

Amelia wrapped her arms around Lisette. "I sang out, over and over, hoping you could hear me. You mentioned a light, so I started running. Then I saw your hand appear out of nowhere." She gave Lisette a slow, lingering kiss. "I thought I'd lost you."

Dazed, Lisette touched her lips. She could still feel the places where Amelia's lips had just been. No one had kissed her like that before. The few suitors who did persuade her to walk with them would have suffered a swift hand across their cheeks.

"I know you're not ready yet." Amelia kissed her gently on the head. "Right now, we should get back to the men. They must be frantic." She stood up and lit the last branch.

An image of William and Geoffrey running around the cave in circles sprang to Lisette's mind. "Those two are more suspicious than a trapped animal."

Lisette and Amelia emerged from the tunnel, ready to defend themselves against their guards' accusations. The men were crouched near the cave entrance. William pressed a finger to his lips, pointing to the outside. Lisette heard the karupa drinking from the waterfall. Her feet glued themselves to the cave floor. The waterfall's incessant roar drowned out their voices and any other noise they might make, but she dared not test her assumption.

She mouthed her understanding and searched for the source of the cave's foul odour. One of the cave walls was partly covered in large patches of grey slimy material. She sat down to remove her boots, then tiptoed over to inspect the material. Scooping the slime up with her hands, Lisette knew she had found what they needed. Once disturbed, the slime's odour intensified, punishing Lisette's eyes and nose. Motioning the others to join her, she covered her hands, feet, hair, and face in the lifesaving gunk.

The men crawled back to their posts. Light streamed in from a small opening at the edge of the waterfall, transforming the men's faces into silver orbs. Lisette sat with Amelia at the farthest end of the cave, debating if they should take refuge in the tunnels. She turned to Amelia, who shook her head.

"Ye don't know what I was going to ask," Lisette whispered.

"We can't risk losing you again," Amelia whispered in return. "We still don't know what happened."

"We're like rabbits waiting to be skinned."

"Rabbits don't have our hearts." Amelia squeezed her hand.

"Our hearts won't be much good if this doesn't work."

"It—"

The sound of bones breaking rang through the cave, followed by a loud crashing noise. The horses neighed and thrashed in alarm. A second crash rang through the air, then a third. Lisette covered her mouth to silence a scream. She could hear flesh ripping from its bone. And for the third time that day, Lisette felt sick as the horror of what was happening punched her in the stomach. The karupa cried out in victory, followed by a fourth crash. Lisette tightened her grip on Amelia's hand, then silence. The horrific sound of limb, bone, and animal suddenly stopped. The karupa landed on the ground with a loud burp.

All four huddled in shock. After the crashing had stopped, William and Geoffrey had crawled over to their charge. The karupa had not moved since its brutal act of savagery. The sky told them morning was fast approaching, and they needed to decide what to do next.

"We can't just walk out of here," Geoffrey muttered.

"A karupa's stomach is even slower than its wit," Amelia said in the same hushed tone. "They need to sleep after a kill. We can't stay here indefinitely."

"What if it wakes up?" William asked. "This slime won't hold under the waterfall."

Lisette rubbed her arm. The slime was sticky. "We could cover our bodies and clothes. The stench would knock out a bear."

"Then what?" Geoffrey asked. "It ate at least one of our horses."

"All the more reason not to wait until it gets hungry again." Amelia took Lisette by the hand. "We can ride together."

"We need to get past that monster first." William paused for an instant. "Or we'll be breakfast."

The men turned their backs to allow the women to strip down to their underclothes. Scraping the slime off the cave wall, they coated their bodies and clothes in the putrid filth. Lisette pulled the slime through her hair again and tied it back with a soft twig. When they finished, Lisette and Amelia turned to give the men a chance to cover themselves in the grey slime.

When all four were ready, they stood at the mouth of the cave. They would need enough distance between each of them to safely manoeuvre the sharp rock. The rising sun greeted their exit, blinding them momentarily. Lisette gazed at the water below. It looked different at first light. For an instant, she was tempted to jump.

"Getting everyone to the ground be bravery enough," Calder whispered in her ear.

She glanced to the left of the pond where the karupa was busy sleeping off its night of terror. Lisette stepped onto a narrow rock adjacent to the cave, focusing on her hands and feet to avoid any costly mistakes. Each climber counted on the other to get them to the ground below, communicating their trust one rock at a time.

The first to arrive at the bottom, Lisette tiptoed onto the grass. Their horses remained blissfully quiet. The karupa stirred and mumbled in its sleep. Lisette froze in place. The others clung to the mountainside, afraid to move. Time watched over them while they waited. Soon as the karupa settled back down, the others resumed their descent to dry land.

Across from the karupa, lay the body of Geoffrey's horse. Its head had been crushed and ripped from the neck. Lisette turned away, heartbroken and enraged. She noticed the trees next, which had somehow managed to twist and turn their branches into a protective shield around the horses. *Florette.* Lisette remembered her friend's promise. *I'll ask the trees to watch out for ye.*

The group followed the trees in search of a way in, sneaking through the grass so as not to spook the horses or wake the karupa. Geoffrey found a narrow opening just above the grass halfway round the wall of trees and branches.

He peeked through the opening, looked back in approval, and crawled inside. The others crawled behind him. Lisette and Amelia wriggled their way over to the horses to calm them. Daisy snickered, halting everyone in their tracks. The karupa snored and turned over. When it relaxed once more, the men leaped into action and pried just enough branches apart for the horses to pass. Geoffrey crept over to Amelia's mare. Saddled up, they led the horses away from their waking nightmare, putting as much distance between themselves and the karupa as possible.

They stopped when the sun reached its peak. The sun's position reminded Lisette of the noon bells. Far from everything she knew, Lisette missed their familiar sound. Looking to the sky, she couldn't remember the last time it had rained. Although the days had begun to cool, she wiped the sweat from her forehead, careful to leave the slime. The stench filled her nostrils. She cast a fond smile at the redwoods populating this part of the woods.

"It might be best to travel with the trees," Lisette suggested to the men. "Their cover will help protect us."

William looked toward the forest bordering their route to Strawbridge. "It'll be slower travel."

"Where do ye suppose that karupa be going? What if it reaches Kingsbridge?" Geoffrey looked around at their group.

Lisette shared the concern she heard in Geoffrey's voice. "They've always stayed clear of our towns and villages. Strawbridge be the first town attacked. Let's hope they didn't get a taste for it."

"I wish we had a way to warn King Eldridge," Geoffrey said.

"Me too, Geoffrey. Me too." Lisette filled her waterskin. "One of us could head back to the castle, although I'm not sure it'll do any good in the long term. We don't know where the karupa be going. It could be headed anywhere."

"Including Kingsbridge," William said. "The king needs to know of the possibility at least. I have no choice but to go back and warn him. Ye three can continue east."

Studying William's expression, Lisette knew his choice was made. "Watch your back," she said needlessly.

After another long day and travelling well past dark once again, their weary group rested by a wide brook after washing off the slime as best they could. They sat eating salted meat and the last of their bread. After William had turned back toward Kingsbridge two days ago, they forewent the trade route to travel through the denser woods. Tomorrow should see them in Strawbridge before night's fall if they set out before dawn. They prayed William was safe.

Lisette hoped his return would be greeted with some measure of gratitude. From what she had observed during their encounters, it was one of the few things King Eldridge lacked in abundance. "Geoffrey, ye know the king far more than us. How do ye think he'll react to William's story?"

"If he doesn't throw him in the cage for breaking an order?" Geoffrey mulled over Lisette's question. "King Eldridge has a quick temper, but he cares about his people. And he likes to win. If ye can convince him the threat be real, the king will go after the karupas with everything he has. From what I can tell of our king, he'd never back down from a fight."

"The king knows about the camp at Metterling Mountains. We

told him during our first visit to the castle, and now there be the attack on Strawbridge. I'm not sure what else we can do."

"It'll take more than words to convince King Eldridge. William knows that. But if he hadn't turned around, I would have. William was right. The king does need to be warned." Geoffrey sighed. "The poor dastard will have a hard time defending his decision to return before us. Once we return with confirmation of the attack and William's story, it should help to convince the king, but we'll need to get back first."

Chapter 25

The sun was preparing to set when they arrived in Strawbridge. Nearly three moon cycles had crossed the sky since Lisette's last visit. The town she remembered was gone, replaced by loss and suffering. Nothing could have prepared her for the destruction she saw. Homes were hammered down to rubble. Part of Mountain Inn was gone, replaced by a gaping hole on the right side. Market square was now a mass burial site.

Throughout the square, bodies covered in blankets strewed the ground. Survivors of the monstrous attack wandered among their loved ones. Others sat next to the blankets. Children clung to their mothers. Amelia and Geoffrey stood next to Lisette in front of the inn, staring in horror at the devastation all around them. Neither of them managed a single word. Death hung in the air.

Bernard almost ran into Lisette on his way to the inn. The shovel in his hand was covered in fresh dirt. "My dear Lisette. I didn't see ye there. But we knew ye'd come, of course. Ye made good timing too. Where are the others?"

"In Kingsbridge."

"Aye. A trader said that he spotted your group travelling to Kingsbridge. We hoped he was right for Lord Stanley's sake. He has his mind set on seeing ye and waits for ye at the manor."

"What happened, Bernard?"

"A large group of karupas and some other beast charged through just under a fortnight ago now. I've never seen anything so vicious. Our walls were no match against them. They destroyed everything they could with their bare hands. Killed as many as they could. Others died from their injuries. We be still burying them."

"How many did ye lose?" Lisette observed a boy sleeping on top of a blanket. Her heart broke for the child.

"Hard to say. Too many for sure. We won't know until we've buried them all."

Lisette took Bernard by the hands. "We should've been here."

"Nonsense, or we might be burying ye too." Bernard glanced at the inn. "Ye'll need to take Lord Stanley up on that offer."

"Do ye know how Deidrik's sister and her family faired in the attack?" Lisette asked.

"The brutes attacked the manor first. They arrived here from the north road. The northern part of town was hit the hardest, the east and some of the west. The brutes never attacked the southern part of town. Ludara's family be taking in survivors like all those lucky enough to still have a home. Her husband was here earlier with his son and food for the hungry. A fine family, they be."

Lisette breathed a sigh of relief. Deidrik rarely talked about his family, but it was clear how much he loved his sister and nephew. She could at least bring back one piece of good news.

The front and left side of the manor lay in ruins. Stones covered the ground next to uprooted trees. The empty courtyard was deathly quiet. Spared during the attack, the great hall beckoned with its welcome light pouring from every window. Halden rushed out to greet them.

"Lord Stanley was hoping ye'd make it," Halden said quickly, glancing at Lisette's companions. But like Bernard, he asked no questions.

They went with Halden inside the great hall. Townsfolk and servants sat throughout the chamber. Children slept next to the adults on makeshift beds of straw and blankets salvaged from the rubble. Survivors looked out from grief-stricken eyes. In a bed next to the fireplace, Lord Stanley observed their slow progress. Lord Aurik waved them forward.

"We came as fast as we could," Lisette said, noticing how weak Lord Stanley looked when he raised his head to acknowledge them.

"Ye will have to forgive my lack of manners, Lisette. I fear my time may be short—" Lord Stanley clutched his chest in pain.

"Lord Stanley underestimates his strength," Lord Aurik said, holding onto the rickety headboard. "He be far too headstrong to let a group of karupas best him."

"Mhutig said a karupa's hunger for blood knows no bounds. I've never witnessed so much destruction or suffering."

"Their hunger will eradicate our people," Lord Stanley replied. "We have to stop them."

Lisette realized the strange whistling sound was coming from Lord Stanley. "We've asked King Eldridge to form an army."

"I need ye to give the book I told ye about to Lisette," Lord Stanley said, looking up at Lord Aurik. "The one I asked ye to get from our chambers."

Lord Aurik retrieved the book from a chest by the fireplace and handed it to Lisette. She lingered over the title in bright yellow.

Millennia. Beneath the bold lettering was the simple outline of a land, which Lisette imagined to be much like Wrunwicks with its forests and rivers. Opening the book to the last page she had read, Lisette gazed at Lord Stanley in bewilderment. Her copy was still in her saddlebag. She had not opened it in more than a moon cycle. Why did he want her to have this copy?

"Go to page 235," Lord Stanley instructed.

Lisette scanned the page, wondering what she was supposed to see. Near the bottom of the page, she found it.

Mrs. Sleets resided at Forty-Six Street, Northbridge, until her death. People still speak of the fiery-tempered woman and the secret she kept, saying it died with her. But Mrs. Sleets was best remembered for her flaming red hair, matched only by that of her daughter's.

As the first light of understanding dawned, Lisette's jaw fell through the floor. Her eyes flew to Lord Stanley in amazement this time. "How did ye know I was reading this?"

"I didn't, although it seems we share the same taste in books. Ye know where ye must go," Lord Stanley said, meeting her eyes.

Lisette nodded. She sensed the author's reference to the ill-fated Mrs. Sleets and her daughter was more than a coincidence. *But why?* Was she making connections where there were none? She had shared her mother's disappearance with Lord Stanley during her last visit. It seemed their lord also saw a link, regardless of how thin that connection might be. Could they have both lost their reason?

"First, I'd like to honour the fallen." Lisette's thoughts twisted around each other. "The people have been so kind to us, I'd like to return some of their charity."

Accepting Lord Stanley's invitation to stay at the manor, the three settled down for the night. The sound of restless sleepers filled the hall. Nearby, a man snored between whimpers of sorrow. Halden informed them the man had lost his wife and two children in the attack.

Pain clawed at Lisette from every direction. It was etched in their faces everywhere she looked. From the child balled up in the corner to the man next to them, it reached out to the town square, destroying the hearts of its people. Lisette searched for Harmony, finding her asleep next to Agnes. Lord Aurik continued his watch over Lord Stanley. What did the future have in store for the people of Strawbridge? How do ye get past so much tragedy?

"Where was Lord Stanley referring to? What does he want you to find?" Amelia asked from her bed, a thin layer of straw next to her own.

Lisette chased the dark thoughts from her mind. It would not help anyone. "I think I'm supposed to go to Northbridge."

"Ye got that from a book?" Geoffrey said in disbelief.

"I can't explain it. Call it a hunch." Lisette knew how weak her answer sounded. But to admit her suspicion would sound even worse. How could she explain there might be a link between Mrs. Sleets, the imaginary character whose name spelled Steels, only backwards, herself, and her mother? Any reasonable person would ignore the flimsy connections, dismissing them as coincidence. And Lisette considered herself reasonable.

"As a breaker waiting for trial, ye'll need more than a hunch to convince King Eldridge," Geoffrey said as he settled down to sleep.

Just as Lisette knew she had to go, coincidence or not, she knew Geoffrey was right. Her odds of being hung for murder were far greater than convincing the king of letting her go.

They rose at dawn with the townsfolk, wolfed down some bread soaked with ale, and followed the procession into Strawbridge. Less than half a mile out, Lisette noticed a small flock of birds encircling the town. Although she couldn't say for certain from such a long distance, the birds looked like purifiers with their bold telltale feathers streaking the sky. If the birds were purifiers, they needed to act quickly. "We have to warn the townsfolk," she told Amelia and Geoffrey, who looked at her in surprise. "They have a problem, and I need to tell Halden." The three of them started running.

"I'm afraid we're out of time," Lisette said when they reached Halden a few moments later.

"Time for what?" Halden threw her a confused look.

Lisette pointed to the sky. "See those birds? If I'm right, they're after the fallen." She went on to explain what Mhutig had told her and what she had witnessed firsthand. "The townsfolk have already been through enough. I don't think they could handle any more heartache."

Halden turned to face the townsfolk and whistled his alarm. "Alright then," he shouted, funnelling his words through cupped hands. "We need to hurry. No time to explain."

The townsfolk charged toward the square in a desperate bid to save their loved ones. The purifiers swooped down, dodging hastily gathered shovels, axes, pitchforks, and flails. Lisette guessed there were at least a dozen birds, hissing and grunting at the townsfolk. Children scrambled to help, throwing rocks and bits of rubble at their new assailants. Lisette swung a shovel at one of the purifiers and struck its wing. The purifier barked in anger and flew up to join the swarm, disappearing behind the encroaching cloud.

"I've never seen them attack like that before," Amelia said, leaning on a shovel to catch her breath. "They must be hungry."

Townsfolk went to work transporting the bodies to their final resting place while others shifted through the debris, adding to the growing pile in the middle of the square.

"The fallen need to be buried before those birds come back. Do ye see Halden anywhere?" Lisette asked Amelia.

Amelia helped Lisette search the square. "He's over by the inn talking to Bernard," she said, pointing him out to Lisette.

"The townsfolk won't listen to us," Lisette said, already walking toward the inn. "But they'll listen to Halden."

Lisette straightened her back as she approached the two men. The townsfolk deserved more than her useless pity. "These people need a leader, Halden," she launched in. "They're in shock. And they're grieving."

Halden scratched his head, staring at the horror before him. "They've been sifting through what remains of their homes and families for days now." He stopped and exhaled deeply. "Walking around in circles, they be."

"Those birds may not be so easily discouraged if they return. The dead deserve a proper farewell and can't wait until people are ready. If those birds return, there might not be anyone left to bury."

"Lord Stanley—"

"Lord Stanley be too feeble, and Lord Aurik won't leave his side. As the manor's next steward and head of the privy council, they trust ye, Halden. And ye're almost an elder."

After word of Halden's impromptu meeting spread through the square, people gathered near a pile of stone that had replaced the well. Four elders stood next to Halden.

"Kind people of Strawbridge, we suffered more loss than

anyone should ever have to endure. We lost more family and friends in a single day than in my lifetime and yours combined. I know we're all mourning and trying to make sense of something—" Halden stopped to clear his throat. "We're all trying to make sense of something that can never make sense. But our family and friends need us to do right by them. We need to pull ourselves together and send our loved ones home."

Lisette's heart broke for Halden and the people of Strawbridge, whose pain and suffering filled the square alongside their fallen. She watched as Halden struggled to maintain his composure.

The elder closest to Halden placed a hand on his shoulder. "Many of us have known this man our entire lives. We will rebuild Strawbridge with the same stones they destroyed. And as we build anew, those stones will not only remind us of the ruin inflicted by the one-horned monsters but of our ability to overcome. Today, we will begin the path to recovery by returning our fallen to Mother's loving hands, so they too may rise to overcome."

The townsfolk spent their day fulfilling the men's brave words. They finished wrapping loved ones in their best blankets before bringing them to their final resting place. A sea of colour spread across Forest Hills. More than two hundred people had been lost in the attack.

Saplings lay on the ground next to the massive burial site. The town's people had agreed to plant one sapling for every ten buried and a winter's flower for each of their loved ones. It was the largest known service in Strawbridge history and lasted until dark. When every man, woman and child had been laid to rest, Lisette returned to the manor with Halden and the townsfolk. Tomorrow, they were leaving for Kingsbridge. Passing by what remained of the manor's dovecote, Lisette decided it was time to resolve the matter of Melvin's treachery.

Lord Stanley raised his head as everyone drifted into the hall and signalled to Halden. Lord Aurik and Harmony were sitting with him.

"Do ye mind if I speak with him as well?" Lisette asked Halden.

"Not at all. Lord Stanley welcomes your company. And Lord Aurik likes what be good for Lord Stanley."

Leaving Amelia with Geoffrey, Lisette accompanied Halden. Harmony jumped up to wrap her arms around Lisette.

"Your smile brightens my heart, Miss Harmony."

"Uncle Stanley and Uncle Aurik said ye were here, but I was asleep."

"Tis true, and I didn't want to wake ye, little one. Ye must've been very tired."

Harmony nodded. "Uncle Stanley be tired too. He's been in bed for days."

"Adults can be funny sometimes. I bet he'll be up in no time and better than ever." Glancing at Lord Stanley, Lisette noticed how pale he looked. "Now, why don't ye go find Agnes? She could use some of that sunshine." She gave Harmony another hug. "I promise to come and say goodnight."

Halden was still filling their lords in on the day's events. Lisette took advantage of the distraction to gather her composure. The day had taken its toll on everyone. Some were already settling down for the night, ignoring the servants circulating with food and ale. Their lords insisted on keeping everyone fed. Fortunately, most of the manor's granaries were still intact along with the kitchen and its adjoining stores.

"I knew ye were a leader, Lisette," Lord Stanley said after

Halden had finished. "I saw it in your eyes. Ye have a rare gift and must learn to embrace it." He studied her for a brief moment and managed a weak smile. "I believe ye will once ye have the proper guidance."

"Ye give me too much credit, my lord," Lisette replied. "But the people of Strawbridge must be praised for their courage."

"And so they shall be." Lord Stanley's chest rattled. "Halden said ye're leaving us tomorrow. Will ye be travelling to Northbridge?" He searched Lisette's eyes.

Lisette wished she could say yes. "I hope to make the journey after Kingsbridge. But King Eldridge may have other plans for us."

"The slaughter will not stop with Strawbridge." Lord Stanley struggled to breathe. "Ye will need to persuade him of the threat. Seek the queen's help if ye must. King Eldridge adores my aunt."

"Melvin Dunstan accused us of murder, my lord." Lisette went on to explain the ambush and Elmer's death. "He was struck down in self-defence, but without a witness to the contrary, we may end up with our necks inside a rope."

Lord Stanley cringed. "That man has never been up to any good. He returned to Strawbridge with the same noxious claim. The elders warned him about making false accusations and advised him to remember what happened more clearly. He disappeared without duty clearance two days later. Then the attack happened."

Lisette sent a silent word of praise to the elders. And for the first time since arriving in Strawbridge, she thought about the elders of Stonebridge, fearing for their safety. She shuddered at the thought of them encountering a karupa.

"That explains why he went missing," Halden said. "I should've known he was up to something."

"King Eldridge sent a message requesting the elders' counsel at his table, but I noticed the dovecote was nearly destroyed," Lisette said to Lord Stanley.

"Thanks to the servants' quick actions, several of the pigeons were saved. Although I haven't received the message ye speak of." Lord Stanley was ashen by now.

"Perhaps a willing elder could accompany us to Kingsbridge?" Lisette ignored the guilt tugging her heart. If only her question had not arrived on the tail of such tragic circumstances.

"Several elders are staying here at the manor. Ye're welcome to speak with them. They have proven themselves a brave lot over the years."

Two elders agreed to make the journey to Kingsbridge. Mr. Cook and Mr. Tanner were happy to accept. Lisette remembered Mr. Cook from Calder's burial ceremony. Both men were widows and well into their sixties. Mr. Tanner had lost his wife during the attack and saw the journey as a means to escape his grief.

"My dear wife would tell me to go. She believed in justice for all," Mr. Tanner said. "Melvin's actions dishonour his poor father. May he rest in peace, ignorant of his son's disgrace."

Before their departure the next morning, Lisette went to see Lord Stanley. To her continued dismay, Lord Stanley's health still showed no signs of improvement. Lord Aurik sat by his husband next to Harmony. Lisette hugged her young friend and said farewell to the people she had grown to care about and admire.

"Remember what I said, Lisette," Lord Stanley said before she left. "We cannot allow those monsters to destroy us."

"The Seekers and I will return someday, and the threat to our people will be no more," Lisette replied.

Chapter 26

ll five kept an ear to the forest as they made their way to Kingsbridge. Neither traveller's experience with the beasts suggested they were stealthy by design or purpose. The karupas feared nothing or no one. Save for Mhutig, the only threat to their deadly power was back in Krousus. And Mhutig had become a prisoner in the hands of those he vowed to save.

"The villagers will need to salvage what be left of the harvest," Mr. Cook said on the third day of their journey, "or hunger will finish what those monsters started." He looked unhinged, like a door forced open once too often.

"You could plead your case with the king," Amelia reassured him. "Isn't it the king's responsibility to ensure the safety of his people?"

"In Wrunwicks, tis the people's duty to obey their king."

"It'll be difficult to perform any duties with hungry stomachs." Amelia leaned forward. "What do you think, Geoffrey?"

Geoffrey glanced at Amelia. "The king provides for his people."

Lisette mentally rolled her eyes at the familiar phrase. She had yet to see any evidence of it. The people worked to provide for themselves and their lords, who provided a regional wron to their king. In return, lords enforced peaceful order through their elders. And the king kept an army of knights to protect his people. It was an accepted system that had long since been taken for granted. Only there was no army, not in the last hundred years.

"If I were younger, I'd show those monsters a thing or two," Mr. Tanner said defiantly.

Lisette smiled. She liked the two elders. They were charming and unaffected by their titles. "Were there any opowaks with the karupas, Mr. Tanner?"

"Aye. There was one. The strange thing was, he didn't attack, just stood around watching the karupas and shouting at them."

"Shouting? Karupas can talk?" Lisette asked. Having only heard a karupa speak once, she assumed them incapable of communicating. At least not beyond that single word: humans, the target of their blood hunger and unfathomed hate.

"Mostly just loud guttural noises from what I heard. But the opowaks seemed to understand."

"We've often asked ourselves if those awful noises were the sounds of a senseless beast or something else," Amelia said.

They had not glimpsed a single monster since leaving Strawbridge. The sun had yet to set and rise one last time, and only then would Kingsbridge appear on the horizon to bolster Lisette's spirits. She looked to the grey sky, but it was of no use with the thick canopy of trees. When they reached an open clearing, she pulled out her knife and twisted the blade until the sun's shadow was no more than a thin line. She guessed they had about ten miles or so to go before sunset.

Geoffrey pointed to a man riding toward them. The man's slow speed meant his wagon was full. As the man drew closer, Geoffrey informed them he knew the trader and swung his arm in recognition.

"Tis Solomon. He passes through Kingsbridge this time each year. Ye can mark the beginning of harvest by his visit." Geoffrey sounded proud of his ability to relay the information. He gestured toward the small stream near their path. "Let's move over to give him some room."

Solomon waved and picked up the pace, causing his wagon to tilt dangerously as he came round a turn. "I thought I was finally in trouble there for a bit," he said, pulling up alongside their horses.

"Fooling around as usual, old friend," Geoffrey said. "Might ye be on your way to Strawbridge?"

"Tis my next stop. And I heard in town that ye were charged with a most important task, although everyone was a little stingy on the details."

Lisette liked the trader immediately. During Geoffrey's hasty introductions, Solomon had simply extended his hand to each of them, appearing not to notice anything unusual about her riding outfit or Amelia's ears and pale skin. While people mostly kept their opinions to themselves, strangers often regarded the women with upturned brows.

"I fear ye won't find Strawbridge as ye last saw it," Geoffrey said gravely. "Tis a tragic time for its people." He recounted the attack on Strawbridge, all the while keeping a protective eye on the elders.

Solomon whistled softly after hearing the story. "I knew it was bad, but I didn't know just how bad."

"Come. Break some bread with us and share our ale, brave friend. We're stopping for tonight."

Lisette looked over to check on the elders. They looked painfully tired, despite their repeated assurances to the contrary. They insisted on not slowing them down as they travelled every day past dark. Rest would do the elders some good. She patted Daisy's shoulder. The long days were hard on the horses too. She looked forward to giving the mare a much-needed break when they reached Kingsbridge.

Lisette had never seen Geoffrey so relaxed or receptive, listening to Solomon chat about his family and life back home.

"I think my mother has given up on me taking a wife," Solomon said while chomping down on some cheese. "She says I'll grow to be a lonely elder with no one to visit or care for me."

Geoffrey laughed complaisantly. "I'll visit ye with my wife and many grandchildren. Ye can tell them stories about when ye were a young and daring trader."

"Barring any problems, I'll be in Highbridge again this year for the wine-crushing celebration. Ye can't change a man's nature."

"The king'll be in need of that wine after the harvest festival. He always drinks too much, claiming tis for a good cause."

Solomon's eyes glowed with merriment. "His stomach be the reigning cause of that."

"Tis true. The king has a fondness for the wines of Highbridge. He says they're the best in Wrunwicks."

"A fact the good people of Highbridge will readily share with ye whenever they get the chance," Solomon replied.

Lisette and Amelia exchanged a bemused look. This wasn't the man they knew. Nor was he the man who had insulted Aspen with such arrogance or regarded them with such unbridled suspicion. Lisette could not help but wonder which Geoffrey was the real one.

"Ye've already been to Kingsbridge?" Lisette asked Solomon.

"I have, m'lady. They're looking forward to the harvest festival."

"Did ye hear of any elders from Strawbridge?"

"From Strawbridge? Not that I recall. But I did hear of visiting elders. They're staying at the castle. I also heard about the prisoners in the castle cellar. Friends of yours?"

"We've been wrongfully accused of murder. I'm returning to clear our good name."

Solomon tilted his hat toward Lisette. "A most heinous and vindictive accusation, m' lady. The owner of such an accusation clearly wishes ye dead. May our Mother favour ye and your company."

"She has yet to steer me wrong." Lisette prayed Utaika would not choose this instance to forsake her or her friends.

The next morning at dawn, Solomon bid his hosts a safe journey before setting out for Strawbridge. Geoffrey cautioned his friend against the karupas.

"Sleep with one eye and both ears open," Geoffrey advised. "If ye hear anything, don't linger. Karupas are soulless creatures who would feast on the heart of our Divine Mother."

"I'll share news of our meeting with the people of Strawbridge," Solomon assured the travellers and left to make good on his word.

Chapter 27

hey reached the highlands of Kingsbridge overlooking the fields and Mukita River. Lisette turned to Amelia and smiled in relief. They had arrived unharmed. And with the elders' testimony, their friends would be released from the king's prison. She felt it in her bones, true as the mountains. Lisette filled her lungs with the cool winds of harvest. The growing season had come and gone unnoticed, and as they rode toward the castle, Lisette felt a surge of renewed strength.

Their group followed Geoffrey past the gate and into the castle courtyard. Two young grooms met them and took their horses. A servant came to escort them to the tower. Geoffrey forewent the meeting to go in search of William but assured the servant he'd speak with their king before the day was over.

Inside the round hall, King Eldridge waited with his elders at the large centre table. Upon seeing them, the king rose from his seat. Another servant left his post next to the king and ushered them across the chamber. The elders rose alongside their king.

"Welcome to Kingsbridge, wise elders." King Eldridge pointed to a set of empty chairs by Master Furlow. "Please, join us at the table. We have anticipated your arrival with great pleasure and look forward to your company." He shifted his attention to Lisette and Amelia. "Welcome back, Seekers. None the worse for your travels, I see."

There were also two elders from Stonebridge at the table, Mr. Walling and Mr. Brewers. The sight of Mr. Walling danced its way straight to Lisette's heart. The elder's kind soul had transformed an impossible idea into reality. And thanks to Mr. Walling's help, they had learned the face of their enemy.

"How was Lord Stanley?" the king continued. "Queen Harriet be most anxious to hear of his health."

"He was badly injured in the attack on Strawbridge, my king," Lisette replied. "But he was in good spirits and sends his respect to ye and our queen."

"What of Strawbridge? How did it fare in the attack?"

"The monsters have left their mark on the town, and much of it will need to be rebuilt, my king. I've never witnessed so much destruction. The brave people of Strawbridge mourn their loved ones who were slaughtered by karupas."

"Its people are strong and resourceful. I have no doubt they will recover with time." King Eldridge looked to the elders of Strawbridge. "It be with great honour that I invite ye to join our council. The journey gets longer with the passing of years. But first, allow me the pleasure of referring to ye by name, wise elders."

Mr. Cook and Mr. Tanner introduced themselves. The elders of Stonebridge and Kingsbridge introduced themselves in turn. Seated or standing, the ten elders formed an imposing group. Dressed in their robes of fine wool, oversized hats with their symbolic feathers of truth, and silver pendants bearing the swords of justice, the men rose above every court in the land. They were the court.

Standing before their king and elders, Lisette knew she should wait for King Eldridge to broach the matter, but her friends' health far outweighed her need for better judgment. "The Seekers, my king. When may I see them?"

"Mr. Walling speaks highly of your fearless spirit, Lisette. He also informs us that ye and your friends are of the finest character known to him, incapable of the charge brought against ye. So with Mr. Walling's recommendation, the Seekers were released awaiting another matter. We will consult with Mr. Tanner and Mr. Cook concerning Melvin."

Her friends were free! Lisette fought to maintain the semblance of composure. "Another matter, my king?"

"Mr. Brewers tells us that ye allowed a woman to consecrate your friend's burial, which took place without his father's knowledge or permission. In so doing, ye deprived the young man's father of the right to honour his son and family, a deliberate and shameful act."

Lisette's mind reeled from the accusation. "If I'm the one being accused, what charge has been brought against the others, my king?"

"Your friends would have been aware of your wrongdoing but failed to stop ye nevertheless. The father requests to know why."

Lisette and Amelia left the castle in search of their friends. While Kingsbridge looked like every other township with its colourful stone houses and cobbled roads, the town distinguished itself by its sheer size. Lisette estimated it to be at least four times bigger than Strawbridge and a good six times bigger than Stonebridge. This evening, the town's streets were empty. The grain moons required everyone on field duty before winter's first frost.

As they rode to the stable behind Deidrik's house, the spicey aroma of Bertha's mouthwatering pottage wafted through an open window. The stable was empty. Lisette coaxed Daisy into a stall and gave her some water from the barrel outside. Amelia returned Deidrik's mare to her stall and gave her a drink. Bertha ran out to greet them, wiping her hands in the same blue apron she had worn the night they met.

"My, my. Ye be a welcome sight for these old eyes, m'lasses. Let's get ye inside. There be plenty of ale to quench your thirst. Tis a good thing I put on extra for supper."

Lisette hugged the woman with a heart bigger than either of them. "What would we do without ye, Bertha?"

"I knew there was a reason I liked ye, my dear Lisette. And now in ye go for a bite."

The house smelled of crisp harvest air, vegetables, rabbit, and custard pie. Inside the kitchen, a pot simmering over the fire was large enough to fit five rabbits. The floors were swept clean with a fresh layer of sage, and the table was laden with enough bowls and trenchers to feed several families. Bertha stirred the pottage, retrieved a trencher from the pile and filled it with cheese, then poured them all a mug of ale. Lisette sat next to Amelia in front of the trenchers and oversized bowls. Bertha went back to check on the pottage.

"I expect ye be wondering where your friends be to. They've been staying here since the king let them go yesterday."

"King Eldridge filled us in on their release," Lisette replied. "We hoped they came here with Deidrik."

"Aye. After being cooped up in that cellar, Deidrik invited them to join him in the fields. As the court painter, Deidrik be exempted from duty, but he likes to help out whenever he can. A day in the fresh air will do them all some good."

"It looks like you have on enough for an entire army, Bertha." Amelia examined the pot. "Is that rabbit pottage, I'm smelling? I swear you can smell it all the way down the street."

"Tis, dear lass. I'll have three houses in need of a hot supper when the bell rings. The elders decided my skills be best saved for kitchen duty this year. Their way of saying I be too old to work in the fields. The small coin they offer in return goes toward extra meat and fish for the families."

"My nose says that'll be three lucky houses." Amelia helped herself to a piece of cheese. "The smell is making me hungry."

"That man from Strawbridge be up to no good, going to the tavern every night he be and telling anyone who'll listen ye killed his friend. Most don't pay him either mind. All bark and no teeth, they be saying."

"In Krousus, we call them foncors, fools of no cause or reason."

Bertha tee-heed, clinking her ladle against the pot as she stirred. "He must be worth a few foncors at least."

Lisette pictured a toothless Melvin barking like a wild dog. The image struck her as absurd and more than a little accurate. "I hope he barks at the wrong person this time." Lisette then explained what happened in Strawbridge, concluding with the elders' visit. "It be up to them now."

Bertha placed a hand over her chest. "May our Divine Mother guide their steps and ours."

The Seekers must have received word of Lisette's and Amelia's return, crashing through the door in their eagerness to confirm the news. With cheeks coloured by the wind, the Seekers hugged their friends among hoots of joy. Shaking her head in disapproval, Bertha ordered everyone out to the back tewk, warning them not to return until their hands were scrubbed clean. Deidrik lingered to ask about his sister and her family. Lisette rushed to inform him of their safety and good health. The relief in Deidrik's eyes filled her with thanks to Utaika.

Bertha sent the last field workers home for supper. After a day of reaping wheat, the Seekers were already wolfing down the pottage.

"I suppose ye heard about Calder's father?" Ewart asked.

"We have to be at the castle tomorrow morning, but I'm not sure what it can accomplish," Lisette replied. "We did our best in the situation."

"I had a feeling it would come back to bite us," Henry said. "We had no right to make that decision for Calder's family."

"We can't change what's been done. And Mr. Reed's opinion can't change it, no matter how upset he be." Lisette didn't want to argue with Henry again. They had argued the issue on at least two separate occasions. Twice was more than enough.

Henry sighed in exasperation. "No, but it could change what becomes of us."

Lisette looked around the table at her friends. Their group had been through so much together in the past few moon cycles. They felt more like brothers and sisters to her now than ever before. "I'm sorry to have dragged ye all into this. It was my idea."

"I could've said no," Aspen replied. "But I wanted to do it. I don't expect ye to take responsibility for my actions."

"Mr. Reed's anger might be tempered by a ceremony in his son's honour without an actual burial," Mhutig suggested.

The others gazed at Mhutig, chewing on the idea. At this point,

Lisette was willing to try anything to make amends. As much as she hated admitting it to herself or Henry, a part of her still felt guilty. The truth was, she had never asked herself why. Not really. Why did she insist on Aspen being head of ceremony? It was unfair to forbid her the honour, but was that the only reason? And who was she to flout a time-honoured tradition, regardless of the reason?

"It might be the perfect solution," Florette said, placing her hand on Lisette's. "Mr. Reed could save his family's honour, and we'd be left in peace, knowing we acted out of love for Calder."

"After your departure yesterday, it came to my attention that young William did not return with ye, Lisette," King Eldridge said.

Lisette sat with her friends in the great hall facing the elders, Calder's father, Melvin, and Vincent. Lisette's jaw slammed shut when she spotted Vincent at the table next to Mr. Brewers, his grandfather. The smug look on Vincent's face told Lisette he was up to no good. Her hand itched. Melvin and his kind had drained the last of her patience bone dry. She was done with the foncors of Wrunwicks.

"He turned around after our encounter with the karupa, my king," Lisette replied. "He should have returned by now."

"It seems that death and destruction follow in your wake. And now it would seem that one of my men has vanished, along with the grievous loss of two fine horses."

Lisette made a note to speak with Geoffrey. She had not laid eyes on him since their return yesterday. "Karupas know no mercy, my king. If allowed, they will destroy our land."

"But here we are, alive and well. Why haven't they attacked more towns or villages?"

"Please forgive my bold tongue, King Eldridge. If there was any doubt before, there can be none at present. Karupas have somehow joined forces with the opowaks, possibly making them even more deadly," Amelia asserted.

"I was born into a war that continues to rage between taupaks and opowaks," Mhutig added from his end of the table. "A war that has never included karupas. However, when we observed their camp at Metterling Mountains, the opowaks appeared to have found a way to control karupas. A union between the two will prove challenging for Krousus and devastating for Wrunwicks."

King Eldridge removed his crown and stared at it. The famed headpiece was made of thick silver and rare stones. "This thing will be the death of me. Made to fit a child's head, but it pleases Queen Harriet." He reluctantly put the obscene decoration back on. "Speculation serves us no good, Mhutig. If what ye say be true, what hope do we have of defending ourselves?"

"To defeat this enemy, you will need the full strength of your people. Even then, there will be much loss to Wrunwicks."

"With harvest upon us, tis unlikely the people will pay much heed to such a remote threat. We will revisit the matter at a later time." King Eldridge turned to Mr. Reed. "Today, we must address the injustice perpetrated in the name of convenience. But first, let us enjoy a morning meal. I cannot think on an empty stomach."

After pleading a lack of appetite, Lisette went in search of Geoffrey. She found him in the stables tending to one of the horses. Unaware of her presence, he spoke quietly to the animal. Lisette remembered seeing the same gentleness in Strawbridge. It was a quality he took great pains to hide from those around him.

"Ye have a way with the horses it seems," Lisette said, smiling. Watching Geoffrey as he brushed down the horse provided a much-needed break from the stifling tension inside the great hall. Theirs would be a long day.

Geoffrey straightened to peer over the stall gate. A sudden smile spread across his face. It was quickly replaced by his characteristic scowl. "My father worked in these stables and his father before him. Six generations ago, my grandfather was a knight in the army of King Lazoran II. He helped lead the king's army to victory during the Salt Wars."

"Quite the family lineage. I've only read about the wars. I've never actually met anyone related to the famous army."

Geoffrey shrugged off her comment. "It means little to nothing to the people of Wrunwicks nowadays, except as stories passed down by our elders. But it does afford me some leniency, like riding with ye to Strawbridge and overseeing the stables."

"The king said William never made it back to the castle. Have ye heard anything from the servants?"

"They assume he vanished like the rest of them."

"What do ye think as his friend? Do ye think he vanished?"

Geoffrey looked thoughtful. "He would never disappear on his own. Thanks to Master Furlow, he be already set to join the privy council in eldership."

"The king's steward?" Lisette asked, frowning at the memory of Master Furlow's expression when King Eldridge had announced William's absence. The master steward looked ready to throw her in the cage himself.

"Aye. That'd be the king's most trusted elder, as I'm sure King Eldridge told ye by now, and William's grandfather. He doesn't say too much usually. At least not outside of the king's ears."

"Let's hope William finds his way back soon, then. We've lost too many good people already."

"That we have. And I fear we'll lose more yet. Those monsters are up to something. Mark my word."

When Lisette returned to the great hall, servants were clearing the last remnants of the morning meal. King Eldridge seemed a little more relaxed than he had before her departure, although Lisette placed no faith in his better mood. The king struck her as someone who could plunge his sword in a man's heart with one hand while the other held one of his ornate goblets of wine. She disliked their king and, try as she might, could not share people's trust in him.

King Eldridge sat strumming his fingers on the table, lost in thought. The elders waited quietly for their king to begin. Master Furlow wore a dark gloom on his face. Mr. Cook and Mr. Tanner offered Lisette a warm smile. She hoped they would find a chance to discuss the matter of Strawbridge with the king.

"Now that we are all back, what do ye have to say concerning the circumstances surrounding your friend's burial, Seekers?" King Eldridge fixed his gaze on Lisette, worming a hole through a spot just above her nose.

"Calder was given a hero's ceremony in Strawbridge. He rests next to lords, their elders, and the knights of old," Lisette replied.

"Why did ye think it fitting to choose Aspen as consecrator?" King Eldridge asked.

"It seemed like the best choice at the time, my king," Lisette said feebly. She suspected there was no answer that Calder's father would accept. "Calder and Aspen were very close."

"Closer than the rest of ye? It hardly seems likely. Why not ask one of these fine young men to bless the ceremony?"

And there it was. The question Lisette had dreaded. She snuck a quick look at Mr. Reed. He sat clenching his fist in ill-suppressed rage. "I failed to consider the consequences for his family, my king."

"If I may," Mr. Cook interjected. "As one of the elders who presided over Calder's burial, my king, I can assure ye that he will be remembered alongside the heroes of Strawbridge. I can think of no greater legacy for his family."

"That and the knowledge his ceremony was consecrated by a woman. She isn't even kin, my king. She be no more than a friend." Mr. Reed's voice rose steadily with each word. "They had no right to dishonour my family."

Mr. Cook looked across the table at Mr. Reed. "Lord Stanley led the procession himself, brave sir. The elders of Strawbridge and the privy council trust his wisdom. Ye will not find a more devout follower of the virtues."

The air in the chamber weighed heavy over the table while the elders waited for Mr. Reed to respond. King Eldridge examined his guest, who sat in rocky silence. Lisette waited for someone to break the tension.

"In Krousus," Mhutig said at last, "when a soldier is lost, the family is compensated to help ease the burden of their loss."

"Coin cannot compensate for my son's death or my family's loss of honour." Mr. Reed's face grew flushed and angry.

Watching Mr. Reed, Lisette feared he would not budge. She could see no way out of the situation. Florette's wings fluttered next to her. Lisette recognized the pattern. They always fluttered erratically when Florette was nervous. Glancing around the table to see how her friends were faring, Lisette recalled Mhutig's suggestion from the night before.

"A second ceremony consecrated by ye would honour Calder and your family," Lisette said, choosing her words carefully so as not to upset Mr. Reed any further. "While Calder may already be at rest, ye could share the story of his bravery with his friends and family back home. It can't change what be done, but it will give ye a chance to pay tribute to his legacy."

Mr. Reed stared unseeing into the emptiness. The rage had been replaced by grief so profound, it was carved into every inch of his face. Observing Mr. Reed in that moment, Lisette realized he was simply a father reacting to a loss outside his control. He had lost his child, the greatest loss of all. A loss she suspected Vincent was manipulating for his own vindictive purposes. She pictured her hand greeting Victor's cheek in the manner it deserved.

"Mr. Reed, your son was a noble and courageous man. Nothing can make up for his death," Lisette began. "Not a day passes that I don't miss him and wish he were still here with us. In my anguish, I acted without thinking or regard for his family. I would take back those actions if I could. The best any of us can do now be to respect his memory."

Lisette kept her eyes fixed on Mr. Reed. There was nothing else for her to say. She had no way of knowing if she would've ever acted differently, but it didn't matter right now. She couldn't undo the past. Mr. Reed sat in silence for a while longer, then slowly, he looked around at the Seekers.

"Ye were all like family to my son. Calder cared little for people's accolades or opinions, but he loved a good story. In the days leading up to your departure, he spoke in earnest of the many stories he would bring home. I will bring my son's story home to share with all of Stonebridge."

"Can we consider the matter of your son's burial to be closed, Mr. Reed?" King Eldridge asked.

"We can, my king." Mr. Reed granted Lisette part of a smile. "I'll give news of your good health to your parents."

Chapter 28

Ewart offered to accompany Mr. Reed to the inn and share Calder's story over a mug of ale. Lisette and the others rode out to the wheat fields. Townsfolk watched with curiosity as they meandered through the busy fields. Lisette guessed word of their meeting had made its rounds. Deidrik looked up as they approached and cut into the wheat with a well-practised swing of his scythe. When his team finished the strip of land they were reaping, he threw down his scythe and ran over to them, jumping over piles of wheat along the way.

"I take it the meeting was a success. Ye didn't come out to share more bad news, I hope," Deidrik said with a sweaty grin.

Aspen explained what happened at the meeting. "It seems we've avoided the cage once again," she said, smiling at her joke.

"Then maybe ye'd like to help out here. Old Fenwick could sure use a break." Deidrik threw a quick look at one of the men on his team. "He be too stubborn to accept his rightful place among the elders. Other teams wouldn't mind ye lending a hand either."

"I'll see if Hattie could use some help," Aspen said eagerly, turning to Lisette. "I'll introduce ye to the team. They already know me and Florette."

Hattie was working three fields over from Deidrik's. She greeted the newcomers with warm enthusiasm. To Lisette, Hattie appeared no older than either of them. She was also very pregnant. Following the direction of Lisette's eyes, the young woman glowed with joy.

"I must look ready to burst." Hattie rubbed her tremendous belly. "It feels like it today." She placed Lisette's hand on her stomach to feel the baby kicking. "This one wants out."

"When are you expecting?" Amelia asked.

"By the end of harvest if Mother wills it. My first baby was born too soon and didn't live to see her first sunrise."

It was an all-too-common story, a baby born too early and too weak to survive outside the mother's protective keep. Some liked to say it was Utaika's way of caring for the frailest of her children, an explanation that offered no comfort to the grieving mother. And if a woman was fortunate enough to birth as many as four healthy babies, it was by the grace of their Divine Mother, earning a woman the respect of her husband and the entire town.

"The baby's kicks are strong and will bring much love to your family," Lisette said brightly.

"I have a good feeling about this one." Hattie smiled and placed her hand over Lisette's for an instant. "Now, we need to get back to the wheat, and with your help, we should have no trouble keeping up with the reapers. We're missing more workers every year."

Florette had already joined the children to glean any grain left behind by the reapers. She waved to Lisette.

"Because of the vanishings?" Amelia asked Hattie.

"That, and wealthy shopkeepers insisting they be permitted to buy their crop in the same manner as tradesmen. Last year, a few of the shopkeepers got greedy and purchased more than their allotted share. It created a shortage of wheat, barley, carrots, and beans. Many were forced to buy the rest of what they needed for more than the shopkeepers paid the king, we think."

"The king permitted such an unfair practice?" Lisette asked in disbelief. She had never heard of field workers buying crops before.

Hattie nodded in resignation. "So long as shopkeepers are more than willing to pay. In return, the king allows men like old Fenwick to fill the shortage of workers. That poor man should have been declared an elder two years ago, but he insists he can still do the work."

"Praise Mother, there be none of that treachery in Strawbridge."

"Not yet," Hattie replied, "but greed has a way of catching on."

With supper over, Henry bid them a good night and went to find a local tavern. The others declined his offer to share a few mugs. Shortly after Henry left to satisfy his thirst, Florette informed them she needed to go stretch her legs. Midst their looks of concern, she explained that her spirit animal liked to run free on occasion, the same as any other animal. Roy opened the door, reminding her of curfew. Florette assured him she would not be long, or he should send the night watchmen, for it would surely mean disaster. Seeing the nervous expression on Roy's face, Florette kissed his cheek.

"I was only kidding," she said. "No harm will come of me, but I'll veil myself just to be certain." And with that, she disappeared into the night.

Glancing at the candle, Lisette saw there were two scores until the last bell. She asked Bertha about the shopkeepers and Fenwick.

Bertha listened, shaking her head from time to time and

enjoying a liberal mug of ale. "Aye. Tis true," she said when Lisette had finished. "Greedy shopkeepers further the king's appetite for silver, and the rest of us further our lot. Poor Oscar, a cobbler like his father before him, had to borrow coin from the blacksmith. The two have long been loyal friends. No one really knows how it happened, except Oscar and Alek. But happen it did." Bertha tutted her disapproval. "And now his wife said he needs to make enough coin to pay Alek and his dues. As for Fenwick, he'll take his last breath in those fields. I thought I would too. Then word got back to the elders I was slowing down the team." Bertha paused to show them her hands. Her fingers were twisted and knotted from age. "They took one look at these, and that was that."

"An unconscionable practice." Lisette was still in disbelief.

"Shopkeepers see it their way," Bertha replied. "The rest of us do the best we can."

The conversation drifted to the harvest, the upcoming festival, Strawbridge, and inevitably, to the karupas. Bertha loved to talk and showed no signs of winding down. The others mostly listened, happy for her company.

"If those karupas have their way, we'll have a lot more than greedy shopkeepers to worry about," Bertha said.

"The king could learn from your wisdom," Ewart said with a bemused smile. "It feels like we're throwing wool at the wall."

"Lord Stanley suggested that I speak with the queen," Lisette replied, "but I doubt she'd hold court with the likes of me."

"What ye need, lass, be a reason to see her." Bertha stopped, then broke into a wide grin. She looked exceptionally pleased with herself. "Florette told me that ye sewed her outfit. And I happen to know the queen's seamstress. Ye leave it up to me, lass. I'll see to it that ye get your meeting with the queen."

Bertha had scarcely finished speaking when Florette burst through the front door. A bruised and bleeding Henry sat slumped between her wings. His right leg dangled in a useless position.

"I wanted to check on him before returning," Florette said. "When I got to the tavern, I saw Melvin and Vincent beating him with a stone. I resumed my animal form and scared them off. But I was too late. I think they broke his leg."

The men had already bolted from their bench to help Henry. Ewart and Roy carried him to his straw bed near the back tewk.

"He managed to climb onto my back before passing out," Florette said, watching the men carry Henry. "He hasn't said a word."

Bertha returned from up top with a blanket. "He'll be needing to keep warm." She cautiously pulled the blanket over Henry. Straightening, she turned to the men, who were standing over Henry. "Do ye think we should wake him?"

"It may be best to let him sleep for now," Mhutig said. "He's probably in shock from the pain. If he fails to wake on his own, I have some herbs left from the last time."

Lisette scooped some water from the boiler and added the cooler rainwater from a barrel in the back tewk. She also retrieved some washcloths before returning to the kitchen. "We can clean his face while we're waiting." She wiped the dried blood from Henry's face. A small gash over his eye and another one next to his left ear were still bleeding. The left side of his face was swollen. Lisette wiped the last blood from his lips. Next, she ripped another cloth to cover the deeper wounds. As she placed a rag over his ear, hate erupted somewhere inside her. She drew strength from its rage.

"We'll need to alert King Eldridge and the elders," Roy said. "For their sake, Henry's leg best not be broken."

"Those two are more trouble than the karupas," Ewart replied. "We should never have let Henry go out alone."

"Was there anyone around, Florette?" Deidrik asked.

Florette sat guard in front of the door. If someone were to enter the house, they would be met by an immovable black wall. Amelia had joined Lisette next to Henry, who was beginning to stir. His face twisted in pain each time he moved.

"A few left the tavern," Florette said, "but no one paid any heed. Too much ale clouds the eyes."

"I'll request a notice be posted in the square tomorrow. Your word might be enough, but a few more can't hurt," Deidrik replied.

Henry moved his mouth to speak, winced, and closed his eyes, opening them again a moment later. "Those balshaks," he finally said between swollen lips.

"We'll get them," Lisette quickly reassured him.

"My leg be killing me."

"We need to check if it be broken," Roy said. "Those two will stop at nothing."

Henry tried to move his leg and let out a sickly whimper. "On second thought, it might be best to wait."

Back from her search, Bertha laid down a basket with splints, rope, some large wood chips, elder branches the length of a thumb, and one long branch with bite marks. "I reckon this should do the trick until the bonesetter can see to ye," she said, placing a couple of wool cloths and some healing salve next to the basket. "It be from the time I broke my arm in the field. Ye won't be using your leg for a bit, I'm afraid. We need to reset the bone and bind it." Bertha kneeled to inspect Henry's leg. "There be no cause for worry, lad. My husband was a bonesetter with me by his side many a time." She stood up and looked at the Seekers. "I'll need two of ye to help me."

Ewart and Amelia offered to hold Henry while Bertha cut his trousers. No broken bone protruded through the skin, although his leg was bruised and swollen around the knee. Using her fingers as guides, Bertha worked her way up from Henry's ankle, all the while focusing on Henry's face. When she reached just below his knee, Henry wailed in agony.

"I can feel the separation." Bertha instructed Ewart to wrap his arms around Henry and hold his hands. She told Amelia to hold his feet. "I need to push the bone back." She passed Henry the long branch to bite down on. The shorter branches had been hollowed out to serve as splint holders.

Florette walked over from the door and placed her front paw over Henry's shin. A flash no bigger than a baby's fingernail of bright emerald dropped from her paw and into Henry's leg. "That should prevent infection and help his bone to heal. Any more would do him more harm than good."

Bertha pushed the bone back in place and smeared the affected area with salve before covering it with the wool cloths. She glanced over at Lisette. "Ye'll be able to hold the splints for me?"

After Roy kneeled to lend a hand, Bertha placed a series of splints lengthwise over the reset bone, covering the area below Henry's knee. Ensuring that Lisette and Roy were able to hold the splints steady, she strung a short row of elder branches together and laid them across the splints, repeating the process until the splints were almost fully covered. Next, she carefully slid each string under his leg and tied them on the side for easy access. The elder branches fastened over the splints, she squeezed two wood chips between each string and tied a set of ropes from end to end where the elder branches stopped on each side of Henry's leg, pulling the strings together to secure the entire cast in place.

"These might need to be adjusted," she said, inspecting the splints, "but they'll do for now. Tomorrow, I'll be getting ye some healing herbs. The herbalist should have some elderflower for ye." Bertha turned to Florette. "Ye'll have to tell me about that light of yours."

"A pardela's light heals from within but can burn a human from the inside out because of their sensitivity to its power. The drop I gave Henry was too small to hurt him."

"Henry has never been known to suffer from sensitivity," Roy said with a sly grin.

"There be nothing wrong with your hands, Bertha," Lisette said, admiring the cast.

"My husband was the best bonesetter in Kingsbridge, but he liked his drink as much as the next man. So when a poor soul came to us, and my Ernest was feeling his ale, I was the one to take care of it. Nobody minded, and not a single person died."

"Well, we owe ye a depth of gratitude." Lisette squeezed Bertha's hand, then turned toward Florette. "And ye too. A dear friend of my father's died after breaking his leg."

"He'll still need time to heal. Some shock be normal as his body adjusts, but it should subside by tomorrow."

"How did ye know to check on Henry?" Lisette asked.

Florette went to lie down between Henry and the wall behind him. She covered him with one of her wings. "This should help with the shivering." She adjusted her wing before continuing. "Melvin and Vincent are cowards. Men like that prefer to attack when the numbers favour their victory."

"They attacked the wrong man tonight," Lisette replied.

Chapter 29

The castle buzzed with men and women starting their day. Lisette, Ewart, and Deidrik waited inside the rounder for King Eldridge. Neither of them had slept much the night before. Bertha rose before the first bell to catch the only herbalist in Kingsbridge, who was scheduled for duty in the fields.

"Mind ye make haste after your meeting with the king," Bertha had warned on her way out the door.

As luck would have it, King Eldridge arrived just after his guests. He directed them across the hall to the fireplace. It appeared to be his favourite place to hold council inside the chamber.

"To what do I owe this early morning visit?" King Eldridge scrutinized his visitors. "The matter with Mr. Reed be closed."

"Henry was attacked last night by Melvin and Vincent, my king," Lisette said in a breathless rush. "They managed to break one of his legs before they were scared off."

King Eldridge warmed his hands near the fire. "A most heinous turn of events. Scared away, ye said?" He turned to them once more.

Ewart informed King Eldridge how Florette had scared off the men after she discovered them attacking Henry in the street. As the king listened, his initial curiosity gave way to doubt. Noticing their king's dubious expression, Lisette realized they had never told him about Florette's ability to transform.

"I fear, my king, that we failed to mention Florette's unique skills," Lisette said and explained the nature of Florette's powers.

"She will have to demonstrate for me," King Eldridge asserted gruffly. "In the meantime, I can have the men brought before the elders for judgment. Did anyone else witness the attack?"

"I did, my king," Lisette blurted out. She avoided the men's eyes. There would be time to explain her deception later.

"I will let the elders know. An unfortunate situation, indeed. Henry will stay at the castle where he will receive the best food and wine to aid in his recovery. The princess has taken quite a shining to your friend and will no doubt insist on it along with our queen."

Lisette wondered how the princess could have possibly taken a liking to Henry. To her knowledge, they had only met once. Not that it mattered. She knew it would appeal to Henry's ego. He fancied himself quite the charmer, though many a maiden fancied otherwise. She smiled at the thought of Henry sharing his story upon their return to Stonebridge. But why? Why, in the name of Utaika, would their king invite Henry to stay at the castle? The question baffled Lisette.

"We will inform Henry of your generous invitation soon as we return, my king," Lisette replied with the respect such an honour was due. An inconceivable honour for a commoner.

Upon their return, Lisette shared the incredible news. Recovered from his initial astonishment, Henry chuckled with satisfaction.

Bertha had returned with enough elderflowers to last Henry a good fortnight. When Ewart questioned the cost, Bertha informed him that her late husband had sent many of his patients to the herbalist over the years. To show his gratitude, the herbalist never charged her full coin.

"It seems I may have some luck with the maidens, after all," Henry said with a wolfish grin.

"The elderflower can help with your fever, not the heat in your blood," Bertha teased.

"Far be it for me to crush your hopes." Lisette sat down next to Henry. "But I don't understand how the princess could've taken such a liking to ye."

Henry scrunched his lips together for a moment, then chuckled softly. "Our dear Lisette, never one to hold back. My charm isn't enough?"

"Your charm isn't the question. I can't help wondering about the king's motives, tis all."

"Princess Rosalyn came to visit us many times while we were in the cellar. She wanted to ensure our good health and even brought food on occasion after discovering the hunger rations provided by the castle."

"Tis well fixed the princess be willful," Bertha said, stirring the evening's pottage. "Princess Rosalyn be two years past the age of marriage and still hasn't taken a husband. Without an heir, tis said Queen Harriet's nephew will assume reign after the king's death."

"King Eldridge has no family of his own?" Ewart asked from the table where he was enjoying a mug of ale with the others.

"None that be known," Bertha replied. "King Eldridge be a proud man and never speaks of such matters."

Lisette wondered if the nephew in question was Lord Stanley.

He would make an excellent king. Wrunwicks could use a ruler with compassion.

"Did ye ask King Eldridge about posting a notice looking for witnesses?" Bertha continued.

"We didn't need to," Deidrik drawled. "Our dear Lisette claimed to have seen the attack."

All eyes turned to Lisette. She had already shared her reasoning with Deidrik and Ewart on their way back into Kingsbridge. Both men expressed their concern that if found out, she would be thrown in a cage for lying to King Eldridge. The twenty-seventh canon stated that no person shall present false information to the king.

"I didn't want to chance Melvin and Vincent walking away while Henry's leg might never be the same, despite Bertha's skill and Florette's healing light. Who knows what they would've done if Florette hadn't shown up when she did? They deserve to pay."

Florette finished washing the plates and flew to sit on the table by Lisette. "Revenge favours no one in their dreams." She placed her hand on Lisette's. "The cost be steep."

"If it means justice for Henry," Lisette said quickly, "I'm willing to accept that cost."

"Don't I get a say in this?" Henry asked. "Tis my leg that was broken."

"What be done can't be undone." Lisette hoped they would come to understand. Some men didn't deserve to be free. "I take full responsibility for my actions. Soon it'll be no more than a bad memory."

"Except for Melvin and Vincent," Ewart pointed out.

"Enough of this dreariness. When do I leave for the castle?" Henry asked.

"King Eldridge will send a cart later today," Lisette said, more than happy to change the subject.

"I almost forgot, Lisette," Bertha interrupted, "but I spoke to Doris on my way home. She said that ye can help carry the samples for Queen Harriet's approval. Ye be going tomorrow."

A cart stopped in front of the house before supper. Lisette went with Deidrik to greet the carters. The two men jumped down and introduced themselves, then pulled a wooden plank from the back of the cart. Lisette noticed that fresh straw and a blanket had been carefully placed on the bottom. Deidrik escorted the men inside.

"I'm not a cripple," Henry protested when he saw the plank. "I still have one perfectly good leg to get me around."

"King Eldridge insisted that we take all necessary precautions," the man, who had introduced himself as Linus, said sheepishly. "He expects his orders to be followed."

"How do ye propose a man keep his dignity on that thing?" Henry said, scowling at the plank. "King Eldridge must think me a weakling."

"Cheer up, good friend," Mhutig advised. "There's no shame in accepting the help of others. Your caution now will favour you later."

"Ye're not the one being carried out on a wooden plank," Henry retorted.

Lisette shook her head in exasperation at the tell-tell look on Henry's face. She loved him, but he could be stubborn to the point of infuriating when he chose to be.

"Princess Rosalyn will undoubtedly want to come to your aid," Amelia reminded Henry. "What better means to recovery than with the beautiful princess by your side."

"The princess may help with your leg, but there be no hope for your sour temper," Roy said, teasing his friend.

The carters listened with helpless expressions. They had politely refused Bertha's offer to sit and enjoy a mug of ale, opting to stand by the door instead while holding the upright plank between them.

"Are they always like this?" Linus asked Deidrik, who sat with a mug of ale in his hand.

"For as long as I've known them." Deidrik raised his mug in a cheerful salute.

Florette flew over to sit between Henry and Lisette. "We'll visit often."

Linus gripped the plank a little tighter. "We really should get going. King Eldridge doesn't like to be kept waiting."

"'Tis true, Seekers." Deidrik stretched his legs underneath the table. "We don't want these poor lads forced to explain why they be late for no good reason."

Lisette turned to hug Henry. "I'll check in on ye tomorrow before I leave. Don't drink too much wine, or the king might send ye back. Then ye'll have to put up with us smothering ye some more."

A smile threatened to break through Henry's dark pout. "I barely slept a wink last night, fearing for my life the way ye kept checking on me." He hoisted himself up on his elbows. "Well, men. Let's go. The plank it be, but I hope ye brought a few more men. I'm no lightweight."

As the second bell rang through the castle, Queen Harriet waited in the same chamber Lisette had visited yesterday with Deidrik and Ewart, although the rounder appeared less imposing this morning. The queen stood by the table with a bright smile for her two guests.

Queen Harriet wasn't much taller than herself, but to Lisette, she looked taller than the king this morning. Draped in a pale blue gown with silver leaves stitched along the cuffs and around the hem, the queen exacted the attention of those around her. She was even more striking in person than in her paintings. Lisette studied their queen's gown with admiration. Its simple lines accentuated the heavy silk and its beauty.

Cut down to the waist, the gown's V-shaped neckline exposed the bodice of Queen Harriet's matching blue kirtle of fine wool. The gown's billowing sleeves invited the kirtle to play peekaboo around Queen Harriet's wrists, where the lace cuffs from her smock flared out. Lisette had never seen such white cuffs. And contrary to royal tradition, the queen's dark brown hair flowed free from her crown with its fabled diamond. Presented to Queen Omira in 896, the knight was said to have found the stone on his way home in the low belt. No other diamond of such magnificence had ever been discovered.

"No need to stand there." Queen Harriet waved them forward.

Lisette and Doris bowed and joined the queen. Doris placed her samples on the table. Lisette helped her spread them out for their queen's approval.

During their supper in the great hall, Queen Harriet had been quiet and reserved, seldom uttering a word to anyone. Lisette had taken the queen for gracious but perhaps a little arrogant like her husband. She now saw her mistake. The queen's eyes possessed a warmth and quickness that reminded Lisette of Lord Stanley. The likeness bolstered Lisette's confidence in her plan to enlist the queen's help.

"These colours are exquisite." Queen Harriet ran her fingers over one of the samples.

"They are, my queen," Doris replied with satisfaction.

On their way to the castle, Doris shared that she'd been Queen Harriet's head seamstress for as many years as Lisette was old. Upon her marriage to King Eldridge, the queen arrived from Westbridge with a young seamstress. When the maiden died of a mysterious illness a few years later, the queen posted a notice in search of a new seamstress. Doris gained the honour after Queen Harriet saw the kirtles she was selling at market. Impressed by the quality of her work, the queen entrusted Doris immediately.

"This would go nicely with the gown ye designed for the harvest festival." Queen Harriet held up the swatch made of a dark purple brocade with flowers in a lighter shade of purple.

"Aye, my queen. If I start today, your overcoat will be ready in time for the festival."

"What do ye think, Lisette?" Queen Harriet asked.

To Lisette, it felt as though the queen could see into her soul. "A pleasing choice, my queen." Lisette thought how stunning the colour would look against Amelia's pale skin and silver hair.

"Which colour would ye choose?" Queen Harriet asked.

Lisette examined the different coloured samples. "The yellow would make an impressive gown."

Queen Harriet's eyes settled on the wool. "What better way to beat the fall chill than with such a delightful colour." The queen looked over to where Doris waited. "I see no reason not to have both made. Ye could trim the overcoat with rabbit fur. I despise the rodent furs some would have us think fashionable."

Doris beamed with pleasure. "Wise selections, my queen."

"Now that we've settled the matter, something tells me ye've not come here to help pick colours, Lisette." Queen Harriet's voice was gentle but firm.

The queen's observation presented Lisette with her opening. Having already explained to Doris the true reason for her presence at the castle, Lisette offered the kind woman a reassuring smile. It was now or never. Other than William, there were no new vanishings in Kingsbridge since her return. But peace was an illusion. The devastation in Strawbridge meant that sooner or later, the enemy would strike again.

"I'm afraid not, my queen. I'm here about the karupas. They represent a threat to our entire land, though we've been unable to convince King Eldridge of the need for action."

"I wondered as much." Queen Harriet raised her left brow. She locked eyes with Lisette. "King Eldridge be headstrong by nature. It be his greatest strength. Although sometimes, it be his greatest weakness. He has yet to pass the canon allowing my dear nephew to declare his union with Lord Aurik. I grow tired of waiting."

"Lord Stanley be a patient man." Lisette suspected the king had no intention of passing the canon, but she preferred to keep any doubts to herself and suspected their queen wouldn't think well of her intrusion into the matter.

Queen Harriet paced the floor. She stopped suddenly. "The Knights Memorial be the day after tomorrow. Enough men have signed up for the jousting event, but we still need one more for the sword duels. If one of your friends entered and won, he would earn the king's ear."

"The deadline has long passed," Lisette said, wishing they had arrived sooner. She had to admit it was a brilliant idea.

"Ye leave that to me, Lisette. We've never had a gentleman outside of Kingsbridge enter the events since their inception four years ago. I could advise the king that such an entry would reflect well on his rulership. Do we have an agreement?"

Lisette nodded in amazement. The queen was a woman of quick mind and action. "Remind me to never underestimate ye, my queen."

The following morning, Linus delivered the king's royal invitation:

> A Seeker be hereby invited
> to participate in the ceremonial
> Knights Memorial sword duel.

Lisette shook her head in admiration. The queen was a woman of sound word. She sent back a message of Ewart's acceptance. Over supper the night before, they had decided Ewart should enter the fight. Roy was also an excellent swordsman. But Ewart had more experience, increasing his odds of winning. At the same time, no one thought the queen was likely to succeed in her effort to help them.

"This be an unexpected turn of events," Ewart said as he tore a piece of bread from the trencher. "How exactly does a person win this competition?"

"It be based on a point system," Deidrik said. "The first man to achieve five points wins. Each time your sword touches your opponent, a point be given. Although the rules are simple, I should warn ye that winning won't be easy. Men who enter the competitions practice hard." He paused, looking up toward the bedchambers. "I have something for ye."

Deidrik climbed up top and returned with a sword in hand. "This was my father's. I'd be honoured for ye to wield it."

The sword had a wave-like pattern engraved on one side of the blade. Its grip was further adorned with a large, crisscrossed pattern. Lisette admired the sword's craftsmanship. Decorated swords were rare in the age of peace. The knights of old owned swords with richly designed blades and symbols on the grips to mark their status within the knighthood. But those swords had mostly disappeared into history.

Deidrik handed his sword to Ewart. "It's been in my family for generations, passed on from son to son. It hasn't been used in years. Tomorrow, I hope ye'll put it to good use."

Ewart held the sword, checking its weight. "It be heavier than mine, but it has a good grip. May it bring me luck in duel."

Chapter 30

pectators lined the grounds outside the castle. According to Deidrik, the competitions were growing in size and popularity every year. Townsfolk set up tables to sell pendants in honour of the occasion. A person with coin to spare could buy a pendant with its engraved medallion bearing one of the five symbols representing a knight's foremost virtues: wisdom, truth, justice, hope, and courage. Today, each competitor would celebrate those virtues.

Lisette and Ewart accompanied Deidrik to inform the king of their arrival. He sat with Queen Harriet at the far side of the field. Along the way, Lisette noticed several people already wearing wooden medallions with the two intersecting swords of justice. She mentioned it to Deidrik, who explained that wooden medallions were the most popular with townsfolk due to their cheaper cost.

"We are honoured by your presence," King Eldridge said when they reached him.

"Thank ye for your kind invitation, my king and queen," Lisette said as she bowed in respect. Ewart and Deidrik bowed beside her.

"These competitions are open to the brave men across our land," Queen Harriet said to Ewart. "Ye will be the first to compete outside our township. Perhaps your presence will encourage other young men from Wrunwicks to enter."

"Ye bestow me a great honour, my queen."

"I look forward to watching ye fight." King Eldridge studied Ewart. "Have ye selected your symbol yet?"

"My symbol?" Ewart asked.

"They have become so popular, I decided that each competitor should wear the symbol of their choosing." The king indicated a small table set up a few paces from the rest. "There, ye will find pendants made by one of our most accomplished silversmiths."

"I will wear it with great pride, my king," Ewart said.

"I suggest that ye hurry," the queen said with a quick smile. "The competitions are due to begin soon."

The trio rushed back to where the others were gathered. Amelia teased Ewart about the fact that he was already sweating. Ewart blamed it on the unusual heat for this time of year. Deidrik updated everyone about the pendants.

"I wonder if I get to keep it?" Ewart said jokingly as they hurried over to the table.

"If ye don't lose it first." Aspen poked Ewart in the arm. "Let's concentrate on ye winning for now."

When they arrived, Ewart gazed down at the pendants. A few remained on the table. Lisette admired the intricate details etched into each symbol.

"These are impressive," Roy said to the elderly woman behind the table.

"The king ordered them himself," the woman said proudly. "My husband made every one of the pendants ye see here."

"Your Milton still has the touch," Bertha remarked.

"That he does, old friend," the woman said, watching Ewart. "Which one will it be, kind sir?"

Ewart picked up one of the smaller silver medallions. "I like this one." He turned it around for everyone to see. A sun reached out from the medallion's centre, the symbol of hope. "For Calder, who always preferred sunrises to sunsets." He hung the pendant around his neck.

"For Calder," they echoed.

"And for Henry. May he walk again soon," Bertha added.

A total of twelve men were due to compete, eight men in the jousting tourney and four in the sword duels. Today's events would start with a jousting match. Deidrik briefed them on the rules of the tourney. Each match consisted of five charges across the grassy field divided by a makeshift fence. The goal was to strike your opponent with a lance or unhorse him for a quick victory. Otherwise, victory went to the man with the most points. Lance tips were blunted for the safety of participants. The men also carried shields to protect themselves from a lance's impact.

Continuing, Deidrik explained that when the tourneys began, the shields were wooden replicates of those used by knights. But by year two of the competitions, the wealthier and more competitive shopkeepers who had entered, flaunted more decorative shields made with reinforced strips of iron along with helmets, chainmail hauberks, shoulder, arm and chest plates. The armour provided them with an advantage over their unprotected rival. By year three, only wealthy shopkeepers had entered their names. Blacksmiths fattened their purses as the need for quality armour grew, and the king ordered hauberks for swordsmen to increase participation.

"King Eldridge be not a man to deny opportunity," Deidrik concluded as an elder declared the winner of the first match. "He set a small price for entering the jousting tourney this year. The sword tourney be still free for now."

"Thank Utaika for that," Lisette said. "Our meagre savings and the coin provided by Lord Sumunder be almost gone."

"Tis Geoffrey," Amelia said excitedly. "He be competing in the tourney."

Lisette looked over to where an iron-plated Geoffrey waited to test his skills. His shield was made of spotted wood with an iron frame. The engraving was difficult to see from such a distance. But Lisette could pick out the outline, two swords with a single drop of blood beneath them. A tree stood permanently etched inside the droplet. Together, the shield's emblem symbolized justice, courage, and wisdom.

"Geoffrey be the king's entry. Given his lineage, King Eldridge saw him as the perfect choice to represent the castle," Deidrik said.

"He never shared a word of it," Lisette replied.

An elder waved a flag bearing the royal crest, signalling the match to begin. The men charged across the field. Geoffrey struck his opponent on the shoulder as they passed each other across the fence. Townsfolk cheered as the elder called the first point.

"Geoffrey was never much of a talker," Deidrik said. "I've known him for years, and he be still just as tightlipped now as he was then."

The men charged for the third round. Neither strike in the second round meant Geoffrey led the match 1-0. Both men managed a point as they passed each other across the field. Florette sat on Lisette's shoulder for a closer look. The crowd's enthusiasm was contagious. Lisette clapped as the elder announced both points.

"I suspect there hides a big heart underneath that sour temper of his," Lisette replied.

Deidrik chuckled. "Not many would agree."

The crowd cheered again as Geoffrey's opponent struck him in the arm to even the score in round four. There seemed to be no loyalty among the townsfolk for either man, cheering equally for each strike.

"Not everyone be who they present themselves to be," Florette said, turning to look at Deidrik.

"I suppose that be true," Deidrik said. "I mistook ye for a timid little creature, but the fault was entirely my own."

It was the fifth and final round of the match. Geoffrey charged across the field and struck the man hard just below his chest plate. The man bent over in pain. Geoffrey raised his arms in victory to the sound of more cheers and hoots from the crowd.

Lisette spotted the elders from Strawbridge. They were talking to a small group of men bordering the thick band of jousting enthusiasts. Apart from a few words at the king's table, she had not spoken to either of them since her return. She wondered if they had procured any help for Strawbridge and decided to speak with them. Inside the castle walls, they were constantly surrounded by the king's elders, meaning this might be her only chance away from meddling tongues.

When she informed the others of her intention, Amelia and Roy elected to go with her. The elders took leave of the group when they saw them approaching. Mr. Cook waved them forward.

"Our noble Seekers, it lifts the heart to see ye again." Mr. Cook offered his hand in friendship to all three.

"As it does ours, wise elders," Lisette said warmly. "Please forgive my silence. These are trying times for everyone."

"Indeed they are." Mr. Cook appraised the scene around him. "A fine spectacle in the midst of harvest and the threat that looms over Wrunwicks."

"Ewart entered the sword duel in a bid to gain the king's ear," Roy said. "Maybe then we can persuade the king to act."

"We wish him every success in his effort. As for us, we leave for Strawbridge at morning's first light," Mr. Tanner said earnestly.

"Will you be travelling alone, wise elders?" Amelia asked. "The forest isn't safe for anyone."

Mr. Cook's face brightened. "Young Geoffrey agreed to ride with us once again. We will be safe in his care. He's proven himself to be a man of notable skill and character."

Lisette smiled at the elders. It was clear that Geoffrey had found himself two admirers. An opinion he would undoubtedly dismiss as biddle-babble. For all his faults, Geoffrey did not strike her as a man who was easily affected by praise, deserving or otherwise. "Did the king approve help for Strawbridge?"

"King Eldridge deferred the matter to his council," Mr. Tanner said. "Meanwhile, we tire of waiting. But the people of Strawbridge are strong-minded. They'll find a way."

"Let's hope the council be swift in their deliberations," Lisette replied.

"The people of Strawbridge speak highly of your group, Lisette. May your spirit never be dulled."

The presiding elder announced the winning swordsmen for the last and deciding match. Ewart, son of Walter and Iris Alderon of Stonebridge, would compete against Floyd, son of Saul and Hazel Braxley of Kingsbridge. Both men wore leather hauberks and iron chest plates to protect them from injury. But unlike the engraved, more expensive plates worn by jousters, Ewart's and Floyd's were plain and poorly fitted.

Ewart raised his sword to salute the cheering spectators, then turned to face his opponent. The men shook hands and assumed position within the designated area of the field. The flimsy fence had been removed to make space for the sword matches.

Pausing while the crowd cheered, the elder waited with his flag in midair, standing halfway between the men. The crowd cheered louder. Several moments passed when the elder finally began to lower his flag. Lisette squeezed Amelia's hand. They needed Ewart to win this match.

After winning his first match, Ewart appeared fearless and ready. But Lisette had an inkling that Ewart's cool composure was a mask worn for the sake of his opponent. Ewart had once observed that sword fighting required skill, speed, and misdirection.

Soon as the elder's flag reached his hip, the men began their slow march forward. The flag dropped to the ground. Floyd lunged his sword toward Ewart in an upward flourish. Ewart deftly intersected the sword's blade just below the edge and slid his blade toward the guard on Floyd's sword. The men walked a slow circle.

Floyd managed to disengage, took three steps back, and stopped. Grinning widely, he leaped forward and crossed swords with Ewart. The crowd cheered and clapped. King Eldridge rose from his chair to wave the royal banner in approval.

The men's swords hovered near the ground while they stared each other down, blades locked in an age-old fight for dominance. Finally, with his usual sheepish grin, Ewart freed his sword, and in a wide sweeping motion, he struck Floyd's arm. The elder declared the duel's first point.

Lisette cried out her support along with the cheering crowd.

Ewart and Floyd were proving themselves to be worthy adversaries.

"Ewart certainly knows his way around a sword." Deidrik whistled in admiration. "Floyd's been entering these sword matches since the beginning."

"Has he ever lost?" Roy asked.

"He lost to Geoffrey the first year of competitions. After that, King Eldridge enlisted Geoffrey's skills for the jousting tourneys."

"He be no match for Ewart," Roy said with conviction. "'Tis well known that Ewart be one of the best swordsmen in all of Stonebridge."

"We've been practising for years," Lisette admitted. "It be our secret obsession. So much so that we never thought to bring a single bow on our journey. It was the perfect excuse to carry a sword."

Deidrik looked to see how the men were faring, then turned to Lisette with an amused grin. "Swords don't make good hunting weapons."

"We paid coin where we could and fished the rivers," Lisette said lightly. "Fortunately for us, Mhutig had a bow."

Oblivious to the conversations and cheering outside the ropes, Ewart and Floyd tested each other with a new line of attack. Floyd's sword struck Ewart in the thigh to even the score. Ewart retreated, then advanced with his sword in striking position. Floyd lunged to block the attack, but instead of striking in the direction that Floyd expected, Ewart stepped to the left. And with a broad sweep of his sword, he struck Floyd's forearm. The crowd roared their approval.

"Ye might be right, Roy," Deidrik said. "The king looks worried. Floyd's swordsmanship has gained a lot of support from townsfolk and helped grow the game's popularity. Everyone loves a winner."

"They seem to be loving Ewart right now," Roy said with a smile that grew even bigger when Ewart scored another point.

The men launched a new series of attacks which included a rapid succession of strikes and blocks. Floyd suddenly struck Ewart in the chest. Moving quickly, he encircled Ewart's sword, effectively locking it in place. He reached to grab Ewart's arm. Ewart seized the opportunity to disengage his sword, and following a daring leap to the right, he swooped in to strike Floyd's shin. Floyd retaliated with a loud strike to Ewart's chest, followed by another strike to Ewart's arm. The score was 4-4.

Both men retreated. Ewart advanced with his sword aimed at Floyd's chest. Floyd grinned. When Ewart was about to thrust his sword, Floyd stepped to the left. But unlike earlier, Ewart held his position with a quick-footed set of backhands and forehands, and soon as Floyd stepped to the right, Ewart lunged his sword toward Floyd's shoulder for the winning point.

The game was over. Ewart waved to them in the crowd. Caught up in the moment, Florette flew over to stand on Ewart's shoulder and raised her arms in victory. Townsfolk clapped and cheered all the louder. Lisette looked over at the king. Surprise had replaced the concern Lisette saw earlier. Queen Harriet observed the crowd with near motherly affection. Contrary to her husband, she looked happy with today's outcome.

Most of the townsfolk had left for home. Those who lingered used their time to catch up with friends and chat about the afternoon's events. Tomorrow would see them back in the fields. But for now, they basked in the day's respite from their labours. Some had bought medallions to toast the winners. Lisette noticed several wearing the symbol of hope. King Eldridge was on his way back to the castle when a thump sounded the alarm inside Lisette's head. The distant but all too familiar sound echoed through the forest.

The king stopped. He grabbed Queen Harriet's hand. The chatter around Lisette slowed, then came to an eerie silence. Her eyes widened in fear. For a moment, she had forgotten about karupas and monsters. She searched for Mhutig. They exchanged a brief look of understanding. The fast-marching karupa meant a confrontation was inevitable.

With no time to waste, Mhutig galloped to inform the king of what was happening. King Eldridge summoned all who remained in the field. He shared what Mhutig had told him, urging every man capable of wielding a weapon to claim one from the tower's armoury. The king ordered the women to seek shelter inside the tower's kitchen.

Geoffrey and the other jousters were still in the field along with Ewart and his fellow swordsmen. King Eldridge instructed them to arm for battle. The jousters would attack from their horses with proper swords or lances from the armoury. The rest would attack from the ground.

As men and women disappeared behind the castle walls, Ewart went with Floyd to retrieve their swords from inside a competitor's tent. Lisette and the Seekers ran to the castle behind the townsfolk. Swords were forbidden inside the perimeter of any town or village if staying the night. A canon which Lisette fiercely condemned as she made her way to the armoury.

Inside the tower, Lisette darted around the men hightailing it back to the field. The armoury was in shambles. Dislodged swords, spears, lances, bows, axes, maces, and daggers clanged against the stone floor. A few men stared at the weapons in shocked fear.

"See to the women and children," Roy shouted at the men. "There be enough in the field." He picked up a sword for himself and Mhutig, who waited on the field with the king.

Lisette grabbed the nearest sword. Amelia grabbed the one next to it. Their weapons in hand, they hurried to join Roy and Deidrik. The men had already left the armoury. As she ran across the empty courtyard, Lisette gripped her sword, an image of Calder's lifeless body obscuring her sight.

Townsmen huddled with whatever weapon they had chosen in their panic. King Eldridge and Queen Harriet stood with them. All attempts by the king to persuade their queen to seek refuge had failed. Queen Harriet refused to hide inside the castle tower. Thanks to Geoffrey, the king and queen held a sword each. Lisette held onto hers alongside Amelia. Mhutig stood beside the king.

Lisette scanned the outlying woods. Judging by the loud thump and steady rhythm rising and falling beneath her boots, they didn't have long to wait. The vibrations' hypnotic pulse coursed through Lisette's veins. *At least there be a lot more of us this time.* A quick look suggested they were about thirty or so.

The karupa held its brazen march through the trees. It was no more than a couple hundred feet away at most. Lisette understood the men's fear back in the armoury. Nothing or no one was safe from a karupa's destruction. She glanced around to see how the men were doing now. They looked just as scared and confused. King Eldridge clutched the queen's arm. Lisette saw the determination in his eyes. And for the first time since meeting the king, she felt a begrudging sense of admiration for him.

The men raised their weapons in preparation for battle. Ewart stood next to Floyd. The jousters waited on their horses, swords and lances ready. Mhutig's ears twitched anxiously. Florette had transformed into her animal form to stand with Mhutig.

When the karupa cleared the woods, King Eldridge signalled for the men to hold firm. The lumbering karupa did not see them immediately. Seemingly mesmerized by the watchtowers' billowing flags, it headed straight for the castle.

King Eldridge lowered his hand. "Watch each other's back, and let's kill this balshak!"

The king's voice was lost in the ensuing chaos. Everyone charged toward the karupa, their feet propelled by whatever excitement besieged them. Lisette's heart filled with rage. She would avenge Calder and the people of Strawbridge. When she reached the karupa, Lisette swung her sword with every ounce of might she could muster, again and again.

Breathless, she stood back. The scene before her unfolded like a grotesque nightmare. Florette circled from above, using her paws to pummel the karupa at every opportunity. She swiped its bald head with her long claws. Mhutig and the jousters circled from the ground, striking it repeatedly. From everywhere, the men attacked.

Uttering a loud combination of strange noises, the karupa bent down to push the offenders away, rising next to take a swing at Florette. It managed to fling a couple of men across the field, but they hobbled back. Wedged among their men, the king and queen sliced into the karupa's leg repeatedly.

Florette swooped in and slashed the karupa's eye. Bright red claw marks ran the length of its forehead and nose. The karupa thrashed in pain. Then, with a loud guttural scream, it turned around, swinging its arms through the mob below. Men rolled across the ground. Lisette rejoined the attackers, striking at will.

From the corner of her eye, Lisette saw one of the jousters cut into the karupa's thigh. She plunged her sword into its foot. The karupa tried to push her off, but she jumped to the left, narrowly escaping its hand. Standing on his hind legs, Mhutig thrust his sword into the karupa's chest.

Reeling in pain, the karupa swerved right, blinded and bleeding. The men scattered for safety. The karupa fell to its knees, teetering back and forth before toppling to the ground. The men cheered as the karupa took its last breath. They had defeated the monster.

"Brave men of Kingsbridge, we have slain the beast," the king declared. "In so doing, we have proven our courage and strength against the enemy."

The blood-soaked men raised their weapons in triumph. Those still lying in the field stirred. Ewart went to check on them with Florette, her claws withdrawn from view.

"The karupa's size and spongy skin indicate that it was still young," Mhutig said. "An adult karupa does not bleed so readily."

"Undone by foolish impudence," King Eldridge replied. "Its days of destruction are over."

Ewart gave them a thumbs up. Lisette breathed a sigh of relief. The men's lives had been spared this time. They might not be so lucky if another karupa showed up to test the strength lauded by their king.

"With Mhutig and Florette by our side, we can't lose," a man said. He looked up at Mhutig. "Utaika led ye to us in her wisdom. May she guide our victory."

That night in Deidrik's kitchen, they sat around the table to fill Bertha in on their battle with the karupa.

"It don't sound like much of a battle," Bertha said after they finished. "More like a butchering."

"Ye should've seen the men. Even the king and queen had a go at it. Queen Harriet be a brave woman. And the beast had it coming," Lisette replied. "They've slaughtered enough of our people. Time for us to fight back."

"That they have, lass. Do ye suppose its kin will come looking for it?"

"Karupas rear their young until they are better able to fend for themselves. This one was well past the need for her mother's care," Mhutig replied.

"Maybe the king'll finally see to reason," Bertha said. "That karupa be only the start."

Lisette pictured the karupa. To her, it looked like any other karupa. And she hadn't noticed a difference in its voice, unlike the one that had killed Calder. "How do ye distinguish the males from the females?"

"The females are two or three shades lighter," Mhutig replied. "You learn to recognize the distinction after you have seen enough of them. They are also smaller and shorter."

"I wonder if it was the same one that destroyed the king's horse. It was the same light charcoal grey." Lisette turned to Amelia. "What do ye think?"

"It could've been, although I didn't really get a good look. And it was scarcely light out."

"It can't hurt anyone now, and that be what matters to Wrunwicks," Ewart remarked. "I'm amazed some have enough control over their hands to take prisoners instead of slaughtering them. Every karupa we've met was bent on killing us."

"Any discipline would originate from opowaks," Mhutig said. "We would do well not to underestimate them."

Ewart appeared lost in thought for a moment. "At least the king saw for himself what we're up against."

Chapter 31

Mhutig, Deidrik, and Aspen took their leave to help a few of the king's servants dispose of the karupa. Lisette and the others continued on with Ewart to his meeting with the king. For the rest of Kingsbridge, it was field duty as usual. A dead karupa guaranteed the day's fodder with speculation and truth spun into a hundred different tales by day's end, each new tale a little taller than its predecessor. Lisette's time in Kingsbridge had shown her that people, regardless of where they lived, shared a love of stories. The stranger the story, the better and wider the reach.

Accompanied by Master Furlow, the king and queen greeted their guests from the table in the round hall. Wrunwicks' most well-known couple sat before a breakfast of fruit, cheese, and sweet tartes. Yesterday's winner of the jousting tourney sat with them and held a mug of ale in his hand. King Eldridge never served his prized wine in anything other than one of his obscene goblets.

"Welcome, Seekers." King Eldridge glanced at the shopkeeper. "I trust ye have met Leeland."

"We met briefly in the competitors' tent," Ewart said cordially. "Though I don't think my friends have enjoyed the same pleasure."

Leeland made his way over and bowed with an absurd flourish. "The pleasure be mine, esteemed Seekers. Leeland Bawling at your service, son of Howard and Clara Bawling of Northbridge."

Lisette stifled her amusement. Whether genuine or affected, Leeland's excessive display of respect reminded her of the fabled peacock. Leeland's grin said he recognized the twitch tugging at the corners of her mouth.

"Ye'll have to forgive my eagerness, Seekers. I'm still basking in the glow of yesterday's victories. How often will I be able to boast of defeating my fellow shopkeepers and a karupa on the very same day? We've all heard of the beasts, of course."

"It was a first for us too," Roy said. "Our previous encounter with a karupa ended with the loss of a dear friend."

"My deepest regret for your friend. I can't help thinking that yesterday's encounter be related to the mysterious vanishings. The thought of confronting one of those creatures without the benefit of weapons or friends be the stuff of nightmares."

"Come now, Seekers," King Eldridge said. "Sit and help us eat these fine tartes. Otherwise, I may spoil my afternoon meal."

Lisette had to admit the tartes looked delightful. "Your cooks are very skilled, my king. And we have yet to eat." She smiled politely at King Eldridge. For a man who had looked so unhappy after Ewart's win, he was almost jovial this morning. She hoped the king's current disposition held fast.

"Ye will be relieved to know that Melvin and Vincent were both sentenced earlier this morning and are being escorted to a cage as we speak." King Eldridge took a swig of wine. "Their fate will deter others from breaking a canon under my nose."

The king's ruling hit Lisette with its abrupt pronouncement. She had expected the elders to hold council before the men were caged. "Have the elders left yet?"

"Mr. Cook and Mr. Tanner left before the first bell. The elders of Stonebridge will be leaving soon."

"I'd like to wish them safe travels," Lisette said. "And offer my regards to Mr. Reed."

"Of course. Hogden will notify us when the elders are ready." King Eldridge gestured to a servant and spoke into his ear.

The servant nodded and disappeared through the far door.

"As my first order of business," Leeland began, "I would like to broach the matter of guild fees. I spoke with some of the men last night, and they argue the fees have increased beyond their capacity to pay."

"What exactly would ye have me do?" King Eldridge asked. "Last harvest's increase was the first in three years. A castle cannot run itself."

"The guilds respect your wisdom, my king. The men humbly propose a compromise by decreasing their fees for this year only. They seek the castle's approval to increase the cost of their services. Such an increase would mean more coin for their shops, which can only be good for the castle."

Listening from her seat, Lisette recalled her conversation with Hattie. A service increase could only increase the struggle for those already suffering at the hands of greed.

"Master Furlow and I will discuss your proposal with the privy council before making a final decision." The king turned to Ewart. "And ye, Seeker. Do ye have any concerns on behalf of the good people of Stonebridge?"

"The townsfolk entrusted us with uncovering the truth behind the vanishings, my king." Ewart paused for a moment. "And while we know the karupas are responsible, we have yet to discover why. Or what fate awaits our people. We can, however, be certain of their destructive nature as shown yesterday. Then there be the prisoners to consider."

"We demonstrated our strength against the monsters yesterday. If any others dare to cross our path, we will slay them as well." King Eldridge pounded his fist on the table. "Let them try to destroy us."

"With all due respect, my king, that was one karupa. A young one at that. If the karupas and opowaks decided to wage a true war against us, we will not be able to vanquish them so easily. They demonstrated their strength in Strawbridge."

Queen Harriet placed her hand on the king's. "What would ye recommend that we do? We have no army, and our people are not soldiers."

Ewart leaned forward in his chair, meeting the queen's eyes. "We need to build a new army and bring the fight to them. The people of Wrunwicks embrace peace, but karupas have proven their taste for death. And if they were to wage war against us, the peace we've enjoyed since the Salt Wars will be gone, replaced by something else." He looked over at Lisette. "Something much worse."

"We cannot conjure an army out of the winds, no matter how hard they might gust," the king said. "And I will not send the good men of Kingsbridge to be slaughtered."

"Ye already have men with the skills needed to fight right here in Kingsbridge. Others can be trained."

"A bold suggestion," Queen Harriet interjected. "Training takes time and men."

"The men of Wrunwicks are brave. I have no doubt that if asked, they would come forward to join our king's new army. Men with the necessary skills could train them. With our king's wisdom and our people's alliance against the beasts, we will know victory and peace will endure."

"Ye speak of victory," the king said, "but at what cost?"

No one dared to interrupt while Ewart pleaded the people's need to act. They sat quietly, absorbed in the conversation and their own thoughts. It was impossible, Lisette reasoned, for anyone to not have an opinion on the events that were unfolding. She knew how her friends felt, but the expressions of the other attendants told her nothing.

"Any attempt to answer your question would be rash and arrogant, my king. But I fear none of us will like the price of hiding like rabbits."

Leeland dug his knife into a piece of fruit. "I commend the depth of your emotion, although I hesitate to call myself a rabbit."

A servant entered and spoke into the king's ear. The king gulped down his wine and turned to Lisette.

"The elders are ready to leave, should ye still wish to bid them a safe return," King Eldridge said. He switched his attention back to Ewart. "A matter of this importance deserves careful consideration, but further discussion here now will not aid our deliberations." He gave Master Furlow a quick nod. "I will discuss your case with our council and inform ye of my decision."

Lisette found the elders in the courtyard. They were speaking to a servant. When Mr. Walling saw them, his face brightened. Lisette ran over to where he stood by the apple tree, relieved to see him. Ewart and the others caught up to her. Florette resumed her post inside Lisette's hood.

"I didn't want ye to leave without saying my farewells," Lisette said, halting in front of the elders. "Or thanking ye once again for riding to Kingsbridge to clear our name."

The servant returned to the castle. Watching as the door shut behind him, Mr. Walling helped himself to some apples and placed them in his saddlebag.

"Thanks to ye, my grandson will rot inside a cage." Mr. Brewers stared at Lisette with dark brown daggers. "Ye may as well have taken a scythe to his neck."

"Come now, Adelard," Mr. Walling said. "Lisette did not force your grandson to help Melvin. We must all account for our actions, including Vincent."

Smoke rose in angry black puffs outside the castle walls. Lisette realized the air's unfamiliar stench belonged to the dead karupa. Too big to move, the only solution was to burn the flesh. Mhutig had warned the karupa would take at least a day to burn completely.

"'Tis never easy to see someone we love inside a cage. Or be the reason a person ends up in the cage," Roy said to Mr. Brewers.

"King Eldridge assured us the privy council would revisit the wretched matter after Swine's Day," Mr. Walling informed the Seekers. "Around the same amount of time it will take for Henry's leg to heal, I should think."

"Swine's day be moons from now, and the council has a short memory." Mr. Brewers almost sneered as he spoke. He sounded none too pleased or convinced by Mr. Walling's remark. The anger in his eyes threatened to burrow straight through the Seekers.

Ignoring Mr. Brewers' scowl, Lisette turned to Calder's father, who had not said a word. "May our Mother guide Calder home."

Mr. Reed looked at Lisette, opened his mouth to speak, then appeared to change his mind. He looked around the courtyard at the fading shrubs. "Calder lives on through her."

Amelia watched the billowing smoke. "Even in death, a karupa infests the air around it."

Mr. Walling glanced over the wall. "Better to infest the air than us. We will inform Stonebridge of what we've learned and instruct our people to be careful. Karupas are a savage enemy that no single man could ever destroy."

"Your wisdom prevails, wise elder," Ewart replied. "We'll need all the help we can muster to defeat those monsters. Our men would do well to practice their sword skills."

After taking their leave from the elders, Lisette fixed her mind on visiting Vincent and Melvin. She had planned to go alone, but Florette and Amelia insisted on making the trip with her. Fearing the cage like any reasonable person, Lisette had always avoided the cage district in Stonebridge. Located on the outskirts of town, each district housed a stretch of cages meant to scare potential breakers with their iron bars. She imagined the cage district in Kingsbridge to be no different.

The amount of time spent inside a cage varied widely from one breaker to the next. Depending on the elders, a breaker could spend as little as days inside a cage or years. Townsfolk knew the stories of breakers left to perish all too well, further inflaming people's fear and imaginations.

When they reached the infamous district, abandoned wails of defiance escaped their iron prisons to join the recurring whimpers of defeat. Mr. Brewers had every right to be concerned, Lisette acknowledged to herself. She tied Daisy to a battered post with its notice forbidding horses from entry. They would go on foot from here. Lisette's stomach churned as they went through the gate. Florette's wings fluttered next to her. Cages were strung around the parcel of mud in no discernable order, as though fate's careless hand had dropped them in a hurry. Perhaps fearing Utaika's mighty wrath, Lisette surmised as she made out the district.

The roofs were covered in dark brown stains like a disease spreading its filth in every direction. Mud around the cages was soaked with last night's rain and degradation. The air reeked of even greater humiliation. Here, men and women were reduced to animals, each one fighting for survival. Some would win, and some would not.

Lisette noticed a couple of purifiers circling up ahead. The birds flew off as they drew nearer. And when they passed by a cage, Lisette saw what had attracted the birds. A man sat in the corner with his tongue stuck out in a final act of rebellion. Whitened by death, his bulging eyes stared out at them, unseeing and devoid of expression. Whatever the man's last thoughts, he kept them trapped inside his blistering flesh. Instinctively, Lisette pinched her nose against the awful smell. She asked herself how many more were left to rot in their own excrement, only to join the other way-ward souls who had turned their backs on Utaika and all that was good.

A breaker tried to grab them while they searched for Vincent and Melvin. The madness lurking in his eyes reached out to them in desperation. Stories spoke of breakers going mad of hunger and cage sickness. Those stories were shrouded in mystery. Although walking through the district, Lisette glimpsed the truth behind the lore. The madness she saw devoured its victim from the inside out, leaving nothing behind of the person. Only sickness remained.

"Are ye sure this be a good idea, Lisette?" Florette asked. She observed the breakers with nervous wings. "Tis not the kind of place that welcomes visitors."

Lisette saw Melvin and Vincent. Their cages were next to each other. The hatred in Melvin's eyes had grown since their last encounter. Its corrupt shadow swallowed the space between them. Lisette shuddered but kept walking. She needed to face the men who had attacked Henry like wild animals.

"We won't be staying long," Lisette promised. "I just need to confirm those two are where they belong."

"I think we've already confirmed that," Amelia replied. "Unless my eyes are playing tricks on me."

Lisette's eyes were glued to the men. She refused to look away. They stared back in a mad rage. Lisette brushed aside whatever guilt she may have felt in seeing them and concentrated on her own hate. They were the guilty ones, not her.

"Have ye come to gloat?" Melvin asked upon their approach. He sized up his visitors like a wild boar closing in for the kill. "I see ye've brought reinforcements."

Lisette smirked. Even now, Melvin could not resist baiting her. "It would be rude of me not to say farewell."

"Ye plan on returning to Stonebridge?" Vincent scoffed at them. "Your actions bring shame to your family and Stonebridge, travelling with these aberrations."

"As hateful as ever, Vincent," Lisette said calmly. "Tis your greatest flaw, although I hear tis not your only one."

Amelia held Lisette by the arm. "We should leave. These two aren't worth any more of our time."

Melvin's lips warped into a cruel snarl. "The pointy-eared mongrel speaks."

"My tongue is pointier still," Amelia retorted.

"I fear neither can save ye," Melvin said. "A pity I won't be the one to put ye out of your misery."

Lisette turned to Amelia and Florette. "I've said my piece. These two can rot inside their cages as fate intended."

They stepped back onto the only path connecting the district and the road back to Kingsbridge. Lisette breathed a sigh of relief. She had seen enough of Melvin and Vincent to last a lifetime. She turned to look at Amelia. The impending war drew a menacing backdrop for their love. Away from itchy noses, she kissed Amelia's hand. Knowing it was futile, she had given up any attempt to hide her feelings in front of Florette.

Amelia smiled. "Someday this will all be behind us, and we'll be free to do as we please."

The light in Amelia's eyes chased the darkness threatening Wrunwicks. "Until I met you, I dared not dream of such joy. Now I dream of our future together."

Amelia squeezed Lisette's hand. "First canon be damned. We'll find a way, even if it means living in secret somewhere. But it'll be our choice to make, not the king's or anyone else's."

Remembering their promise to hurry back, they went to untie the horses. Lisette noticed that every tree bordering the path leaned forward at a dangerously sharp angle. The trees should have broken from the impact of whatever had caused their trunks' unnatural position. Lisette searched her memory, unable to summon an image of the trees from earlier. She turned to Florette, who was inspecting the trees with a thoughtful expression.

"What do ye think might have caused the trees to bend like that?" Lisette asked.

Florette flew over to one of the trees and placed her ear against its trunk. She flew back moments later. "The flame grows dark."

"It sounds like a children's riddle." Amelia stared at the tree. "Is it a message?" she asked Florette. "We could use a few more clues."

"Ye never ask a tree for understanding. The meaning belongs to the listener."

"Do ye know what it means?" Lisette asked. "Is that why these trees were almost destroyed?"

Florette shook her head. "A tree's meaning can take some time to understand. We need to be patient."

The trees reminded Lisette of the horror outside the cave. She had completely forgotten to mention it. "When we escaped from the cave on our way to Strawbridge, the trees had formed a shield around the horses. Without their help, it might have been a lot worse."

Florette contemplated her surroundings with a loving eye. "The trees are guardians of our land and its creatures, providing shelter to all those in need. They know neither hate nor malice and live in accordance with our Divine Mother's wish for us.

"Did you have anything to do with their protection of the horses?" Amelia asked.

"As long as there be breath in them and me, ye will never be alone."

To Lisette, Florette's words sounded almost as cryptic as the tree's. "Ye speak of the trees like they're human," she said.

Florette led them to one of the trees. "Place your hands on its trunk."

Lisette and Amelia did as they were instructed. Her hand on the tree, Lisette asked Florette what they were supposed to feel.

Florette placed her hand next to theirs. "Feel the tree's pulse. It be much slower than our own."

"I don't feel anything," Amelia said, looking a little frustrated. "Maybe I'm not doing it right."

Florette raised a finger to her lips. "Patience. A busy mind cannot hear," she whispered. "Nor can it know what be true. We hear when our minds grow still."

They waited while time slept beneath the trees. Then Lisette felt the slightest tremble beneath her fingers, then another, stronger this time. She took Amelia's hand and gently placed it inside hers. Amelia frowned in concentration. Florette placed her hand over theirs. Eventually, a wide smile brightened Amelia's face.

"I feel it," Amelia whispered and began keeping beat with the tree through her index finger. She looked at Florette in amazement. "It feels like a heartbeat."

"Just as we breathe," Florette said softly, "so too breathe the trees of our land. They aren't human, but they do live side by side with all of Mother's children."

On their way back to Kingsbridge, Lisette studied the rows of worn-out dwellings facing the road. The crude homes were divided by paths so constricted, an adult could scarcely lie across them. Those paths led into Ribald Reach, the district of miscreants. Placed next to one of the main roads leading into town and market square, the reaches reminded townsfolk and visitors alike of their good fortune.

No one wanted to live in Ribald Reach, and no one knew how many lived within any given district. Births and deaths were never recorded by stewards. Reach dwellers kept to themselves, growing crops and caring for their own. And so long as dwellers paid their dues, they were left to squat on the land without interference from the council. Lisette mused it would have been a fitting home for Melvin and Vincent.

After supper that night, Ewart filled everyone in on his meeting with the king. Their nightly gatherings around Deidrik's table were a much-needed excuse to unwind. It was also a time to enjoy the company of friends away from the threat that had taken hold of their lives. Deidrik and Bertha made them feel welcome, despite the lack of space. They all made do, bumping into each other on occasion and navigating around Mhutig, whose large frame dwarfed the kitchen. Everyone acknowledged the fact with a sense of humour and belonging.

When Ewart finished speaking, Lisette shared the details of their visit to the cage district. Bertha raised her eyes to the sky in her usual manner and thanked Utaika for two problems less to solve. They all agreed Lisette's deception was justified. But knowing their king and his elders would disagree, they vowed to keep the truth to themselves. The only one who appeared worried was Florette. Seeing her concern, Lisette attributed it to Florette's protective nature.

"There be nothing to fret about," Lisette said to convince Florette. "The only people who know are us."

"I pray your words be true." Florette's mind seemed elsewhere for an instant. "The price for deceiving the king has never been cheap. He knows only one truth."

"Did anyone see Henry today?" Bertha asked. "He'll be needing a walking stick for the rest of his days if he be lucky enough."

"The pardela's light should help his recovery. It may not prevent him from needing a walking stick, but I was afraid to give him any more," Florette replied from Lisette's shoulder.

"Myself and Roy saw him earlier." Ewart glanced at Roy and chuckled. "He said the king's wine helps with the pain."

"And the princess sweetens his days," Roy added. "A good thing since he'll be there for a while."

Bertha raised an eyebrow. "The princess has a wounded pet to nurse. I noticed she wasn't at the Knights Memorial. No wounded pets to keep her company, I suppose."

Bertha's words dripped with rare sarcasm. It was long apparent the kind woman didn't like their king's only child. She had once mentioned Princess Rosalyn's disdain for townsfolk and preference for the horses in her father's stables. It seemed the princess shared their king's affinity for horses, Lisette had mused at the time. It now seemed Princess Rosalyn's affinities included Henry, at least for the moment.

"What happens if the king agrees to build an army?" Aspen leaned forward to rest her elbows on the table. A nearby candle cast a warm glow over her delicate features.

Lisette once again noticed Deidrik's appreciative looks in her friend's direction. Aspen, of course, was oblivious to his admiration. She had a face that drew men to her, but it being the only face given to her at birth, Aspen remained blind to the fact. And Lisette respected her friend too much to ever mention it. Some things just were.

Mhutig turned to Ewart. "An army needs training. I would be happy to assist you."

Ewart shifted uncomfortably in his chair. "Assist me? I'm scarcely the one to train an army. Winning a sword fight doesn't qualify me to train anyone, especially not for battle."

"The men would need someone to lead them. As the new sword-fighting champion, they would trust your leadership. And with me as your second in command, you could use my knowledge to help you." Mhutig smiled reassuringly as he finished speaking.

The weight of Mhutig's words crashed into Lisette. If the king agreed to form an army, they would wage war against an enemy three times their size. And if Mhutig proved correct as he often did, Ewart, a blacksmith's apprentice from Stonebridge, would lead that army. Her wildest imaginings could not have foreseen such a moment, or most of what had happened since their departure from Stonebridge for that matter. Regardless of whatever else befell them, Lisette had the uneasy feeling their lives would never be the same again.

Chapter 32

The Seekers spent the next day in the fields waiting for news from King Eldridge. With the grain nearly reaped for another year, most of the work had moved inside the granaries that stored the town's fruits, vegetables, and grains. Contrary to the wooden granaries in most townships, the sprawling barns just outside Kingsbridge were built of stone. The heavy wooden doors at both ends were open to allow the winds of Arias passage, creating a cold draft from the back to the front of the barn. The roof trusses backed up the craftsmanship of its carpenters.

Field workers gossiped and shared stories as they threshed and winnowed. Lisette took solace in the familiar work of separating the wheat from their husks. Holding the winnowing basket, her thoughts travelled back to Stonebridge and the baskets she helped Nora make. They'd sit by the fire to weave the rushes while another layer of snow blanketed the earth outside their window. At times like today, she missed her stepmom and wondered how her parents were faring. Returning to the task at hand, Lisette topped up her basket. Winnowing kept her hands busy, if not her mind.

Toward the other end of the barn, Deidrik was teaching Mhutig how to properly thresh the sheaves of grain. It gave workers a reason to smile as they watched. Mhutig's previous efforts in the fields had not gone unnoticed either. The people of Kingsbridge had come to embrace the taupak, whose contribution to this year's harvest would prove invaluable throughout the cold winter moons.

Amelia was also watching Mhutig work. "Now, there's a sight I never expected to see in my lifetime. The prince of Krousus taking farming lessons from a commoner."

"And that be a sentence I never expected to hear in my lifetime." Lisette shook her basket to dislodge the larger pieces of chaff that fell back in with the grain. "Until we met Mhutig, I had no idea taupaks or Krousus existed. No one did. It heartens me to see how well the townsfolk have adapted to the idea."

"In Krousus, the castle's off-limits to the likes of us. We hear of the king and his family, but the people in my village have never been within twenty paces of the royal family. It's just as well, I guess. The stories tell of a cruel king. Mhutig's rise to the throne may finally bring peace for our land and us."

"I can't imagine how hard it must be to grow up in constant fear." Lisette paused to straighten the dress borrowed from Bertha.

Disappearing into her bedchamber one night, their kind host had returned with three dresses for them and a smock for Amelia, who was still wearing the sleeveless dress she had arrived in. "From my younger days. They're old but in good repair and will be warmer in the fields," she had explained.

And while the coarse wool provided a shield against the cold whipping through the granary, Lisette's skirt had the annoying tendency to twist around her legs with every gust of wind. She had opted to keep her shirt and trousers under the dress in the absence of a smock. So when a strong gust lifted the bottom of her dress, Lisette sighed with relief. At least the trousers hid her knees and shins. She threw the wheat into the air with a light flick of her wrists. "We still have to free those prisoners."

"And get to Northbridge," Amelia said. "We'll be short a few bodies if all goes well."

Lisette turned to Florette next. She was helping the children again. Florette had once observed that like the flowers of Wrunwicks, a child faced the rain, snow, and sun with equal enthusiasm. Today, Florette was helping the children collect the discarded husks and straw for livestock. "At least we'll have Aspen and Florette with us. It might be wise to veil ourselves too. The extra caution can't hurt."

"Do you think King Eldridge will stop us from going?"

During one of their rare moments alone, Lisette had told her about Mrs. Sleets, the secret she kept, and her flaming red hair like that of her daughter's. Apart from Harmony and Lord Stanley's sister in the painting, Lisette had never met or seen anyone with the bright red hair of herself and her mother. Four details that Lisette couldn't ignore when put together.

"Thank Utaika we're no longer prisoners, and King Eldridge would never allow women to join his army. I doubt the king will even notice our absence. And I have to see what be in Northbridge. My heart says it can't be a coincidence, no matter how hard I try to dismiss it."

Chapter 33

nother day inched forward without a word from the king. Then on the third day, a knock sounded at the door. King Eldridge was ready to speak with Ewart. A meeting he would not attend alone. Soon as Ewart had finished reading the king's message, the Seekers insisted on accompanying him. Gulping down the last remnants of breakfast, they set out for the castle.

As they rode down the waking streets of Kingsbridge, the chantry bells rang in the new day. An ambitious sun peeked over the hills once more. Soon it would chase away the morning dew and warm the still-damp earth. Inhaling the crisp morning air, Lisette smiled with determination.

The longer she waited in Kingsbridge, the harder an invisible rope tugged, pulling her west toward Northbridge. It was past time to leave. After speaking with Amelia in the granary about going to Northbridge, Lisette had tried to explain the best she could to her friends that same night. And with unquestioning support yet again, they accepted her explanation. Even to Lisette, her reasons for travelling to Northbridge sounded feeble when said out loud but had the value of truth behind them. She then invited Aspen and Florette to join her. They quickly accepted and dared her to leave without them. The men's only condition was their promise of a swift return to Kingsbridge. A promise each of them had happily provided.

Right now, however, Lisette rested her hope on King Eldridge. She would not leave until the king agreed to form an army. Along with her friends, Lisette came to Kingsbridge in search of help to free the prisoners and defeat a growing threat. One moon cycle and a fortnight later, they had yet to receive that help. She prayed the king's decision would end their wait.

A servant instructed them to wait in the great hall for King Eldridge to arrive. They stood just inside the door, unsure of themselves and afraid of taking liberties not afforded mere commoners. It was not the time to offend their king.

Moments later, King Eldridge and his elders entered from the side door. Lisette squashed her disappointment when she noticed the queen was not with them. Every ally was crucial in a time of war. And whether King Eldridge realized it or not, the karupas and opowaks were already at war with the people of Wrunwicks. Now they needed to bring that war to them.

King Eldridge and his elders took their place at the table. It was impossible to read their sober faces. Master Furlow met Lisette's eyes while he sat and waited for King Eldridge to speak. Her heart skipped a beat. She had managed to track down Geoffrey before he left to escort the elders back to Strawbridge. According to Geoffrey, Master Furlow blamed her for his only grandson's disappearance. Lisette feared the king's steward would allow his dislike for her to interfere with what needed to be done. The prisoners had no more say in William's disappearance than she did.

King Eldridge motioned for the Seekers to sit down. "The queen views your devotion to Wrunwicks with an admiring heart. Time to see if her opinion proves accurate. After a long and careful deliberation with my privy council, I have decided to create an army to defeat the karupas and opowaks."

The king's words were met with relieved expressions from his guests. Lisette wondered if Queen Harriet had come through once again.

"The enemy will meet their end at the hands of this new army," Ewart said calmly.

"I trust ye will help train the men. I will be sending a notice to every part of the kingdom within the day," the king said, swinging his arm over the full breadth of the table. "Let us hope that others share your devotion."

"If I may, King Eldridge," Mhutig said, weighing his words. "It has been my experience that a small token of gratitude increases the likelihood of success."

"The council and I have agreed upon a more than reasonable compensation for the men. I am not so naive as to expect our men to risk their lives for nothing in return."

Lisette recognized the look in Amelia's eyes. She was biting her tongue. They had already agreed to let Ewart and Mhutig lead the meeting, which required decorum and extreme delicacy. It meant the rest of them needed to sit tight and allow the meeting to unfold.

"I should also like to assist with the men's training. The Order of Taupaks has been hunting karupas for many years now," Mhutig replied.

"Will ye be joining as well, Deidrik?" the king asked hopefully.

"Of course, my king. Have ye ever known me to back down from a challenge?"

King Eldridge chuckled. "No, I suppose not. Your father would be proud of the man ye've become."

Roy sat up straighter than a board. "Allow me to offer my skills as well, my king." He smiled at Ewart. "It'll be my honour to fight alongside my friends."

King Eldridge appraised Roy a moment. "Wrunwicks would do well to have more young men with your loyalty and courage. I would not have to persuade them with coin."

Lisette squeezed the handle of her mug. It was her turn to bite back the words. A few wren would scarcely be noticed by a king with his wealth on display in every corner of the castle. Raised like all commoners to value stories over coin, Lisette remained at a loss when confronted with the castle's extravagance.

But it was the wine cups that baffled her the most. Made of utekan rock, the goblets willingly flouted their Divine Mother. The divine metal was reserved for chantries to symbolize Utaika's enduring presence across all of Wrunwicks. Apart from its use in chantries, uteka was left undisturbed. It seemed the king respected his wine more than their provider.

"I will do my best to defend our land and its people," Roy said humbly. "To Wrunwicks and our people's victory," he concluded with unfailing optimism.

King Eldridge raised his goblet. "To Wrunwicks."

Sitting with her friends, Lisette toasted to their land and the new army along with Roy and their king. They had finally secured a means to free the prisoners and save Wrunwicks. Now they just needed enough men to form the king's army.

Chapter 34

efore dawn the next morning, Lisette set out for North-bridge with Amelia, Aspen, and Florette. Deidrik loaned his mare to Amelia for their journey. Aspen remarked they had become an all-female band of travellers, horses included. Amelia agreed, declaring they needed a new nickname to seal the occasion. With a lighthearted smirk, Aspen proposed they call themselves the Stubborn Ones. Amelia erupted in a fit of laughter, nearly falling off Clover in the process.

While Amelia struggled to regain her seating, Florette suggested the Keepers of Hope.

"It reminds me of the moon keepers. I'd rather an ounce of hope than two full moons any night of the year." Aspen turned to Lisette with a smile. "I like it."

And so they became the Keepers of Hope, or Keepers for short. Their new nickname resounded on the empty street. Except for the odd rat or dog scrounging up food, the town was still asleep. Soon, the day's first bell would interrupt their dreams and nightmares.

In the spur of the moment, Lisette asked if they could visit the chantry on their way to the northwest road. Amelia accepted with a quick nod and grin. Observing Amelia's enthusiasm, Aspen and Florette shared their own grin and shrugged. Aspen reasoned they had plenty of time, given their early start.

When they arrived, the stained glass windows blinked as night retreated behind the sun. They secured their horses to the railing in front of the stately temple and found the footpath leading to the main entrance, bell tower, and rear of the building where the chantler resided. Lisette stopped outside a set of doors. Enclosed by the tree of wisdom with its intertwining branches rising toward the sky, the door's imposing sculpture eclipsed its humble neighbour leading up to the bells. And in the tradition of all chantries, the tree was forged entirely out of utekan rock.

Opening the chantry door, Lisette admired the magnificent windows. They were larger and higher than the windows in the Stonebridge chantry, measuring almost the same height as the chantry walls. The left and right walls formed a mirrored line of six windows each. The first five windows showcased the cherished symbols of their revered knights. The sixth and final windows near the altar served as sunlit frames for Utaika's tree of wisdom.

Benches ran the length of the temple on both sides with a wide passageway in the middle leading to the statue of Utaika. The elders were already in their seats to thank Utaika and ask for her guidance and wisdom. During the cold mornings of winter, townsfolk and villagers filled the less ornate benches for the daily thanks led by their chantler. But with prayers suspended until after the harvest festival, a temple's chantler saw little company outside the elders. Absorbed in prayer, the elders ignored their visitors.

As the first bells chimed, Lisette and Aspen led the way to the front of the temple. They kneeled twice to honour their Divine

Mother, once at the beginning of the nave and once at the nave's midway point. Arriving before Utaika, they lit a candle each to help guide their loved ones, both alive and gone. Lisette had not lit a candle for her mom since Mother's Day. This morning, she would also light that candle for Calder.

Their candles burning, the Keepers kneeled at Utaika's feet to demonstrate their humility. Atop her stone base, she towered over them. Like the sculpture cradling the entrance, Utaika was forged entirely of her own untarnished essence. Her arms and hair were shaped like the branches of the tree of wisdom. On a necklace around her neck, hung the three stones of life: first birth, death, and rebirth.

Three utekan butterflies rested on a branch of Utaika's hair. The butterflies symbolized the transition from one life stage to the next. Admiring the butterflies as she always did, Lisette noticed how the wings resembled Florette's. The butterflies could just as easily be fair folk, she thought, motioning her intention to sit on one of the far benches. The others nodded and followed. Apart from chantlers, nobles, and elders, speaking inside a temple was deemed profane and thus forbidden without explicit permission.

When the bells stopped, Lisette invited the silence to wash over her and cleanse her thoughts. She sat picturing Melvin and Vincent fading from her memory. Stuck inside their cages, they posed no further threat to anyone. Next, she pictured the karupa outside Kingsbridge plummeting to its ugly death. She promised herself and Utaika to destroy the danger to their land and restore peace to Wrunwicks. In so doing, Calder would be avenged, and Wrunwicks would finally be rid of its monsters.

The Keepers followed the river for six days without incident, much to everyone's relief. After another supper of bread and fresh fish, they settled down for the night. The days were growing short and the nights cold. Lisette took out her map and unfolded its treasure. Most maps were crude and made of poorly prepared sheepskin. The resulting parchment was prone to more wear and rarely made its way into books. But thanks to Lord Sumunder's generosity, she was able to purchase their current map. Drawn on the carefully prepared parchment favoured in most books, it showed all the major rivers and towns without a single hole in sight.

The map had also proven itself to be reasonably accurate throughout their journey. People's preference for home meant that mapping was a scarce and underappreciated art. The maker of this map had invested a lot of skill and knowledge into its creation.

Peering over the map, Lisette guessed they had six more days of travel, just two days shy of the harvest festival. A realization that reminded Lisette of her parents. They were undoubtedly looking forward to the festival. This would be her first year away from Stonebridge during the biggest celebration of the year. So far as she knew, none of her friends had ever travelled beyond Woodbridge until now either. It struck her once again how much their lives had changed since leaving home.

Glancing up, Lisette noticed Aspen watching her. She saw the question in her friend's eyes. It burned brighter than the fire between them. Lisette smiled reassuringly, a habit she seemed to have picked up during the course of their journey.

"Ye may as well ask whatever be on your mind," Lisette said. "Ye know we don't keep secrets from each other."

Aspen remained quiet, shifting her gaze from Lisette to Amelia, then back again. She stoked the fire, deep in thought. "I've noticed for some time now that ye two have become very close."

Lisette looked over at Amelia before meeting Aspen's eyes. She trusted Aspen and was relieved for the opening into a long-overdue conversation. "We have." Lisette searched for the right words. "We're very fond of each other." Lisette's smile turned apologetic, knowing her words had come up short by several miles long. An affliction she appeared to suffer more than most as of late.

Aspen's eyes shared their understanding with Lisette. She turned to Amelia. "Lisette has been my dearest friend for many years. I love her every bit as one loves a sister and would never let anyone hurt her."

Amelia reached over to take Aspen's hand. "I love her too, dear friend. And I have no intention of hurting Lisette or you."

"Tis not ye that I'm concerned about. I can see how much ye love Lisette." Aspen squeezed Amelia's hand. "Tis everyone else. Lord Stanley said the king was going to create a new canon allowing men and women to wed whomever they please, but I saw nothing in his demeanour to suggest such a thing."

Lisette threw a nearby pebble into the river to vent her frustration. Like it or not, she agreed with Aspen and wouldn't be able to ignore her situation indefinitely. "The king strikes me as a man of tradition like all good Wrunwickers. He may also prove to be a man of empty promises, who prefers to appease our queen than speak his truth."

Aspen nodded thoughtfully. "So where does that leave ye? If the king were to discover your secret, ye'd both be thrown in a cage."

"I fear the answer may not agree with my heart," Lisette replied.

Aspen turned to Florette. "Did ye know about this?"

"Since their return to Kingsbridge." Florette smiled at Lisette. "Their love shines true as the sun, but it wasn't my place to share with anyone."

Amelia scooched over to wrap her arms around Lisette and kissed the top of her forehead. "We need not torment ourselves about that which can't be known just yet. We have enough to keep us busy for all foreseeable moons and then some."

"We must trust Utaika's wisdom." Florette stretched out her wings. "She will guide ye both."

"May she guide all of us," Aspen said brightly, although her eyes were dark with worry.

Chapter 35

True to Lisette's prediction, they arrived in Northbridge three days later. Deidrik had forewarned them about the increased lodger's fee due to the ongoing reconstruction at the town's manor. When the town's outer walls were demolished and made into roads during the renovation period, it forced lords to find more creative ways to collect the gate wron from visitors. Many lords placed a user's fee on inns and common ruchtons. Stories told of visitors skirting the ruchton fee by using whatever public space was available, causing King Lazoran III to issue a new canon prohibiting the practice in its entirety.

The subsequent rise in the popularity of ruchtons required more people to empty the barrels. Nestled halfway in the ground beneath their benches, the job of emptying a barrel's waste was not an enviable or easy one. Barrellers were young men looking for extra coin to spend at taverns like Henry, whose height and strong build made him a natural choice for the gruelling work.

Lisette sometimes teased Henry about the smell at the end of market day. Henry would respond by saying it made the ale taste all the sweeter. Far from the ruchtons of Stonebridge, it seemed that Henry still found ale just as sweet. And Princess Rosalyn found Henry to be even sweeter, Lisette mused to herself, then questioned whether the princess would be so sweet on Henry if she knew he was a barreller. But the answer remained with Henry and Princess Rosalyn.

As they entered the city, Lisette shifted her thoughts to the task at hand. Deidrik had informed them of an inn with far cheaper rates than the one on market square. Knowing the owner, Deidrik wrote them a note to give the man. The problem would be finding it. According to Deidrik, the small inn was tucked deep within town limits. It was late afternoon, and with the work of harvest just about over, children were free to play while their parents finished up the season.

Spotting a small group of children playing hoods, the Keepers approached them for directions. Most children relished the chance to display their knowledge of the streets and buildings, making them the first point of contact for many a wandering traveller. Upon seeing the Keepers, the children came to an unruly stop. In the middle of the group, a young girl pulled down her rearward hood to reveal what had startled her friends. Seeing the source of disruption, she ran over for a closer look.

"Greetings, travellers. Ye're here for the festival?" The young girl inspected the Keepers with enthusiasm.

Lisette saw no reason to disappoint the child. "We are, young dweller. What may we call ye?"

The young girl called out for her friends to join them. "Iris, daughter of Hoyt and Edna Cooper of Northbridge."

Lisette introduced herself and her friends. The children stared at Florette with their mouths ready to run away from them. Lisette suppressed her laughter. She did not want to disrespect their new acquaintances. "We'll be needing a place to stay during our visit. Might ye be able to point us in the direction of Brown Rabbit Inn?"

The children clamoured out the directions to the inn. Lisette fetched half a wren and gave it to Iris. It was more than she had intended to give for the information, but the children's gaunt frames told their own story while they spoke. The Keepers bid the children a bright farewell and set out to make sense of the children's eager, albeit obscure directions.

They found the shoemaker's shop after a long series of twists and turns leading to the old district. According to the children, they should take the path by the shop. Some twenty paces later, they came onto Trade Street. Lisette scanned the short row of tired shops and broken-down signs. Before the renovation period, the street would have been bustling with commerce from Northbridge and the neighbouring villages. She guessed the street catered strictly to those who lived in the district now. Children, who were still too young to venture outside the district, played among themselves. One small child was drawing in the dirt with a stick. A future artist or mason, Lisette thought hopefully as she looked over. A few shopkeepers watched suspiciously as the women followed the row of signs to the inn.

Brown Rabbit Inn was nestled several paces back from the end of the street. The courtyard was devoid of the weary travellers normally seen outside an inn. The crumbling building was made of wood, unlike the newer inns found in market squares. Light spilled through the holes in the second-floor walkway of the inn. A brown rabbit hung from the railing in a rare demonstration of defiance, daring the winds to rip it apart. And unlike its modern counterpart, the inn's door was in the rear of the building. They dismounted and made their way to the backyard. The open gate informed them there were chambers available, while the absence of a groom meant they should escort their horses to the stable at the innkeeper's behest. Their horses tended to, the women ventured inside.

A welcoming aroma of sweetgrass filled the air. Freshly strewn from one end of the hall to the other, the fragrant herb showed pride in the inn. The smell reminded Lisette of Nora, who liked to add sage during the growing season. Lisette's nose also detected the pungent smell of candles made from tallow. They were cheaper and dirtier than bee candles. Taking a closer look at her surroundings, she noticed the cleaner candles on each of the hard-scrubbed tables. It seemed the innkeeper was doing his best to balance care and cost.

Upon seeing the Keepers, a woman tending to a large pot at the end of the hall walked over to greet them. Lisette suspected the sharp-looking woman was responsible for the inn's sparkling care.

The woman smiled invitingly. "Welcome to Brown Rabbit Inn, travellers. I be Mabel, the innkeeper's wife. Might ye be in need of lodging?"

Aspen introduced them and offered Mabel the note from Deidrik. "We'll need a chamber along with food for ourselves and our horses. We just finished putting them in the stables." Aspen glanced around the busy hall. "Ye keep a fine inn."

Mabel read Deidrik's note with one eye on the Keepers. "Ye be in luck, fair travellers. I have some fresh pottage ready and a private chamber with three beds if it pleases ye to stay. Your horses will be well taken care of. Friends of Deidrik are always welcome, provided ye have coin to pay."

They paid for their chamber in good stead and sat down to their first true meal of the day. Given the lack of horses in the small but well-appointed stable, Lisette scarcely expected to see so many patrons at the inn. Only two of the twelve tables in the hall were empty. Travellers like themselves sat enjoying their pottage and washing it down with ale.

As a precaution, Amelia had borrowed a hooded cloak from Bertha to hide her ears. Florette would earn them enough attention for the time being. But they could do nothing to hide Amelia's pale skin. Lisette ignored the furtive looks from other guests. They had already decided to only address people's curiosity when it became necessary. Until such a time, neither of them wanted to attract any unwanted questions or owned the slightest intention of explaining their presence in Northbridge.

That time came while they were enjoying Mabel's pottage, thick enough to stand a spoon in. The burly innkeeper approached their table and introduced himself as Oscar. After examining Florette, whose feet dangled just below the table as she helped herself to some bread and cheese, Oscar turned to the three women.

"We don't normally see maidens like yerselves travelling on their own. A dangerous undertaking to be sure, even for the Seekers. Many mouths speak of your journey and battle against the beasts of old. Some say ye possess the magic of the first ones."

Lisette considered just how much they should tell the innkeeper. They had not travelled to Northbridge to encourage stories about magic. "I can assure ye that we possess neither the power to heal nor the power to conjure death. We want what ye want, to put an end to the vanishings and the beasts that would see us destroyed. Wrunwick or not, they aren't invincible. One of the monsters was destroyed in Kingsbridge by a group of brave men and the king himself. King Eldridge will need many such men for his new army."

"A note's been posted in the square, promising coin for every man who joins the king's army against the wrunwick. The king's note also exempts men from the planting of winter crops if they join. I don't know about the rest of Wrunwicks, but the note's been met with skepticism aplenty in these parts. People are asking how the king can afford such generosity and at what cost to towns and villages."

"An understandable concern," Amelia said. "But without men willing to fight, there can be no victory."

"And without men to work the land, there can be no Wrunwicks," Oscar replied with growing exasperation.

Oscar's last remark suggested their conversation with the innkeeper was heading down a path that led to nowhere, with one wrong turn leading to an argument. The innkeeper had his mind made on the matter, Lisette decided as she signalled to Mabel for some ale. She was far from in need of more ale. But she would gladly drink the whole pitcher to end their current conversation. They needed a roof to shelter them and could not afford to offend the innkeeper. "Who else could use another swig after that delightful pottage?" she asked her friends.

"I could use some," Aspen said to Mabel. "Riding all day can make a woman thirsty."

Mabel obliged by filling everyone's mug. She scooped up a full thimble for Florette. "Drink up, m'ladies. I brewed a fresh batch just yesterday."

Taking advantage of the distraction, Lisette inquired about the true purpose of their visit to Northbridge. "Would ye know of a street with forty-six in its name, kind innkeeper?"

Oscar's frown darkened further. He whistled softly, observing his guests. "That be no place for a fine group of ladies such as yerselves, Seekers. The only street I can think of would be inside Ribald Reach, where the untrue number their streets without bothering to name them. A Motherless place that ye best be staying clear of, lest ye be killed wherever they should find ye."

Lisette thanked the innkeeper for his wisdom and promised to heed his advice, though she had no intention of backing away now. They had not travelled this far to turn around empty-handed.

Chapter 36

hey rose to the sound of rain, crept down the ladder at the end of the walkway, and retrieved their horses. A guest opened the ruchton's door as they were about to leave. He wished them good morning with a cheerful wave. Lisette politely wished him the same. Fearing the man might seek their company for the swapping of travel gossip or want to pry, Lisette exchanged a quick look with her friends. Aspen bid the man a prompt farewell and turned Silver toward the gate. Lisette and Amelia followed Aspen onto Trade Street.

According to Mabel, Northbridge had two main roads leading to market square. They had not passed the cage district on their way into town yesterday from the east, so if they used the square as their starting point and took the south road, they should be able to find the district and Ribald Reach. Lisette hoped it was a simple matter of retracing their steps until they reached the market. In any case, they all agreed it was worth trying.

To Lisette's unexpected pleasure, once past the old district, finding market square proved easy as joining the townsfolk. The streets were filled with men and women on their way to prepare for the harvest festival. Some rode with wagons hitched to their horses. Others walked with their baskets while children trailed behind with their own carefully guarded wares. The overnight rain subsided as the sun began its climb over the Northbridge highlands, bestowing a determined kiss upon the wet stone.

At the square, preparations for tomorrow's festival were well underway. Pennons hung throughout the square in white, purple, red, and yellow. Stalls, tents, and platforms were in various stages of setup for the celebration. Later, the manor would send barrels of ale to be replaced as needed during the festival. No one would go thirsty. Nor would they go hungry. The town's lord always made sure there was plenty of food and drink for everyone.

The town's watchtowers would be manned by a series of elders for the festival, including the four towers cornering the square, to ensure everyone's safety and adherence to the king's canons. The festival marked the last day of late curfew, so most townsfolk would stay until the very last bells rang out. Villagers would trickle out in time to meet curfew in their villages, but leniency was invariably afforded latecomers. Lisette asked Utaika to guide the villagers as they travelled to give thanks for another bountiful harvest.

The Keepers followed the south road out of town. They were nearing the town limits when Aspen signalled to her right. Lisette could just make out the cluster of buildings. Like all commoners born outside Ribald Reach, Lisette had never stepped foot inside the notorious district.

Rumours of the districts' people were more colourful than wildflowers. One popular rumour spoke of the people inside Ribald Reach wearing little more than their own filth. Another spoke of men and women riding horses that looked like giant bats. Such outlandish accounts served to entertain, frighten, and often disgust those who listened.

Lisette stopped outside the entrance to Ribald Reach. A single alley led into the district. Taking a calm breath, Lisette thanked her friends for being so willing to come with her, despite not knowing what they were searching for or what to expect. She proceeded to enter the district, patting Daisy to assuage both their trepidations. Aspen, Amelia, and Florette rode next to Lisette into the uncharted stretch of land.

After about ten paces, the alley branched off into several muddy paths, scarcely wide enough for two horses. They chose the nearest path to see where it might lead. The old wooden houses lining the path appeared empty and in desperate need of repair. Many had shutters hanging from their windows, while some houses were missing shutters altogether. Pails outside the homes were partially filled with rotting scraps. Lisette noticed several rats foraging for food. Thanks to the ubiquity of cats and a canon requiring people to empty their pails at least once a day, rats were seldom a problem within a town's limits. It seemed the rats of Ribald Reach roamed free inside the district.

Lisette kept watch for a sign indicating which street they were on. Finally, with the sun near its peak, she saw a post one lane over with the number forty carved into the wood. Squeezed between two houses, the lane was scarcely wide enough for a horse. The Keepers dismounted and led their horses over to Forty Street, where they rode north. They passed a butcher shop with three large rabbits hanging outside but still no one in sight. Lisette feared their journey would prove to be a fruitless waste of their time.

They rode in silence, not wanting to disturb whatever ghosts had taken residence inside the forsaken homes. Lisette imagined the ghosts staring out at them with the unblinking eyes of a snake. But other than ghosts, the district appeared deserted. Its people now vanished with their clothes still hanging from wash lines strung haphazard between muddy windows. As she appraised their surroundings, it dawned on Lisette they were lost inside a deserted maze. She cast a long frown on some rats scurrying off with their reward. A sudden gust of strong wind took hold of a door somewhere nearby. Startled, Lisette peered in the direction of the loud banging. She located a post with the number forty-six.

Lisette turned right onto the path. She looked back at Amelia and Aspen. Their expressions said they held little hope of finding much beyond more desolation. Skimming the shops that made up the lonely street, Lisette saw an open door at the far end. She threw another quick look at Amelia and Aspen, pointing toward the door this time. Florette scratched Daisy's neck to soothe their skittish companion.

While Lisette tied Daisy to a post outside the shoemaker's shop, Lisette heard a muffled sound from within the shop walls. Friend or foe, someone was in that shop. She opened the door to its fullest capacity to look inside. A woman stepped out of the shadows.

The red-haired woman smiled in recognition. Lisette's knees buckled beneath her. She tried to breathe—the air forced from her body in a single swoosh. Amelia grabbed her by the waist. Lisette fell limp in her arms. The woman ran to their side and gently brushed the hair from Lisette's face.

"We need to get her inside," the woman said. "She be in shock."

Tightening her arms around Lisette, Amelia obeyed the woman, guiding Lisette through the door and onto a chair. The chamber smelled of leather and mint. Lisette's mother had always scattered a few mint leaves during the growing season to ward off ants. Summoning her strength, Lisette looked up at the woman she had mourned for nine years. Save for a few grey wisps and the first wrinkles of time, her mom had not changed. She still had the same kind and caring eyes as the woman in Lisette's memories.

Years of unshakable longing rose to the surface. Lisette felt the tears streaming down her cheeks. Her heart ached with utter joy and disbelief. She sobbed uncontrollably in loud, clumsy bursts of grief buried for too long. Then slowly, she became aware of Amelia stroking her hair, bringing her back to the present.

"Ye must have many questions," Lisette's mom said.

Not yet ready to speak, Lisette nodded, absorbing the sight of her mom through every fibre of her being. The slow drumming of her heart reduced time to an uphill crawl. Each moment, a heart-beat. The air vibrated around her. It raised the hair on her arms, each strand swaying in unison.

"Allow me to introduce myself. I'm Waverly, Lisette's mom."

The Keepers introduced themselves. Waverly appeared not to notice when Amelia mentioned Krousus. Lisette listened to her friends, the timbre of their voices causing the air to vibrate in rapid succession. The hair on her arms began a new dance every time the pattern changed.

"If it pleases everyone, I'd like to invite ye to my house not far from here." Waverly smiled at her daughter. "Are ye up to walking?"

Lisette managed to return her mom's smile and nodded. She looked to her friends for confirmation.

"We'd be honoured," Aspen said.

Amelia lifted Lisette from the chair. Lisette waited for the floor to stop spinning, then steadied her feet. Florette reclaimed her spot inside Lisette's hood.

Chapter 37

averly led the way through the district maze. She was on foot, citing the need to stretch her legs. The Keepers walked behind her with their horses next to them. No one spoke, happy to trail behind Waverly. Lisette took refuge in the silence. Every few paces, Waverly looked back to smile. Recovering from her initial shock, Lisette noticed her mom's hair was a much darker red than she remembered. Questions began to form in her head, like what was her mom doing here in Ribald Reach, and why?

"We're almost there," Waverly said. "It be just after that sign." She directed their attention to the post with a sun carved into it.

Lisette blinked. It was still there, just beyond the post. A translucent wall that rose higher than Metterling Mountains. The wall crisscrossed in what looked like a multicoloured basket woven into the air itself. She blinked again. Beyond the wall, she could see the blurred outline of what looked like a town.

"At my signal, ye'll need to walk in a straight line," Waverly said when everyone had caught up to her by the post. She took Lisette by the hand.

Waverly led them about ten paces north of the post and stopped. "Stay close, follow me, and keep the line straight." She let go of her daughter's hand.

Lisette examined the wall. It looked brighter now and seemed to vibrate. No one had mentioned it or appeared to notice. Had she finally lost her mind for good this time? Should she say something? And what would she sound like? Lisette shook the rocks from her head. Florette placed a hand on her shoulder.

They followed Waverly some five paces west to where she waved her hand and a passageway appeared in the wall. Waverly led them thru the invisible opening. Lisette stopped in amazement. A town reaching higher than any town in all of Wrunwicks stood before them. It stretched for miles inside a low-lying wall made of the same stone used throughout the kingdom.

Lisette glanced back at the wall and knew it was somehow real, whether her friends saw it or not. Why didn't her mother mention it? Overhead, Lisette spotted a horse swooping through the air. It flew over and landed in front of them.

"Welcome to Northbridge District," the horse said. "Waverly said ye'd be coming. Greyson at your service. What the name lacks in originality, it makes up for in directness. I have my parents to thank for that."

Greyson was light grey with a silky white mane and wings. In addition to the wings on his back, he also had two small sets of wings in the place of fetlocks. Lisette guessed he was a couple hands shorter than Mhutig.

"Greyson be a questier, one of the many animal guides that live in the district," Waverly explained. "And now, ladies, allow me to offer ye a meal after your journey." She took them through another passageway in the town wall that led straight to market square.

An elder descended one of the watchtowers and sequestered their swords. To be returned upon departure, he told them. Lisette scanned the square. The high, narrow buildings making up most of the square were no less than five floors each and as many as seven. Wooden stairs provided quick access to doors at every level between each set of adjoined buildings. Shop signs hung from the bottom levels.

To Lisette's right, the library stood beside a stone archway through which people came and went. Engraved in the archivolt was a set of wings, the knightly symbol for truth. The library was at least six times wider than the other buildings in the square. Two tunnels cut into the first floor of the library and connected the market to the district. A statue of Utaika watched over the people from her place next to the library doors. She was carved entirely of wood with her dress painted in yellow.

Streets branched out from the square between every three sets of buildings. Brightly coloured pennons hung from one corner of the market to the next, intersecting in the middle where stalls radiated outward from a round wooden platform.

People and the occasional winged animal filled the market with their comings and goings. A few people were finishing preparations for tomorrow's festival. As Waverly and the Keepers made their way across the square and through one of the library tunnels, men, women, and animals alike saluted Lisette's mother. Lisette mused that either her mom was very respected, or the people of Northbridge District were exceptionally polite.

Once through the tunnel, Waverly led them down Grove Street with its houses packed in sets of two like the shops in market square. It seemed the district's people had used every available space to build their town with its high buildings and narrow streets.

Looking up at the tall, thin-necked homes, Lisette's eyes grew large at the sight of men and women flying atop a group of animals.

Partway down the street, Waverly stopped to announce they had arrived. She directed them to the rear of the house using a side lane. Lisette was struck by the presence of a small well in the middle of the two adjoining yards. Aside from manors and the castle, towns and villages used large communal wells, so a well this close to home represented an impossible luxury. Lisette marvelled at the district's attention to detail and apparent disregard for cost.

Careful not to stumble over the chickens running around the yard, the Keepers led their horses inside the stable, leaving them in the company of two other horses. Lisette's mom waited by the stairs to usher them up to the kitchen on the second floor. The ground floor was mostly reserved for bathing, Waverly explained. In the corner, a private ruchton spoke of more luxury. Most families in Wrunwicks shared a ruchton with at least three other households.

Upon entering the kitchen, an elderly woman ran to hug them and introduced herself as Hilda, Waverly's longtime companion. Lisette remarked on the enticing aroma coming from the pot over the fire. Still smiling at her guests, Hilda offered them to freshen up at the basin by the hearth.

Light streamed into the kitchen from its large windows, spilled over the table to their right and onto a mat woven from sweetgrass in the middle of the chamber, where two stone pillars supported the ceiling and hangers made of bulrushes. The hangers were laden with fresh fruits and vegetables waiting to be cooked and baked.

A butcher's table ran below the left side window, stopping only for a ladder that disappeared into the third floor. Like the district, no space had been wasted. The final result was warm and inviting.

While everyone washed their hands, Hilda poured a pitcher of ale from the barrel by the door. She placed it on the table before resuming her meal preparations. After Waverly had washed her hands, she set out mugs and filled them. Lisette settled onto one of the benches. She had so many questions to ask her mother, without a clue as to where or how to start.

"I thought ye were dead," Lisette mumbled at last.

"I wanted to tell ye, sweet pea, but I couldn't," Waverly said softly, her voice filled with anguish. "I returned to Stonebridge, but your father had already remarried. And tis forbidden by the canons for a man or woman to commit chetuk. As a man with two wives, your father would most certainly have seen the cage. I couldn't do that to either of ye."

No one had called Lisette by that name in nine years. Sweet peas were her mom's favourite flower. After harvest, she would mix the dried petals with sweetgrass to sprinkle over the kitchen floor and fill the house with their lively scent.

Lisette held onto her mother's gentle gaze. "Ye could've let me know somehow. After ye disappeared, I spent years wondering what happened to ye and thinking the worse when ye were right here, safe and alive."

"So be your father. I don't know if it was the best choice, but it was the only one I had."

"And now?" Lisette knew she sounded stubborn and childish, reduced to the little girl hiding in a cave. But she couldn't help it. How could her mother leave her like that?

"Now it be ye who has found me. After writing *Millennia*, I asked Utaika to guide your heart to me. I knew since the day ye were born the legacy had been passed on. It was simply a matter of time."

"Legacy?" To Lisette, her mom may as well be talking in obscure riddles that only she understood.

"I was born into a legion of women able to use the sun's energy to build bridges across vast distances. Light masons used the bridges to access the far reaches of their land in search of food and materials to help their people survive. Eventually, they shared their bridges with a nearby band of people. But when the band's people began to die of a strange illness, they blamed it on light masons and their people, saying their bridges brought death. Enraged, the band declared war on light masons and their tribes." Waverly stopped to look at Hilda.

"No need to concern yourself with me," Hilda said, reaching into a hanger. "Your help isn't needed today. Our guests are more important than these turnips."

Waverly smiled gratefully. "Now, where was I?" she asked herself. "Oh yes, the war. Outnumbered and scared, our people feared a war between the two bands would not end well for our tribe, so one young light mason suggested they build a bridge between our land of old and this one. Some light masons glimpsed this land when creating the original bridges, but no one had constructed a bridge across the stars before. Wary of its ability to hold over such an incredible distance, masons refused to attempt what they feared amounted to folly." She took Lisette's hand into her own.

"Undaunted, the light mason built the bridge and travelled here. When she returned, the mason spoke of a wondrous land with two moons and rocks the colour of the sun. Awed by the news and desperate to survive, our people travelled here. Though a few of our people travelled with their families to remote parts of the old land to start anew." Waverly grew quiet, appearing lost in her thoughts.

"Are ye saying that Lisette be a light mason?" Aspen asked. She turned to stare at her friend in astonishment. "I always knew there was something different about ye and that proves it."

Lisette found the information much harder to digest or accept than Aspen. She could no more build a bridge than either of them. What did her mom mean by a bridge able to cross the stars? And what did it have to do with her mom's disappearance or the North-bridge District?

Waverly smiled in response to Aspen's question. "Light masons are all born with red hair. The brighter the hair, the more power a light mason possesses. Lisette was born with hair brighter than the brightest of flames. But masons need to grow into their powers, which are much too big for a child to harness. I've never known of a light mason able to use her power before reaching maturity."

"Where does the power come from?" Amelia asked.

"It comes from the sun itself and its unlimited supply of energy. That energy be invisible to us, much like our own energy. But light masons can harness it and use it to build bridges like the ones from our birth land. Although these days, we prefer to build bridges using less energy than the masons of old. The bridges are just as easy to use and safer for travellers. The process be much like building a table with just a little more space between the boards. But the boards are still made of wood, and the table be still usable."

"Can ye use the energy to build other things?" Aspen asked.

"We've never tried or needed to use it for anything else. The bridges serve us well. Every district like this one be connected by a bridge, suspended well above the ground to prevent people outside the districts from accidentally stepping onto one."

Lisette remembered the wall and knew it somehow protected the town. "Why aren't people able to see the districts?"

"Like the sun's life-giving energy, the air around us be also made of energy. That energy be made of star ash, the building material used by light masons for their bridges, like the boards used for a table. Masons long before me mixed star ash with the spittle from fair folk who possessed veiling abilities. They used the mixture to build a wall around each district." Waverly paused for an instant. "So I guess we've used the energy to build something apart from bridges, after all," she said, sounding a little surprised.

"In any case, it hides us from outsiders, who only see the forest. At the bottom of the wall, there be a narrow bridge leading outside the district for anyone who might cross the wall. The only opening be where we entered, but we keep it closed to outsiders." Waverly paused again, this time to direct her attention toward Florette. "Ye might be interested to know that Northbridge District be the home of an entire band of fair folk. Ye've already met one."

"Greyson," Florette said happily.

Waverly nodded. "I think that be enough talk about bridges for now," she said, looking around the table. "How would ye ladies like to see my scriptorium?"

Located on the top level, the scriptorium was decorated with a mat woven from sweetgrass like the one in the kitchen, a fireplace with a chair on either side, a desk, and a book wheel below the chamber's only window. Lisette had never seen a book wheel outside of the Great Library. This one was smaller with six shelves instead of twelve but no less impressive. And to her delight, the walls were lined with books rising toward the vaulted ceiling. A ladder stood against one of the bookcases, providing a way to the higher shelves. Lisette fell in love with the chamber instantly.

Lisette turned to her mother. A forgotten memory of Waverly reading to her jumped in front of Lisette. Meeting Lisette's eyes, Waverly invited her over to the desk where a book lay closed. Three inkhorns protruded from their brass rings in the right corner. A small stand next to the desk held more scribing tools. Lisette picked up one of the pens. It was made of bone with a copper nib.

Waverly remained by her desk and passed a light hand over the book's leather cover. "The second *Millennia* book, back from the binder. I started the books for ye, Lisette. Ye always did love books and stories about faraway lands. I hoped that when ye were ready, ye'd know where to find me."

"I wouldn't have found ye without Lord Stanley's help. He was the one who pointed out the address to me."

"Lord Stanley's mom was a light mason, and his sister had the makings. His mother would sometimes bring him here as a child during her visits. He liked to visit, though not since he married. Outsiders are forbidden to enter the district."

"He never said anything about his mother being a light mason or his visits," Lisette said, floored by her mother's revelation. *Why didn't he say something?* "He had to know what the address meant."

"Light masons must discover their powers without any direct interference from the legion. We can only show the way through hidden clues inside the books we write. So we teach our children to read and share our love of books, then we recommend the books that contain clues to potential masons but no more. Lord Stanley be versed in our customs. Daring to point out the address would be met with much criticism from our sisters. Unfortunately, there be fewer of us left to criticize anyone with each generation."

Going back, Lisette admitted to herself that her mom's words made sense. It explained why Lord Stanley was so happy to see her that first night in Strawbridge according to Florette. "He was badly injured in the attack on Strawbridge. I fear his life be in danger."

"Although a man has never been born into the legion, Lord Stanley has his mom's strength. Let's hope it be enough to save him. And ye, sweet pea, will need to destroy the bridge to Krousus. I suspect Lord Stanley knew this and nudged ye forward.”

Overwhelmed by the suggestion, Lisette stared at her mom in a mute state of disbelief. Listening to Waverly in the kitchen, she came to understand that a bridge had to exist between Wrunwicks and Krousus. It was the only possible explanation. However, her understanding failed to explain how she was supposed to destroy it.

Waverly tucked an unruly strand of hair behind Lisette’s ear. “Districters may live inside a bubble, but we do travel outside its walls for trading. It be how I knew ye were coming. A couple of districters were eating at the inn and overheard ye speaking to the innkeeper. We keep up with what be happening in the rest of Wrunwicks too. The people are right to be scared.” Her face grew tender. “Destroying the bridge may seem impossible now, but it won’t. Ye’ll need to trust your heart. Only then can ye harness your power.”

“Shouldn’t the bridge be destroyed by a much more capable light mason?” Lisette didn’t want to disrespect her mother, but the idea of dismantling a bridge made from an invisible material, and the sun no less, struck her as beyond impossible for herself or anyone else.

“Others have tried and failed. The bridge was built by a light mason with great power and skill. I wish we knew who it was, but most of our light masons have been accounted for. We do have a mason who travelled to Krousus to uncover more information but has yet to return. She would never do anything to hurt the people of Wrunwicks.”

“She used the bridge?” Lisette wondered how it would ever be possible to get past the karupas and opowaks.

“The energy needed to build a bridge over such a long distance can create rifts in the space around it. Those rifts allow people and animals to go through, depending on their size and the size of the rift. But space rifts are dangerous and grow with time. They might not be stable enough to ensure safe passage for non-masons. Amelia was very fortunate."

"I still don't understand how the bridges allow people to cross between distant lands." Lisette tried to wrap her head around the notion, but it was proving useless.

"How about I show ye? I know just the place. Your friends are welcome to join us."

The yardok was the second-largest building in the square. Serving as an inn and gateway to the other districts, it housed the bridges on the first floor and guests in need of shelter on the upper floors. Inside the yardok, people came and went through tall doors with yellow signs indicating their destination. Elders greeted visitors at the doors, then directed those without lodging to the inn upstairs. Lisette noticed a door with "Galak" written on it. She asked her mom where it led. Waverly explained the bridge was reserved for traders who transported goods to and from Millennia, the word used in her book for Galak, the land of their ancestors.

"Traders bring back spices and other items to be sold in town," Waverly said as they headed to the only other door without a line of people. "We monitor the kingdom for rifts and close any that might appear as quickly as possible. The bridge takes a little longer to cross than our district bridges."

Fascinated by the information, Lisette wanted to ask more. But it would have to wait. They had just arrived in front of the elder manning the door to North Falls. Standing behind Waverly like timid children, the Keepers waited patiently. The elder bowed and asked Waverly about the nature of her trip. Waverly informed him she wanted to show her daughter the waterfall and promised to be back before the high tide. Smiling cordially, the elder opened the door to a short, rectangular corridor.

Waverly instructed them to follow her. Inside the luminous corridor, there was a second door. Pulling it open, Waverly jumped onto the sand outside. When it was Lisette's turn to jump, she stopped to commemorate her first view of the ocean. Crossing the sky above its unknown depths, Thomas Waters splashed a deeper shade of blue over the horizon. What lay beyond the horizon? Would she fall ever downward into a bottomless pit as the ancients believed? Or was there another land like Calder had suspected? Overhead, seabirds squealed their message of welcome and waltzed in the late afternoon sun.

A patch of moss stretched up and down the cove's rocky cliffs. To their right, North Falls barrelled down to wash the sand below and deliver its gift to Thomas Waters. Lisette could taste the salt in the damp air. Florette flew to the ground and ran her fingers through the sand on its way to the ocean. Amelia scampered to the shore's edge, removed her boots, and dipped a foot into the water.

"Lisette, you have to try it," Amelia sang out.

Lisette and Aspen ran across the beach to where Amelia stood, kicking the water. Aspen nearly fell in her bid to rid herself of the clunky riding boots. Waverly and Florette joined them moments later.

"North Falls be one of my favourite places to visit in all of Wrunwicks," Waverly said. "It be outside the district limits, but the people of Wrunwicks never travel this far, so we keep the bridge open."

Lisette spotted three men in the distance with their trousers rolled up. They were hauling a fishing net through the water. A bit farther in the distance, a dock of about twenty feet jutted out from the shore with two partly filled wheelbarrows. Lisette asked her mom what kind of fish the men were trying to catch.

"Mostly the blue fish that roll in this time of year. Districters harvest a lot of the fish ye see in Wrunwicks. We manage to keep some for ourselves too, of course. Thanks to the king's penchant for sarik, the fish harvesters of Kingsbridge District earn enough coin from their fish to pay wron for the year."

"The king has agreed to form an army to fight the karupas and opowaks invading our land," Lisette said.

"So I've heard. I wish the army well, but the bridge must be taken down if we are to be rid of them for good, or the war will never end." Waverly gathered two pebbles and placed them several inches apart. "These pebbles represent the lands connected by the light mason's bridge. The sand represents the star ash surrounding our land, us, and everything around us. But they're so small that people can't see them. Like these grains of sand, each star ash be unique and forever moving through the space around it. And for reasons we have yet to discover, light masons can see the ash once they grow into their ability." She rubbed the damp sand between her thumb and finger.

"We use the sun's energy to interlock and hold the ash together. Masons named it after the wood ash used to make soap. If ye placed a block of soap between the pebbles and hollowed out the middle, ye'd have a bridge connecting the two. An insect could easily travel through the tunnel inside the bridge. Pressure from a bridge causes the space and time around it to crumple so tightly, it allows us to travel its length in mere blinks of an eye. It be as though the bridge was folded onto itself."

Amelia stared at the pebbles. "How do you build the bridge?"

"Like the sun, each of us be filled with unlimited energy. It comes from here." Waverly placed a hand over her heart. "The sun's energy lights the many paths before us. The light from within gives us hope and strength. Our light can also tell us which path to take if we have the courage to see. But we also have a dark energy inside us. And if allowed to grow, its darkness begins to cast shadows all around us. If the darkness grows so big that it turns to hate, there be no room for anything else. Hate knows only itself. The karupas are filled with that hate, as are some people. But we can't allow their darkness to take away our light too."

Waverly drew three circles to form a triangle. Next, she drew a series of squiggly lines projecting outward from the circles. The lines intersected, connecting each circle in the centre of the triangle and along its sides. It reminded Lisette of three interlaced suns.

"Masons link the strings from star ash much like these circles. We noticed that star ash always connects in the form of a triangle. Once we've connected enough ash, we shape the blocks." Waverly drew a rectangle, hesitated, then divided the rectangle into two squares. "Ash blocks are the basic material needed to construct any bridge. Each light mason uses a different technique to shape and assemble the blocks. The same goes for dismantling the blocks."

"The bridge to Krousus?" Lisette asked. She still had no idea how any of it allowed her to destroy the bridge.

"Masons must find their light and let it grow until there be no room for anything else. Only then can she see the star ash and harness the sun's energy. A mason can't be taught to see or use their ability." Waverly placed a hand over her heart once again. "It must come from within. I see that a dark shadow surrounds your heart, sweet pea. It casts long shadows in the light and dims your flame."

"Is that what be happening to Lisette's hair?" Aspen asked. "I swear it grows darker with each passing day."

"Like day turning to night." Waverly reached over to take her daughter's hand. "I sense your heart be troubled, sweet pea. I can't help ye with that, but Florette can."

Lisette gazed at her mom with an image of Melvin and Vincent standing between them. Calder and those killed in Strawbridge were also there. She pictured the child balled up in the corner at Lord Stanley's and the pain pressed onto the faces of survivors. Why were men like Melvin and Vincent spared while Calder and so many innocent people were not? "I don't understand," she said, fresh anger rising to her throat.

"I don't think it was by chance that your paths crossed. A rider and their spirit animal are drawn to each other. For every animal guide, there be one true rider. An animal guide heals and protects their rider. In return, the rider frees their animal guide, their two forms balancing themselves out. As a light mason, Florette's spirit animal will help restore your light and help guide ye to watika, the realization of your full power."

"Transformation be dangerous," Florette said with alarm. "It can lead to madness if a fay transforms too often. Some lakiyas have even attacked humans."

"When your spirit animal finds its rider, it can finally coexist with your fay form. We call them wimals, and there be no danger to either of ye."

"So I could transform as often as I wish?"

"Ye'll both be stronger for it." Waverly stood and brushed the sand from her dress. "We should head back before the tide comes in. Will ye be staying for supper?" She smiled hopefully. "And the night if it pleases ye."

They were enjoying Hilda's impressive cooking skills when Lisette told her mother about what had happened inside the cave on their way to Strawbridge. Waverly listened carefully, weighing Lisette's words without interruption.

"Though rare," Waverly said after Lisette had finished, "there are stories of light masons who claimed to see the space between kurucks, like the one who first saw Wrunwicks."

"Kurucks?" Aspen asked.

"Each kuruck be made up of many different lands separated by vast distances. Wrunwicks be part of one kuruck, Krousus another. Theories about what lies between kurucks have come and gone. A once popular theory said it was the place between the living and the dead, the in-between. A cold and dark place where souls of the wretched are condemned to spend eternity, far from our Mother's guardianship. But of course, the theory was never proven."

"What became of the light masons who said they could see the in-between?" Lisette asked, picturing herself stuck on that ledge for all time. She couldn't imagine a worse fate.

Waverly offered Lisette a reassuring look. "No harm ever came to them according to the surviving stories. I pray ye never find yourself in that situation again, sweet pea. Tomorrow be the harvest festival. We can go, or we could begin your flying lessons."

Lisette squeezed her mother's hand before letting go. Waverly helped herself to another piece of pork pie with almond cream, made in honour of the Keepers. Hilda had also prepared sweet dough, a fried dessert made with bread dough, almonds, honey, ginger, and wine. Lisette helped herself to the sweet dough and turned to Florette. She considered her mother's proposal. What exactly were flying lessons?

Florette finished her dessert and sat on Lisette's shoulder. "I'm to teach Lisette how to fly?"

Waverly laid down her fork and smiled gently. "Ye must learn to fly as one. The natural bond between a rider and their animal guide grows stronger with each flight as they learn to draw strength from one another."

Although Lisette trusted Florette with her life, she still couldn't imagine flying with a pardela or any other creature and found the idea fantastical at best. She also trusted her mother and recalled the group of people flying above them that afternoon. If they could do it, so could she. "There'll be plenty more harvests. I'm willing if Florette be willing."

Chapter 38

As the people of Northbridge District woke to celebrate the harvest festival, Lisette and Florette made their way back to the yardok while the Berion Star made its yearly appearance just before dawn. Waverly accompanied them with Greyson, her animal guide.

The yardok was empty, save for the elders who were already at the doors. Waverly greeted the elder in front of the door to North Falls with an affectionate grin and introduced him to Lisette and Florette, explaining that he was an old friend. Mr. Craters tipped his hat to Lisette and Florette, welcomed them to the district and wished them well before ushering them through the corridor.

The air was cool and damp as the Berion Star faded from view for another year. Lisette watched her first sunrise above Thomas Waters. The ocean lay quiet and still. She had never thought to ask herself if Utaika slept until now. The ocean had spread out a silk blanket for their Mother to rest, who stirred when the water touched the sand like feet at the edge of a bed. Utaika would soon wake from her slumber. Moments later, a flock of seabirds flew across the horizon to greet their Mother as she rose. Lisette turned to Waverly, who was removing her saddle from Greyson's back.

"Ye'll need to start low and slow," Waverly instructed, handing Lisette the saddle. "In time, ye'll be able to fly without this. But right now, ye need to get a feel for each other's movements. Then before ye know it, ye'll be riding saddle-free." She studied Lisette's face. "Don't worry, sweet pea, ye're meant to do this. With a little practice, ye'll even be able to see through each other's eyes."

Nervous and unsure of herself, Lisette placed the saddle on Florette and fastened it. She checked to make sure it was properly cinched. Florette assured her the strap was comfortable. Lisette hoisted her leg over Florette's back. Sitting in the oversized saddle, Lisette looked to her mom for further instructions.

"The rest be up to ye," Waverly said, taking hold of Greyson's white mane. "I won't be far."

"Ye're lighter than expected. Not that I have much experience, mind ye," Florette observed in what had become one of her rare moments of levity.

"That makes the two of us," Lisette said, smiling at her friend's joke. She missed Florette's lighthearted humour. "I guess we'll learn together."

"As it should be." Waverly grinned proudly. "I'll see ye over there," she said, glancing toward the dock.

Florette straightened, and with a graceful flap of her wings, rose into the air. Lisette gripped the reins and took a deep breath. They hovered for several moments to adjust their balance. Once ready, they flew over to where her mom and Greyson waited. Florette stayed clear of the water, flying no more than five feet above the shoreline. Lisette's heart pounded in her chest. She could hear Florette's heart beating with her own.

Waverly pointed to the cliff. "We're going up to Ashwood Rim. We'll wait for ye by the outlying hills. Take your time and try to anticipate each other's movements."

Florette flew to the top of the cliff and across the field of ash trees. Lisette concentrated on her breathing. She watched Florette's wings move through the air, creating ripples in the space around them. Astounded by what else she saw, Lisette let out a sharp breath. She could see the two of them in the moments leading up to now and in the moments ahead of now. The past, present, and future were strung together like a chain of images merging and shifting at every point in time.

Below, the trees swayed to the rhythm of the cool harvest winds. Lisette ran her hand through the ripples travelling over Florette's wings, leaving a crystallized greenish-blue trail behind them. Spotting Waverly and Greyson at the foot of a hill, Florette changed course and increased her speed ever slightly. Lisette tightened her grip on the reins. The treetops grazing Florette's feet sent Lisette their silent assurance. If she fell, the trees would at least cushion her landing.

"Ye're a natural," Waverly said after Florette landed next to Greyson. "But ye need to unburden your heart, sweet pea. It clouds your mind, even now."

"'Tis an honour to fly with ye, Florette," Greyson said. "Stories speak of pardelas, but ye're the first one I've met."

"There be only a few of us left, far as I know. According to the Grand Oak, most pardelas disappeared from Wrunwicks hundreds of years ago."

"Legend has it that when our people arrived here," Waverly said, "the land was inhabited by fair folk capable of transforming into winged animals of immense beauty. The magnificent creatures help protect forest animals from the wrunwick who ruled this land. So when we arrived, they swore to protect us as well. The wrunwick terrorized our people, creating a war between wrunwick and pardelas. It wiped the wrunwick from our land and nearly wiped out pardelas. As legend tells it, pardelas chased the wrunwick through a rift created by the original bridge."

"Does the original bridge still exist?" Lisette asked. After she had shared her story about the cave, Waverly explained how she had accidentally gone through a space rift while fleeing from a karupa and found herself on Galak, lost and alone. Lisette was struggling to come to terms with the knowledge. She loved her mother, but years of grief demanded her mother be made to pay. Lisette pushed her grief aside. Her mother was alive, and she had no intention of allowing her pain to ruin that.

"Destroyed long ago. No one knows exactly when it was taken down," Waverly replied. "And when ye be ready, sweet pea, I'll go with ye to the bridge at Metterling Mountains."

Lisette feared she would never be ready. She was still having trouble wrapping her mind around the idea of being a light mason. "Destroying the bridge won't rid us of the monsters already here," she said quietly.

"No, sweet pea. It won't. Even after the karupas are gone, there will always be monsters in our midst. A few are born that way, but most travel blindly toward the evil that awaits them, losing their hearts to the darkness somewhere along the way."

"Our land be stained with the blood of too many innocent in their fight against an evil spit out by Balsha," Greyson said. "I'm afraid more blood will be spilled before the wrunwick are defeated once again."

Chapter 39

In the days that followed, Lisette and Florette visited North Falls often. Lisette eventually gave up her saddle and reins, preferring the feel of Florette's smooth coat warming her hands. After their first flying lesson, Waverly opted not to go with them, saying this was their time to connect. Both friends grew more confident with each flight and now shared the common sight that Waverly had mentioned. Lisette could also see across distances that she would have never thought possible, and the distance continued to grow. With enough focus, she could now see the king's castle. The image was still blurry but unmistakable. And like Lisette's newly discovered ability to fly, it never failed to amaze her.

On their sixth day of practising alone, Lisette was ready to leave the security of Ashwood Rim and suggested they fly to an island she hadn't noticed until two days ago. Remembering their promise to Waverly, they veiled themselves before venturing from shore.

In a cloud of pulsating colour, they came to the island with its gentle cliffs rising above Thomas Waters. Shielding her eyes from the bright sun, Lisette squinted for a better view of the island. It appeared occupied. Houses, buildings, and roads stretched across the land from shore to shore. Turning her attention back to the cloud of colours, Lisette knew it had to be star ash. Everywhere she looked, the ash churned in luminous swirls.

Lisette scooped up as much as her hands would hold. She had never witnessed so many different colours. Some were familiar, while others were entirely new. The vibrations from the ash ran the length of her skin in waves, mimicking the ocean below. Taking a closer look, Lisette inspected the star ash. Each star was made of strings that resembled branches rippling and coiling around each other as they spun in all possible directions.

And like strands of hair escaped from their confinement, wayward strings contracted while others expanded. Each string varied in colour, creating more shades than Lisette could ever hope to identify. She blew the ash back into the air.

Picturing the strings from her mother's sketch, Lisette placed two pieces of ash between her thumb and forefinger, squeezing the ash together to connect the strings. Once the strings connected, they bonded to create a new colour. She grasped another star ash and held it next to the first two. It bonded immediately to form the triangle her mom had mentioned and yet another colour. She tried to describe the colours to Florette, realizing it was beyond her.

"Like ye, I've never seen so many colours before and wouldn't be able to describe them any more than ye can. Not everything can be expressed through words," Florette said, breaking into Lisette's thoughts. "A box was never meant to hold the stars."

Florette's observation reminded Lisette of the island's strange machines that were scattered everywhere. She pointed to a street in a small town. "Do ye see those metal boxes moving between the houses?" Lisette asked. "They're moving faster than any horse in Wrunwicks."

"It might be wise to keep our distance until speaking to Waverly. I did promise to be careful and watch out for ye."

They turned toward the safety of North Falls. Florette spotted the karupa first. It thrashed about in its usual savagery, destroying ash trees as it headed toward the hills. The district was just a day's ride behind those hills, maybe a little less. Neither of the Keepers had thought to ask how safe the district would be in the presence of karupas, and Lisette had no intention of finding out by allowing this one to attack.

Determined not to shirk in fear this time, Lisette searched her mind for a way to divert and defeat the karupa. She remembered what Florette had said. The stars might not belong inside a box, but maybe she could use the stars to build a box for the karupa.

Unwilling to debate the absurdity of her reasoning, Lisette went to work building a trap at the edge of the cliff. She opened her arms to their fullest extent and scooped up the star ash, then closed them to see if connect the strings would still connect. They did. When she had connected enough ash to create dozens of large, misshapen clusters, Lisette joined the clusters and shaped them into three-sided blocks. When she had created enough blocks, Lisette tried joining two of the blocks. They connected like the ash. She hurried to add the other blocks.

After a quick look at her progress, she connected as much ash as possible to create more clusters and added them to the blocks. When the walls grew too high for her to reach, she asked Florette to fly up so she could stack the remaining clusters and create a roof for the bridge. She repeated the process until the bridge began to take shape. Lisette was relieved to note that each new section pushed the other sections forward, extending the bridge out to sea.

She felt a new energy coursing through her body while she worked. The star ash seemed to have a pulse of its own, radiating outward through its strings. Her hands grew so bright that she could no longer distinguish them from the ash. And inside each star ash, newly formed light served as mirrors that shimmered and reflected everything around it.

"We'll need to force the karupa to turn around and onto the bridge," Florette said after Lisette had finished building their trap.

"I'm not sure that it'll work." Lisette sat back down to examine the hastily constructed bridge. Would it hold? She considered the ends. From what she could see, the bridge connected Ashwood Rim to a point above Thomas Waters. "If we fly in front of the karupa, I can throw ash into its eyes." She scooped up more of the ash. Her hands began to glow again. "When my hands glow like this, they infuse the ash with light. It might blind the karupa or at least throw it off guard long enough for us to attack."

"Mhutig would never agree to your plan. And neither would your mom. They'd call it dangerous and reckless." Florette stretched her wings to their full length. "But my heart says victory awaits us. We just need to find the courage to claim what be ours."

"We have to at least try. That balshak be too close to the district for my liking." Lisette fixed her eyes on the target.

The karupa stopped and sniffed the air. It turned around and started toward them.

"That solves one problem," Lisette remarked. "This one must have a weak nose. It should've detected us before now."

They flew straight ahead. Their veil offered some measure of protection, or so they hoped. When they were no more than ten paces away, Lisette pressed the ash into a ball, grateful for the years of aiming snowballs at trees. She aimed for the chest and swung. The first one missed by a good two feet. She threw a second, third, and fourth star ball. The fourth one struck the karupa on the left shoulder. Florette cheered in admiration. The karupa brushed the offending ash from its shoulder.

Lisette rolled and pressed the star ash as fast as she could throw. After the eighth strike, it was clear the karupa was growing furious, yelping and swinging its arms in the air. They were less than five paces away now. Florette veered to the left while Lisette rolled another star ball. This time, she infused it with the light in her hands.

Taking a deep breath to steady herself, Lisette aimed between the karupa's eyes, hitting it in the forehead. "Close enough." She scooped up her next handful of star ash.

The karupa blinked and stopped to inspect the area. Lisette threw another star ball. This one hit right between the eyes. She struck again before Florette rose to fly over and around the now infuriated karupa. Lisette stirred the ash, creating a windstorm over Ashwood Rim. She watched in triumph as the ash funnelled around the karupa. It thrashed the air in a useless attempt to crush the assailing wind.

"We still need to get it on the bridge," Lisette exclaimed. "Or our efforts won't mean much. Can ye nudge it a little?"

Florette kicked the karupa's shoulder with her front paws. It took a swing, narrowly missing Florette's leg, who kicked it again, harder this time. Lisette threw a star ball, slamming the back of its head. At last, the karupa moved forward with only three paces to go. Lisette asked Florette to fly higher.

Hovering high above the karupa, Lisette dropped a flood of star ash over its head. The karupa weaved and ducked to escape the onslaught. Lisette maintained her frenzied pace, rolling, pressing, and striking with every ounce of strength she could muster. The star balls found their mark. The karupa's left shoulder made a loud cracking noise. It hobbled forward. Lisette wondered where it hoped to go. The trees offered no refuge against her determined hands. At its current trajectory, the karupa was headed straight for the bridge. Lisette threw another star ball to push it forward.

Injured and raving like a mad dog, the karupa stumbled onto the bridge. It disappeared for an instant, then emerged over the depths of Thomas Waters, plummeting to its watery death. Lisette and Florette cried out in triumph. They had vanquished the enemy from Wrunwicks. Lisette basked in her newfound confidence, throwing ash into the air to celebrate their win.

"What of the bridge?" Florette asked when they sobered up. "Can ye take it apart?"

Lisette assessed her work with the budding realization of what she had done. She had forged a bridge of light and ash.

"A light mason must accept her gift with humility and courage," Florette said. "No power should ever be taken lightly. It can destroy as easily as it can create. Power requires great strength to bear its weight."

"Our Divine Mother has given me a friend to share that weight." Lisette wrapped her arms around Florette's neck. "I could never have done it without ye."

"It be my honour to serve. I believe Waverly was right. The Grand Oak wasn't due to wake for another spring. Perhaps it was our Mother who woke her so that we should meet."

"Our Mother's wisdom reaches far and wide," Lisette said. "It isn't for us to question her reasoning, but to express our gratitude for the gifts bestowed upon us."

"Spoken with clarity and humility. Ye'll make a fine mason."

Lisette finished telling Waverly about the island with its strange metal boxes. They had retired to the scriptorium after supper, much to everyone's delight. Enjoying the night calm, Lisette sat across from her mother. Waverly was taking advantage of the fire's crackling light to braid a new rug for the kitchen. Her fingers wove the sweetgrass with the skill afforded by many years of practice. The light from the fire softened the years outlining her face, reminding Lisette of a simpler time. As a child, she would sit between magical tales to watch her mom mend, weave, and sew in front of the fire. Other times, Waverly taught her the words in their books. Lisette never expected to sit with her mom again and thanked Utaika for the blessing. And while she still didn't know the entire story behind her mother's disappearance, they now had a lifetime to catch up.

Waverly's fingers interrupted their work. She studied her daughter's face. "Over time, there have been light masons who could traject from one place to another without bridges. We call them lighters. They inspired respect and jealousy for their power. Not surprisingly, those masons who claimed to see the in-between were also lighters. It seems ye have the gift, sweet pea, and visited Galak. A kuruck much like this one, but more advanced in time and knowledge. Thank Utaika that ye had the good sense to turn around. After all these years, I wouldn't want to lose ye again. We trade in that kuruck, but only Utaika knows where ye might've ended up."

"Districters travel to Millennia?" Lisette asked, still fascinated by the idea. Townsfolk and villagers scarcely ventured far, much less another kuruck.

"Only light masons and the men and women trained in the ways of Galak. Their people and customs are different than our own. We've shared some of their children's stories, scribed in our own language and adapted where needed to best suit our land."

Lisette pictured the metal boxes. She preferred travelling with Daisy to the idea of riding inside a box. Did the people use them for protection? "Are there any creatures like karupas in Galak?"

"No, but they definitely have their share of monsters. Evil be common to people everywhere," Waverly replied.

"Did ye destroy the bridge after the karupa fell off?" Amelia sat on the wall bench in front of the window, breathing in the cool air. "And to think we missed all the fun."

Not even the star-strung sky could compete with Amelia's grace, Lisette marvelled as she smiled at her beloved's words. Their love for each other remained a secret, although she suspected her mother knew. Lisette noticed Waverly observing them on occasion with one of her knowing expressions. Amelia had also taken note and mentioned it during one of their rare moments alone. She had promised Amelia to share their secret with her family and friends when the time was right.

"The bridge came down faster than it went up." Florette stretched out in front of the fire. "Ye would've been proud of her, Waverly."

"I've always been proud of my daughter's abilities." Waverly peered over her spectacles to smile at Lisette. "Your hair be brighter tonight, sweet pea. Tis a good sign. Ye'll be ready soon enough."

"Are there many light masons in Wrunwicks?" Aspen paused in front of the bookshelf she was inspecting.

"Not anymore," Waverly said. "There be me, the young mason who travelled to Krousus, a handful more scattered throughout the districts, and now Lisette. We were many, but after a strange disease began to spread across Wrunwicks, people accused us of bringing death once again. Desperate and dying, the people lashed out. Light masons were declared the messengers of death who needed to be destroyed. Unable to reason with our people, light masons went into hiding and built the first district. Fearing they were next to be killed, fair folk also retreated. Some joined the light masons, while others simply disappeared." She paused to stoke the fire, causing the round spectacles to slip further down her nose. She pushed them back up before returning to Lisette.

"When King Izrek began imposing stricter rules to better control his people and reduce the demand on resources from the growing populace, he introduced a new canon forbidding marriage before the age of twenty-five and many other new rules. Declared traitors by the king and unfit to live among those faithful to the throne and our Mother, protestors were forced to live in cheaply built homes outside the towns. The number of houses grew and became known as Ribald Reach.

"The reaches were hailed as a demonstration of the king's mercy. Light masons invited the people from each Ribald Reach to live inside their districts, leaving the houses as a front for busy tongues. We started rumours to dissuade others from venturing near the districts. And thanks to our prodigious trading success with neighbouring towns, the districts grew into what they are now. The fabrics our queen and ladies are so fond of come from the districts."

Lisette listened in disbelief. How could she and the rest of Wrunwicks be so completely ignorant of the truth? "None of our books describe any of what ye've said, Mom. How is it possible that not a single story exists about what happened?"

"Scribes and bards were forbidden from sharing the events through their stories. It was declared a time best forgotten and never to be spoken of. The king even went so far as to ban the books describing Galak and our role in settling Wrunwicks. Eventually, the long history of our people died with them. The king got his wish, but not until after his death."

"What happened to the books that were banned?" Aspen had joined them in front of the fireplace and now sat next to Florette.

"Light masons saved as many as they could from fire. The books are safe inside the masons' library."

Lisette felt like she had been turned around and upside down. The land she knew was gone, replaced by a land of shadows and secrets buried with their ancestors. "Does King Eldridge know?"

Waverly studied her daughter. "Ye're feeling the effects of star ash. Light masons feel its energy inside and out. For star ash, up, down, left, and right can't be separated. It exists in every possible direction at once." She paused to inspect the mat still in her hands. "As for King Eldridge, no one knows if our true history survived his family tree, other than the king himself."

Amelia tucked a thick wool blanket around her legs. "The inn-keeper said the people of Northbridge have little interest in joining the king's army."

"A few pieces of coin are of no value to a dead man." Waverly placed the mat on the floor next to her chair. "It'll take more than a promise to convince our men to fight such a formidable enemy."

"The karupas and opowaks care nothing of scared men, women, or children," Amelia said. "They kill without distinction."

"Our people need someone to make them understand. Taking down the bridge won't stop those already here," Waverly replied. "It will only give them another reason to war against us."

Florette's eyes searched Lisette's. "I could accompany Lisette across Wrunwicks. We could call upon the people to stand in the name of our families, friends, and Divine Mother. It be up to all of us to defend our land. If karupas are allowed to roam as they once did, it will affect everyone."

Although Lisette felt confident after defeating the karupa, the idea of persuading Wrunwickers to join the king's army opened an old wound. After her mom's disappearance, she spent years fearing that she had somehow failed. She had wanted to go in search of her mom but lacked the courage to try. Nor could she find the courage to ask her father's permission. And with her mom gone, she tried to care for her father and their home as the lady of the house. She failed on all accounts. Despite her father's assurances and praise of her housekeeping skills, she had not been able to keep up with the never-ending demands of a home.

Waverly removed her spectacles. "Ye've come so far, sweet pea. A part of me was afraid ye would never get past the shock from that day."

"Shock from what?" Lisette looked to her mother in confusion. She had no idea what her mother meant.

"When ye were five, I took ye to Rocky Falls after the snow moons like every other year since ye were two. Ye liked to watch the water after the snow melted. Only that year, I noticed a rift in the rock behind the falls. As a light mason, it was my duty to close it. But there must have been a karupa inside the rift. Half its body fell into the lake. It was no more than eight feet tall, a child that had probably wandered off. Ye screamed so loud, I was sure they could hear ye all the way to Stonebridge. A band of light masons took care of the body before hunting and killing whatever karupas had passed through the rift. After that, karupas started using the bridge."

Lisette stared in astonishment. She went back to her childhood, but there was no memory of that day or the horrific accident just described by her mother. *How could anyone forget something like that?* "I don't remember," she said. "It was so long ago."

"Ye had nightmares for more than a fortnight before they finally stopped. Ye never asked about the monster after that. So I let it go, hoping it was over. But we never went back to the falls again. I was too afraid of the nightmares starting again."

"Children are stronger than they look sometimes," Lisette said quietly, remembering what Lord Stanley had said about Harmony.

"Ye grew into a woman of unstoppable courage." Florette was contemplating her friend. "And ye were always good enough. A child should never carry so much burden. Now be time to break the shackles around your heart."

"But what am I to say? In Stonebridge, the people knew me, and I had the elders to back me."

"We'll back ye," Aspen said. "Leaving Stonebridge was the best decision I've ever made. I'd rather face the truth, no matter how dangerous, than live in fear. The people of Wrunwicks deserve to know what be truly happening, so they can face it too."

Lisette pictured the karupa falling into the ocean. If she could take on a karupa, surely she could address a few people. She was about to ask Amelia and Aspen to go with them when Florette shook her head.

"Ye must travel the path alone," Florette said. "My role will be to guide ye."

"Perhaps it be time for light masons to finally emerge from the shadows," Waverly said quietly.

Chapter 40

The next day, Lisette and Florette said their farewells. They were at the yardok and would begin their journey in the neighbouring town of Waterbridge. Aspen and Amelia would stay with Waverly in the Northbridge District, awaiting their safe return.

Waverly extracted a promise from Lisette to use the bridges for their journey across Wrunwicks, all the while gathering men for the king's army, or so everyone hoped. Waverly explained that although Lisette was a lighter, she was also inexperienced and therefore more prone to travel sickness, an illness that befell those who wandered through space rifts.

"But travel sickness can affect inpatient lighters who don't take the time to master their rare gift just as easily," Waverly added with a stern look at her daughter.

Lisette repeated her promise. She found the reference to travel sickness alarming. Her thoughts immediately zoomed in on Amelia and Mhutig. They had travelled through space rifts. Her mother finished by saying no one survived once the illness took hold. She asked Waverly if Amelia and Mhutig were bound to the same fate.

To Lisette's relief, Waverly said that if Mhutig or Amelia had contracted the illness, they would have shown signs within days of their arrival. Lisette recalled Amelia's sudden illness that night on their way to Metterling Mountains. She told her mother about the incident and Florette's quick intervention. While Waverly could not say for certain, she admitted it might have been the onset of travel sickness.

Waverly's admission prompted Lisette to hug Amelia longer than she would have dared before embarking on her next journey. A journey that would begin without pomp or praise but with a new promise to herself. Surrounded by her loyal friends, she had left Stonebridge on a quest for truth.

And during her search for answers, she found the truth about herself, hidden deep inside her heart. But did she have the courage to hold onto that truth? Or would she back away yet again, unable to leap into its unexplored waters? She vowed to chart the entire ocean or sink by trial, whichever came first.

Lisette opened the door to the yardok's receiving hall in Waterbridge District, where an elder greeted them. Lisette introduced herself and Florette before handing him the note from her mother. It granted special permission to use the bridges as an outsider. The elder returned the note, introduced himself in turn, and said that news of Waverly's daughter had spread throughout the districts. He then invited them to stay at the inn on the upper floors. Lisette thanked Mr. Bloomings for his gracious hospitality but declined his invitation. She explained the purpose of their visit to the elder's courteous nods.

"Monsters have always lived inside our myths and fairytales,"

Mr. Bloomings remarked after Lisette finished. "They were best left in stories to scare our imaginations. All we had to do was close the book on them. Now they live in the darkest corners of Wrunwicks."

"We can still close the book on these monsters, but it'll require an army of men instead of one." Lisette bowed her respects and said her farewells. Their business waited in the town of Waterbridge, not its district.

Outside the yardok, Lisette glanced around the square and saw that it was built to the same specifications and splendour as its northern neighbour. She climbed onto Florette's back. They would fly to Waterbridge and over the square, knowing such a grandstanding entry guaranteed some raised eyebrows at the very least. They hoped it would also guarantee people's interest.

Lisette crossed her fingers on their short flight, aware that too many angry tongues could land them in a cage for disturbing the peace. And she didn't fancy waiting for more elders from Stonebridge, preferring not to test their elders' patience a second time.

Lisette and Florette circled the square. Lisette observed the men and women below. It was market day, and everyone was busy with the post-harvest rush. Dressed in the duller colours of their villages, husbands and wives bartered with the brightly dressed townsfolk. Husbands with a pig to spare argued for the fairest price from the butcher, while their wives sold the nuts gathered after harvest alongside baskets and needlepoints. Like her husband, a woman would spend the coin on supplies like honey, salt, and materials needed for winter.

Traders preferred to deal with the more established shopkeepers and seldom travelled to the villages outside town limits, keeping shopkeepers busy and their purses fat. On the tail of the busiest moon cycle of the growing season, Srumoks was the busiest of the entire year with the planting of winter crops, and everyone set to begin preparation for another snow season. But right now, towns-folk and villagers alike turned to the sky.

Florette circled twice more for good measure. The Keepers landed among gaping stares and open mouths. Ignoring the shocked expressions of those around them, Lisette and Florette walked the ten or so paces to the town's well. Lisette straightened her back. She had not prepared a single word for the speech she was about to give, knowing it might prevent her from giving the speech at all. Fear was not the answer, nor would it defeat the enemy.

Lisette introduced herself and Florette, bowing once again to show her respect. The people greeted them with jeers and cries of suspicion. One man called them balsherons, a term used to describe anyone with an unnatural propensity for villainy. The epithet also conjured up dark images of men and women driven to madness by a demonic spell, only to be tormented after their death by Balsha's demons who lived thousands of miles below the surface with the wrunwick. Stories spoke of demons who dug their way up from Balands, lurking in the black of night to cast their frightful spell over the innocent. Once under a demon's vile curse, a person was capable of unthinkable evil. It was not the kind of description to inspire allegiance.

"I can assure ye, kind people of Waterbridge and its region, that we are not balsherons but concerned Wrunwickers like ye. A balsheron could never speak with such reason, their minds locked away in the dark." Lisette scanned the crowd for a friendly face, finding it in that of a young man. "Do I sound like a balsheron to ye, brave sir?"

The young man looked hesitant. Lisette smiled to reassure him. She waited for him to answer, mentally counting each time the man blinked. After about thirty blinks, the young man shook his head.

"Thank ye, kind sir. I promise that we're nothing of the sort. Last spring, my friends and I left Stonebridge to discover the truth behind the vanishings occurring across our great land. Less than two moon cycles later, we found that truth. A band of giants and half-men, half-bulls have joined forces to destroy Wrunwicks and its fine people.

"It be up to us to defend our land and children from this most vicious of enemies. Our wise king himself has agreed to lead an army of men to wage war against the monsters who dare to enter our land. Make no mistake, the enemy will be defeated. But it will require our daring, strength, and fortitude. The knights of old were a true and brave clan of warriors. Now it be up to us to carry on that tradition.

"King Eldridge offers recompense to any man willing to march with him to Metterling Mountains. Though it isn't much in the face of such danger, the army fights not with coin, but with honour and courage. Upon your return, ye will be heroes. And your name will live on in the stories of our children. What say ye, brave men?" Lisette searched their expressions. She saw a mixture of suspicion, fear, and disbelief. But at least no one called them balsherons this time.

After Lisette finished her address, the sound of voices rose above the square. The mid-morning bells rang out, adding to the clamour. Lisette turned toward Florette with a grim smile. They were getting nowhere, she thought to herself. Florette nodded her understanding and stretched her wings to their fullest extent. She flapped them once, then twice more.

"Which of ye brave men will fight to protect our Divine Mother?" Florette asked in a booming voice. "The knights of old may be no more, but their hearts of fire and iron beat inside every man here. Our Divine Mother has provided for us since the first dawn. Now she needs us to defend her land. Who among ye will rise to the task before us?"

The people had grown quiet while Florette spoke. Lisette opened her mouth to add more but decided against it. They had said enough. She could think of nothing more to say.

"Why haven't we seen these monsters?" A man in his thirties emerged from the crowd in a brown farmer's tunic. "How do we know ye speak the truth? The king's notice offers coin in exchange for our service in a war against the wrunwick of old. Yet he makes no mention of the giants or half-men ye speak of."

At least he didn't contest the coin. If the discussion focused uniquely on compensation, they had scarce hope of enticing anyone to join the army. Lisette had no experience with war, but she doubted they were waged or won because of monetary reward. "Although there be no proof, we believe the giants are indeed the wrunwick of old. We've seen too many of the monsters and helped slay one of them in Kingsbridge. At Metterling Mountains, we saw their camp firsthand and the buildings where our people are being held captive."

The noise rose higher and louder this time until Lisette was left with no choice but to shout above the racket.

"Our loved ones must be freed. And that can only be won by the might of Wrunwicks. The people must unite and march to Metterling Mountains," Lisette cried out.

"What of our homes, women, and children?" the farmer asked. "We'll be preparing for winter in earnest soon."

"Your women will miss ye, but they'll have plenty to keep them busy," Lisette said, eliciting laughter from the crowd. She could not recall a sweeter sound.

"And what of the work to be done?" The furrow between the farmer's eyes suggested he lacked the crowd's sense of humour. "Are we to abandon it?"

"Ye won't be leaving for good. Until ye return, your wives are capable of managing homes and land with the ready help of your children." Lisette threw a quick look at Florette. It was time to go. The rest was up to the townsfolk and villagers. "King Eldridge awaits your arrival in Kingsbridge. Meanwhile, the day continues in its usual haste. So now, kind people, we, too, must make haste. May our Mother guide your steps." She bowed a closing farewell.

The Keepers visited Westbridge next, followed by Cornbridge, home of the largest salt beds in Wrunwicks. They were nearing the end of their address when the fifth bell sounded to hail the closing of shops. Lisette glanced over to where a small group of night watchers waited to begin street duty. Excused from the fields for their service to the privy council, night watchers were despised and feared by many. Some argued the watchers made a mockery of the justice symbol, prominently displayed on their light green overcoats. Lisette still wondered where the watchers were the night of Henry's attack.

As townsfolk drifted from the square and with scarce coin in her purse, Lisette approached the cobbler who was shuttering his windows. She asked the man about an inn within her budget. A passing woman heard her query and offered lodging for the price of their company. Unable to refuse such a generous offer, Lisette and Florette eagerly accepted the woman's proposal.

They entered the courtyard through a gated entrance. The house more closely resembled a manor with its architecture and layout. Briony ushered her guests up a set of stairs to their right where a servant waited. Lisette relinquished her sword.

Briony led them to a window bench at the far end of the hall. Admiring the feather cushions with their cheerful designs, Lisette welcomed the opportunity to rest. Florette sat next to them, ever protective of her charge. A second servant kept vigil near an ambry. Lisette resisted the urge to inform the spindly youth they had no interest in plundering the cupboard's wealth.

Seated on the bench across from Lisette, Briony peered out the blue-stained window overlooking the courtyard. She seemed lost in her thoughts. A heavy melancholy surrounded her, impressing it-self onto her face and manner. And although Briony had been more than willing to share her story on their walk back, Lisette imagined the only person allowed past their host's impenetrable sadness to be her husband. Married for two years, she wore loneliness as the knights of old wore their armour.

A salt trader like his father before him, Briony's husband often travelled the low belt from Cornbridge to Eastbridge. His long trips left her in charge of their home and its affairs. Briony admitted that she liked being in charge but also missed her dear husband. At twenty-eight, Briony had lost two babies. Lisette could see their loss weighed on Briony, despite her quick smile.

Briony diverted her attention from the courtyard, surrendering its secrets to the night. "Tell me, fair guests, what brings ye so far from home in aid of the king?"

"I fear that without an army, the beasts will eventually take over Wrunwicks and there'll be no one left," Lisette said honestly.

"Please forgive my bold lips, but would a man not be more suited to the task? I should think men more apt to follow another man."

Lisette was reminded of her conversation with Florette the night before. She had voiced the same concern to her loyal friend. Florette had assured her of the contrary and now smiled patiently at the suggestion.

"The messenger isn't as important as the message," Florette said to Briony. "Passion must be tempered by reason if we expect people to listen. Lisette speaks with her heart, all the while holding onto her wit."

"If only my brave husband were here. He'd gladly ride with the king to Metterling Mountains. Julien was never one to walk away from a fight."

"King Eldridge could use a man like your husband in his army," Lisette said earnestly.

"I'd spare the servants if they were mine to spare. Wrunwicks belongs to everyone. My husband has many connections. He be also in the good graces of our town lord. In his absence, I see no reason not to use those connections to help your cause if needed."

"I'm appalled by people's lack of interest in the threat that looms over all of us," Lisette said.

"The king be too far removed from the low belt and most of Wrunwicks. King Eldridge might be a wise man, but he knows little of his people. Many of us have only seen him in the paintings that hang throughout our libraries. While a number of men have left to answer the king's plea, it would do much to further his cause if he travelled beyond the walls of his castle more often."

However puzzled by the observation, Lisette knew Briony to be correct. Until leaving home, she possessed almost no knowledge of their king or Kingsbridge. People spoke of King Eldridge with a blend of loyalty and fear. No one disputed his rule from afar, lest an elder overheard them. Anyone opposed to his reign whispered behind deaf walls and then only with the trusted few. Speaking ill of the king was an unforgivable breach of trust, for a king's ancient bloodline flowed from Utaika. To dare question his reign was to undermine their Mother's wisdom.

"Wrunwicks be a vast and beautiful land. King Eldridge denies himself the pleasure of its many charms," Lisette replied. "It be with a grateful heart that I accept your generous offer. The strength of Wrunwicks resides within its people."

"To Wrunwicks and its brave citizens." Briony grew quiet as a servant approached to inform her the cook worried their meat might become tough if not soon eaten. "To our victory and the cook's expertise," she concluded.

Chapter 41

isette and Florette travelled east throughout the low belt for the next two days. They stopped each night with the fifth bell, finding shelter in lonely inns, long forgotten. But after a meal of bread and watery pottage, exhaustion softened their pillow. On the third day of travel, they made their way to the mid-belt of Wrunwicks. After visiting the town of Woodbridge, they looked forward to spending the night in Stonebridge.

They went directly to Lisette's house, skipping market square. Lisette counted more than four moon cycles and a fortnight since leaving home. It felt like four years of yesterday. Florette landed in the backyard among the chickens, pig and sheep. The windows were shuttered to banish the gusty winds.

Lisette opened the door and ran through the back tewk on her way to the kitchen. She could already smell her stepmom's pottage simmering over the fire. Standing at the butcher's table, Nora was chopping cabbage. She turned around to see Lisette standing in the doorway. With a cry of delight, Nora rushed over to squeeze her stepdaughter. Florette poked her head around the door.

Nora cried out again, this time in astonishment. "My failing sight deceives me. Surely tis not a pardela I'm seeing. I heard the stories but didn't know what to believe."

"Mom, I'd like ye to meet my good friend, Florette. And your eyes aren't deceiving ye," Lisette said, still holding onto her stepmom. She smelled of soap and cabbage. Lisette took a warm breath. "I promised her she could stay with us tonight."

"My word. A pardela in my house. I thought they disappeared into legend before my great-grandmother was born."

"Pleased to meet ye, Mrs. Steels. Ye've raised a fine daughter." Florette stayed at the door.

"A smart pardela at that." Nora gestured for Florette to enter. "Well, no need to stand there. Come in. I was getting supper ready. Ye'll be staying, of course."

"It'll be my honour." Florette sat next to the table. "Lisette told me about your pottage. The best in Wrunwicks."

Nora chuckled with pleasure. "Lisette may have exaggerated just a little. But I'll let ye be the judge of that."

"Soon, ye'll meet my father," Lisette said to Florette. "He'll back my claim. After he's had his fill, mind ye."

Nora's eyes grew sombre. She hugged Lisette again, harder this time. "I'm so sorry, Lisette. This isn't the news ye be wanting to hear after getting home, but I'm afraid your father won't be home for supper."

Confused, Lisette studied her stepmom's face. "Is he away on a trip?" Lisette wished she could have sent word about her visit. Her heart sank at the thought of not seeing her father.

"Your father was accused of stealing from Lord Sumunder. Ye might remember young Dottie. She claims to have witnessed your father sneaking out of the lord's granary."

"But tis nonsense. Dad would never steal from Lord Sumunder or anyone else, for that matter," Lisette said after Nora's words sank in. She couldn't think of a more outlandish claim against her father.

"Your father be an honest man, loyal to land and king. But twas your father's word against hers. And there be turnips gone from the lord's reserve. They even withheld his share of the prized pig."

Lisette looked around the kitchen she had grown up in, settling on her father's bench at the end of the table. She knew in her gut that Dottie had mistaken revenge for her father in the granary. *Cage for a cage.* She imagined Vincent leering in satisfaction.

"Your father be in a cage like a common thief." Nora clobbered the cabbage. "He won't last the snow season."

"Dad won't be in that cage come snow. He won't," Lisette said, determined to free her father. She would not let him rot in a cage. "Florette, ye stay with Mom while I see to this outrage."

"Dottie won't change her claim, Lisette. I pleaded with her to see reason until my tongue went numb. She laughed and said it was out of her hands. A rotten seed, that one."

Lisette found Dottie tending to the chickens. How fitting, Lisette mused as she opened the gate. When Dottie straightened to greet her visitor, Lisette noticed she was pregnant. After a twinge of guilt for what she was about to do, Lisette walked over to where Dottie stood, rubbing her belly.

"How dare ye accuse my father of stealing," Lisette said with slow deliberation. "Have ye no heart?"

"So, the prodigal daughter returns while my brother rots in a cage. I have plenty of heart, shrew. And it breaks because of ye."

"Vincent should never have gone to Kingsbridge in search of trouble. Because of him, Henry be stuck in bed unable to walk."

"Word has it, he lies on a mattress made of the finest feathers. I hear it be your word that sent my brother to the cage. Ye stole him from me. We all know the privy council's promise be empty as a poor man's purse. So now I've taken your father from ye."

If not for the unborn child, Lisette would have slapped her. As it were, the baby had no stake in the matter. "What did ye hope to accomplish? It doesn't change Vincent's fate."

"No, but ye can, just as I can change your father's fate. I may be a shrew, but I don't pretend otherwise. And I'm smart enough to know how to barter."

Lisette glared at the woman standing in front of her. "My father isn't livestock. He can't be bartered like swine."

"I see that ye have much left to learn. Little Lisette, always so naive. My word for your word. It be simple enough. Tis high time to get those squeamish hands of yours dirty. All ye need do be to tell the king ye made a mistake, claiming your eyes deceived ye, or some other biddle-babble. Ye'll think of something if ye want your father home before the snow fills his cage."

Nora and Florette were still in the kitchen when Lisette returned. Florette had transformed back into her fay form and was assisting Nora at the butcher's table. They stopped, transfixed in a single moment of time. Nora searched Lisette's face for the slightest hint of hope. Lisette forced her brightest smile, resolved to make good on the promise she made.

"I spoke to Dottie, and we've come to an agreement. If I can convince the king to release her brother, she'll withdraw her claim."

"That dastard deserves his lot." Nora's voice shook with anger. "A rotten seed like his sister. They didn't get it from their mom, I can tell ye that. A better woman, ye'd never find."

"Vincent's lot will need to wait until after Dad be back where he belongs. I'll address the people by day's end with Florette, then tomorrow we'll make Kingsbridge long before nightfall. If it works, I'll have to get word back to Dottie. But first, I need to see Dad."

Nora accompanied them to the cage district for her twice-daily visit. Sam was sitting with his head resting on both knees when they located his cage. At the sight of his daughter, he scrambled upright, exclaiming his amazement. He reached out to take her hand. Lisette insisted on hugging him through the rusty bars. Nora gave him some bread, pottage, and ale to wash it down.

"If I knew ye were coming, my dear Lisette, I would've made better arrangements," Sam joked, laying his food to one side. "I swear ye've grown over the past four moon cycles." He stopped at the sight of Florette. "And who do we have here?"

Lisette forced down the lump in her throat. Growing up, it was easy to take her parents for granted. But here in the cage district, she realized they weren't infallible. Her father had always looked so strong, the tower of strength protecting her with the fierceness of a bull. She wiped her eyes, blaming her tears on the dusty road.

Sam squeezed her hand. "I won't be in this cage forever, Lisette. And I need ye to stay strong for when I come home. Promise me ye will."

Lisette managed a nod. She was afraid to speak. The lump in her throat had grown so big, she couldn't swallow.

"Ye need not worry." Nora winked at Lisette. "There be a flame inside our girl that no wind could ever extinguish."

Lisette threw her stepmom a grateful look. She was blessed to have Nora in her life. They both were.

"And what brings ye to Stonebridge?" Sam asked once Florette had introduced herself. "Surely ye haven't travelled all this way to visit me in a cage."

As she stood there fighting for control, Lisette felt a surge of admiration for her parents. Neither had thought to question Florette's presence. Both her parents accepted Florette with the same open hearts they had always shared. The same open hearts that embraced all of life, balshaks included. Even now, inside the cage district, their spirits could not be broken.

Florette had already begun to share the details of their journey across Wrunwicks. When Lisette recovered her voice, she added the occasional detail of her own between pauses. They finished with their upcoming address to the people of Stonebridge.

"Ye might want to hold off on that," Sam advised. "After ye left, some folks took to shaming your group for leaving during the growing season. And now, ye've been branded the daughter of a thief. Folks were already sore about Calder's death, blaming ye for what happened."

Lisette suspected her father was underscoring the true ugliness of people's reactions. "Calder's death was an accident. We had no idea of the threat we were facing." She refrained from mentioning her guilty conscience. It was her burden to carry. And saying it out loud would only deepen the wound left by Calder's loss.

"The people here are scared. Calder's death gave them a place to focus that fear. When his father returned from Kingsbridge, their fear turned to anger."

"We have to at least try. They deserve to know the truth about what be happening."

"They know enough. Your mother told me there be a notice posted in the square asking men to fight in the king's new army. Ye can't save everyone, my dear Lisette. I remember ye mending your dolls when ye were little. Ye refused to let any of them go. I think your mother still has a couple stored in a basket somewhere."

Sam opened his mouth to continue, but Nora interrupted him to share Lisette's plan to free him.

"I'd insist that ye give up your plan if I thought it would do any good. Ye're too headstrong for your own good, Lisette. What if the king decides to make an example of ye? Ye could end up in a cage yourself."

Lisette assured her father that no harm would come to her. "I share your mind, Father."

"And look where that got me." Sam turned to Florette. "I'm counting on ye to help keep my daughter safe. We all need someone to walk with us, no matter how brave we are."

Lisette gave her father a tender look. She placed a hand over her brooch. "It reminds me that I'm never alone."

Chapter 42

A servant escorted Lisette and Florette through the courtyard and up the tower stairs. King Eldridge sat with the queen in front of the fireplace. Queen Harriet looked up from her needlepoint to welcome their guests with a warm smile. She summoned them to come forward.

"What brings ye to the castle after so long an absence, Seekers?" King Eldridge studied his subjects. "Bring ye some much-needed good news, or should I regret your visit?"

Where to begin? "We stand before ye after our journey to spread word of the new army, my king. Just this morning, we visited Shewbridge and Highbridge. Ye'll need many soldiers to help gain your victory. The likes of which will surely become legend." Lisette stopped to catch a breath. "Your defeat of such a renowned enemy will be an achievement few kings can boast."

"Your loyalty and dedication to the king be most admirable," Queen Harriet said. "It will serve ye well."

"I hope your faith does not prove itself premature, my queen," Lisette said. But bolstered by Queen Harriet's words of praise, she continued. "It might favour your victory to add such able-bodied men as Melvin and Vincent to your army, my king."

King Eldridge flushed a beet red. "I shall not be known as the king who allowed breakers in his army. Victory belongs in the hands of the true, not miscreants."

Lisette sighed inward. As much as she did not care for their king, she agreed with him on one point at least. "Your wisdom shines through once again, my king. Wrunwicks belongs to the brave and true. And so the reclamation of our land must reside with them." She pictured her father inside his cage. "However, it be with a heavy heart that I must inform ye of my grievous mistake. I fear that I was mistaken in my claim against Melvin and Vincent, my king. The dark of night deceived my senses, ensnaring me in its treachery." Her mouth tasted like spoiled cabbage.

"I've often mentioned the need for an earlier curfew during the growing season," Queen Harriet said, coming to Lisette's rescue. "The dark be a false mistress who cannot be trusted by those who follow the virtues. She protects the disloyal who more often prefer the company of her toads to that of our Divine Mother."

"Queen Harriet speaks true. Although it saddens me to say, false claims do occur from time to time. I will need to seek the counsel of my elders, of course. And if agreeable, Vincent will receive a full pardon. Melvin incited this sorry calamity by bringing the matter to Kingsbridge, so he will be permitted to join the army as a fair requirement for his pardon. The seat of judgment frowns heavily upon those who waste their time with matters best settled at home."

"Most wise, my king. Melvin be a notable swordsman." Lisette bowed. The king's words were more than she had allowed herself to dream.

King Eldridge looked to Queen Harriet. She nodded briefly. Observing their exchange, Lisette feared she had said something to offend the king. *I should never have praised Melvin.*

"Ye can trust these two," Queen Harriet said to the king. "They're true and sound in mind and character."

The king turned to Lisette. "In return, I ask for your continued dedication to the crown and to be my eyes and ears when required. My suffering prevents me from knowing what be happening in the distant regions."

"Our king suffers a debilitating and most painful illness that renders travel over long distances near impossible," Queen Harriet explained. "It would not do well for the people of Wrunwicks or his council to see their king as weak. This knowledge cannot be shared with anyone. To do so would be seen as treason by myself and our king."

Could she refuse their king and queen? She was already indebted to Queen Harriet. And without her, Lisette knew the king would not listen with such willing ears. She glanced at Florette. What had she dragged her friend into? To Lisette, the king's request was a small price to pay for her father's life, but she had no right to exact the same price from Florette.

"It will be my honour to serve our king and land," Florette said.

Lisette snuck a grateful peek at her dear friend. It would seem they had just become the king's messenger and opened the door to her father's freedom, allowing her to keep at least one promise.

Lisette bowed. "And mine as well, my king. I can think of no greater honour."

Outside the castle gate, Lisette noticed a large group of tents. Pitched in the same field that hosted the Knights Memorial, the tents ushered in a new dawn. The age of war had begun. They could burrow inside the safety of their homes or march toward it. Either way, the war would find them.

Ewart stood outside a tent with Mhutig. They waved to the Keepers. Florette landed next to Mhutig.

"There be a sight," Ewart said. "Ye look made for each other."

"We've had a lot of practice," Florette said. "It was slow going at first, but Lisette be a fast learner."

Lisette asked how the training was going. She was heartened by the number of men at the camp. A few were practising with swords, while others were tending to the makings of supper. At the far end of the field, she spotted Roy in a line of men sharpening their bow skills. The man next to Roy shot his bow at one of the straw targets. The man's arrow hit the outer circle. Roy smacked him on the shoulder. Lisette could see that Roy was pleased with the shot.

"'Tis better than expected." Ewart pushed the hair out of his face. "Men have been trickling in from all over the high belt. To our surprise, many came in from Strawbridge. They need the coin to buy grain for the winter. We're expecting more from Strawbridge over the coming days."

"Ye may be seeing a lot more men too," Florette said. "Lisette's speech should rally the low and midbelters here as well."

"Don't let Florette's modesty fool ye," Lisette said. "She saved my blundering tongue more than once. I can only pray our efforts won't be in vain. Some were already on their way, thank Utaika. But we still visited every town in Wrunwicks except Northbridge and Strawbridge, thinking it best to forego Strawbridge given the attack. Though it seems they've made up their minds."

"Every man who makes his presence known is welcome," Mhutig said. "The king instructed the blacksmiths and bowyers of

Kingsbridge to fashion additional weapons for the men. We plan to march by the end of the moon cycle. Any other training will need to be completed on our way to the mountains. Until then, we have plenty of work to do. Some of these men have never held a weapon until their arrival, but they have the will and the might to learn."

Atop the highlands of Kingsbridge, Lisette squinted in the dark. While Ewart and the men trained beneath the moons' watchful gaze, she prepared to set course for Stonebridge. With night under-way, Lisette suggested they forego the district bridges to save time. Florette insisted they veil themselves in case some poor bystander looked up and panicked at the sight of a woman riding a black cat with her head swathed in fire.

Past the hills, valleys, forest, rivers, and blue murkiness, Lisette could see Stonebridge and Woodbridge. Her sight was growing stronger. At first, the towns appeared smudged against the skyline. Blinking to adjust her eyes, Lisette separated the smudge into two distinct, sprawling towns. She zoomed in on Stonebridge. It drew closer. As Stonebridge approached from the south, Lisette and Florette were pulled from the north. Then without warning, they trajected to the bridge outside Stonebridge.

"That'll take some getting used to." Florette swooped upward to avoid the tree in front of her. "If we manage to stay alive long enough."

They flew straight to Dottie's house. Florette transformed back into her fay form to avoid startling the chickens. Lisette was about to open the back gate when Florette remembered their veil. Lisette rubbed her forehead. It would do no good to knock on Dottie's door in their current state. She might have laughed at the prospect, but she couldn't find her sense of humour.

The pig lifted his head high and squealed, mocking her feeble attempt to be heard. She knocked harder while Florette lingered next to her. The sixth bell rang out, announcing curfew. Lisette's heart jumped. They should have refused Ewart's invitation to stay for supper. A damp wind found its way inside and slithered up her back. She pictured a snake with bloodthirsty fangs and shivered.

"Little Lisette," Dottie said, arriving at the doorway. "Twice in as many days. To what do I owe the misfortune?"

"I've come to inform ye of your brother's release. Vincent will receive a full pardon."

"I was unaware he needed to be pardoned. If hate were indeed punishable, we'd all find ourselves in a cage." Dottie sneered at her visitors. "Ye take me for a soft wit to present this news just one day after our agreement."

The biting cold Lisette saw in Dottie's eyes reminded her of Vincent. She sympathized with the unborn child. Motherhood would not become this woman. "I assure ye my words are true." Lisette gestured toward Florette. "We travel faster than any horse."

Dottie scoffed at Lisette. "No animal can travel that fast. Ye've been drinking too many blue leaves."

Lisette wanted to ask if Dottie had emptied a pitcher. In large quantities, blue tea was known to play tricks on the mind. Yet the prevalence of blue flowers made it the preferred tea of Wrunwickers when the days grew cold and the pipe leaves of choice during the growing season. *Still your tongue.* "I give ye my word."

"Your word be of no value to me, little Lisette. I prefer to trust my eyes. When Vincent returns to Stonebridge, I'll stand before the seat of judgment. And not before. Now, if ye'll excuse me, I have more pleasant matters to attend."

Chapter 43

Lisette and Florette opted to spend the night with Nora. Her stepmom was thinner than Lisette remembered. She worried that in caring for her father, Nora forgot to also care for herself. After convincing her stepmom to sit and eat with them, Lisette eagerly shared the details of Vincent's release, their meeting with Dottie and her promise to stand before the seat of judgment. The news brought a fresh set of tears for Nora.

"I don't know how ye did it. Convincing the seat of judgment be no easy task," Nora said. "The king's seat, no less. But convince them ye did. Tis nothing short of a miracle."

"We still need to wait for Vincent to come home," Lisette said, wishing she could shake the sense that Dottie sorely lacked into her thick head. *Maybe I could mix it with her tea.*

"We've waited this long. We'll just have to wait a bit longer, tis all. Your father be a patient man. He'll be so pleased when I tell him what ye've done."

Mouser sauntered into the kitchen and stopped when he saw Florette in her animal form. His fur stood on end. Florette turned toward the old grey cat and purred in a low, crooning voice. Mouser's fur settled down. He meowed, walked up to Florette, and sat next to her.

"I should've asked ye to speak with Dottie in my stead," Lisette remarked, stroking Mouser's long fur coat. "Maybe she would've retracted her claws for ye. I swear she wanted to tear me to shreds. I'm not sure who's worse, Dottie or her brother."

"Dottie's heart be closed to love and her mind to reason," Florette replied. "Let's hope Vincent possesses enough for the both of them and makes haste."

"Until then, I'll take care of your father, Lisette. He won't want for food or ale so long as I'm here. Dottie won't get the better of us, or my name isn't Nora Steels."

"Promise ye'll put some of that food into yourself as well, Mom. It won't do Father any good if ye get sick. We both depend on your strength and would still be lost without your love to guide us."

"Tis hard to remember sometimes, but I promise to try. And soon I'll have your father back with me."

The Keepers returned to Northbridge District the next day before noon. Waverly waited for them in the scriptorium with Amelia and Aspen. After a round of hugs and exclamations of relief, Lisette updated everyone on their journey. She finished with the release of Vincent and Melvin. All three women agreed Lisette's deal with Dottie was a small price to pay for Sam's freedom. Lisette abstained from mentioning the king's illness or his request of her. She was still unsure what her role as messenger would entail and didn't want to burden her friends.

Waverly asked Florette and Aspen to help her retrieve the overcoats she had purchased while Lisette and Florette were gone.

When they disappeared behind the door, Amelia wrapped her arms around Lisette and placed a tender kiss on her lips.

"I was so worried about you," Amelia said. "Your mother might not admit it, but I could see the concern in her eyes too. She loves you, Lisette. As do I."

Lisette took in Amelia's face. She savoured the unique joy of Amelia's arms around her. "My heart leaps at the sight of your smile. I want to shout our love into the kurucks, but such a love be forbidden."

Amelia kissed her again. Slower this time. "Tis not forbidden in Krousus or the districts. I've seen it with my own eyes. When I asked Waverly about it, she said they've never followed the king's rule, including the first canon."

Lisette held onto Amelia like a drowning woman. "The districts feel like a different land. When I'm here, it be easy to forget about the canons and the busy tongues of townsfolk. They'd be all too happy to report us to the privy council. Especially in Stonebridge where I'm now the daughter of a thief."

"A land hidden inside another one," Amelia replied softly. "Wrunwicks is a strange place. But I have you next to me." She pressed her body against Lisette's. "And that's what matters. Your father's name will be cleared soon and so will yours."

Waverly knocked and opened the door, prompting Lisette to let go of Amelia. Waverly held a purple woollen overcoat in her arms while Aspen held a breen one. Breen was a blue-green dye that first appeared around two years ago. It was growing in popularity among nobles and the few townsfolk who could afford the more expensive colour. Lisette had always found the bold colour to be stunning.

"These will keep ye warm," Waverly said. "I had them altered using Aspen's measurements. Ye'll still be able to ride with them on." Waverly turned toward Amelia. "Please forgive my silence, but I didn't want to give ye the chance to refuse my gift." She handed her the purple overcoat. "The colour will compliment your skin and lovely hair."

Lisette smiled in agreement with her mother, admiring the round buttons that ran down the front and forearms. They were made of bone instead of the cheaper cloth buttons.

Aspen handed Lisette her overcoat. "She swore me to secrecy. Mine be sleeveless like yours but dark green with a straight hem like Amelia's. It has a slit on each side and one in front like Amelia's too. Tis a lovely coat. I tried to refuse, but it was of no use. Your mom can be very insistent."

Florette flew over to Lisette. "Ye have to try it on. They look delightful and elegant."

Grinning at Florette's description, Lisette and Amelia tried on the overcoats. Amelia's coat fit perfectly over her dress. Lisette pulled hers over her jacket and buttoned it up. The silk lining matched the fine wool exterior. The coat was warm, light, and fit comfortably. It was longer in the back, extending past her knees and V-shaped like the two front panels. At their longest point, the front panels reached just above her knees. The front buttons went down to her hips. A leather belt completed the overcoat with a single purse loop. Lisette tied the belt and turned around for her mother. She had never worn anything so luxurious.

"I chose long sleeves for ye, Amelia," Waverly said, admiring the two women. "Ye don't have a jacket to keep ye warm like Aspen and Lisette."

"Thank ye, Mom. They're stunning. But they must have cost a king's purse," Lisette said.

"I rarely have occasion to spend the coin I've earned from silk and spice trading. It pleases me to spoil my beautiful daughter after all these years." Waverly directed her eyes toward Florette. "I would've chosen one for ye too. But they had none in your size."

"My body's temperature remains constant throughout the year," Florette said. "We don't feel the cold like humans."

"One day, I'd like for us to visit the masons' library on the other side of Metterling Mountains. And when that day comes, I'd like to make a stop on the way, so we'll need to dress warm." Waverly's face glowed with pleasure

Chapter 44

Metterling Mountains stretched clean across the horizon, offering shelter to the passing cloud in its weathered valleys. Lisette reached up to welcome the early morning sun. After King Eldridge had abruptly postponed their departure days before they were due to leave, the men were finally set to begin their long march to the mountains on the first aromons of Romoks. The king's delay put the soldiers a fortnight behind schedule, which gave the last men to arrive a chance to settle in and practice their weapons skills. Notwithstanding another delay, the soldiers were set to leave in two days.

Ewart hoped their journey would take no more than one moon cycle. But with the first flakes already on the ground, Ewart feared more snow would slow their progress. He also expected the terrain between Kingsbridge and the mountains to be rough going after an unseasonable amount of rain, further impeding their race against winter.

Upon hearing Ewart's concerns, Lisette had travelled with Florette to inspect the route, a kind term for the narrow paths they used during their journey from the camp to Kingsbridge. The paths were muddy and nearly impassable in some areas. Lisette had suggested building a bridge to Waverly, who promptly advised against the idea, saying the bridges could serve dark ambitions in the wrong hands.

Lisette looked to her mother now. They were finally going to the masons' library. And true to her word, Waverly had stopped along the way. They were standing in a large field at the bottom of a valley. Nestled between the mountain's peaks, the valley and its flowers went on for miles.

Waverly's eyes followed the flowers across the snow-powdered valley. "The library be only accessible through a chain of bridges like the one we just used," she said eventually. "During the reign of King Izrek, masons and districters used the bridges to transport stone for the districts."

"Does anyone still use the bridges?" Amelia asked.

"Not anymore. I can't remember the last time a mason travelled to the library. When the last rayiok died ten years ago, the library and its books were left to the trees."

"The last rayiok?" Lisette searched her memory, but she couldn't recall hearing the word before.

"The old word for bookkeepers. Rayioks lived at the library and cared for the books." Waverly kneeled to inspect one of the purple flowers. "I always check on the flowers before my visit." Waverly held one of the star-shaped petals between her fingers. "They bloom all year long, but their colours are especially vibrant this time of year."

Aspen hugged her overcoat. "I don't know how they survive this cold."

Waverly tracked the mountain's dense profile before settling on

Aspen. "Our Mother never makes mistakes. These flowers need the mountains like we need air. Thinking they were like snow flowers, I planted them in the district some years ago. But they perished in the summer heat."

"No matter how hard I try, I fail to understand our Mother's wisdom behind karupas," Aspen said. "The lands would be better served without them."

"I'll never understand their hate of humans," Waverly said. "And yet, we're stronger because of the karupas. Men from every belt have united in a common goal. An event that hasn't occurred since the ancient ones."

"An impressive feat," Amelia said. "In Krousus, we've grown too dependent on taupaks to protect us. Fear is all we know."

"Our people live in fear too, living out their lives without ever knowing what lay beyond field duty, preferring the toil they know to the unknown. And while fear be natural in the face of danger, we can't let it control our fate." Waverly pointed to the mountain flowers. "Like these flowers, we can rise above that which seeks to destroy us. Or we can lie down in defeat."

They stepped off the bridge and onto a narrow path that led from the library to a lake. Waverly said the object near the dock was called a boat or dory. The dory's design was fashioned after the small boats of Kavora, the island to which Lisette had travelled with Florette on Galak.

Intrigued by the dory's simple frame, the Keepers walked the overgrown path for a closer look. Made of wood, the dory looked timeworn but otherwise solid. Waverly picked up one of the sticks lying inside the dory, saying the sticks were called oars and that they were used to steer the dory out to the lake's deeper waters for fishing. She wagered the dory would still float as the others took in its battered appearance.

"We can take it for a trip sometime." Waverly placed the oar back in the dory. "But right now, I'd like to show ye the library."

Built on a gently sloping hill, the library stood in the permanent shadow of Metterling Mountains. A series of vines crept over the walls and maintained their upward journey onto the roof. Stripped of their leaves, the vines shielded the entire library in a prickly layer of defence against intruders. Beneath its protective layer, the library looked almost as worn as the dory. It too had weathered its share of storms. The entire area was enclosed by a thick forest of redwood trees that hid the ancient library from view, although Lisette failed to see how someone might stumble across the remote location. She wondered what lay beyond the forest.

Waverly opened the door onto a large chamber. The fresh breeze merged with the smell of dust and old books. Shelves lined the walls on three sides that gave way to a table and chair every ten feet or so. Lisette counted eight tables with candle holders on the walls above for reading. Waverly opened the shutters, found a fire striker on the mantle over the fireplace, and lit the candles. When the candles had chased the gloom from every corner, she stacked a small bundle of wood and twigs into the firebox, lit a handful of dry moss stored in a nearby basket, then carefully laid the moss in with the kindling. Satisfied with her efforts, she invited the Keepers to poke around.

"The place could use a little freshening, but it'll do for now." Waverly looked around the library. "It used to be so busy here with light masons coming and going. There was always pottage over the fire in the kitchen and ale to wash it down." She gestured toward her right. "The rayiok welcomed everyone who came through that door. Though most masons preferred the back door for a taste of her pottage.”

“I can still feel the energy of times past,” Florette said. “This was a place of great warmth.”

“What happened to the light masons?” Aspen asked. “Why did they abandon this place?”

“Over time, fewer women were born with the light,” Waverly replied. “We were always outnumbered by those around us.” Her eyes clouded over. “I fear there’ll be none left eventually. Our search for others has proven fruitless, but I refuse to give up.”

“There has to be more,” Aspen said. “Maybe they just aren’t aware of their power, like Lisette.”

“The young child in Lord Stanley’s care has the makings of a mason,” Waverly said hopefully. “She has the hair and heart to match. When she be ready, she’ll find us. We can’t interfere in a mason’s fate. They must choose for themselves.”

“But if they don’t know, then how can they choose?” Aspen persisted. “How could anyone not want such an amazing power?”

Waverly studied Aspen’s stubborn expression. “’Tis how we’ve always done things, but ye could be right. It might be time to find a new way.” Waverly smiled at Lisette.

Lisette combed through the dusty library shelves, stopping in front of a book whose copper trim had turned green around its soft leather binding. *The First King*. Her interest piqued by the simple title, she sat down at a reading table and opened the book.

hey came from across the mountains, a group of twenty men in need of shelter. Like those before them, the men spoke of villages much like our own and shared their language and

customs with our people. Finding the people of Wrunwicks to be most generous and fair, the men stayed for more than three moon cycles, speaking of the riches throughout our land. One man spoke of his king and the reward they would surely receive for the biggest discovery of gold ever known.

The men travelled throughout our noble land, stirring imaginations with their promise of coin for all who helped amass the gold. They shared stories of a great ruler who led his people to victory across many kingdoms. Their powerful king would rule Wrunwicks too and add it to his mighty kingdom. The good people of Wrunwicks did not like these stories of a king who would come to rule their land. Our people had many wise leaders of their own and did not want a king from across the mountains.

Upon hearing of the men and their claims, Sianna, a young and courageous light mason with hair redder than the boldest of feathers, sought counsel with the leaders throughout Wrunwicks. She travelled near and far to discuss the threat to our people. Her counsel achieved, the leaders agreed we needed to protect this land from anyone who wished to own it.

One leader asked the fair folk of Evergreen Forest to help protect our land and theirs by casting a spell. The fair folk agreed, and so a spell was cast to conceal Wrunwicks. Grown tired of the men's presence, the people of Wrunwicks slew the visitors and once more called upon the fair folk to help. And once more, the fair folk obliged. They cast a second spell to close the passage running through the mountains.

Fearing that other men might still find their land, Radifur, a leader from the north, suggested the people choose their own king to rule alongside their wise leaders. Radifur argued that a king would make Wrunwicks a kingdom of its own. As such, it could never be added to another kingdom or placed under the rule of an unwanted king.

Radifur left his village to seek counsel with the leaders, travelling with Sianna throughout Wrunwicks. Sianna's ability to light travel enabled Radifur to journey the entire land in just three days, sharing his idea and gathering support from the other leaders, who loudly declared Radifur's idea to be most wise—

"I see ye found *The First King*. The author was never known." Waverly placed her hand on Lisette's shoulder. "The history of Wrunwicks, or at least what's been scribed, be in this library. Ye're welcome to visit any time with your friends. Like our districts, the library has always been forbidden to outsiders, but I think tis time we changed that. We already have."

"The first king was a commoner?" Lisette asked in disbelief.

"A commoner with an uncommon ambition. King Radifur wasn't happy to stand among the other leaders as equals. He wanted to stand high above his people and rule from his place in the sky. So when he was chosen as king by the other leaders, he built the castle of what would become Kingsbridge. The people of Wrunwicks had never laid eyes on such an impressive home. They lived in houses scarcely taller than a man. The castle included a stone tower and was a good sixty feet high. Over time, future kings replaced the original castle, but the tower still stands."

"The story says the men found gold too. Is it a precious stone?" Lisette stared at the book in front of her. And again, she felt herself turning upside down, downside up, and in every other direction imaginable.

"Gold be what we call uteka. In other kurucks and on this side of the mountains, it be worth much coin." Waverly took in Lisette's flushed cheeks. "Lighters are said to be even more sensitive to the effects of star ash than light masons. The dizziness should pass once ye've fully adjusted to your power. The amount of time it takes be different for every mason. Some hardly feel the effects at all while others suffer for many moons."

Lisette's stomach lurched. "It started after we left Stonebridge to uncover why people were vanishing. I haven't noticed it as much lately, but it's started again. It feels like my body be spinning in all directions."

"Star ash being part of all things, it connects each and every one of Mother's children. We breathe it into our bodies and absorb it through our skin. The dizziness ye've been feeling be caused by the ash's constant motion. Lighters can absorb more energy from the sun than masons. The extra energy causes the star ash to spin even faster."

Lisette rose to put the book back in its resting place. "How far can lighters travel?" The back door creaked open. Lisette imagined the voices of light masons echoing through the library. The masons might be gone, but their ghosts survived.

"I've never heard or known of a lighter travelling outside the kuruck triangle." Seeing the confusion on Lisette's face, Waverly explained that it referred to Wrunwicks, Krousus, and Galak. She paused to listen while the Keepers returned from their exploration of the area. "No one has ventured beyond Krousus or the old land in fear of getting lost."

Chapter 45

On the eve of the army's departure, Lisette promised Ewart to keep an eye on the camp's activity. While there was nothing that she could do to help the prisoners, Lisette needed a distraction from her gloomy thoughts. For just as winter chose the wrong year to arrive early, Vincent had chosen the wrong season to sprout a backbone. Upon receiving his pardon, Vincent joined the king's army alongside Melvin.

However much she hated Vincent's decision, Lisette's hands were tied until after the battle. While Vincent grew a conscious, Sam was stuck in his cage. So in keeping with her promise to Ewart, Lisette observed the camp from the safety of the mountains. She stood with Waverly on the same ledge used by her friends over three moon cycles ago. And like that day, Lisette watched from afar, wishing she had the power to do more.

The prisoners were carting utekan rock to three wheelbarrows large enough to fit a horse each. A different group of men and women waited to carry the rock up a ladder and into the gigantic barrows. Their carts emptied, the prisoners trudged back toward the mountain to reload. More prisoners emerged from the cave to repeat the process. The prisoners looked cold, scared, and weak.

A karupa grabbed one of the wheelbarrows, sending ladders and men toppling to the ground. The karupa let out a grotesque sound that loosely mimicked laughter, then headed to a post near a scruffy group of trees and disappeared. Lisette blinked to adjust her eyes. The post marked the bridge's starting point.

Made of densely packed star ash, the bridge glowed in a brilliant fusion of colour and light. When the army arrived to destroy the balshan spawn, Lisette planned to destroy the bridge. She disliked overusing the word beautiful. Used to describe everything from a woman's smile to a flower, the description sometimes lacked any real meaning. But overlooking the camp, she conceded the bridge's unrivalled beauty and told her mother as much. On the day of its destruction, Waverly would accompany her to the mountain.

"I'd destroy it myself if I thought it was possible," Waverly said, observing the bridge. "My light has grown too weak over the years. But ye never know what can go wrong, and I can always help free the prisoners."

Directing her attention back to the camp, Lisette watched as an elderly woman turned a boar over the hungry fire licking its burnt flesh. The woman was pale and dirty. She wore the same broken expression as every other prisoner. For these men and women, hope had died at the feet of their captors.

A gaunt and dishevelled man approached to speak with the woman. Lisette dug into Florette's fur and skin. Florette flinched. Lisette recognized William's face under the grime and exhaustion. She exhaled a trembling sigh of relief and sent thanks to Utaika. It seemed that for the time being, the invaders were more intent on mining the mountain than slaughtering their prisoners.

Lisette and Florette flew to check on the men. The army had grown to more than a couple hundred men from every belt in Wrunwicks. They were still riding with the north river to the karupas' camp. According to Ewart's calculations, they should arrive in less than a fortnight. They had already been travelling across the northern belt for a full moon cycle.

But thanks to more snow, the army's size, and their supplies, progress was even slower than Ewart had feared. The forest was also scragglier this far north and offered little protection from the cold winds of Maomoks.

The soldiers had set up camp for the night and were finishing their supper when Lisette and Florette arrived. They landed next to Ewart, who offered them some salted meat, bread, and ale. The Keepers sat next to Ewart while they ate.

"The men are cold and getting colder." Ewart regarded his men with admiration. "Winter challenges their will with each passing day. But their stomachs are full, and their spirits remain high."

It was clear to Lisette that in spite of Ewart's reassurances, the men were suffering from the hardship of travelling so late in the year. She had mentioned to Waverly once again about building a bridge to allow swifter passage. And once again, Waverly cautioned against alerting the king or others to her power, reminding Lisette that not everyone possessed steady hearts or minds.

"Even those who start with good intentions sometimes fall prey to greed," Waverly had said in conclusion.

Her mother's reasoning did nothing to assuage Lisette's guilt as she observed the men's faces. She spotted Vincent. He sat next to Melvin, rubbing his hands over the fire. Lisette breathed a sigh of relief. She needed him to live so her father could live. Three days after hearing the news of his decision to join the king's army, Lisette had gone with Florette to inform Dottie, knowing it would make no difference to the woman's original position. But Lisette also knew she had to at least try. And true to form, Dottie had simply commented that Sam's survival depended on Vincent's safe return. If Dottie possessed so much as an ounce of decency hiding somewhere behind her relentless smirk, Lisette had yet to see evidence of it. Left with no other option, she kept a watchful eye on the man who held her father's life in his balshan clutch. She spotted Deidrik and Roy coming their way and smiled at the men.

"We should all be able to travel so quickly," Deidrik said. "Could ye teach our horses to light travel?"

"And deprive us the pleasure of these visits?" Lisette said, feeling another twinge of guilt. *What if I built a bridge anyway?*

Deidrik stared at Lisette's hair. "Your hair grows brighter with every visit it seems. The sun will soon meet its match at this rate."

"Too many days without a hat." Lisette smoothed her hair in a useless bid to tame it. She put up her hood to cover the unruly curls.

"How are Aspen and Amelia?" Roy asked when he finished the bread in his hand. "Knowing Aspen, she be already making herself indispensable."

Lisette chuckled softly. True to Roy's observation, Aspen spent her days helping Hilda as she had helped her mother. A nurturer, Aspen appeared happiest whenever she was tending to those around her. Waverly often remarked their guests were intent on spoiling them. In addition to her own time in the kitchen, Amelia was practising book lettering and helping Waverly scribe a small group of books for the Northbridge library. Lisette had also begun to practice her book calligraphy, a task she looked forward to with increasing joy.

"Waverly and Hilda are gracious hosts," Lisette said to her friends. She missed them dearly and had yet to share her mother's true identity with them. Not due to a lack of trust but to a lack of favourable circumstances. There would be plenty of time after the balshaks were defeated.

"In Krousus, the winters are cool but never cold enough to snow," Mhutig said, looking down at the ground as he joined them. "I just spoke to King Eldridge. He appears to be suffering more than our men."

Bound to secrecy, Lisette kept quiet on the matter. She had not spoken to the king since their meeting in the round hall. During her visits to the soldiers' camp, King Eldridge mostly stayed inside his tent. She had seen him talking to his men a couple times but preferred to maintain her distance.

"To think this might all be over uteka," she said, referring back to their last conversation about the karupas and opowaks mining utakan rock.

"I should have realized the opowaks were after the gold," Mhutig repeated from that same conversation. He stopped to cast an eye over the soldiers. "The cost of war in Krousus has grown considerably over the years. With such an abundant supply of gold at their disposal, they could increase their army tenfold."

"We can't retrieve what's already been stolen," Ewart replied. "But we can stop them from stealing more of our land and people."

"We could veil the men," Lisette said. "It would at least offer some protection against the balshan spawn."

"They'd never agree to the idea," Deidrik said, glancing around the camp, "and see it as cowardice. A stubborn lot like someone else I know. They've travelled a long way to fight for their king. Every man ye see here has the heart and courage of a true knight."

Chapter 46

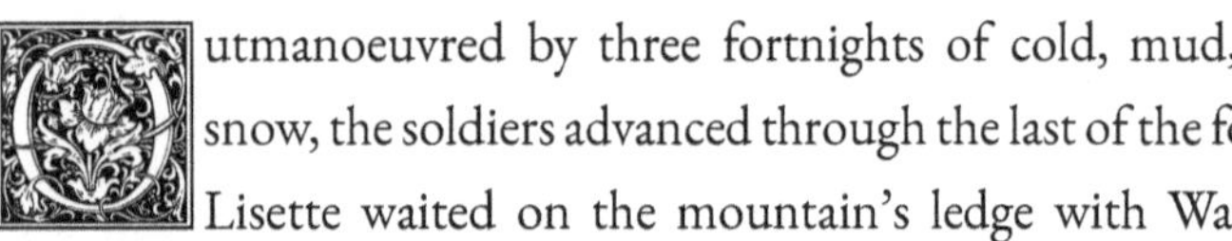

utmanoeuvred by three fortnights of cold, mud, and snow, the soldiers advanced through the last of the forest. Lisette waited on the mountain's ledge with Waverly, Florette, and Greyson. A karupa stopped suddenly and let out a thunderous cry. No matter how often Lisette heard a karupa speak, she would never get used to the piercing sound of their voices.

"Humans!" An opowak shouted and ran to retrieve his sword from a nearby tent, returning moments later. He barked orders at the karupas, who were growing increasingly agitated, stomping the ground and sniffing like wild animals. More opowaks ran from the cave, their swords already in hand. Based on her visits atop the ledge, Lisette estimated there were fifty or so karupas and opowaks in total. The numbers were in the men's favour, but each karupa possessed the strength of at least a dozen men. The opowaks were not as strong but still stronger than any human.

The soldiers cleared the tree thicket bordering the camp and charged toward the enemy. Most of the men were on foot. The thicket made it near impossible for their horses to pass through with the speed required once detected. Several karupas cried out in what Lisette guessed was a declaration of battle. Stunned by the events unfolding around them, men and women scrambled for shelter beneath the wheelbarrows and inside their prisons.

An infuriated karupa picked up one of the first men to arrive and swung him like a doll. The screaming man tumbled through the air, smashed against the mountain, and collapsed in a pile of flesh and bone, his head crushed beyond recognition. A woman shrieked when another man slammed the ground next to her and splattered her face with his blood. Lisette watched in horror. The men were no match for the stronger karupas and may as well be jumping off the mountain.

"We need to free the prisoners and help the men. The king be blasted," Lisette said to her mother. "Florette and Greyson can help the men while we get the prisoners to a bridge."

"A bridge to where?" Waverly asked. "We can't send them home or to one of the districts."

Lisette's mind raced. "We can send them to Kingsbridge. Queen Harriet will know what to do. If not, at least tis far enough from here to protect them."

"And the bridge to Krousus?" Waverly asked. "Ye can't destroy the bridge if ye're hurt or worse."

"I have no intention of giving a single one of those balshaks the pleasure." Lisette steadied herself to let Florette know it was time to leave. She didn't want to give her mother a chance to argue.

"I'll go for help," Waverly sang out as she and Greyson headed back to the mountain bridge. "The wimals will be eager to join the fight."

"Where to?" Florette asked after they were in the air. "There isn't much room down there."

Lisette searched the camp. Bent on slaughtering every man standing, karupas hammered the ground, pounding everything in sight. There would be neither man nor camp left at their current rate of destruction. She spotted Mhutig in time to witness him plunging his sword into the chest of an opowak. Continuing her inspection, she found King Eldridge at the edge of the woods with a handful of men. His illness made him an easy target. Lisette held little respect for their king, but he was the only king they had. Wrunwicks would need him when the battle was over.

"Bring us to the king, Florette," Lisette instructed. "He'll not die here today."

Florette swooped down and landed in front of King Eldridge. Lisette dropped to the ground. King Eldridge stared at the bloodshed in shock.

"I've led these men to slaughter," the king said. He looked at Lisette in despair.

"The people of Wrunwicks will need your strength, my king." Lisette jumped to the ground. "Go help the men best ye can, Florette. I'll take care of the prisoners."

"Time to balance the scales." Florette turned and flew toward the battlefield.

"I implore ye, my king," Lisette said. "Leave the field to those trained for this battle." Behind them, the blood-freezing screams of men and women rose through the air, punctuated by battle cries and the clanging of swords in search of their next victim.

"The men are scarcely trained to fight these monsters. There will be neither man left by night's fall."

As much as Lisette wanted to reassure the king, she was too scared and desperate to save the prisoners. "At least wait for help. There are more like Florette on the way. Together, we will win this fight." Lisette refused to think about the cost of their victory right now. They would mourn later. "I need to check on the prisoners, but I'll return soon."

King Eldridge opened his mouth to speak. Lisette raced toward the prisoners. The king's words would have to wait. Before landing, she noticed it was empty behind the mining shelters and planned to build the bridge there. She would need to be quick before the balshaks detected her presence.

Lisette pinpointed Kingsbridge to the southwest. Blocking the screams and battle cries from her mind, she constructed the bridge at breakneck speed, discovering that when she scooped up the star ash, the strings connected on their own if allowed to do so. The bridge walls needed to be near seven feet high and three feet wide to safely accommodate the prisoners. Without Florette to assist her, she tried throwing the ash into place when a block's sides became too high for her to reach. After a few failed attempts, Lisette could accurately aim the ash from the ground to finish the walls and top of each block, then connect it to the previous block.

The bridge ready, she marked it with three stones and left in search of the prisoners. On her way to the front of the buildings, Lisette felt the air vibrate. She looked up to see the wimals arriving. Greyson flew down to drop off Waverly.

"It will be our honour to serve alongside humans as our forefolk did." Greyson flew off to join the battle.

"I saw your bridge," Waverly said, wasting no time. "Well done."

"Now we need to gather the prisoners and get them to Kings-bridge soon as possible. They've been here long enough." Lisette headed to the front of the buildings.

The prisoners scurried to the back wall when Lisette entered the first building. Without so much as a bench, the small rectangular shelter offered no comfort to its occupants. The floor was covered in deep mud and wet hay. The shuttered window kept the sun out, increasing the building's damp cold. Lisette ignored the mouldy smell and fixed her eyes on the prisoners.

She placed a finger on her lips, then craned her neck around the door to check for danger. The balshan spawn were too busy fighting to worry about their prisoners. She signalled for the dozen or more men and women to follow her. Stepping outside, Lisette saw her mother peering out from the second building. Lisette pointed to the rear of the buildings. Waverly nodded.

As the battle raged around them, Lisette led the prisoners to the bridge. Waverly stayed close behind. Next to the stones, Lisette whispered instructions to the prisoners, who listened but refused to move. Waverly exchanged a look of understanding with her daughter. Suffering from shock and enough torment to make their Mother weep, the prisoners could do no more than stand with empty eyes.

Lisette threw a small, oddly shaped stone across the bridge. It disappeared. She stepped across the bridge herself. It opened onto the field outside the castle. There was no one in sight. Lisette found the stone and picked it up. She also picked a snow flower, shaped like mountain flowers but with white petals and a thicker stem able to reach the height of a man. She turned around and walked back across the bridge. Her return elicited amazed expressions and wide-open stares from the prisoners. *Finally, a reaction.* She explained where the bridge led and assured the prisoners of their safety.

"Ye have to go now," Lisette pleaded, "before they notice us."

One of the men walked up, stopped to look at the flower in

Lisette's hand, and stepped over the middle stone. He took a step forward and disappeared on the other side in two blinks of an eye. One by one, the others stepped over the stone.

When the last prisoner was about to leave, Lisette instructed her to go to the castle and ask for Queen Harriet. The woman nodded, then disappeared. Lisette and Waverly ran back to the front of the buildings.

"The wimals are making progress," Waverly said.

To their right, a liara struck a karupa from the air and sent it to the ground. A stockier kin of pardelas, liaras possessed the same black coat but with slightly wider wings and a long black mane.

"Without their help, this camp would be a butcher's dream for those balshaks." Lisette counted a good thirty men on the ground. "Time to destroy the bridge."

The bridge was located on the other side of the camp, near the mountains. Between Lisette, Waverly, and the bridge, karupas and opowaks fought for supremacy over humans and uteka. Men and wimals fought for Wrunwicks, attacking with all their strength. The men attacked from below while wimals attacked from above. The fallen spilled their blood, leaving a stain that no amount of rain or snow would ever wash clean. The remaining prisoners watched in a terrified stupor, unwilling bystanders trapped inside a new nightmare.

While Lisette and Waverly ran toward the bridge, they watched an opowak walk past the bridge post and disappear.

"Gone for reinforcements," Waverly said breathlessly. "He won't be returning."

A few moments later, Melvin ran past the post and disappeared behind the karupa.

"What in the name of Utaika was he thinking?" Waverly stared at the bridge. "We've lost enough men without them running to their death."

"That was Melvin. There be more reason inside a rock," Lisette said.

"The bridge must be destroyed." Waverly turned to Lisette. "And we still have the other prisoners to save."

"Melvin could worm his way up from Balands. If anyone can survive the karupas, it be him," Lisette replied. She might not wish Melvin dead, but she had no intention of running after him either. He made his choice, and she wished him well. "It seems fate has her own plan for Melvin."

Lisette adjusted her eyes to examine the bridge. Its blocks were made of large triangular prisms that sloped upwards for about forty feet, then projected straight into eternity. The star ash was bound so tightly, the strings extending from the ash curled around each other in oversized knots along the entire bridge.

The knots created an impenetrable seal, making it almost impossible to distinguish one block from the next. Almost, but not quite. Lisette noticed that a band of light ran around the width of the bridge every five feet or so. The light was slightly brighter than the light surrounding it.

Under different circumstances, Lisette might have admired the light mason's craftsmanship. Instead, she was already loosening the first set of knots. She started with the bands. The bridge was strong, but it was about to meet its match.

"Absorb as much energy as possible," Waverly instructed. "Then funnel that energy through your hands."

Lisette removed her overcoat, jacket, and boots. The cold air whipped her skin. She shivered from the attack, then ignoring the pain, she focused on the sun. A warm energy poured over and into her exposed flesh, including the skin under her thin linen shirt and wool trousers. Within moments, an intense heat replaced the cold. Light radiated from beneath her skin. It shot out in all directions. The snow beneath her feet began to melt. She diverted the light to her hands.

While men and wimals waged war for their king and land, she deconstructed the first section of the bridge, block by block. Once the bands were sufficiently loose, the blocks were easier to detach from the bridge. Next, she separated the knots from each block back into star ash. After she had removed twelve blocks and freed the ash, Lisette stood back to appraise her work. That should do for now, she decided and asked her mother's opinion. Waverly agreed, examining her daughter's handiwork.

"I've never seen a mason work so quickly." Waverly eyed the bridge a little closer. "Any creature that tries to use the bridge will find themselves stranded once ye're done." She turned to observe the battle behind them. "They'll never survive the space between our lands."

Lisette held no sympathy for the balshan spawn. "I'll come back to finish destroying it later. Right now, we need to help the rest of the prisoners."

Many of the male prisoners had joined the fight, William among them. A few men continued to watch helplessly next to the women. Lisette and Waverly hurried to collect the prisoners in view. They navigated between karupas, opowaks, and soldiers, ducking and weaving their way around the battlefield to the prisoners.

Unlike the first group, the prisoners who were left on the field did not hesitate when Lisette informed them of what to do. They ran from the field, stopping only to wait behind the buildings. And soon as Lisette explained about the bridge and where it led, they stepped past the stone in their rush to freedom.

The last prisoner gone, Lisette remembered her promise to the king. "I need to check on King Eldridge. He'll be no good to anyone dead."

Waverly spotted the king fighting alongside Roy and Mhutig. "A king who fights with his army be met with much respect."

Lisette observed King Eldridge with begrudging admiration. Though his flaws were many, their king was not a coward. She drew her sword. "I can't stay here." From where she stood, it seemed the scales had tipped in their favour.

A handful of karupas and even fewer opowaks survived. Bodies covered the ground. Wimals and the surviving men attacked with claws, swords, axes, and bows. Karupas fought with their fists and feet while the few opowaks still standing wielded swords the length of men.

"Time to join the fight," Waverly said, recruiting the nearest sword.

With their swords raised to Utaika, they ran toward the battle, stopping behind an opowak who had just plunged his sword into a man's chest. Lisette jabbed her sword into the opowak's hind leg. He reared in anger. Waverly leaped into the air and stuck her sword between his lower ribs. The opowak landed with his front legs on the fallen soldier's back. Florette swooped down to dig her massive claws into the opowak's eyes. Waverly withdrew her sword from its ribs and pierced the opowak's chest to inflict the final blow.

"One less monster to worry about," Waverly declared. "They might be big, but they bleed like the rest of us."

The women soldiered on in their quest for blood, striking every monster in sight. And everywhere, monsters and men fell to their death. They were running toward another karupa when Lisette caught sight of Vincent among the bodies on the ground. She ran to his side and dropped to the ground. Blood oozed from his mouth. Lisette inspected his sunken chest. He was gone.

Vincent's death shattered all hope of saving her father. Lisette bent her head in grief. The ground spun around her. She clutched her chest. It hurt to breathe; she had failed her parents.

"Your spirit did not die with Vincent," Calder whispered in her ear. "Just as ye fight for Wrunwicks, ye must fight for truth."

Lisette turned toward Calder's voice. Through her grief, she saw him standing no more than a pace from Vincent's body. Calder met her eyes and smiled.

"Fight for hope," he said and faded into the star ash.

Lisette searched the battlefield for her mother. Waverly fought next to Ewart. After a final look at Vincent's body, Lisette scrambled upright to help Waverly, who was ducking below a karupa's fists. Catching sight of an axe wedged between two soldiers, Lisette grabbed it and ran toward the karupa with her sword and axe ready. She channelled the sun's energy into both weapons, heating the star ash inside their steel blades until they burned a dazzling white.

The karupa flung its arm at another soldier. Lisette swung her axe and sword at the karupa's ankle, slicing through scale and bone. The karupa careened to the side. Lisette sliced the other ankle. With a surprised yelp, the karupa fell backwards, leaving its severed feet where the rest of its body had stood. Ewart ran to plunge his sword into the karupa's heart. Waverly stared at Lisette's weapons in amazement, grinned, and raised her sword in victory.

Ewart pointed to a karupa on their left. Lisette nodded, and the three of them ran to where the monster stomped the ground, searching for its next victim. Lisette slashed through its ankles, sending the karupa to the ground. Waverly and Ewart plunged their swords into its heart, crying out in triumph. Lisette surveyed the battlefield. Snow had begun to fall, covering the soldiers in a white burial cloth. The bodies of karupas and opowaks lay next to them in their shrine to hate and greed.

Lisette spotted a young soldier still holding his sword. The man's strength and sacrifice reminded her of the bridge. They had lost too many men and would lose more if the bridge survived.

She turned to Waverly and Ewart, gesturing toward the bridge. With its front section destroyed, the bridge dangled carelessly in midair. Unable to see what Lisette was pointing at, Ewart stared in bewilderment.

"Ye can't see it," Lisette said, "but I need to finish destroying the bridge." She singled out one of the opowaks. "They use it to travel here."

"I'll go help Roy and the others," Ewart said quickly. "Ye clearly have it under control." He headed to where Roy fought with a group of soldiers against a karupa.

Waverly followed Lisette. On their way across the field, Lisette sliced into the monsters, severing ankles, knees, arms, and the trunks of opowaks. When they reached the bridge, Lisette began dismantling what remained of the light mason's legacy.

She managed to separate four blocks when a karupa appeared on the bridge and toppled thirty feet to the ground. It stood and shook the fall from its bones. Waverly charged the karupa, striking its leg. The enraged karupa flung her beneath the bridge. Lisette's heart stopped. Without soldiers to distract it, she would need more than her blades to kill the monster. Waverly stirred. Lisette let out a sob of relief.

Florette landed next to Lisette. "Come! We'll destroy this karupa together!"

Lisette gawked in surprise. "My mother."

"We'll get her to safety." Florette kneeled on all four. "Now climb on!"

Lisette climbed onto Florette's back with her sword and axe. When Florette flew level with the karupa, Lisette heated her blades. Eyeing the clumps of ash still left from the bridge, she instructed Florette to approach. The karupa headed straight for them.

Using her sword and axe to balance herself, Lisette kicked the dense ash toward the karupa. And judging by the dazed expression on the karupa's face, it struck with a force equal to small boulders. Not enough to be deadly, but enough to stun the balshak until that moment arrived. The karupa raised both hands in a futile attempt to protect itself.

Lisette saw her moment. Informing Florette of her plan, she raised her sword and axe for the kill. Fixing her eyes three feet above the karupa, Lisette trajected behind the monster. She garnered her strength and cut through the karupa's skull, neck, and torso. An image of a karupa sliced in half flashed somewhere inside the dark recesses of Lisette's memories.

The karupa's cleaved body dropped where it stood. Lisette turned to check on her mother. Waverly was removing a block from the bridge. Lisette flew over to help.

"Ye go destroy the bridge farther north," Waverly said. "I'll keep at it from here."

Lisette turned toward the upper reaches of the mountains and trajected to the northernmost coast in Wrunwicks. When she had disconnected several blocks, Lisette looked to the grey skies. The next section sloped upwards past the clouds. They trajected above the clouds to continue their work. To save time, Lisette heated her weapons and cut along the bands of light. Once the blocks were free, Lisette unravelled the knots.

"Why didn't ye think of that sooner?" Florette teased.

"Patience, dear friend. Tis not like I've done this before."

"How much do ye plan to destroy? We can't travel all the way to Krousus."

"One more stop should do it. Brace yourself." Lisette trajected them as far into the sky as she dared. The sky turned a deep blue.

She cut seven more blocks loose and released the knots. She needed to get back to see how her mom and the soldiers were doing.

Waverly was still dismantling the bridge. She had freed at least twenty blocks and continued her work on the next one. Star ash turned all around her.

Pleased to note the colour in Waverly's cheeks, Lisette threw her mother a quick smile. "I'll separate the knots. I'm not sure what would happen to them over time."

Florette kept guard while the women worked. A loud tremor ran through the field. Lisette looked to see the last karupa fall to its death. And for the first time, she noticed the swarm of purifiers circling overhead.

Lisette informed her mother of the danger presented by the birds. "We need to get our fallen off the field."

The women left the bridge to go find the king. They found him at the edge of the field with a group of soldiers. Lisette explained the threat to their king and told him about the bridge crossing over to the castle grounds. The king launched into action, summoning the soldiers scattered around the field. He relayed what Lisette had told him and ordered the men to begin transporting the fallen.

Lisette led King Eldridge to the bridge. "The stones mark where the bridge begins. If the men stay within these limits," she said, pointing toward the two outer stones, "they won't have any trouble crossing the bridge." She removed the middle stone. "It'll just get in the way. I placed it there as an extra precaution for the prisoners. They were more likely to cross safely by staying in the middle."

The first men arrived with their fallen comrades. The liara walked behind with a soldier on her back. King Eldridge instructed them about the stones. The men and liara disappeared, returning moments later. They raced back to the field. Lisette and Waverly offered to watch over the men as they carried their fallen back home. The king nodded gratefully. He went to oversee his men on the field. Florette went with him to help in the rescue mission.

As the soldiers and wimals rushed to save their dead from the purifiers, Lisette and Waverly kept their eyes on the birds. A scatter bird swooped down, only to be scared off by wimals. But despite the wimals' efforts, the birds circled and barked from overhead. The bodies of the karupas and opowaks would be left for them to feast on later.

The men worked late into the night. King Eldridge and Ewart carried the last soldier across the bridge. Lisette and Waverly crossed the bridge behind them. Florette and Greyson waited with the men and wimals. The fallen soldiers lay throughout the castle grounds, but at least they were safe. The purifiers should have enough food to keep them busy for the time being.

The surviving soldiers retreated to their camp adjacent to the field. Tonight, they would sleep alongside their fallen. Lisette flew back to Northbridge District with her mother and the wimals.

Chapter 47

Four days had passed since the soldiers' return. And four days had passed since the prisoners walked to the castle gate, requesting Queen Harriet. The prisoners' sudden appearance caused a ripple that began in Kingsbridge and spread its way across Wrunwicks by the third day. The ripple was largely due to King Eldridge, who had sent an urgent notice to every town in the land announcing people's imminent return. The king's notice also requested that any unusual activity, sightings, or vanishings be promptly noted and sent to the castle.

King Eldridge subsequently named the field after the men who had fallen in battle. The soldiers were to be buried by the bridge in three days, giving the caretakers of Kingsbridge just enough time to build the burial boxes.

Determined to free her father still, Lisette invited Amelia and Aspen to accompany them on their visit with Briony. Lisette's first visit had suggested Briony would make a good ally in her ongoing dispute with Dottie. Vincent was not going to sign her father's death sentence. Not while she drew breath.

After an evening meal of blue fish in sweet onion sauce, they sat in the dining hall discussing the battle at Metterling Mountains with Briony, whose husband was away on his last trip of the trading season to Hillbridge. A trip made longer by the snow.

"I trust ye'll be spending the night," Briony said. She peered at the fire for a moment, then shifted her attention to Aspen and Amelia. "A chance for us to become acquainted."

"Of course," Amelia replied, smiling graciously at their host. "We thank you for your hospitality."

"Will ye be attending the burial ceremony in Kingsbridge?" Briony inquired. "A tragic end to a vile story."

They had lost ninety-two men in total, nearly half the army. In addition to the burial ceremony in Kingsbridge, towns and villages would hold their own ceremonies to honour the fallen on the same day. King Eldridge declared it a day of mourning for all of Wrunwicks. The wimals were invited by the king himself. Lisette would have preferred to attend the ceremony in Stonebridge, unable to deny the king's request to stand with the prisoners she had helped to free. When asked about the mysterious woman who had also helped, Lisette spoke of a brave woman from a small village outside Northbridge. The story might not hold indefinitely, but it held for now.

"I fear the king would be most displeased if we failed to make an appearance," Lisette replied.

Briony nodded in agreement. "A wise woman. Over the years, I've found it most auspicious to uphold a sense of goodwill with those who hold the power to affect us."

The conversation then drifted to Lisette's bid to free her father. Lisette filled Briony in on the details of her deal with Dottie and her deception before the king. Admitting her wilful breach of canon twenty-seven was risky at best, but if Lisette hoped to gain Briony's confidence, she first needed to demonstrate her trust in their friendship.

"My father's life depends on Lord Sumunder's ability to see past Dottie's preposterous claim," Lisette concluded.

"Tis an awful injustice for an innocent man to die in a cage," Briony said. "I'll write to Lord Sumunder by night's end." She stopped to meet Lisette's eyes. "It's long been my experience that power preoccupies itself more with the appearance of justice than its provision. Your story be safe with me. Our land was built on as much deception as it was truth."

In the not-so-distant past, Lisette would have considered Briony unusually bitter. But instead, she saw her as unusually perceptive and smiled in gratitude. "I own nothing more than the truth. My father didn't steal from Lord Sumunder. He be an honest man."

"Ye don't need to convince me, Lisette. I can assure ye the chance to defend your father. At least I can promise ye that, but the rest will be in your capable hands. Ye'll need to convince your lord and elders by whatever means at your disposal."

"Then we'll find more means," Aspen said. "Mr. Steels be a good man. Everyone knows that. They're just too scared to admit it and be branded the friend of a thief."

At dawn, Lisette set out with Florette. Aspen and Amelia accepted Briony's offer to stay while their friends travelled to Stonebridge. Florette could not accommodate all three, and Greyson had already travelled back to Northbridge District. He was due back for them in two days.

So with Briony's letter tucked inside her pocket, Lisette waited anxiously outside the manor gate for permission to enter with

Florette. A servant came to their rescue and ushered them to the great hall. The large chamber resembled Lord Stanley's with its high vaulted ceiling and white plastered walls. But unlike Lord Stanley's, neither portrait graced its walls. In their place, wide-sweeping landscapes had been painted directly onto the plaster. An immense tapestry hung on the far wall facing the lord's table. The tapestry portrayed King Lazoran II as he gave his famous speech in Stonebridge.

Lord Sumunder entered from a door next to the tapestry and greeted them with open arms. "To what do I owe this unexpected pleasure, my child? Have ye come to share the story of your daring adventure that we've all heard so much about?"

Lisette explained that she brought an urgent message from Mrs. Darkwood of Cornbridge.

"Urgent indeed if I am to trust my eyes," Lord Sumunder said, accepting the scroll. He promptly broke the seal and read the letter, pausing on occasion to glance up at Lisette. "Mrs. Darkwood be a most compelling woman. Her husband and I have enjoyed many meals over the years. I've always felt he allowed his wife too many liberties. However, she does make a convincing case. This situation with your father has never agreed with me, Lisette. I can offer ye an audience before the seat of judgment the day after mourning. Ye'll need to speak on your father's behalf to any elder who can testify to Sam's good character. Although I've always held your father in the highest regard, I hesitate to interfere in matters of the court without just cause."

Emboldened by the opportunity to prove her father's innocence, Lisette resolved to visit every elder in Stonebridge who had ever known Sam. Most dismissed her at once, declaring Sam a breaker and therefore unworthy of their consideration. Undaunted by their rejection, Lisette persisted. Townsfolk avoided her as they passed on the street or glared in contempt. Some were polite enough to hide their scorn, but Lisette recognized the cold look in their eyes. Vincent had viewed her with the same expression. Florette stayed inside Lisette's hood to avoid further insult. Lisette pretended not to notice their insolence. She had a more pressing matter to attend.

And by day's end, a total of five elders had agreed to speak on Sam's behalf, each one echoing Lord Sumunder's esteem for her father. On her last visit of the day, Lisette sat with Mr. Walling in his kitchen. She was sipping a mug of hot tea to chase the cold from her bones. Mrs. Walling maintained a discreet silence, checking on occasion to see if their guests needed more tea or ale.

"A terrible thing," Mr. Walling said after Mrs. Walling refilled his mug with ale. "Thrown in the cage like that and without a single elder to defend him. I must confess the whole sordid affair baffled me. Between us, Dottie's word still amounts to little more than that of a capricious child, though it was widely accepted by the elders that justice had prevailed. But the type of justice, no one ventured to say."

Lisette declined Mrs. Walling's invitation to supper and took her leave of the charming couple. She wanted to share the news of Sam's defence with her stepmom before returning to Briony's. Nora would want to be at her father's side for the meeting.

On the eve of the burial ceremony, the reunited Seekers hurried through the snow in the castle courtyard. Winter had settled over the land without further question. Wrunwickers were finishing the final preparations for the harshest moons ahead. Men coppiced firewood and made any neglected repairs to homes and stables.

Women were equally busy making blood puddings and cheese, tending to the livestock, and assisting their husbands with the butchering left from Swine's Day. Said to bring an early spring, it was custom to delay butchering of the last pig until after Maomoks.

Sensing its close demise, a pig squealed in the distance, followed by a loud thwack. Lisette pulled up her mittens to ward off a gust of wind. Henry had sent a message that morning to Deidrik's house where the Seekers were staying for the burial ceremony. Henry's cryptic message wrote of an important announcement for them. Accompanying Florette, Greyson and the liara from battle entered the great hall alongside the Seekers. All three had opted to travel in their smaller fay forms.

Henry sat with Princess Rosalyn next to him at the table, while a servant stood nearby with a richly carved walking stick. Henry motioned for them to take a seat. A second servant poured wine for the guests.

"Ye've had quite the adventure in my absence," Henry said brightly. "Thanks to ye, our land enjoys peace once again. With William back home and fully recovered, even Master Furlow has regained his good spirits. And who are these noble fair folk, I see next to ye?"

Lisette introduced Greyson and Violet, explaining their role in the army's victory. "Ye look to be in fine health," Lisette continued, noting the plumpness of his cheeks. "It does the heart good to see ye back on your feet."

"The favour of King Eldridge knows no limit. He be a wise and benevolent king." Henry took Princess Rosalyn by the hand. "As ye know, I have some news to share. Now that we're all here, I'd like to announce my marriage to our lovely princess."

The Seekers sat in silence, stunned by Henry's announcement.

He would be of marital age in one moon cycle. The next one to reach that all-important milestone after Henry would be Ewart, whose birthday fell three days short of Mother's Day.

Princess Rosalyn beamed at their guests. "We are to be wed on Mother's Day so that Utaika might bless us with many children. Ye are the first to be informed outside the castle walls. Although in her excitement, the queen has already sent word to Uncle Stanley."

"How is Lord Stanley?" Mhutig asked.

"He continues to need additional rest," Princess Rosalyn said. "But he has promised a full recovery by our wedding."

"Ye're all invited to attend, of course," Henry added. "It'll be a grand ceremony befitting our princess."

"I also hope to have a celebration for our people," Princess Rosalyn said. "I know what the townsfolk say about me. I've never been good with people like Henry. I believe he has the entire castle charmed, but perhaps a celebration will help our people view me more favourably."

"May Utaika sing with joy on the day of your wedding," Roy said, grinning from ear to ear. "Hail Prince Henry and Princess Rosalyn!" He raised his goblet.

"Hail to the prince and princess of Wrunwicks," the Seekers sang out. "Blessed be your union."

"For my first official act as Prince of Wrunwicks, the king has tasked me with the pronouncement of our soon-to-be knights." Henry raised his goblet in turn. "Ewart, Roy, Deidrik, and Mhutig, ye are to be knighted in the service of our king and land."

Lisette glanced at her friends. The first knights in more than a hundred years. She was still digesting the staggering thought when Greyson flew to the middle of the table with Florette and Violet. He turned to face Henry and bowed.

"It will be our honour to stand with the knights of Wrunwicks, just as our ancestors once stood with the people," Greyson said gravely. "If ye will have us."

Henry's face lit up like a candle. "The king will make a public announcement after a sufficient period of mourning has passed. The people need time to heal."

"King Eldridge honours us," Ewart replied. "I swear to carry my sword with wisdom and humility, upholding the virtues passed down by the knights of old."

Roy raised his goblet once more. "May we serve with courage."

Chapter 48

A tall stone rested in the field to mark the final home of the soldiers, the monument's humble beginnings left untouched by the engraver. Its dull surface bore the field's name in careful lettering: Heroes Crossing. King Eldridge stood near the stone with his family and future son. They waited in the snow as the fallen soldiers arrived.

The procession marched its way from the chantry to the field. Lisette watched as the soldiers and townspeople carried ninety-two burial boxes across the snowy field to lay them in the ground. Their comrades put to rest, the soldiers joined the men and women they had fought to free, eleven of whom were from Krousus. For now, the Krousians appeared content to stay at the River Inn with the others. The Wrunwicks prisoners would be leaving for home in the morning.

Lisette suspected the Krousians would also want to return home once they recovered from their nightmare. *What then? Do we leave them stranded in Wrunwicks?* She knew that regardless of her mother's warnings about building another bridge to Krousus, she would. And Mhutig would want to return home before long.

His family was probably frantic with worry. Then there were the prisoners who were still missing. Where were they? Did they all meet their death at the cruel hands of the first karupas, or were some stuck in Krousus as the Krousians suggested? No one knew the answer or whether there were any other monsters left in Wrunwicks. No sightings or vanishings had been reported, but they needed to remain cautious. Feeling Amelia's eyes on her, Lisette took her hand.

They still needed to find the time to discuss their future. But regardless of what life held for them, Lisette knew in the depths of her heart that she wanted to spend it with Amelia. After her father was back home, and he would be back home, Lisette vowed to herself for the umpteenth time, she would share their love with her parents. Amelia gently squeezed Lisette's hand as if to reassure her. Together, they would face whatever obstacles lay ahead.

As the crowned leader of the army and appointed consecrator in the place of family, Ewart presided over today's proceedings with the master of ceremonies. Ewart began by reading the names of his soldiers from the royal scroll, followed by the master's invitation to Roy, who shared the men's tale of bravery and sacrifice. When Roy fell silent, the people entrusted their fallen heroes to Utaika, singing the familiar words of praise.

While they sang, Lisette heard the low, sonorous voices of the wimals behind her. She had implored her mother to attend as well, but Waverly insisted on attending the ceremony in Northbridge District, fearing someone might somehow recognize her. A slim possibility, but not a risk her mother was willing to take. Lisette dropped the matter, knowing how stubborn her mother could be. Among the voices rising to the sky, Lisette imagined she could hear Calder. The sound of his rich singing voice warmed her soul.

With their voices still lingering in the air, Ewart led his men to sprinkle the first soil. They marched between the burial plots aligned in seven rows, each man dropping a handful of snow and earth over the soldiers. Next, King Eldridge, Queen Harriet, and Ewart placed a single snow flower at the foot of each soldier for transplanting. And while soldiers planted the flowers, the master of ceremonies recited the final prayer.

"To these flowers, may your spirits return when they have grown tall and proud, their roots planted firmly in the ground to stand with your brothers, old and new. And may these flowers be made ever strong by your eternal light."

Chapter 49

The five elders who had agreed to speak at the hearing sat with the privy council across from Lisette, Sam, Nora, and Dottie. Lord Sumunder chaired the meeting from his seat at the head of the table in the great hall.

It was late afternoon, and the sun had begun to set outside the manor. Servants filled the table with wine, ale, cheese, and tartes. Lisette tasted the wine to respect Lord Sumunder's hospitality. She could not bring herself to try the food.

"Now that we've all had the opportunity to replenish," Lord Sumunder said after dismissing the servants, "I'd like to reacquaint myself with the situation which has brought us here today, starting with Sam."

"I was at home with my wife for the night, my lord. It was late. And like all respectable citizens, I had long retired for the day."

Lisette turned to look at her father. Nora's cooking had kept him fed, but his face was drawn and pale. His clothes reeked of the cage. Yet he spoke with strength and dignity. Her father had once said that a man's worth came from within and could never be taken against his will, no matter the weapon wielded against him. Seeing her father now, Lisette finally understood what he had meant that day in their kitchen.

Lord Sumunder looked over to where Dottie was sitting. "That brings me to my next question. What were ye doing around the granaries so late at night, my child?"

Dottie shifted uncomfortably. "I needed berries, my lord." She placed a hand on her rounded belly. "The baby grows with each passing day. I fear my appetite grows with it."

Lord Sumunder's expression softened. "May your baby be born strong and healthy."

So that be how she did it. Dottie's pregnancy created a blind spot in Lord Sumunder's reasoning. Lisette looked toward the privy council, who should be impervious to the wench's lies, pregnant or not. Nora had speculated that Master Geraldson was a distant kin of Dottie's family. And while the council of elders was respected for its virtue in all matters of justice, Lisette had learned justice was also a weapon. Like the two swords that symbolized justice, it served to protect and maim. In the wrong hands, justice became deadly.

"I think now might be a good time to hear from our esteemed elders who join us in council," Master Geraldson said. "Supper be fast approaching, and my wife likes for me to be on time."

The master elder's words enraged Lisette, but she held her tongue. It would do her father no good to offend these men. She fiddled with her brooch. It was a constant reminder of her parents and their love. She needed to hold strong for them.

The visiting elders spoke of Sam's dedication to Stonebridge and steadfast loyalty to his lord and king. Lisette observed the privy council. Their expressions remained calmer than a windless night.

Lord Sumunder cast a quick look around the table after the men had finished speaking. "We've heard all that we need for our deliberations. The council will arrive at a decision within a few days at most. Until then, may our Mother guide us ever forward."

Aspen returned home from her journey. She visited Nora every night after supper while Lord Sumunder and the elders deliberated Sam's fate. Amelia and Florette stayed with Lisette. During the day, they helped tend to the livestock, cook, and scrub the linens in preparation for Sam's return, hanging them to dry in the back tewk. At night, too anxious to concentrate on chores, they played dice to keep busy, avoiding any mention of what would happen if the council decided against Sam. Lisette maintained a brave face for her stepmom.

On the fourth night, as Lisette threw the dice, her eyes skirted around the table. Nora was miles away. Amelia handed a gaming bone to Florette, who had scored the highest and won the round. Florette laid it next to three other bones. Lisette had planned to wait until her father came home to share her love for Amelia. But as the days crawled to their slow demise, the silence grew heavier. She looked to where Nora kept her box of flowers on the mantle. From that box, Lisette summoned the courage she needed to break the silence.

She reached over to bring Nora back to them. "There be something I need to share with ye."

Nora grasped her stepdaughter's hand. "Sam'll be home soon. I know it in my heart."

"'Tis something else I need to share. It be about Amelia and me."

Nora fixed her eyes on Lisette. "Amelia be welcome to stay for as long as she needs." She gave Amelia an encouraging smile.

"Thank ye. I may have to accept your offer." Amelia returned Nora's smile.

Lisette turned to the woman she loved more than she could have ever thought possible. Amelia waited for her to continue, the full realization of Lisette's next words written in her eyes. There was no going back.

"Amelia and I have grown very fond of each other." Lisette took a deep breath. She owed her stepmom the truth. She owed Amelia and herself the truth. "Our love grows stronger with each passing day." Lisette's heart fluttered like a new set of wings.

Nora drank in her stepdaughter's face. She was about to speak, then stopped to consider Amelia for a moment before settling her attention back on Lisette. "Before ye left Stonebridge, I said it was your life. And I prayed for your safe return. Utaika answered my prayers, and it seems that in her infinite wisdom, our Divine Mother brought me a second daughter. Who am I to question her wisdom or refuse her gift?"

Lisette's heart took flight over Wrunwicks. Tears spilled down her cheeks. She went to hug her stepmom. "Utaika has blessed me with the gift of your love. The greatest gift I could ever hope for."

Amelia rose from the bench to wrap her arms around the two women. "Your strength and wisdom rival that of knights," she said, planting a gentle kiss on Nora's cheek.

Lisette held onto her stepmom a while longer. She still had to speak with her father. But first, he needed to come home. She feared he wouldn't last much longer with the days long grown too cold for the sun to compete. And all the blankets in Wrunwicks would not save him, nor the winter's tunic Nora had given him with an extra layer of fur to wage her own war against the cold.

Chapter 50

wo more days passed when they finally received a knock on the door. The man introduced himself and presented Nora with a scroll bearing Lord Sumunder's crest. Nora ripped the seal open and read it in silence, mouthing the words as she went. Lisette watched her stepmother, afraid to speak. She waited with Amelia for Nora to say something.

Moments later, Nora looked up and sobbed as she met Lisette's eyes. Sam was to be released immediately. It was the privy council's decision that due to the unpredictable nature of childbearing and the dark's deceptive powers, Dottie had mistaken another man for Sam.

Lisette's knees buckled beneath her. After six days of imagining the worst, she relinquished her fear in a sudden outpouring of joy and relief. Her chest hurt from the onslaught. *Dad be coming home!* She ran to her stepmom. *He be free!* Nora grabbed Lisette, her tears shaking them both.

"I told ye he'd be home," Nora said between sobs. "He'll be needing food when he gets here." She let go of Lisette and looked around the kitchen. Her eyes grew frantic. "Do we have ale? He'll be needing ale."

"We have a barrel near full," Amelia said, smiling foolishly. "And enough pottage to feed at least ten men."

Nora ran over to check on the pottage, stirring furiously. "Sam loves his pottage, don't he, Lisette."

Lisette nodded, wiping the tears from her lips. She watched her stepmom tending the pottage and sweeping the ashes back into the hearth with her foot. Nora was stirring the pottage so hard that it splattered over the floor.

The door swung open. Sam walked into the kitchen and looked around, taking in the sight of his wife and daughter. Nora froze with her ladle still in the pottage.

"Might that be rabbit I smell, my beautiful Nora?" Sam asked with a lopsided grin. His eyes were brighter than stars as he breathed in the aroma.

Lisette and Nora stared at Sam in surprise, then ran to hug the man who had never asked for anything, save for an extra helping of his favourite pottage.

"There be no need to cry, m'ladies. Tis finally over. I'm home now." Sam kissed his wife and daughter. "Tomorrow, we rise to a new day."

Looking up from her father's shoulder, Lisette caught Amelia's gaze and smiled. Next to Amelia and Florette, Calder stood in a swirl of star ash. Lisette blinked, but he was still there.

"To truth and courage," Calder said, smiling from ear to ear.

"To sunrises," Lisette said through fresh tears.

Moon Cycles O/O

<table>
<tr><td>April

Neomoks</td><td>May

Saromoks</td><td>June

Luomoks</td></tr>
<tr><td>July

Raomoks</td><td>August

Winomoks</td><td>September

Laromoks</td></tr>
<tr><td>October

Srumoks</td><td>November

Romoks</td><td>December

Maomoks</td></tr>
<tr><td>January

Swomoks</td><td>February

Kaomoks</td><td>March

Drumoks</td></tr>
</table>

A new moon cycle begins on the first day of uomons when both moons are full for three nights. The first of uomons also marks the last day of the former moon cycle, dividing each moon cycle into 30 days, denoted by O/O. Aromons marks the middle of a moon cycle when both moons are dark for three days. The first day of aromons divides each moon cycle into two halves of fourteen days on each side to represent Utaika's fourteen virtues for Wrunwickers, denoted by /OO\, where the arms of Utaika light the dark and point to her wisdom. The people of Wrunwicks pay little heed to specific days within a moon cycle, a task left to the moon keepers.

The King's Canons

1. No man or woman shall court before an age decreed by their king or court another of their own kind.

2. No man or woman shall commit chetuk.

3. No man or woman of courting age shall appear in a state of undress in public.

4. No man or woman shall marry before their twenty-fifth birthday.

5. No man or woman shall marry without the blessing of their lord or king.

6. Every child and citizen shall obey their parents in all matters until the age of twenty.

7. No person shall steal from their lord, king, or other citizens.

8. No person shall contradict the wisdom of their elders, lord, or king.

9. No wife shall contradict the wisdom of her husband.

10. No person shall be found wandering after the seventh bell from the first uomons of Neomoks to the second uomons of Srumoks and the sixth bell thereafter without reasonable cause.

11. Street lanterns shall be lit after sunset and extinguished no later than the seventh bell from the first uomons of Neomoks to the second uomons of Srumoks and extinguished no later than the sixth bell from the second uomons of Srumoks to the last moons of Drumoks.

12. Overnight guests in a town or village shall yield their swords.

13. No person shall relieve themselves within town or village limits.

14. On the second uomons of Srumoks, wron shall be paid as determined by and payable to their lord and king.

15. Each house shall pay wron in keeping with the number of citizens living within.

16. A house or shop unable to pay wron in part or its entirety must notify the steward and will be assigned additional field duty.

17. Children must learn the king's canons before receiving citizenship clearance. Each child shall stand on their fourteenth birthday and recite the canons to the satisfaction of their elders.

18. Every citizen shall participate in field duty unless deemed too old, infirm, or exempted by their council of elders, lord or king.

19. No citizen shall arm themselves within town or village limits. All visitors shall yield their swords in keeping with the twelfth canon.

20. All shops must close to coincide with the end of field duty.

21. Taverns shall close in keeping with the tenth canon, closing one-half score ahead of curfew.

22. An unmarried woman or widow shall not manage a shop's business without supervision from a male kin or partner.

23. Salt and honey shall each be sold at one wrunsos for a ten-pound drum.

24. Excluding special circumstances, citizens with a dispute must present themselves to their town's privy council for resolution.

25. The decision of the privy council and its chair is final in all disputes and other matters of the courts.

26. The privy council and its chair's decision in court matters cannot be appealed without consent from their lord or king.

27. No citizen shall present false information before their king, lord or privy council.

28. Each citizen must uphold peace throughout the kingdom.

29. Each citizen must uphold the virtues of truth and justice and conduct themselves with honour.

30. A citizen shall defend themselves under the threat of death by another citizen. Murder shall be punished by death.

31. Each dwelling, shop, and other shall maintain their dwelling, shop, and other in good repair.

32. Each dwelling shall gift a minimum of a yearly wrunsos to their chantry so that it too be in good repair.

33. Each dwelling, shop, and other must empty their pails into the street barrels a minimum of once a day for transportation.

34. The king may introduce land ordinances, while his lords may introduce regional ordinances to be observed with the canons.